THE QUEEN

Also by
NICK CUTTER

The Troop

The Deep

The Acolyte

Little Heaven

The Breach
(audio only)

The Handyman Method
(with Andrew F. Sullivan)

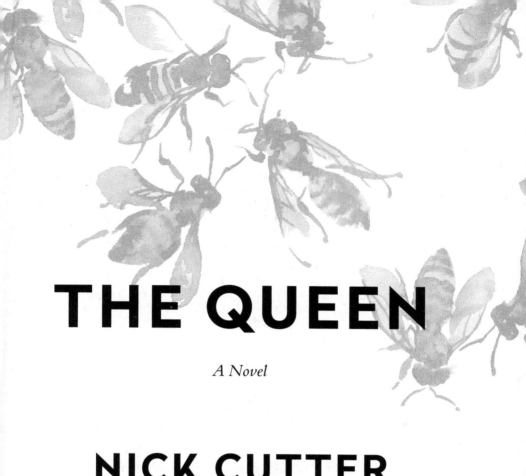

THE QUEEN

A Novel

NICK CUTTER

GALLERY BOOKS

New York   London   Toronto   Sydney   New Delhi

Gallery Books
An Imprint of Simon & Schuster, LLC
1230 Avenue of the Americas
New York, NY 10020

First Gallery Books hardcover edition October 2024

GALLERY BOOKS and colophon are registered trademarks of Simon & Schuster, LLC

Simon & Schuster: Celebrating 100 Years of Publishing in 2024

For information about special discounts for bulk purchases, please contact Simon & Schuster Special Sales at 1-866-506-1949 or business@simonandschuster.com.

The Simon & Schuster Speakers Bureau can bring authors to your live event. For more information or to book an event, contact the Simon & Schuster Speakers Bureau at 1-866-248-3049 or visit our website at www.simonspeakers.com.

Interior design by Erika R. Genova

Manufactured in the United States of America

1 3 5 7 9 10 8 6 4 2

Library of Congress Cataloging-in-Publication Data has been applied for.

ISBN 978-1-6680-2097-5
ISBN 978-1-6680-2099-9 (ebook)

For Charlotte
Long may you reign

"Bugs are not going to inherit the earth. They own it now. So we may as well make peace with the landlord."

—Thomas Eisner

"Bringing Joy and Happiness by Spreading Death and Destruction"

—Slogan for Pete's Pest Control, Mission, Kansas

PROLOGUE

IN THE NEST
Saturday, June 16, 2018

It's impossible to know another person, isn't it? To step past that locked door of their secretive inner self. Sure, you might suspect you can, even broadcast that suspicion to the world: *My best friend and I are so tight that we finish each other's sentences.*

But honestly, do you even want to know? What if science found a way—and science is always finding ways—to string two brains together? What if you could hear the running hum of your closest friend's thoughts? What if you find out she lusts to skin you alive, harvesting Kleenex-sized sheets of flesh to consume like Fruit Roll-Ups?

But I bet it would be a drabber truth. You'd find out she just doesn't hold that special space in her heart for you, the one you hold for her.

If that's what's in her head, it's better off not knowing, right?

". . . better to stay conned."

My voice is a dusty croak. Have I been talking to myself again?

You got to pull yourself together, Meadow. You'll never get into college acting like this.

Tony Soprano's sitting in the darkened office whose door faces the basin sink I'm slumped against. Kicked back with his shoes on the desk, legs crossed in a pair of khaki slacks, mustard-yellow bowling shirt, puffing on a Montecristo cigar.

Tony tsks. *You're about as goofy as a bedbug, Mead. Smarten up, daughter of mine.*

Apparently, my brain's summoned Tony out of some psychological backwater to push my gathering insanity away. Why my id chose a sociopathic New Jersey mob boss in my time of need is a question best left unanswered.

You're getting as bad as my great-aunt Wanda. Tony takes a haul on his cigar, its cherry glowing. *She used to chase terriers around Liberty State Park, foaming at the mouth.*

"I'm not your daughter, Mr. Soprano. I don't look anything like her."

Hopping off the sink, I head down the tiled hallway to a set of double doors marked LOADING BAY. They're locked shut. Just a regular old Master Lock, the brand gracing lockers in schools crisscrossing this great land of ours.

A pair of bloody combination wrenches lie on the floor. I'd scrounged them from a toolbox in the same office Tony's now occupying. For hours, or what feels like, I've been trying to use the wrenches to snap the Master Lock.

Past these loading bay doors, unless someone's played another rotten trick, lies freedom.

We find our heroine, one Margaret June Carpenter, picking up those wrenches for the latest in a series of futile attempts to escape her prison—which, just to get the facts straight, is the banquet kitchen of the St. Catharines Golf and Hunt Club.

YouTube provided the idea. Some survivalist neckbeard in a flannel shirt. *How to Break ANY Lock!* I'd watched the video while tucked behind the industrial dishwasher, making sure the phone's volume was dialed way down.

According to the video, all I've got to do is sock the rounded head of each wrench into the metal U of the lock, then squeeze the wrenches together until the shackle snaps. *Easy as shit through a goose*, so says Mr. Neckbeard.

I give it yet another go. The wrench handles pinch my palms as I struggle to close the distance between them . . . My hands don't hurt anymore: they've gone numb, the joints now oiled with blood—

The wrenches slip in the lock's hasp and snap on my fingers, flaying more skin off my knuckles. Dipping my head, I toss a question to the universe.

"So, you're telling me I'm gonna die in here?"

Instead of the voice of the cosmos, Tony's drifts down the hall.

Oh, poor baby. What do you want, a pat on the head? I can picture Tony's plump rosebud lips blowing a raspberry.

Dropping the wrenches, I hunch back through the kitchen, keeping my profile below the line of the porthole window that looks out into the ballroom. The light hangs thinly in that nightmarish space, which I'm separated from by a flimsy two-inch-thick laminate door.

. . . I can hear things *breathing* out there. At least I think that's breathing. A hissing, zippering rasp coming from under the door—

Something passes through the air right behind me.

I duck, stifling a screech as it arrows overhead, close enough to lift the feathery strands of my hair.

The air goes leaden. My head swivels in syrupy slow motion—

To the walk-in freezer.

I checked it out hours ago. Frozen fish fillets, McCain fries, hash brown hockey pucks. I'd left the door ajar, thinking I could lock myself in if something busted the kitchen door down and came shambling in from the ballroom. Sure, I'd probably freeze to death, but there were worse ways to go.

After that, I'd plugged up every entry point I could find. Stuffed tea towels down the sink drains. Slapped duct tape on the hood vents. Wadded rags under that swinging porthole door leading to the ballroom—that was my first move, as soon as I dead-bolted it.

Why all of this, you might ask?

Because death was throwing an unspeakable rager out in that ballroom. A party that, each time I gaze out at it—and I can't *stop*, same as how I couldn't stop scratching at the poison ivy I'd picked up down at Martindale Pond, rashing it all over my ass—a little piece of my mind goes screaming off into the dark.

Except I'd forgotten to shut the freezer door. I assumed it'd be too cold.

Too cold for the wasps.

This wasp—there's only one so far—banks sharply, wings glittering. For an instant I think it's oriented on me, but instead it switches course to settle atop the office door.

I don't dare move. If I do, the wasp will spot me with its disco-ball eyes. But what if this one is a scout? Once it sends word back to its nest-mates—and it has billions, if not trillions—the kitchen air will be alive with them, too thick to breathe.

Forcing my knees to unlock, I slide my right foot over the tiles. The wasp's wings burr—the sound of a thumb riffling a paperback book—but it doesn't take flight.

Oooh, that's one mean bastard, ain't it?

From his office seat, Tony seems unfussed by the wasp. *Say, I bet it'd sting you six ways from Sunday.*

Ten steps separate me from the freezer. I try to progress without giving the impression of movement. I am the wind on a summer's day. A glacier melting too slow for a human or insectoid eye to see.

Noises from inside the freezer. A bristling, angry hum.

My shoulders jerk, adrenaline spiking. One foot in front of the other, left, right, left, right, I'm getting there . . . gripping the freezer's

THE QUEEN — 5

handle, I set my shoulder to the door. Can't slam it, though every atom in my body wants to. The noise is liable to set the scout wasp off.

The hum gathers to an agonizing pitch. I imagine wasps crawling from a busted cooling pipe in the freezer, their thumb-sized bodies clinging to the frost-pebbled meta—

Click.

A heartbeat after the lock catches, they're ricocheting off the inside of the freezer door: *pok! pok!*, balls of aluminum foil launched with a slingshot.

Jaw clenched, our heroine manages not to scream. Now, did a drop or three of pee squirt into her underwear? Not gonna lie, yeah, that probably happened.

When I hunt for the scout wasp, I'm dismayed to discover it's not where it was. I drop into a crouch, eyes dodging wildly . . . a muffled buzz from the office.

Taking frictionless steps, I feel myself not walking so much as being *pulled* across the kitchen; it's as though I'm locked onto a conveyor belt, winched relentlessly forward.

I can't see the wasp through the glass fronting the top half of the office door, but I can hear the drumbeat of its wings. Tony's still behind the desk, except now his face is the enameled shell of a wasp. His chest strains against his shirt buttons, the stout cask of a wasp's thorax.

I got my eyes on you, Mead, Wasp-Tony purrs.

Gripping the knob, I ease the office door shut.

The moment the hasp clicks, the wasp smashes into the glass. Its wings scissor, *zzz-zzz*, beating not with the dopey confusion of a bluebottle fly but in crazed anger. Its stinger is a silvery sewing needle; it *tinks* off the pane.

Its attack is aimed at eye level. If that glass wasn't there, that's what it'd go for, wouldn't it? My eyes. Try to blind me. This comes as no shock.

I'd seen these things at work already, out in the ballroom. Hours ago, before I'd gotten myself trapped in here. As I was trucking at a dead sprint toward this very kitchen as everything had gone haywire—a rip in the fabric of reality, my terror so intense that every sense got heightened.

I saw a man in a turquoise suit squeezing one of these wasps in his hand, his grip tight enough to crack a walnut—then another flew at his face, landing on his naked eyeball. The man's eyelid flapped uselessly against the wasp, trying to shut like an elevator with a filing cabinet jammed between its doors; the wasp's stinger jabbed into the man's eyeball, which collapsed, some of it spilling down his cheek like curdled egg white as the rest foamed in his socket with the velvetiness of my father's Gillette shaving cream from a spray can.

The wasp gives up or gets bored. It buzzes away from the office door. My heart claws down out of my throat. I can see it on the desk blotter in there, perched on the clear barrel of a Bic pen.

Crossing back to the freezer, I jam more rags into the eighth-inch gap between the bottom of its door and the floor, stuffing them tight using the tip of a butter knife.

Will they freeze in there? I don't think so. These bastards are tough. Pressing my ear to the door, I listen to their pissed-off buzz—

POK!

I rear back, one hand slapping my ear. For an instant, my brain tells me that I've been stung right through the door, but no, no—

"You're okay." My voice is not at all steady.

Sure, Mead. You've got this little caper on a string.

"Oh, fuck off, Tony." I unleash a mad shriek of mirth. The wasps respond by pelting the freezer door in a frenzy.

When they finally settle, I catch another noise. A much more worrisome one. The gaunt, somehow hungry scratching of fingernails.

It's coming from the other side of the kitchen door.

Oh fuck oh fuck oh fuck me . . .

Breath bottomed out, I wait to see if anything will appear at the porthole, peeking in from the ballroom . . . a face greenly bloated with venom, goggling back and forth like a jack-in-the-box on a coiled spring—

Nothing appears, but that kittenish scratching persists. Could it be Harry? God, I hope not. I hope Harry's dead. I mean, for Harry's own sake I hope that.

The one thing I shouldn't do is go look through the porthole. One-hundred-percent *no*. But it's like telling myself not to scratch that poison ivy, to not doomscroll my Instagram (@LlamaDelRay), Twitter (@ChigurhWasFramed), TikTok, my YouTube account.

There's nothing nourishing there, I'd tell myself. *It's all sick meat.*

But in the end, I'm no better than a bug to a zapper.

When I take a peek into the ballroom, not much is moving out there. The fundraiser guests and the policemen are still lying under the tables. If not, they're slumped against the walls like sacks of potting soil. Fangs of char climb the walls. I never saw how the fire started—it had been one chaotic element among many when the shit truly hit the fan—but it only raged hotly for a few minutes before petering out.

The yellowy stink of that fire crawls under the door. The soggy reek of mulched leaves and a fricasseed top note that reminds me of the spring buck hunt. Every year the men of the Woody Knot trailer park set off in a checker-shirted, fur-hatted flotilla, returning drunk and stinking of gunpowder with some poor deer splayed across the hood of a shitkicker pickup. The guys would field-dress it down by the water, near a bonfire. All the parts they couldn't use—the bones and viscera and testicles, or buckyballs as they were known—got tossed on the fire. You could hear those buckyballs explode on the coals as sharply as Black Cat firecrackers.

My eyes snag on her. The Queen.

She sits atop a makeshift throne at the farthest edge of the ball-room. Some part of her moved; on another, saner timeline I'd've guessed it was her arm, but there were other parts of her now, parts I'd never known her to possess. Parts no human could possess.

The wasps in the ballroom stir at her command. They thunder up around the throne in a hazy cone, webbing out across the ceiling.

Pikachu!

The digitized chirp had come from inside the office.

Backtracking over the kitchen, I spotted the iPhone on the desk inside the office. Tony had vanished but the wasp is still in there.

Shit, shit, *shit*.

That phone represented my frail link to the outside world. And now the wasp owned it.

I rest my forehead against the door. "Our heroine has regrets."

The wasp rockets right at me, smashing into the glass so hard that the vibration quivers across my brow. I flinch as the wasp's stinger jabs and stabs, wings fluttering along the pane.

My jaw tenses. "I'm going to murder you."

Gathering the dregs of my resolve, I grip the knob and ease the door open a quarter of an inch. My thumb acts as a stopper, prevent-ing the door from opening too far . . . the edge of the door sticks in the jamb, gritting threateningly, shit, *shit* . . . The wasp hurls itself at the glass, energized by this new development.

When I get the door open two-thirds of an inch, I settle my lips near to the gap I've created between its wooden edge and the frame, no more than a millimeter of open air, a millimeter I'm doing everything in my power to maintain . . .

. . . and I hum.

It's hard to summon much vibration; my breath is jumpy, my lungs full of static spiders.

My hum attracts the wasp; it bumps along the glass to the door's edge, *zzz-zzz-ZZZ*. The muscles cramp in my forearms from keeping the door pinned *just so*. I can partially see the wasp in that millimeter-thin slit between door and frame, its Brazil-nut body vibrating like a tuning fork; I resist the urge to pull my lips away as it squirms deeper, squeezing into the space between the door and frame—its stinger scrapes against metal and I'm scared that it might elongate somehow, articulating on a ninety-degree angle to pierce my lips through that wafer-thin opening.

Oh so gently, I reapply pressure to the door. The hinges grit as the gap narrows . . . the buzzing cuts out. I can *feel* the wasp through the entirety of the door: its body now pinned between the wood and the frame. Trapped in the jaws of a vise.

The buzz rises. The fucker's trying to wriggle out. Maddening, deafening, enraged—

I slam my shoulder into the door.

The crack is that of a glossy candy shell. A giant goo-filled M&M splintering.

When I open the door, the upper half of the wasp falls to the floor. It zizzes around and around, a shook-up Coke can stabbed with a nail. Worst part is, it's still trying to sting me. Even though the part of its anatomy required for that is now paste in the doorjamb.

I step on it. *Crunch*. Very satisfying.

I retrieve the phone from the office desk. Opening YouTube, I surf the main broadcast feeds . . . CNN, ABC, CBC, NBC, FOX. Every news camera on earth is pointed at the St. Catharines Golf and Hunt Club, which by now is beginning to resemble a madman's idea of a sandcastle.

And in there somewhere, watching her predicament worsen on live TV, is our heroine. Margaret Carpenter, the girl in the nest.

The kitchen lights flutter. Are the wasps chewing on the power lines? They can do what they did in light or darkness, surely it makes no difference to them. But me? If the lights go out, trapping me with that blackening buzz . . .

Exiting the office, I return to the kitchen door. To the porthole.

The atmosphere in the cathedral-like ballroom is somber, brown, the air salted with wasps that flit above the few tables that haven't been digested into pulp. Light seeps through the skylight, but most of its panes are now covered with the carbuncled comb of the nest. The ballroom's main doors are encased in a slope of nest material, pocked by funneled exits or maybe entrances, papery and baffling like the webs of trapdoor spiders.

Something begins to move out there. I screw my eyes into the murk, trying to figure out what . . . oh Jesus. No. *No.*

It's the guests.

They've begun to give birth.

I guess you'd say that's what they're doing. I can only force myself to watch the first, my tongue stapled to the roof of my mouth in horror.

That one is a woman, beautiful in an old-movie-star kind of way. She's watching me. She's not quite dead, though I'm sure we both wish she were. Her stare has the eeriness of a portrait's eyes tracking you from inside the frame.

She's up on her knees, spine ramrod straight. Her fingers quiver at her sides. Something's moving behind her wide-open eyes. Larval twitches and scurries, the kind a pollywog makes as it cracks out of its egg sac.

Her throat swells. I picture a golf ball pushed through a garden hose. She gags silently, lips stretched into a sick head-splitting grin as some horrid interior pressure forces her mouth open. What I spy (*with my little eye*, goes a queasy voice in my head) through her spread teeth reminds me of a subway train flashing under a sidewalk grate, a thundering glimpse of a great ribbed engine racing past (*something that is red*). It tears up her ballooning neck, shredding her soft palate and breaking her jaw—her lower teeth get shoved out three inches past her bottom lip, the look of a sprung typewriter carriage—as something thick and tendon-cabled slams into the roof of her mouth. The woman's head snaps back as whatever's inside her flexes in a vicious corkscrew that cores through the fragile obstruction as it enters the vault of her skull, funneling into her head, the warm memory-rich oatmeal of her brain, her skull bulging so obscenely that her eyes drift apart, the sockets splintering and compressing in horizontal slits until her eyeballs burst, her nose flattening as her skull continues to expand, the bone held in check by the elasticity of her skin—finally, I catch a raw flapping, the sound bleeding past the tea towels plugged under the door: the snap of wet laundry in a high wind that is in fact her unrooted tongue, thick and purple as a skinned snake, flapping against her cheek.

For a heartbeat, it's as if the woman and I swap bodies. I can taste the thing inside her on my own tongue . . . the rasp of its ungodly body against my taste buds, a sensation that registers as petting a cat's fur in the wrong direction—

A barbed appendage stabs through the top of the woman's head. Retreating, it punches out again and again and again. The relentless pump of a piston. The woman's skull comes apart with each puncture, her scalp separating from the underlying bone and peeling down her forehead and the back of her neck in ribbons.

A creature that seems to be almost all mouth tears its way out the top of her head. Its roach-colored appendages find purchase on the shifting slob-ice of her skull as it *puuushes* itself out the same way you'd shimmy out of a pair of ass-hugging jeans.

The woman's torso caves in, her skin wadding up as her chest folds like a squeezed accordion. She folds again, backward this time, her spinal column bowing gruesomely, her ribs punching through the front of her little black dress as the thing sluices out of her, a tendon-slabbed shucked oyster.

The worst part isn't even that, though. It's that when the thing comes out of her, knobbed with wet gristle and trailing bluish veins, it comes out *eating*.

Once I witness that, I back away from the porthole, retching. All I cough up are strings of bile. I crawl onto the countertop and picture myself in a coffin six feet underground. Rather that than this. Rather there than here.

But before I do that, my eyes flee to the porthole one last time.

I see someone out there I used to know. Allan Teller, a boy I'd grown up with. Allan's eighteen years old. A senior at Northfield High, same as me.

Unlike me, Allan's capering on the ballroom floor, naked and threadbare, smeared in a substance that looks like crankcase oil but is probably something far worse.

I used to be partners with Allan in sixth-grade science, a million years ago. Allan had scorched his hand on the Bunsen burner and whimpered like a little bitch, sucking his fingertips.

Allan is down on all fours, snaffling at what's left of the woman in the black dress. Seizing her in his jaws, he shakes his vein-threaded skull, a terrier with a chew toy; a rag of organ meat bounces off his cheeks like a paddle ball, painting his face with blood.

Next, Allan squints into the light streaming through the porthole: it casts a funnel into the ballroom, the beam of a lighthouse. He looks shriveled in it, his sticklike arms seized with tremors: the look of a bug when you lift the rock it's been hiding under, half-pupated, covered in cottony webbing.

I note that Allan Teller's privates are no more. Two hardened, beef-jerky-like prongs jut between his thighs. His seminal vesicles, if I recall my ninth-grade sex-ed poster correctly. But to me they look like antennae . . . as if a massive ant has crawled inside him, its feelers piercing the walls of his bladder to wriggle between his legs.

"Oh, fuck me, Allan," I hear myself say, clinging to the bitter dregs of my sanity. "Who did that to you?"

THE QUEEN — 13

Except I know exactly who. She's out there with Allan and the trilobite-like thing that was once Chad Dearborn and Will Stinson, now a serpentine freight train patrolling the shadowy scrim of the ballroom.

The Queen's eyes—those complex, inhuman eyes—crawl over me. Our heroine, her moony face in the porthole.

That'll be my best friend out there, watching me back.

Pikachu!

The new iPhone.

I pull it out of my pocket.

It's a text. From her.

> This shit's crazy, amirite?

Oh, this phone. This life-eating, sanity-destroying, motherfucking—

PART I
MORNING

One Day Earlier

Friday, June 15, 2018

ONE
6:58 a.m.

—phone. I could hear one ringing somewhere.

The sound fell from the sky over Saint John's Anglican cemetery on Main Street in Port Dalhousie. Tombstones poked out of the
earth, gray as bad teeth.

My feet carried me down a corridor of graves. Reaching the
end of one row—*Conrad T. Bellweather 1877–1878 Rest in Eternity
Little Dove*—that ringing intensified: a cricket lodged in my ear canal
rubbing its legs together, *creee-cree-crrrreeeeeee* . . .

A trio of gravestones lay heaved up on a bulge of earth. Two were
slanted crookedly; the final one had toppled over, ripped free of the
roots knotted to its plinth.

The ground trembled under my feet (which were bare, toenails
painted aquamarine). The turf made a Velcro-ing tear as a ragged
mouth opened in the earth.

The ringing was coming from that emptiness.

Down there with the beetles and earthworms, something else
moved too . . . something large and possibly larval.

I could see them. Three bodies . . . or how bodies might look after being sunk underground for a month.

The tombstones were new enough that the moss hadn't yet had a chance to fur them. Their owners' names were etched in the granite and filled in with weatherproof paint.

Allan Teller, Will Stinson, Chad Dearborn.

They were crawling from their coffins, which had coughed their corpses out like half-chewed morsels of food. Their funeral suits, the kind that zipped up from their ass-cracks in the style of toddler's jammies, hung off their carcasses in worm-eaten tatters.

Their bodies were deflated pods. Their heads were flat and flounder-ish, their skulls spread into thick pancakes. Some unguessable pressure had drawn their features together, eyes and nose and mouth pinched into a knot and shoved back on the wadded flesh of their foreheads.

Their eyes—those dead, festering eyes—stared mindlessly from their hairlines. They still had that, though. Hair. Thick, curly, and wavy, oh yes they did.

The missing boys issued glutinous noises as they sucked out of the earth, not so much climbing as sidewinding in the manner of millipedes. They didn't speak, but that didn't mean they were incapable of sound: they emitted the hiss of compressed air from a beach ball, which made my skin creep helplessly across my hip bones.

The phone's for you, Margaret.

Allan Teller's voice. But it didn't come from his mouth. How could it, when his lips were pinched into a coin-purse that flapped and bubbled over his nose? It emanated from some other, secretive part of him.

Answer it, you sloppy trash-can bitch.

The dead boys slithered toward my bare feet carrying the gagging stench of the grave. Their arms ribboned over the dirt, six wind socks in a dead calm; their chests were yard bags filled with soggy litter, eyes flickering with a malignant spark.

Useless as we look, Margaret dear, we can still hurt you.

Even worse was the sense something else was down there, under the boys' caskets; a terrible *something* that filled the boys' bodies with its capering, chuckling animus, registering as a scrape across my pineal gland—a thousand watchful yellowed eyes observing me with a festering intellect.

The boys, or whatever was puppeteering them from the guts of the earth, whispered:

You'll go mad the moment we touch you, don't you think?

If I let their decayed limbs coil round me—Christ, wouldn't that drive anybody crazy, oh wouldn't it just make you scream your goddamned lungs out?

ANSWER THE FUCKING PHONE—

TWO
7:01 a.m.

I rocketed out of sleep to the ping of my Samsung Galaxy.

I reached for it, bleary-eyed. Knocked it off the nightstand into a half-eaten bowl of Calbee ponzu-flavored potato chips. Shit. Fishing it out, I flicked chip shards off its screen.

A text bubble hovered between the spiderweb cracks on the Galaxy's screen.

> Go downstairs.

Unidentified caller.

I could still see Allan Teller's caved-in head, his mouth gold-fish-popping as he slunk from his casket. . . .

Ping!

> Come on, Cherr. Get up. Hurry.

The trapdoor feeling in my stomach—yeah, *that* made me sit up.

My feet hit the carpet. The sky sat low and woolen through the Venetian blinds. I hadn't looked out that window for weeks.

The floor was carpeted in dog-eared mangas and Books of Blood paperbacks and dishes stuck with scabs of spaghetti sauce. My hip struck the edge of my desk, sending the pages of my newest short story—tentative title: "Steel Window"—fluttering to the ground.

Who was texting me? Was it someone from Northfield messing with me?

No, unlikely. Nobody at my high school called me Cherry. Plus, I hadn't showed my face at Northfield in a long time.

Ping!

> Go downstairs. It's waiting.

The next heartbeat, I heard the rumble of a truck coming down the block.

THREE
7:05 a.m.

I stumbled to the front door in my underwear and a sweatshirt stained with crime-scene spatters of Mountain Dew Code Red. Screwed my eye to the peephole in time to see a dude climbing back into his FedEx truck.

When I opened the door, a box sat on the stoop. It was addressed to Cherry June Carpenter. The "Shipped From" info was all of two words: *Plum Atwater.*

My name's Margaret. Maggie to some, Mags to others, "The Beefster" to one absolute shit-for-brains who thinks he's funny.

But only one person called me "Cherry." My best friend, Charity Atwater. Her private nickname for me was Cherry. Hers was Plum.

And Plum was dead.

Confusion bristled at my temples, but what ran up on the heels of that was harder to gauge. Fear? What was there to be scared of? The sun was shining and I was in my home. Still, that nightmare kept cycling in my under-brain. Chad Dearborn and Will Stinson resembling a knot of mushy pool noodles as they zephyred out of that hole.

With quiet steps, I returned to my room. The box was tucked under my arm. My folks were still zonked out in bed.

I cleared space on my desk, slit the packing tape with an X-Acto knife. Sifted through packing peanuts until my hand closed around—

I almost dropped the thing. It felt repulsively warm, an excised tumor or . . . or a monkey paw. We'd read that story in English class last semester. The final scene of Mr. and Mrs. White in their shack while their son, Herbert—dead from a machine accident, but now something other than dead—knocked restlessly at their door.

It was a brand-new iPhone. Nothing else was in the box. Just the phone.

Curious, I thumbed it on. A burst of tinkly, Apple-y music like Steve Jobs whistling from the afterlife. The screen lit up.

The photo on the display was an old one, snapped back at the Woody Knot trailer park, where my family used to live before my father's invention made us rich.

Plum and me. We're standing side by side, arms slung over each other's shoulders out front of the Hallmark double-wide I grew up in. Sun on scalded grass, three skinned knees between us, I'm missing a tooth, Plum's hair's up in pink barrettes. We're stupid-happy.

The iPhone *ping*ed in my hands.

How are you this fine morning, Cherr?

Rage broadsided me (*Who the fuck sent this?*) followed by a second barrage of confusion (*Why would* anyone *send this?*), but the steadiest drumbeat was:

What the hell is going on here?

Could I be looking at a text sent by my dead best friend?

Dead. That's right, I said it. That was what my fellow students and everyone else in this glue-trap burg had been left to thinking for the last month. The police evidently shared that belief. Yeah, officers knocked on a couple doors. They'd beaten the bushes around the dump, the riverbank, the rowing club. After that they threw up their hands. I kept at it. Tacking up *MISSING* posters on telephone poles. Talking to everyone who'd known Plum and more than a few who didn't. But even I'd lost hope, gripped by the nagging worry that she didn't want to be found—specifically by me.

I'd come to accept that my friend Plum—our nicknames sprang from the roads we'd grown up on: Cherry Close and Plum Lane— was gone. God, I'd imagined her dead. Her body unraveled in a field, picked at by crows. I couldn't stop the image from popping into my head, the equivalent of those shitty McAfee ads.

But this phone . . . Could it be from Plum? Or was it a prank so mean-spirited that someone needed to die?

Ping!

> Get dressed, ok?

> Gonna be a big day!

Wait, why am I doing this?

That was the question I asked myself while snapping on my last clean bra, the one with gunshell cups that bit under my armpits. I tugged on a fresh shirt and slung into a pair of jeans.

Ping!

> Hurry, Cherr. Please.

Why would I consider, in a million years, doing what a phone told me to do?

> Remember we used to stage our own funerals?

"I remember," I whispered, staring open-mouthed at the screen.

The spring we were eleven, when the tulips had started to pop over Woody Knot, Plum confessed that she often lay awake at night imagining people's funerals. Her mom's, or our fifth-grade teacher, Mr. Lambert's. She asked me: *Is that weird?*

I'd said: "If it is, then why do I imagine the exact same thing?"

It was my suggestion that we hold funerals for each other. We took turns lying on the picnic table out by the horseshoe pits with our hands crossed over our chests.

We are gathered here to celebrate the life of Charity Atwater, who died fighting ninety-nine ninjas. She killed ninety-eight but got cut in half by the very last one. We celebrate her life, her love, her passion for killing ninjas . . .

The iPhone's clock read 7:08 as I tiptoed downstairs to the door. Didn't want to wake my parents. They'd have questions. My Samsung phone was sunk into my back pocket, the new iPhone in my hand.

Ping!

> Corner of crestview and lonnigan.

I relented, typing back for the first time:

who is this?

> You know who

I texted:

fuck off

I'd already learned all about the stages of grief, and "Accept Your Best Friend's Shocking Return from the Dead" wasn't one of them.

Ping.

WTF? Would you prefer if it WASN'T me?

I could almost hear Plum asking this: her chin tucked as she looked at me with hopeful, solemn eyes.

people think you're dead.

Everyone at school.

It's been a long time since

How could I finish that? There were too many ways it *could* be finished.

. . . since everything went to shit?

. . . since that horrible thing happened to you?

. . . since we stopped being best friends?

. . . since you—

Since what, Plum? Since you *what*?

I eased the front door open. Without being consciously aware of it, my feet carried me onto the front steps. Before I knew it, I was on the sidewalk.

Ping!

Don't you trust me, Cherr?

How could I respond to that? My best friend recrosses the river Styx—

Hang on. Nobody knows that for sure, the voice in my head interrupted. *Her body was never found.*

Well, missing then. Missing at a bare minimum. And by the way, how does a teenage girl even *go* missing of her own free will?

Wasn't it possible? that same voice asked.

No, quite frankly. Primarily because Plum was poor. Brown-sugar-sandwich-eating, washing-clothes-in-the-sink poor, the kind of poverty that was dug into my own bones because I grew up same as her: seventeen years in a scratch-ass trailer park until my dad's patent got approved and we became millionaires basically overnight. Next came the grisly McMansion in Executive Acres, a nitrous-oxide funny car in a five-car garage, Dad off racing in the beer milers at Merrittville Speedway on Friday nights. A purple-flake Mercedes for Mom, and dye jobs at a salon rather than out of a Nice 'N Easy bottle.

But see, Plum never left the trailer park. Girls like her don't craft elaborate plans for fresh starts. In what universe do they have that luxury? Poor girls get plucked off the side of the highway and cut into bits, encased in concrete and sunk in lagoons. Poor girls go missing and life carries on. So once Plum's case had gone cold and everybody faced the fact she pretty much logically had to be dead—

Now, of all possible ways to reconnect, my best friend reaches out in a *text* from a new iPhone dumped on my porch?

FOUR
7:21 a.m.

When it dawns that I'm actually outside for the first time in forever, I'm rocked by a lightheaded spell. The sun stings my scalp. I'm an infant waddling around without a sun bonnet.

I thumb the iPhone and start scrolling. An involuntary reflex.

It takes a second to register that the iPhone's not set up to my accounts, feeds, channels—it can't access my online life, so I thumb it off.

I'd pretty much ghosted social media after Plum's disappearance. It made me sick to see people who'd never known her posting tributes.

A bright flame snuffed out too soon. 😞 😧

I only posted about her once. A quote she'd always liked from S. E. Hinton's *The Outsiders*. Later, I found out it was from a poem by Robert Frost.

Nothing gold can stay.

The line captured Plum, sure, but it was as much about, I guess, how briefly any of us are really young. The part of our lives that was shortening by the minute, slipping through our fingers, and we'd never guess where the finish line lay until our chests snapped the tape.

After posting it, I felt shitty. As if I'd turned her into clickbait, same as everybody else.

Reaching Crestview, I headed out of the sterile wonderland of my new subdivision, Executive Acres—what, was Pretentious Prefabs already taken?—past lumpy lawns where strips of sod had been rolled over construction scrap. I was breathing hard, beads of sweat springing out on my neck. The iPhone *ping*ed. I hauled it out to find a news alert.

SEARCH EXTENDED FOR MISSING AREA TEENS

My dream rolled back to me. Those three students from my school—seniors, same graduating class as me—crawling out of their coffins.

Getting under the iPhone's hood, I checked its alert settings. They must have been inputted by whoever had sent the phone.

Five Google alerts. For five names.

Chad Dearborn. Allan Teller. Will Stinson.

Charity Atwater.

Finally—and this sent a jolt through my guts—*Margaret Carpenter.*

Quickly, I thumb-scrolled the photos attached to the article.

The first was of Allan Teller, thin of neck and adenoidal with his shit-eating grin . . . next, Will Stinson, nicknamed "Biebs" on account of his unthreatening YouTuber features . . . finally, Chad Dearborn: fearless leader, charisma for miles, smirking like a country gentleman enjoying an endless procession of golden days.

And why not? The three of them came from old-stock families, drove cars bankrolled by the Corporation of Mom and Dad, and as Northfield seniors, they ruled the school alongside their female counterparts: Instagrammer Miranda Lancaster, Wanda Hollis with the silky curls, Glenda Curtis and her silly-big tits.

The Beefster. That was the nickname Allan Teller tried to pin on me after the last Christmas break. He'd spotted me coming down the hall and dropped into a wrestling announcer's patter:

"Making her way to the ring wearing a muumuu, hailing from the buffet table and weighing in at half a ton, she ain't lean and she ain't clean—it's the Buh-Buh-Beeeeeefster!"

Okay, had I put on a pound or two over the holidays? I'm a fan of eggnog, sue me. Not the kind of thing anyone was bound to notice aside from Allan-shitbag-Teller.

"Body shaming," I'd replied to Teller's wrestler bit. "Interesting tactic. What's next, you're gonna start deadnaming Madison Snell, go around calling them Maury?"

"No." Allan's shoulders hunched, his eyes close-set and ferrety. "Take a joke, Margo."

Even though that marked the end of it, it stunned me to think that

Allan Teller would be a grown-up one day—he'd be *old*, like forty, explaining to his brat of a son how he once, back in high school, had actually called another human being "The Beefster":

It was all perfectly acceptable in those days, Frederick my darling! For, you see, she'd put on noticeable chunk around her brisket and buttocks. It also bears mentioning that she was exceeeedingly poor at the time.

Teller had been one of the guys that night at the party, at Burning Van . . . the three of them were involved with what went down with Plum.

Allan Teller, Chad Dearborn, Will Stinson.

As of today, the three of them had been missing for—I scanned the article—right, just about two weeks. Plum had been gone for a lot longer.

Ping!

> Keep going, Cherr. Tick, tick, tick . . .

Five alerts. Four of the five names belonged to missing students at my school. Shit, was this how they'd vanished? Had *they* received a phone, too, and idiotically done what it told them to?

> Plum. Is it really you?

> You bet. The killer of ninety-eight ninjas, cut in half. But back!

It is *her*. Has *to be.*

This was messaged from the rational layer of my brain. Plum was the only person who could know such intimate details. But the layer under that rational one, the lizardy cortex whose sole concern was survival . . . it sent out a signal that arrived as a cool prickling over my scalp.

What if Plum *was* alive? What did that mean? My friend who I thought was dead had let me go on *believing* that. She'd let me suffer for over a whole goddamn month?

What if she really *had* made herself disappear via sheer force of will? That she hadn't caved while the cops hunted for her, never calling her own bluff . . . all to prove that nobody gave a shit when someone like her evaporated?

That would be the most rock star thing anyone in our piss-ass city had ever done.

I was walking head down, staring at the phone with a clenched jaw until, without realizing it, I hit the corner of Crestview and Lonnigan.

"Margaret?"

FIVE
7:24 a.m.

He straddled his BMX bike, front wheel popped up on the curb. Skinny jeans with rips at the knees—not designer rips, the regular kind—plain T-shirt and all bony underneath, denim jacket that could've been stolen from some '80s hair band roadie, but he wore it with a sincerity that made it all work.

He toe-walked his bike toward me. His Converse All Stars dragged the pavement. Harry Cook, that mythical one-percenter: a teenage boy who didn't suck.

"Hey, Mags."

"Harr, what are you doing here?"

Pinning the crossbar between his legs, he tucked his hair behind his ears in that way of his—as a preparation to say something earnest, usually, earnest being Harry's default mode.

"I got these texts." He pulled out his battered Motorola to show me. "Crestview and Lonnigan, Crestview and Lonnigan, go, go, go . . . so . . ."

"So you just did what some rando texts told you to do?"

At this, Harry seemed unsure in some deep-down way, as if the fact he couldn't say why he had come here worried him. That in itself was unsettling, because there wasn't much on earth that worried Harry Cook.

"I've gone off my meds, milady," he announced faux-grandly. "Those pills make me fuzzy and"—he held his arms up, elbows hinged, bringing them down in twin ax-chops—"I am an engine of *focus*. You get me? Clean lines, Mags, straight and true."

"You couldn't have, like, halved the dose?"

"Clean lines don't waver."

Ping!

> Is he there?

Ping!

> He's there, isn't he?

I typed back.

> so you got us both here. Whee. Where are you now?

Harry had drawn close enough to check out the iPhone. He whistled.

"It's not mine," I told him. "It just showed up on my front step this morning."

Harry's scent hit me as a contact high: crankcase oil and WD-40 and something else, alkaline and wild, that resisted identification.

"Who'd mail you a phone?"

I showed him its screen. "I think it's Charity."

"Bull*shit*."

Gently gripping my wrist, he angled the phone so the sun wasn't shining on the screen. He read our last few texts.

"Killer of ninety-eight ninjas?"

"I really think it's her, Harr."

Ping!

> You should be sitting down for this. Use the bench behind you.

The bus bench was adorned with the lusty face of local ambulance-chaser Leo Zlatar. *Hit by a car? Call Leo Zlatar!*

The lacquered wood was wet with morning dew. Harry sat down first, scooching his butt across the slats to dry them.

"Sit, sit," he beckoned, damp-assed.

As soon as I sank down on the bench, the phone went off.

Ping!

> LONGSTORY.wav

I stared at the file, open-mouthed. *Tap to play.* I shared a look with Harry. His expression said: *Hey, you do you, Maggie.*

I thumb-tapped the icon.

"*Cherr. Hey, listen, I'm so sorry . . . I've missed you so much.*"

There was a frayed edge to Plum's voice, but it was unmistakably her.

"*Hey, Harr. Thanks for coming too. There's a big crazy story still to be told, okay? It took me a long time to come to grips with, but I've reached what the Buddha calls the second noble truth.*"

My heart was jackhammering. Sweat was just dumping out of me.

"*Cherr, you know I'd never hurt you, right? And whatever went down that night at Burning Van, y'know, with those boys . . . we weren't in the best place when we last spoke . . . Anyway, this story I'm a part of—that I've been part of for a long time, it turns out . . . you need to understand. To do that, you've got to see some things today. It's like Mr. F told us in English class: show, don't tell. You with me? You come along too, Harry. It'll be good to have a second set of eyes. And please, don't tell anyone. I'm*" *dead serious. You have to keep this to yourselves for right now. Trust me. Please, okay?"*

When the file cut out, Harry shot off the bench, stabbing his hands through his hair.

"She's Hannah Baker–ing us!" He spun behind the bench, Leo Zlatar's mustache forming a furry girdle at his hips. *"13 Reasons Why,* remember? Charity's just updated things. A phone instead of cassettes."

"Yeah, but she's not dead. We just heard her."

"We heard her *voice,* Mags. She could have recorded it before, y'know, she—"

"Stop. *Don't.* Okay, then who mailed this phone to me? Who's texting us right now?"

Harry's Adam's apple punched at his throat. "I'm not saying I *want* to be right. But, I mean, she was going through some seriously bad stuff, right?"

"She wouldn't kill herself."

Harry re-straddled his bike, picking at a curl of electrical tape unraveling from one of the handlebars. "You'd know better than me."

Ping!

> I didn't kill myself, if that's what you're wondering.

When Harry saw that, he took the phone away from me.

"Is the mic on? You hearing all this, Char? It seems like a lot of friggin' work, y'know?" He inspected the phone as if it were a sinister artifact. "It's *definitely* got mapping software. She knows wherever this phone is."

Taking the phone back, I typed:

> help me understand

. . . ping!

> Go to school.

SIX
9:18 a.m.

When Harry saw Plum's reply, he said: "I can drive . . . unless you want to ride double on my bike?"

"On what planet, Harr?"

He gave me his crooked, bashful smile. "My car's over at my house."

So there I was, dogging Harry home. There was a sensation of being buckled in on a roller coaster as the cart clicked toward the Drop of Doom.

Why not go to the police? I was in possession of a phone that received texts from a missing girl. If not the cops, then Ms. Aceti, the school guidance counselor, or—

Because they're the enemy, Cherr. Plum's voice, sharp as a quill. *They're all the things we don't trust.*

Walking up the sidewalk, I found myself slipping into conversation with my oldest friend.

Plummy, seriously, what's happening? You disappeared on me. Did you actually fake your own death? That's a fucking baller move, but *why*? To punish everyone? Because nobody really *got* you?

Plum's reply, which I logically understood to be my own:

Is it so corny to feel that way, Cherr? Do your folks or teachers really get you? Don't they say you're acting all hormonal? What was it your mom called you, a total drama llama?

My mom's exact quote was: a total drama llama *ding dong*. As for my dad, he's spent the majority of my teenage years building ships in bottles.

I'd never been to Harry's house, but I knew the neighborhood: Western Hill. Native habitat for the Skids, as Harry and his buddies got labeled around school.

"I texted you a bunch of times after Burning Van," he said, not looking at me. "I even *called* you."

Harry had, too. Four or five times a day for a week after the party where Plum had gotten out of control—no, worse: She'd become a different person.

I hadn't responded to Harry's calls or texts. After I stopped searching for Plum, I withdrew into my room, to my shelves full of books. I wrapped myself up in stories, pushing away the painful edges of reality, locked in with heroes and heroines who weren't freighted with the frailties of regular people.

Harry's house came into sight. A patch of shingles was rotting off its roof, and plastic sheets hung over a few windows in place of glass. Still, it was bigger than the Hallmark double-wide I'd spent my formative years in.

The yard was littered with the remains of Harry's YouTube stunts. It beggared belief that his folks could be casual observers of their son's attempts to maim and cripple himself on their own front lawn, his exploits filmed by his buddies-slash-enablers Darcy Simp-kins and Teddy Cosgrove. The mini-trampoline with a hole burned through it was familiar (YouTube title: "Flaming Hoop of Death"); ditto the crash mat covered in rain-rusted thumbtacks ("Thumbtack Face-Plant"). A haystack of bikes that had been variously set on fire, crashed into walls, or jumped off garages was heaped up next to the side-yard shed.

Everyone at Northfield thought Harry Cook was nuts. Not A.J. Slanker nuts, who sold his cousin's prosthetic leg for booze money, or über-keener Amy Coolidge nuts, who got a B-plus in biology and stuck a steak knife into the tire of Mr. Rose's Prius. Harry was a deeper breed of crazy. Strap-one-hundred-packs-of-Black-Cat-firecrackers-to-his-chest-and-light-them-up crazy—a stunt that earned Harry three days in the burn ward and a warning from the doctor that if he tried anything like that again, he'd end up with his ass-skin grafted onto his face.

The thought often came to me that Harry had a wartime soul. Seventy years ago, he would've been conscripted and sent off to fight Adolf Hitler; all that self-destructive energy could've helped rid the world of a great evil, right?

He ushered me into the mudroom. "Bless this mess. My dad needs to invent a robot to pick up after him." He winked. "He ought to talk to your dad, huh?"

"Million Dollar Mags" was Harry's nickname for me. Our family owed our newfound wealth to my father's invention, which could be found in just about every box of cookies on the supermarket shelves. Dad had worked at the Nabisco plant on Lewis Avenue since graduating high school. He toiled on the Nutter Butter line; his skin smelled faintly of peanut butter, no matter how often he showered. He'd noticed how a lot of cookies ended up chipped or dinged and came up with a modification to the cookie tray, a raised squiggle that prevented cookies from jostling into each other during transport. He walked his prototype to the patent office, got it stamped, and within six months it had become the new industry standard. Oreo, Chips Ahoy, Fudgee-O—even the Girl Scouts adopted Dad's tray for their Trefoils and Thin Mints.

I was proud of my dad. He couldn't have forecasted the distance his invention would put between our family and the place we came from. The *anger* it would bring out of some of our old friends and neighbors at Woody Knot.

Crabs in a bucket, was how Mom dismissed their behavior. *Anyone tries to climb out, they want to drag you right back.*

A ruckus kicked up inside Harry's house. He shouted: "Calm

yourself, Goldie, she's cool!"—next, a black Heinz 57 came bounding down the hall. Her nails skidded on the scuffed linoleum, her tail *whap-whapping.*

"Why did you name her Goldie?" I called, scratching her under her ruff.

Harry's voice echoed back: "Look at her eyes."

Ah, I get it. There were tiny flecks of gold in Goldie's corneas.

Harry came back spinning a set of car keys on his finger. "Let's roll."

Before going, he knelt with Goldie and gave her a scratch. "You be a good girl, okay? Mom and Dad will take proper care of you."

Walking out to the car, I caught the steady *thak* of helicopter blades from someplace over Lake Ontario.

SEVEN
9:32 a.m.

If asked to pinpoint the singular event that held dominion over their lives and governed their pursuits, most people would draw a blank.

But Rudyard Crate? Oh, he could define that moment perfectly.

He'd been ten years old, in sub-Saharan Africa with his father, a mining executive, and his older sister, Elizabeth.

On a sweltering day in June, Rudyard watched his sister get devoured by ants.

The *Dorylus* ant, also known as the driver, safari, or siafu ant, is the largest genus of army ant found in the continent. They are territorial and rarely stray from their anthills, but during seasonal droughts it is not uncommon for a colony to march, in ranks of several trillion members, in massive war-parties. They attack and consume anything, regardless of size. They are the only African insect species known to eat flesh.

In 1978, Rudyard Crate's father, Augustus, was CEO of an emerald mining concern with interests in the Kinderson claim in the Northern Cape. He had come with a crew of surveyors to investigate the potential of the area. His children, Rudyard and Elizabeth, accompanied him—Rudyard excitedly, Elizabeth less enthusiastically. It wasn't the heat or the tinned food that bothered her. Elizabeth felt what they were up to was inherently wrong.

"We're wrecking everything," she'd told Rudyard one night, under the mosquito netting in the bed they shared in the barracks. "For what? Want to know the smartest thing De Beers ever did? Making their shiny rocks shorthand for love."

Sometimes Rudyard would wake with the moonlight bleeding through the barrack's eyelets and observe Elizabeth as she slept: the blue of her nightgown frilled at her throat, the milkiness of her scalp under the stiff, short red of her hair (everyone's hair was cut in Marine whitewalls on account of the heat), the freckles on her cheeks collecting the light . . . and a feeling swelled within him, somewhat painful and confusing, but dominant in it was an unquestioning adoration for his sister.

Except even then, Rudyard realized an element of that adoration was jangly and not-quite-right, same as when the doctor struck Rudy's knee with his rubber mallet.

He had no other companions other than Elizabeth and one of his father's men, a German, Carl Leiningen, who ran the camp. Its location had been carefully chosen: the barracks were surrounded on three sides within a crescent-moon cliff that resembled the heelprint of a man's dress shoe in dense mud. The cliff, of red sandstone, rose fifty feet to the veldt beyond. The jungle met the half-moon clearing to the south, hemming the camp within that heelprint.

The site lay in shade half the day, which was of value in the heat of the sub-Saharan summer. At night, the proximity of the jungle made it a source of uncanny sounds: the snaffling of pygmy boars, the glassy slithering of rock pythons, the occasional shriek of a leopard.

Every day, his fearless sister led Rudyard under the forest canopy to explore the hanging vines and lanai, the tangled roots of the baobab and acacia trees.

"If Dad gets his way, all this will be gone," Elizabeth told him.

Every so often, the ground trembled. This was their father's survey crew boring hundreds of feet into the earth using a narrow-vein surface rig and employing dynamite to loosen the earth.

One of those explosions created a fault line into what experts would later call the largest known ant colony in the southern hemisphere. It had lain undisturbed for decades, inhabiting an underground vault the length of a dozen football fields, with an immense bell-like dome that rested quietly under the hills.

With their home breached, the carnivorous siafu ants poured out of the earth—an uncountable number, a total dwarfing the total of every human being, animal, invertebrate, and fish species on planet Earth. The ants streamed over and through the jungle canopy in a living wave.

Rudyard and Elizabeth had been the only two at the barracks when a family of ibexes leapt from the walled strangler fig trees, hacked back to make room for the camp. The animals vaulted madly about, oblivious of Rudyard or his sister. The ibexes approached the jungle again . . . but shied away, stamping their hooves as do cattle trapped in a barn fire.

Elizabeth said: "Something's wrong."

Making their way to the cliffs, the male and kid ibex followed the female up; their hooves found the narrowest outcroppings, scaling the nearly sheer face in a manner so eerie it was as though they were floating. Reaching the top, the kid turned, looked down at Rudyard and his sister, issued a stiff snort—*sorry about your luck*—and vanished.

Their father and his crew were miles away on a survey. Elizabeth marched determinedly toward the only vehicle in camp, a Jeep Willys.

Meanwhile, an unaccountable sound had begun to bristle from the jungle: the whisper of thousands of silk sheets rubbing against one another.

"I'll get the Jeep going," Elizabeth called over to her brother. "Then we'll get out of here."

It was Carl Leiningen who'd taught Elizabeth to drive. Rudyard had watched her take clumsy loops around the camp with their father's hired man, working the gearshift with a teak knob on its end.

Elizabeth cranked the key in the Willys, but the motor refused to catch. The frantic pump of his sister's foot on the gas pedal must have flooded the engine.

Rudyard could see something moving in the shadow of the jungle's hanging fronds. Pulsating strands crisscrossing the ground, fibrous-looking, the appearance of mobile ivy . . .

"Get over here, Rudy!" Elizabeth twisted the key, again, *again*. "I'm gonna get it started!"

He dashed over and slid into the passenger seat. A smell wafted off his sister, a tang both acidic and electric—or was that coming out of the jungle?

"Come on," she said. "Come *on*, you stupid thing."

The strands thickened across the parched earth, splitting and branching. Rudyard recognized the individual links on those enormous chains. He'd seen them before, same as anyone. But never so large, so fast, or so purposeful.

Ants.

The whisper grew louder: a dark, glass-like voice coming out of the foliage.

"Forget the Jeep. We have to run!" Rudyard said. Elizabeth seemed not to hear, her lips peeling back from her teeth in a terror-filled grin.

Ants poured out of the jungle, ants to rival every grain of sand in the Kalahari, more than Rudyard would've thought existed. They enfolded the landscape in a vast creeping carpet—the ants only had tiny little legs, but they moved swiftly as a group; in a wink, their colony had spanned from cliff face to cliff face, penning in the camp. They smothered the hacked-off stumps marking the edge of the jungle. Choked the bonelike strip of roadway that offered their only escape.

"Come on come ON—"

The Jeep's engine coughed, ground, then caught with an earthy rumble. Elizabeth let go an uncontrollable laugh as she sunk the shifter into first gear.

"We're getting out of here, hold on!"

The road was indistinguishable under the ants; the creatures pressed forward, sinewy and blackish-brown, cresting and ebbing in a tidal wave that rose three feet thick in places.

Wired on adrenaline, Elizabeth stood too heavily on the gas pedal; the Jeep shot across the camp and hit the advancing ants broadside. They burst against the grille, the collective weight of their bodies slowing the Jeep as if it had plowed into a snowbank. Ants crunched under the tires with the mad *pop-pop-pop* of bursting corn kernels. The Jeep's tires churned, sending insects up in a mad brown fan; they splashed across the hood, surging over the windscreen to come down on Rudyard's lap, his hands, his face.

Abruptly they were all over him, their legs and antennae tickling before the pain set in, and, oh god, the *pain*. It was like being lanced with needles, like getting every inoculation known to man—mumps, rubella, common flu, malaria—over every inch of bare skin in one agonizing dosage. They were down his shirt and up his shorts, clinging to the tops of his wool socks and biting, biting, mindlessly biting—

Elizabeth's hands slipped off the wheel. The Jeep slewed and struck a stump buried under a shifting hillock of ants. The collision threw them against the windshield, which cracked under the impact of their skulls, the glass turning milky and opaque.

The pain brought Rudyard instantly back. He blinked at the ants streaming around the Jeep, rising past the wheel wells. They hissed and foamed against the tires and were crawling inside now, no different than if the Jeep had driven headlong into a river and he was watching water surge in.

Elizabeth sagged behind the wheel, her head dangling bonelessly. The ants were everywhere, *everywhere*, the world was ants and Rudyard's skin was on fire, his forearms almost invisible under the dark gleam of insects.

"Elizabeth!"

Her eyes snapped open as ants trooped up her neck, gnawing as they went; her hands were bloody sticks and Rudyard knew she'd never be able to use them again, but their father was rich, very rich, and they could do wonderful things with plastic hands and feet—

He tried to drag her up, but no sooner had he pulled than she unleashed a scream. He could see—barely, it was so hard to distinguish anything amid the industry of the ants—her foot had gotten wedged under the brake pedal, pushed off at a ruinous angle.

Elizabeth moaned as the ants crawled over her lips and into her mouth and she bit down, mashing them up as blood trickled down her chin.

A gas can was strapped to the back of the Willys. With numb hands—he caught the giddy wink of bone at his fingertips—Rudy unstrapped it and unscrewed the cap.

Upending the can, he doused himself with gasoline. Its greasy weight clung to his dungarees, the heady stink almost knocking him out—but the ants didn't like it, falling off his arms and legs and face.

When he turned to his sister, the ants had colonized her. Elizabeth was a shapeless heap in the driver's seat.

An image darkened his mind, a hideous equivalency. When his father hosted parties, the maids would pile the guests' coats in the spare bedroom. That's what Elizabeth looked like. A quivering pile of brown coats.

Shrieking, the air swimming with gasoline fumes, he plunged one hand into the ants. He grasped something that felt like his sister, except hard where it ought to be soft and oily, tacky, a rubber inner-tube swollen to a thrilling tension.

Oh god no please, Elizabeth, don't go you can't die on me—

In her final moments, it was as if his sister harnessed all the electricity of youth to make one last defiant and ultimately useless stand.

She stood. On one leg, it must have been—impossible to know, really, as the ants went up with her, never letting go. Bearing that smothering coat of ants, Elizabeth blindly mounted the Jeep, hauling herself over the collapsible windscreen onto the hood.

Then, amazingly and for the briefest moment, she brushed them off.

Slinging both hands down her thighs, she scraped off tens of thousands of those ripping, consuming ants as if she was brushing crusted snow off a pair of snow-pants. She did the same with her arms, and Rudyard would never forget the red state of them, these flayed cuts of beef. Finally, she tried to clear as many as she could off her head and when she had, her eyes locked with Rudy's. She may even have been smiling.

Next, the ants roped up her in a breathtaking flex—in *wires*, was how it looked: tapered, kinky wires that built themselves back up Elizabeth's body. Her chest swelled as she took her last breath, as the ants costumed her in a bristling drapery. Billions upon billions bubbled over the Jeep: the Willys looked somehow deep-fried, coated in a crackly, spuming brown layer.

Elizabeth's arms went up: *hallelujah!* The ants climbed higher than her fingertips, linking to each other like beads on a chain, until her digits resembled icicles that bent forward before breaking, the ants coming apart to fall back into the rush.

When his sister's carotid artery blew out, it was as if a small fire hydrant had been uncapped within the swarm. Ants spat off in the blood spray with the glint of shrapnel.

The shock of realization—*she's dead, and maybe that's for the best*—caused Rudyard to lose his balance. His heels hit the rear gate of the Jeep and he tipped backward, arms pinwheeling, to splash down in the mad river of ants.

It was unlike anything he'd ever experienced. The closest would be falling into scalding water, but this was much more intimate. Their sound was an endless silken tearing; an echo of that note would live in Rudyard's blood for the rest of his natural life. For the briefest moment, the swarm accepted him; the air and sunlight disappeared under the moving, questing, carnivorous stream of their bodies, and Rudyard felt in his core a beat of harmony—his more developed brain melding with the primitive communal mind of the creatures with whom he'd briefly become one.

With a closemouthed moan, Rudyard heaved himself up. Broaching the tide, he surfaced from the colony and stood in the surge, now rising to his kneecaps, dizzy from blood loss, gasoline fumes, and the rancid stink of the ants.

The gasoline was still working; the ants were all over him, but in a single and somewhat painless layer. Or had he surrendered the ability to feel pain by then?

He staggered through the toppling current until he found himself at its breach. Blundering away from the swarm's advancing edge, feet squelching in blood-filled boots, he dug a finger into his ears—little bodies popped and crunched, their corpses driven into his eardrums.

His final sight of his sister was of her deflating like a parade float with a gash in its nylon . . . her legs met the Jeep, becoming part of it, then her chest and arms . . . her head bobbed up on the spume of ants—*only* her head—her red hair glowing as the sun burned within it, her eye sockets stuffed with writhing darkness . . .

He retreated into the shadow cast by the cliffs. He couldn't climb them like the ibexes had; he'd get ten feet up, if that, before he lost his footing and fell helplessly into the sea of ants—or else they'd climb the cliff and devour him where he clung to the rocks.

The ants were going to eat him, same as they'd done to Elizabeth . . . except *would* they? The prospect of what was about to happen unlocked a new fear. Of being torn to pieces and carried back to the ants' nest, lovingly cradled in their mandibles; the bits of him heaped in a dark spot clung with quintillions of bean-shaped egg sacs—sacs that would split to release wriggling larvae that would consume those little parts of Rudyard Crate in a manner he could scarcely comprehend.

Howling, he'd dragged himself toward the only safety to be found.

———————

Rudyard Crate—now a fifty-five-year-old man, decades removed from that sunlit afternoon—sat on his private Falcon 6X as it pierced a cloud bank with its nose arrowing downward. Soon, its tires touched on a landing strip that shone white as bone in the morning sun. The plug door opened. A set of stairs lowered.

As he deplaned, he watched two airport porters guide a black trunk out of the Falcon's baggage compartment. They muscled it onto a motorized carrier, which was piloted between the jet and a waiting helicopter.

Rudyard wore tan pants and boots, an oiled deerskin jacket, and a belt with a buckle that flashed in the sun. His tan gave him the look of a rancher—the owner, not one of the wilty-mustached cowpokes.

A slim briefcase hung at the end of his left hand. To the east, the spire of the CN Tower rose above the skyline, rung by the glittering high-rises of downtown Toronto.

Two men waited for Rudyard in the helicopter's rotor wash. The first, Roy, was tall and broad across the shoulders. He wore faded chinos and a light jacket over an olive V-neck T-shirt. The second, Jameson, was not wearing a lab coat but had the look of someone who usually did: a spare frame, coffee-round eyeglasses, fingers that thrummed nervously at his sides.

"Is that—?" Jameson asked, head tipping to the trunk that the porters were now settling into the helicopter's freight hold.

"None other than, yes!" Rudyard shouted over the chopping blades.

Jameson's face folded in on itself, but he said nothing.

Rudyard's own face would be familiar to the Silicon Valley crowd, but not nearly so much as a Zuckerberg or a Musk. He'd adopted a near-frictionless way of navigating the world. A former business rival once said, "Seeing Crate walk into a boardroom is like watching a shark's fin slit the water."

He was the tenth-richest man in the world, according to *Forbes*, yet was secretly worth a great deal more than that dime-store rag's estimate. He was the owner of SysWell Dynamics, a multinational corporation with ties in pharma, telecom, tech, wireless, agriculture, and broadcasting. Corporate organisms ought to be anonymous, was Rudyard's sense. The octopus must remain un-grippable to the general public. The name of his company had been carefully chosen. SysWell Dynamics, what *was* that? Oh, nothing. Word salad. Pay no attention.

Once Rudyard, Jameson, and Roy were belted in, Rudyard's briefcase resting between his ankles, the helicopter's doors *thunk*ed shut. The chopper lifted. The men donned headsets as they glided over the downtown skyscrapers, on across Lake Ontario glittering pale gold.

"I want you to know I'm not angry," Rudyard told Jameson, this being a colossal lie. He was in fact furious, molten-fucking-lava. "I am resigned to the fact that I'll be working from behind."

Jameson had labored on Project Athena since the beginning, before the initial specimens had even been seeded. Rudyard conceded that Jameson would likely be dead by day's end, but in benefit of hindsight, he was nearly certain that would have happened no matter what. They might all wind up dead, even Rudyard himself, although he personally hoped for a better outcome. He'd cheated death a few times—none more obviously than on that day in the jungle. But everyone's number got called, and one never knew when the reaper's blade might swing.

He faced Jameson: "Do we have any bead on the subject's whereabouts?"

"Best guess is she's still local. But she—"

"I don't think we should use those terms, should we? Gender-specific. He. She." His lips pursed. "Even *they* doesn't quite fit."

Tense silence. Then Jameson said: "*It* is still at large."

Subject Six had disappeared some time ago. Rudyard had been heartbroken at the possibility it could have gone someplace dark and quiet to die, no different than a sick hound crawling under a porch. Its remains may've been found one day by a hunter or some kids playing where they shouldn't; Rudyard may've caught wind of the discovery, but of what value would it be then? Still, he'd never lost hope that his most intriguing subject might resurface.

And by the sounds of it, Subject Six had made quite the re-entrance into public life.

"What about the Minder?" Rudyard asked.

"As before. The subject hasn't made contact with her."

"What about the best . . . ?" Rudyard's brain vapor-locked. "*Bestie?* Is that what the kids call each other these days? Where's the subject's bestie?"

"She hasn't moved in weeks. We can send someone to check on her again."

"Do that, *now*. Keep a thumb on her."

Rudyard would very much relish striking Jameson right this instant, if only to give his fists something fun to do. Jameson with his waxy, chinless face.

Instead, Rudyard closed his eyes. His sister came to him, as she often did.

Their father had kept the official report of her death vague. She'd died of untreatable fever in a foreign land. It was the kindest thing he'd ever done for her. The truth of Elizabeth's death, its sheer absurdity, held the power to reduce her to a morbid punch line.

Rudyard saw Elizabeth now, exquisitely frozen at the age of sixteen. Sometimes he pictured her face plated in the moonlight falling through the eyelets of the barracks. Other times, in the chlorophyll-green light that hung under the jungle canopy.

Yet most often it was just before the ants shuddered over her.

In that moment, his complicated, inexpressible feelings for his sibling—an urge that at ten had only burbled in his primal hindbrain like water down a sluggish spillway—sharpened to a fine point.

Elizabeth's eyes, shining stark white from the center of her face. Eyes that *continued* to stare—defiantly, if terror-stricken—as the ants made a home of them.

That was where Rudyard had lived ever since: in his sister's expression, and the ants, a merging and melding of one into the other like the river mouth meeting the ocean.

In that crushing moment so long ago, Rudyard Crate had discovered his life's purpose.

He was intelligent enough to realize it was wrong. Also clear-sighted enough to see that his experience had left him with significant mental instability. Hell, he may even be full-on demented! But who gave a ripe shit? Of every benefit conferred by obscene wealth, the best was that people treated you as they would a toddler waddling around with a load of shit in his diaper: everyone smiled pleasantly and plugged their noses, so long as the check cleared.

EIGHT
9:50 a.m.

There was this game Plum and I used to play. Except you couldn't really call it a game—at its heart, it was too serious to be that.

Tell Me.

Tell me what scares you so bad you can't sleep.

Tell me what makes you so crazy you can't sleep at night.

Tell me where you're going and what you'll be when you get there.

Tell me who you love so much you can't think straight.

It was the closest thing we had to a confessional, seeing as neither of us were churchgoing types.

The last time we played was my final night at the Hallmark double-wide where I'd spent my life until then. My folks had already moved into our sterile McMansion in Executive Acres. That night it was just Plum and me, alone in the cleaned-out unit. Closets bare, bright squares on the sun-faded wallpaper where pictures had once hung.

We'd spent that afternoon getting sun-crisped on the busted tongue of the old Niagara River bridge. I lay face down in bed while Plum peeled sunburnt skin off me: that delicious sensation of fresh skin taking its maiden breath along my shoulder blades.

"Oooh, this is a good one." Plum displayed a strip so translucent the bedroom light shone through it. "You're shedding. You're a snake."

That night felt different. An endgame sense to things.

"Tell me what you don't want people to know about you."

I rolled over to face her. "You know already."

"Tell me."

"I don't want people to know I'm not . . . put together. That I'm scared of a lot of stuff." Pulling my elbow under me, I traced one finger over her arm, raising goose pimples. "Your turn."

I realized then that Plum was dangerously close to tears. They'd been hanging in the atmosphere all day, waiting on a cue.

"I don't want people to know that I don't feel as if I'm part of things. That people go around me and not *through* me. I'm a rock in a current." Stroking my arm back. "All except you."

All except you.

From my earliest memory, Plum had been there. Us two as toddlers in a Mr. Turtle pool on the sunbaked grass outside my trailer.

Plum always was a bit odd. I'd dwelled on that after she went missing. She had tendencies that were, hmm, *off*. But I never took direct note of them, and I wonder now if it was the same as growing up near a faulty nuclear reactor: You get so used to the black rain that you figure it's normal.

I pictured us as two trees planted side by side. We'd grown into each other, our roots entwining so it got hard to tell where one ended and the other started. Which was great when we were kids. But kids get older, don't they? Find different interests, begin to define separate paths.

All except you.

My mom said Plum marched to the beat of her own drummer. But did she need a drumming partner, and did it always have to be me? And sometimes . . .

Tell me, Cherr.

. . . sometimes I hated your clinginess, Plum. It was getting hard to breathe with you down my neck. I hated being your social crutch.

Tell me more. Every little thing.

I noticed how our mutual friends seemed turned off by you in the months before you vanished. The shift was subtle, but . . . People would angle their shoulder to you, their body language cutting you out. You had this new laugh—*yee-hee-hee*, so weird—and you laughed at the wrong times at the wrong things.

I guess I was changing.

I never wanted to resent you, Plum, but our friendship began to carry a debt. I figured moving out of Woody Knot would kick-start the process. After that, an effortless separation: an iceberg splitting, the two halves drifting away on a moonlit sea.

I used to tell myself that I'd have done anything for you, Plum. *Anything.* But now a part of me—the part my brain sprints away from when I'm awake but circles back to like a shark when I'm sleeping— doesn't believe I was being truthful about that.

". . . Mags, you okay?"

NINE
9:58 a.m.

"Hmm? Yeah, Harr. Just spiraling a little bit."

Harry was behind the wheel of his 2001 Geo Metro. I sat in the passenger seat. Harry had bought the car off his neighbor, who'd left it sitting conked out on his lawn over the winter. Harry bought it off the guy for four cases of Molson Golden and gotten it towed to Northfield, where he'd worked on it under the harassed guidance of Mr. Killbride, our auto shop teacher.

Plum and me had been in Killbride's class, too. That's where the rich pissbabies at our school expected us to be: the Skids all grease-monkeying it up, getting a head start on our manifest destinies.

After a few weeks, Harry got the Metro to fire up. I'd stayed after school that afternoon to help. I'd loved the sound of the Metro's sewing machine engine as it finally turned over, and how brightly Harry lit up. Man, he'd hugged me *so* hard.

Harry drove onwards to Northfield. With its tin roof and brickwork the color of a dead tooth, to me it looked like a factory that spat out frozen toaster strudels. Harry pulled into a space near the tech wing and parked with the beaters driven by his fellow Skids—not that most Skids owned cars, hence the bike rack packed with rust-pimpled BMXes. The rest of the student body parked their mom and dad's Mazdas and Chevy Cruzes in the general corral.

Standing apart from those, in a cluster that may as well have a red velvet rope strung around it, sat Miranda Lancaster's Audi and Cole Lavender's Lexus ES. They were nicer than the teachers' cars. Nicer than Principal McKinney's Subaru.

But Allan Teller's hunter-green Range Rover wasn't there.

Ditto Will Stinson's powder-blue Corvette Stingray.

And Chad Dearborn's jacked-up Lincoln Navigator.

Ping!

The phone. It'd been sitting silently in my pocket, a wad of cancerous tissue.

> Armor Up!

Back in tenth grade, me and Plum walked to school together. She'd fly out of her trailer's screen door and beat her chest with her fists, looking like a pissed-off gorilla. One morning I asked: *Why do you keep hitting yourself in the tits?*

Checking the armor, Cherr. We're in high school now. Gotta armor up.

Ping!

> Head to the smokehole

Harry glanced at the text. He lip-farted. "No risk outside a touch of lung cancer, right?"

With first period still in session, the smokehole was deserted apart from Northfield's custodian, Dickie O'Reilly. He was sucking on a deep-bowled pipe—a real Sherlock Holmes–looking thing—while he scrubbed at graffiti spray-painted across the cinder block:

FUCK DICK PICS, SOMEONE SEND ME A REASON TO LIVE

And below that, the words faded to transparencies now:

GONNA EAT SOME SKINNY BITCHES

O'Reilly clocked Harry. Tossing the scrub brush into his bucket of suds, he folded his arms.

"You'd better not be contemplating any sort of nutty bullshit, young master."

"No deviltry at all, Mr. O'Reilly," Harry said, showing Dickie his palms.

"You and I both know that any ferret-legged imbecile with a death wish can scamper up to the roof using that as a foothold." O'Reilly nodded to the steel drainpipe bolted to the wall, running up to the eaves. "You're tellin' me that you're not plannin' on being that particular imbecile this morning?"

"I wouldn't put you through that, Mr. O'Reilly," Harry said seriously. "I might die today, but not here."

There was something about the solemnity of Harry's statement that made the custodian pause. Smoke curled over O'Reilly's rigid upper lip.

The bell rang, breaking the strained silence.

TEN

10:22 a.m.

Dickie O'Reilly got back to his scrubbing as the smokehole filled. I rarely made the pilgrimage to the realm of vapers and butt-bummers, not because I had anything against these fine citizens, but more be-cause the mingled smell of cigarettes, vape pens, and the odd try-hard Gauloises made me a little sick.

Dennis Weeks, who used to split his Twinkies with me back in kindergarten, sauntered through the doors. Spotting me, he gathered me into a hug.

"Heyyyyy, Carpenter, you old horse thief!"

He crushed me against his wide, freshly deodorized chest. I could feel the *lub-dub* of Dennis's heart against my cheek, envisioning a fist covered in gristle bapping behind his ribs.

"It's good to see you, Maggie." He gave my shoulders a squeeze. "Been a minute."

"Ripping darts, art thou?" Harry said to Dennis in a plummy English accent. "Pray, may I bummeth one, my fine chap?"

"Keen to practice the dangerous sport of lung rocketry, my lad?" Dennis pinched a smoke out of his deck for Harry. "Then fly, fly where only eagles dare!"

Their whole "Talking Like an Eighteenth-Century Dandy" schtick was new. Den lifted one eyebrow at me.

"Do you dare, milady?"

"I do not, noble sir."

He crooked a Du Maurier between his lips and lit it. "Mmm-hmm, thou art wise to avoid yonder popcorn lung. Hey," he said, serious now. "I never believed it. You know that, right? All that bullshit they spread about Charity. That she—"

"I know, Den. You don't have to, y'know . . ."

He exhaled smoke through his nostrils. "Okay, right, cool."

The edge on my anxiety, which had been peaking since the phone showed up, dulled just a bit. The welcoming crowd, the zip of conversation, familiar faces and voices . . . I let the good feeling wash over me, the microscopic molecules that formed one Margaret June Carpenter pinging off the like-minded molecules forming Harry Cook and Dennis Weeks and—

On the next breath, I was gripped by phantom hands and ripped back to that night. To the party at Burning Van. To the sight of Plum dragging herself out of that charred Econoline. How everyone recoiled as she shambled into the firelight . . . how it felt that to touch her would be no different than slipping your hand into a pool of lit napalm; that to breathe her in would be like inhaling an alien fungus designed to cannibalize you from the inside out.

Now, in the sunlit smokehole, I recalled Dennis Weeks as he'd been that night: with a red Solo cup stunned at lips which bore the same half smile they did now, but there hadn't been an ounce of joy in that smile then; no, it was the expression of someone beholding a sight their minds can't make rational sense of.

Ping!

> Go inside.

I showed the text to Harry. He ground his dart out under his boot.

"Thanks for letting me suck on one of your dandy nicotine delivery tubes, Den. We've got to jet."

"Fie, what waste!" Den said, frowning at Harry's half-smoked cigarette.

ELEVEN
10:39 a.m.

The crush of bodies in the tech wing felt assaultive after being cooped up in my room. Bros bodychecked one another into lockers while girls walked four abreast with their faces plunged into their phones. A half-dozen disconnected conversations washed over me.

"—I couldn't afford the Uber surge charge, so I just stayed home and drank a bottle of Mom's pink Zinfandel—"

"—before my dad got put on Flomax, he urinated all stutter-y, dude; I'd hear him in the bathroom taking a piss in Morse code—"

"—being sexually active is a big time-sink. My YouTube channel's losing subs—"

"—dropped a hundred on White Claws, *all* mango, total fucking flex—"

It took a minute for it to twig that the halls weren't as busy as usual. A lot of students weren't here. And maybe it was just Big Mood, but there was more laughter (of the wild and hysterical sort) and stretched-out grins. This sense that the whole student body was stuck in an unrehearsed play. Up onstage, everyone was dancing around the rim of a bottomless pit, their feet kicking with desperate glee—but their eyes were black with fear.

Welcome to today's performance of *Everything's Okay, It's All Perfectly Fine!!*, starring every single soul at Northfield High. But then, having four students go missing during the second semester would tend to have that effect.

Four. God, that number hit hard. My own parents hadn't exactly been crowbarring me out of my room to get my ass back here, either.

Harry and I made our way toward the caf. The bell rang. The halls began to empty as everyone slouched off to make class. I stopped under the banner hung above the cafeteria doors:

THE FINAL DANCE
PRAYERS FOR A SAFE RETURN

Allan, Chad, and Will: their photos were slapped on the banner, blown up big. A trio of grinnin' Daddy's Boys. Running along the bottom in smaller print:

**All profits to be donated to the families'
ongoing efforts to bring their sons home safely**

There was not a single mention of Charity Atwater.

Pikachu!

That was the phone. The ringtone must've been changed remotely.

> Go to the pool.

> why?

No reply. I punched the letters so forcefully my thumbs ached.

> im scared ok? tell me what's going on

Pikachu!

> I can't tell you Cherr only show you

Pikachu!

> Its the only way any of this will make sense

Pikachu!

> So pls

Pikachu!

> for me

Pikachu!

> The pool

As I stared numbly at the string of words, Harry reached over, snatched the phone, and marched off.

"Hey! What the fuck, Harr?"

He didn't stop, not even when I caught up to him by the vending machines. He shook my hand off his shoulder and continued down the hall in the direction of the pool.

"She texted me too, remember?" he said. "Told me where to meet you and all that."

He pivoted to face me—I leaned back under the fleeting impression he was going to slug me—and pressed the iPhone into my chest.

"Sorry. *Fuck*. Here, take it."

"Why are you being such an asshole?"

He threw his hands up. "Just, all this crazy shit. Also the wild and, uh, sorta self-destructive decision to go off my Paxil?"

"What about those clean lines?"

"I may have been overly confident on that, because this has got me in a choke hold." Harry tried to smile, but something lunged up from the pits of his eyes. "It's activating *that* part of me, y'know?"

I knew precisely the part he was talking about. I called that part *Bad Harry*.

My first glimpse of Bad Harry was one morning in Auto Shop. Harry and me were asses to elbows under the power jack; Harry had been struggling with an oil pan, straining to get a seized hex bolt to loosen. He'd cried out, hands upflung. His head hovered in the crosscutting shadows under the jack, disembodied like a sideshow oracle at a county fair—one half of his face had gone pocky black from the oil pouring from the pan; his left eye, rung in that oil, glared at me with baleful glee.

The memory clung to me. How one side of his face was just regular ole Harry. The opposite side mottled and disfigured, somehow poisonous. It would be easy to say I was looking at the true version of Harry, his Jekyll and Hyde, but it was more complex. Harry had a side that was pure spirit, pure energy and joy for life . . . and another side that was jealous of its counterpoint, and when circumstances let that side out of its dark little box, it'd do everything in its power to corrupt its better half.

There in the hall, I said: "We can't have Bad Harry showing up now, okay?"

Harry jammed his hands in his pockets, his fingers stimming under the denim.

"Bad Harry? Okay, I get that. Trust me, I'm trying. But on a day like today, Bad Harry's gonna be lurking."

"Okay. Thank you for your honesty."

"We're in a school full of teachers and students," he reasoned. "Five hundred witnesses. If we scream, people will hear. This isn't midnight in the middle of the woods, right?"

TWELVE
10:48 a.m.

The pool sat on the east side of the school, past the gymnasium. Dickie O'Reilly's understudy, a long-ago graduate everyone cryptically called Bone-Man, didn't look up as he doodle-bugged the floors at the end of an intersecting hallway.

Chlorine tingled my sinuses as we reached the pool viewing area. The water was empty, its glass-like blue shining behind tall viewing windows.

Pikachu!

> The door on the left.

So weird. I must have walked this part of school two hundred times. But if you'd asked me before then, I'd have told you there was no door at all. Yet there it stood.

Its paint was scuffed, the words FURNACE ROOM stamped on a black plaque.

Pikachu!

It'll be open.

I gripped the knob. The clammy metal made me think of a fireman's pole. The door opened onto a cement landing. I stepped through. My sneakers didn't make a sound. Harry came in behind me, edging around my hip. The doorknob hit my ass as it closed behind us on the pneumatic elbow-hinge.

We crowded together on the landing. Two staircases. The first led up to a part of the school I'd never visited. "The Garret," as it was nicknamed, where the wrestling team held their homoerotic grappling jamborees.

The second set led down into a sketchy darkness under the main floor of the school.

"There's a door down there," said Harry, pointing. "Can you see it?"

He was right. Another landing lay at the base of the stairs. And another door.

"That must be the old furnace," Harry said. "The oil one. The new natural gas one is over by the . . . the . . ."

From where we stood, I could see that the furnace room door was open. Half a foot or so, but open. Maybe someone had forgotten to close it behind them when they came out.

Or left it open when they went inside, came the nasty whisper from my lizard brain.

There was this TLC reality show Plum and I used to watch: *My Strange Addiction*. It followed subjects whose compulsions ranged from odd—a dude who ate the stuffing out of couch cushions—to deadly. This one girl mixed toilet cleanser powder and water into a green paste, eating it with a Royal Doulton spoon. You could *see* the spoon was all eaten through, and it made you wonder what the girl's insides looked like. A doctor told her if she didn't stop, she'd die.

Your stomach lining is obliterated. That's the word the doctor used. His decree held a simple certainty, same way you'd tell a child the sun is hot. But at the end of the episode the camera snuck up to find that girl shoveling Ajax stew into her mouth, crouched in the bathtub with the shower curtain pulled shut, sobbing.

This came back to me as my foot touched the first stair leading down to the furnace: the unhealthy, even lethal things we humans do.

The topmost sounds of the school dimmed as I went down that staircase. The soles of my sneakers gritted on the pebbled cement. It was easy to believe I wasn't *in* school anymore. The dust running on the railing under my fingers told me that, in a way, this feeling was correct. I'd come to an uncharted area of the beast, one off-limits and seldom visited.

By the time I reached the bottom landing, my chest was crawling: My skin hooked into a million fingers creeping across my rib cage. Harry bumped into me. His arm brushed mine. His skin felt sickeningly overheated, as if he'd been boiled alive.

"Sorry," he said in a voice that had gone very small.

I shook the iPhone to activate the flashlight, which lit up right in our faces, so bright we flinched. I pointed it the other way round.

Pikachu!

SOLONELY.wav

I pressed play.

"There's this other version of me, Cherr. But she doesn't exist anymore. People liked that version. That person fit in; she felt happy and even confident around her small friendship circle. But that person's gone. What's left is someone nobody likes. Someone other people talk over or pretend never spoke at all."

Harry prodded the door with the toe of his Converse. The darkness leapt out hungrily, pooling over our legs.

My hand rose with the phone: Its light washed over the jungle of pipes running the length of the furnace room, at least the part we could see. Thick pipes, thinner ones, a few wrapped in shiny metallic tape sagging from the ceiling. The phone's light went grainy along its edge—I waited for a hand or leg to invade that weak coin of brightness, for something to step from the surrounding darkness. My mind couldn't make a shape of whatever that could be, only that it had been waiting down here for such a long, long time.

"I can't remember when this new person crept into me, but I think loneliness put her there. The kind that twists you out of shape, making you a sad, mangled version of who you'd been. People didn't like to be around that version, even the ones I know loved me. The old me understands why that is. I'm no fun anymore. I'm like a, a . . . a glowing plutonium rod. Stay close to me long enough and you'll get sick."

I swung the phone. Its light crawled over a stack of ancient, water-fattened boxes. Some hung open, their dusty cardboard flaps lolling; inside I could see unused equipment left over from gym classes of yore: pink two-pound barbells, the ones Mom used for her DVD aerobics classes; a coil of gym rope, the fibers smoothed out by thousands of hands, resting on the floor like a slumbering serpent. Down the limewashed wall, past the boxes, and under the pipes sat the furnace, hunchbacked and spidery. A metallic chuckle rolled out of it . . . only the pop of cold metal.

But it was the smell that got me. A wet, rusty stink knotted with something else, somehow malty.

"At night, I'd twist and turn in bed, my mind replaying all the stupid things I'd said or done that day . . . an endless fixating loop of people looking away as though there was something the matter with me. They couldn't wait to get away from me."

I wasn't going any farther. The stairs were just behind us. We would go up them and back into the hallway where Bone-Man would still be doodle-bugging the floor—

But when I looked back, the door had shut behind us. On its own, maybe, so silently I'd missed the catch of its latch. Or had something slipped in from behind us—a hand with dead black blood collected under the fingernails—to ease it closed?

I turned back to catch Harry walking toward the furnace.

"Harr?" My voice could have been coming from the bottom of a well.

His head had become one with the blackness. The radish-y stalk of his neck jutted from his white tee. Above that was darkness. For a moment I saw Plum standing there instead of Harry, but Plum how she'd look after being dead for a month, her face the bloated black of a decayed banana and her nose caved into a festering pit, grinning at me with empty gums.

I jerked the phone up. The light framed the back of Harry's head under the draping pipes. When he reached the furnace, he stopped.

"I didn't want people hating me, so I put on a mask. With the mask on I could be whoever people needed me to be—so long as I screwed it on so tight that nobody could see what was underneath. Nobody would understand that new person who'd started crawling around under the mask. That person scared people. Did she scare you, *Cherr?"*

I approached Harry, clutching the phone. He knelt by the furnace. Two charred glass portholes looked in on its flame jets, dead now, staring like cataracted eyes.

"Shine the light over there," he instructed.

I swung the phone until its light fell on a bed . . . no, only a bare mattress. Squashed flat with springs poking through, lying on the dusty cement behind the furnace.

"All I'd ever wanted was to be myself without feeling ashamed or stupid. I wanted to be anyone else other than who I was . . . but who was that?"

The mattress was shoved roughly in a corner; part of it had folded up against the wall. It had a dent in it, as though someone's head had been squashed into it hard enough to leave the permanent impression.

That smell was worse back here, solidifying into a taste that filmed my tongue.

There was a stain on the mattress—dead center of it, as though someone had squeezed a whole bottle of Hershey's syrup onto it.

"Mags?"

I turned to Harry. The phone came around with me.

YAS KWEEN

The words had been written on the wall in yellow spray paint. The *Y* in YAS had an *X* spray-painted over it, and the letter *D* had been laid over it in red.

"*Das* means *the* in German," Harry said. "My dad and I watched this movie, *Das Boot*, about a submarine. Dad said *Das Boot* was German for *The Boat*. I never got that because it was a submarine, you know, not a . . . a . . ."

He trailed off. I was only half listening, anyway. My brain was kicking out an emergency broadcast signal: *This is not a test. If you are hearing this, you need to go to a brightly lit area. Repeat, a brightly lit area.*

In a high corner of the furnace room, jammed into a crevice where the bricks had been cut down to accommodate a sewage pipe, I caught the blink of a red light.

I pinned it with the phone. A white device the size of a goose's egg. The red light was blinking from its convex face.

"Is that a Wi-Fi cam, Harr?"

He nodded. "Looks like it. It, uh, probably switched on the moment we stepped in here. Activated by our movement."

are you watching us?

But my text didn't send. Zero bars. Too far underground for the satellites to find us.

I forced myself to crouch by the mattress. Up close the stain was thicker, the dried patch studded with hardened chunks.

THIRTEEN
11:09 a.m.

Harry shouldered through the door and back into the main-floor hallway. I staggered after him. I'd been holding my breath, and my lungs had become a pair of flaming bags inside my chest.

"I'm gonna puke."

I made it to the wall and rested my forehead on it. I inhaled the industrial paint on the pebbled concrete. It struck me that every wall in every school I'd ever been in smelled the exact same, and in a funny way that calmed me.

I wasn't going to puke. Scream, quite possibly. But not puke.

"What the actual fuck?" Harry breathed from somewhere behind me.

"We need to tell someone about this."

Harry straightened up, arms dangling. "Makes sense. Who?"

"Principal McKinney. Vice Principal Grayson. The cops."

"Okay, but tell them what?"

He came over to me. His palm pressed flat on the wall beside my head, blocking me in.

"I'm not saying we *don't* do that, Mags. I'm just saying . . ."

The fingers of his other hand found the bulge of the phone in my front pocket, applying soft pressure.

"Charity *knows* where we are, right? If she's got mapping software, then she knows exactly where we are *inside the school*, right this minute. If she put that camera down in the furnace room—if she was watching us just now—then she knows—"

Pikachu!

"—what we saw down there."

"Yeah? *And?*"

"So she'll know if we go to the principal's office," he went on, his head bobbing as he worked his reasoning out. "And she'll know if we go to the cops, too."

Pikachu!

Harry was probably right. But we could leave the phone on the ground, couldn't we, and get the principal . . . and so what if Plum *did* know? Why should that even matter, unless her aim was to pull us so deep into this (God, what *was* this?) that we'd lose the option of getting help from the teachers or the cops or anyone who could—

Pikachu!

Pikachu!

I yanked the phone out and scrolled the influx of messages:

Just to make sure you're safe.

That was her reply to the text I'd sent from the furnace room, asking about the Wi-Fi camera.

The next ones read:

Please

If you're still my friend

PLEASE

Don't tell anyone

"Fuck you!" I screamed, flecking the phone's screen with spittle.

WHY ARE YOU DOING THIS?

No reply.

"Is she listening in on us?" Harry's suspicion that the phone was feeding audio back on some kind of loop didn't seem at all far-fetched now. "It's like she's right-*fucking*-here."

Harry's own phone vibrated. He fished it out of his pocket and frowned through a text. He stuffed it back in his jeans and said: "I need fresh air. Getting squirrelly, walls starting to close in."

"Who was that?"

"Nobody." A distracted hand-flap. "My dad got a call from the truancy officer."

Harry made his way to the exit near the pool, slamming his hip into the crash-bar. The door popped open, spilling Harry outside.

I could go to the office. Harry didn't need to come. Maybe he shouldn't. This was too big for us. Plum *knew* that. Neither of us handled stress well. Plum got bloated and gassy. Me, I bit my fingernails to the quick.

On cue, my hand rose to my lips, teeth hunting for a ragged edge of thumbnail to gnaw at—*ugh, oh god.*

That smell perfuming the furnace room. A trace of it clung to my fingertips.

That *smell.* I recognized it now.

Back in third grade, Plum and me overheard my parents having sex. I'd never caught them at it before. Amazing, considering we shared a fifteen-hundred-square-foot double-wide. Either they'd figured out how to have subsonic sex, or they didn't have much at all.

That night they'd come home from the beer milers at the Speedway. The two-buck Buds must've been flowing pretty freely. Plum and I pretended to be asleep as they stumbled in to give us beery good-night kisses before retiring to their own room.

We didn't know what to make of the soft gut-shot sounds that seeped through the presswood wall. Could have been a pair of big cats tussling in the jungle. *Are they playing a game?* Plum whispered.

Until then, our knowledge of the act had been restricted to school-yard innuendoes. A boy in our class, Dickie Travis, lectured a rapt group of us on the elementary schoolyard: Dickie explained that a man bought a special seed at a drugstore and placed it in the hole of his penis; he then poked his penis into the woman's belly button, planting it. Nine months later, the woman felt a huge dump coming on and sat on the toilet, but—surprise!—it was a baby.

Embarrassed, wanting it to end, I went into my parents' room and said: *I had a nightmare.* The two of them were off in a corner, not even in bed, their bodies locked in a perplexing human origami. When my father saw me, he went *"Ho-ho-ho"* like some naked, bewildered Père Noël; after awkwardly slinging his underpants on, he led me back to bed.

What came back to me now was the smell hanging in their bed-room. That adrenalized, malty, animal one. It was the same one I'd caught down in the furnace, except much staler.

The smell of sex.

FOURTEEN

11:14 a.m.

I found Harry smoking a joint under the football bleachers.

Eventually I'd followed him out. I couldn't quite grip my own reasoning for not going to the office, but it had something to do with Plum's confession on the .wav.

. . . did she scare you, Cherr?

Had I sensed a shift in my best friend's personality in the months before she went missing—something creeping into her that filled me with low-key fear?

Loneliness put her there . . .

"Where'd you get that?"

Harry sat smoking a joint. "My dad's stash," he said, eyes hooded as he held the smoke in. "You wanna hit it?"

"What about Charity?"

"Has she texted you since?"

"No."

"Then I say we chill until she does."

"Yeah, but don't you think we should—"

Which is when a childish voice said: *Uh, get high?*

Harry held the joint out. I took a puff, had a coughing fit while Harry watched with polite concern, and hazarded a deeper drag. Dizziness hit me instantly, the blood running warm in my veins.

"Wheeee," said Harry.

I sunk down beside him on the dirt. "So, you hooked this from your dear old dad?"

Half our parents were medicating. I kinda wondered if they only noticed their kids were experimenting with drugs when their own supply got raided.

"*Gabagool.*"

Harry laughed. "Wait, *what?*"

I'd watched *The Sopranos*, seasons one through six, during my long hermitage.

"*Gabagool,*" I repeated. "It's fun. Funny word."

Harry plumped out his bottom lip, really drawing it out. "*Gaaaaa-bagoooool.* You're not lying. Say it together on three. One, two, three—"

"*GABBBAGOOOL.*"

After another hit, the furnace and the phone felt far away. The sun carved through the bleachers in bright, sparkly rails, warm on my skin. A big melty pat of butter.

"Do you think," Harry said, "Charity wants to show you all this so you can, y'know, write about it one day?"

"What, like I'm her official biographer?"

"You have to admit, you do use a lot of big words."

"I read books, if that's what you're implying."

Harry went: "*Ah-duuuuuuurrrrh*" with his jaw hanging slack.

"Do big words intimidate you, Harr?"

"Nope." He performed a languid cat-stretch. "Big *sharks*, on the other hand . . ."

In last year's English class, each student had to write a short story. "Balloon Dog" was mine. It was about this guy who got a balloon dog at his niece's birthday party. His loneliness brings the dog to life. He comes to love it. But life's scary for a balloon dog. Every busted shard of glass or stray pine needle could end its life, right? The guy and his dog became shut-ins. They never left the house. But eventually both of them resolve to go outside, where the first gust of wind sweeps the dog out of the guy's arms. The last paragraph is from the dog's perspective as it's being carried up into the sky, to these dizzying elevations—the breathless joy you must feel the moment before you explode.

My teacher, Mr. Foster, held me back after class. *This is a really good story. You're a natural wordsmith, Margaret.* When I tried to shrug it off, he said: *You managed to make me care about a balloon dog, okay? In only ten pages.* He seemed borderline pissed, as if I'd been handed this rare gift that I wanted nothing to do with.

Mr. Foster asked my permission to submit "Balloon Dog" to a province-wide contest sponsored by the school board. From over two thousand entries, mine won. I got a plaque and a check for three hundred bucks. Ms. Crimsen made an announcement on the loud-speaker.

"Your dad's weed is . . ." I licked my lips. My tongue had the warm fuzzies.

"Dank? Yeah, he smokes a shitload. He needs to."

"Why?"

"You really want to know?"

I kicked back, brandishing an invisible notepad and pen like a therapist. "Tell me your troubles, my son."

Harry's look said: *You're weird, but I dig it.* "My dad was in a war, okay? Iraqi Freedom. He came home on furlough, Mom got pregnant, he went back over and came back for good when I was born. Except I never saw him as this army dude. He's been a mechanic as far as my memories stretch back. But he had this whole other life before I was born, right?"

I wiped my face; my skin felt hot, feverish. The sight of that mattress—that dried splash of deep, *clotted* red—kept trying to spoil the nice high I had going.

"Last fall, an old army buddy came by. Him and Dad got high on the porch. Late at night, I'm up in my room listening to them through a rip in the plastic of my bedroom window. Dad told him about an Iraqi soldier he shot over there. *I put it right through his eye.* He was crying, he repeated it a few times. *Right through the poor dude's eye.*"

Harry looked at me. Even through the haze of pot I could see he was scared in a way I couldn't understand, and that scared me.

"It really fucked him up, y'know? But I never knew about it. Like, Dad never shoved his fucked-up-ness on me. And I thought: If he's so good at that, why aren't I?"

"What do you mean?"

"It's like," he said, digging a circle in the dirt with his finger, "I transmit or, ah, release something that weirds people out. Scares them, even. My dad has that in him, too, but he's a good enough dude to keep it hidden."

I wanted to tell Harry he didn't scare me, but I'd be lying. Except it was different, I guess—I wasn't scared *of* Harr, I was scared *for* him.

Another thought hit me as my high glided upward into the blue sky of clear thinking. The notion that adulthood is this place Harry and I were moving toward, and right now we're collecting baggage, suitcases stuffed with stress and sadness, but we actually *need* those because what's inside will furnish our new homes over in Adultland. And as soon as we get there, we'll start collecting more so that when we die, the coroner'll say it was anal cancer or heart failure, but really it was the weight of all we'd been carrying.

"Oh shit," I said. "I'm way too fucking high."

Pikachu!

FIFTEEN

11:26 a.m.

The phone sent a joy-buzzer vibration down my thigh. I dragged it out all dumb-fingered, nearly dropping it.

> Time for English. Go to Mr. F's room.

Oh, *what?* I bared my teeth, molars grinding. My high was mutating— it was getting away from me, going all stringy and decentered.

I tapped a sluggish reply. My nerves fired like bubbles rising through maple syrup.

> not gone to class in forever. Mr. F's gonna be possessed

Shit. Stupid autocorrect.

> piiiiisssssssssed

Pikachu!

> No he won't. He'll be happy to see you. Harry can go too.

Class had already started. Only half an hour until the lunchtime bell. My high was curdling into paranoia. I watched helplessly as my arms elongated, producing new joints, taking the phone with them. The sound they made growing was the crack of deep blue ice.

"Harry, what's in this weed?"

Harry chortled. "Weed, silly. The weed is in the weed."

Oh god, Harry had mutated into a nitwit. I swayed to my feet and began walking toward school, very deliberately. What had I done? What kind of idiot was I?

"Seriously, Harr," I whispered, suspicious that ears may have sprouted from the football field's grass, "was that joint dipped in embalming fluid or some shit?"

"Hee-hee, fentanyl."

"Don't even *joke*." My voice was full of horror.

By the time we stepped inside the school, I was 100 percent positive that Harry's father's joint *had* been dipped in fentanyl. This was bad, ohhh it was so bad. I walked stiff-legged as a toy soldier: nothing to see here, good citizens, just a regular not-stoned girl doing regular not-stoned things.

To clear my head, I tried to focus on concrete memories. I thought about Mr. Foster, my favorite teacher.

Of all my courses, I liked Mr. F's best. I got the impression he'd been a shit-disturber himself in school and found it karmically justified that he'd now have to deal with the same class of asshole he'd once been. Mr. F didn't dress like Mr. Rose, our biology teacher, who wore corduroy blazers and smelled absently of formaldehyde; he didn't get all chesty like our history teacher, Mr. Turpin, with his small-dick energy.

Mr. F wore T-shirts and ripped jeans; one pair was *so* ripped that Plum and I got a peek at his boxers this one time: They had a *Sesame Street* pattern, Cookie Monster slapped on Mr. F's butt cheek. Following a second Cookie Monster sighting, Plum and I printed up a note in the PC Lab and slipped it under his door.

C is for Cookie, is good enough for me.
U is for Underwear, your students all be seeing me.

—With Love, Cookie Monster

That was the last time those ripped jeans were part of Mr. Foster's wardrobe.

Other than Auto Shop, English was the only class Plum and I took together. The fact that we both liked Mr. F couldn't protect him from our scorn. It was common knowledge that he had an unfinished manuscript in his desk. Rumor held that he'd been working on his novel for as long as he'd taught at Northfield. Plum and I came up with titles for his opus:

The Sassiest Werewolf

Sweatpants Boners

The Bi-Curious Cyclops: An Erotic Odyssey

TV Dinners & Elderly Cats with Diabetes

The Butler Farted Blood: A P.I. Deke Fudge Mystery

Wait, is this working? I thought as Harry and I walked up the stairwell to the second floor. *I feel fractionally less stoned.*

It was Mr. F who'd put in motion the two biggest upheavals in my life. The first was him pestering me to enter "Balloon Dog" in that contest. That led inevitably to the second, which is a secret not even my parents knew about yet. The one I'd kept from Plum.

Next September, four provinces and four thousand kilometers away, I'd be a freshman in the University of Victoria's creative writing program.

At the start of winter term, Mr. Foster had handed me an application packet. *I wish I'd taken this opportunity.* I brought the packet home and stuffed it under my bed. After a week, I'd pulled it out. Read it front to back. The next day after class, I handed it to him all filled out. We added my high school transcript, "Balloon Dog" as the writing sample, and an endorsement letter from Mr. Foster. I'd mailed it without telling anyone, slipping it into the mailbox outside the Shoppers Drug Mart on Lundy's Lane.

A week or so before Plum disappeared, a letter showed up. I'd snatched it from our mailbox before my folks got home.

The Victoria University's Faculty of English is pleased to extend an early offer of acceptance for the upcoming academic year...

I'd stashed the letter at the bottom of my desk drawer. But sometimes I took it out, turned it over, *caressed* it. Who knew a piece of paper could feel like freedom?

The only person I'd actually told so far was Mr. F, who gave me a huge and somehow desperate hug. *I knew it. The first step of many.*

And suddenly—like a smash-cut in a horror flick—Harry and I were at the door of Mr. Foster's class.

SIXTEEN
11:31 a.m.

Mr. F's room looked exactly as it had the last time I attended class.

The Christmas garland stapled above the chalkboard. The READING IS FUN-DAMENTAL poster featuring a caterpillar with eyeglasses reading a book that Mr. F had taped, assumedly ironically, to the front of his desk.

Attendance was thin. I counted eight of us. Mr. F was at his desk with his arms hanging at his sides and his forehead resting on the desk blotter. A zag went through me at the sight of him slumped there, a toy with its batteries ripped out.

Harry and I sat at the same two-top desk in the middle row that Plum and I once shared. To my left, Triny Goodhue whispered: "Look at you, touching grass. You're late. By, like, three hundred hours."

"I went down a needlepoint rabbit hole," I whispered back.

I hooked my eyes at Mr. F and cocked one eyebrow: *WTF?*

Triny mimed puffing a joint. "Think he's high," she whispered, giving me some major side-eye. "Bitch, are *you* high?"

"*Nooooooo*," I drawled, my voice doing some weird slide-whistle thing.

Mr. F's phone chirped on the desk. He jolted up in his chair. Patches of sweat bloomed under the armpits of his shirt. He glanced at his phone, then blearily out at the class.

His face. His *eyes*.

I'd been worried in the furnace room. Scared, even. But Mr. F's eyes offered the day's first true dread. They carved through my high like a razor blade.

"Ahhh, Margaret," he sighed. "Aren't you a sight for these sore eyes. So lovely of you to grace us with your presence after lo these many weeks."

The instinct was to drop my gaze, but I kept my eyes on him. "Sorry, Mr. Foster. Y'know, been going through some stuff."

"Sure, sure." His lower lip pooched out in a pantomime of concern: *boo-hoo*. "And you've brought a friend. Terry, right?"

"Harry, sir."

"*Harry*." Mr. F's smile widened into a gruesome slash.

Gooseflesh crept up my arms as something insinuated itself within the classroom. It was almost as if that smell from the furnace room had wafted through the vents, traveling two stories up and across the breadth of the school to find its way here.

Mr. F stood unsteadily. My toes curled painfully inside my sneakers. His face was pale under the halogens; balls of perspiration stood out on his forehead and the sunken furrows under his eyes.

There was another smell now, too. As a little girl, I'd busted my arm when the rotted teeter-totter in Woody Knot's playground snapped under me. When the doctor cut the cast off, exposing my fish-belly-white forearm, the examination room filled with the funk of a month's worth of unwashed skin. The smell coming off my teacher was *that*, but worse.

Pikachu!

I nearly screamed as the vibration ran down my leg.

"Margaret, was that you?"

"Sorry. I'll turn it off."

"No," Mr. F said. "Take it out. In fact, I insist."

I did as he said. Laid the phone on the table and read the new text.

Honesty is the best policy.

Mr. F's own phone went off again. He checked it, swallowed—his Adam's apple joggled, the look of a light switch getting thrown on—and unfolded a piece of foolscap from his pocket.

"Class, stay tuned for an important announcement."

That sense of unreality thickened. Was it the weed? I wish, but . . . this felt more like that point in a dream where it crossed into nightmare: when the tall man with the bent fingers shows up at the edge of the sunlit meadow.

"You all know that relationships between students and teachers are forbidden," Mr. F said. "Teachers must hold ourselves to a higher standard—"

Mr. F choked, gagged, then did something that made everyone recoil.

He spat. Right on the floor.

"—to deny our animal instincts," Mr. F went on, a fleck of spittle stuck to his chin. "Our students are our vulnerable wards."

Everyone stared at the hawked loogie. A shucked oyster full of bloody red threads.

"Now, I must confess that I . . . I stepped over the line with one of my students. Took advantage of my power."

He dragged his head back up. Looked at us with those sad, sick eyes.

"Honesty is the best policy, isn't it? The truth can be cleansing. This student . . . some of you may know her, though she's new to school. She's in this class, though not here today."

Mr. F nodded at Plum's old spot, where Harry now sat.

Triny said: "Are you talking about Serena?"

"Serena, yes, her."

I only knew of one Serena at Northfield. Mrs. Serena Kennedy, the drama teacher. Mrs. K was at least fifty years old, and she was nobody's innocent.

"Serena and I had an inappropriate relationship."

"Oh my fucking *god*." Triny spoke in a horrified hush.

"I was fully the initiator." He stared down at his foolscap like a politician reading off a teleprompter. "And our relationship *was* sexual. I need to be patently clear about that."

Abby Langston unleashed a semi-hysterical titter. "This is *so* inappropriate."

Mr. F continued his confession, oblivious to the gathering groundswell of disgust that shot through the classroom.

That's when I saw the first phone.

A Samsung Galaxy belonging to Ethan Collins. He had it out, pointed at Mr. F. His eyes seemed to be marking the light composition or the framing.

Logan Jackman had his new-ish Pro Max out, too. Smita Acharya, her Google Pixel in pastel pink. Triny was pulling her Xperia out as I watched. She looked hypnotized, acting on generational instinct.

"I should have known better." Mr. F wrung the foolscap in his hands. "I took advantage of a girl who had an innocent crush on her . . . on her . . ."

"Say that again, sir," said Ethan Collins, angling his phone with a grin that was all teeth. "*Enunciate.*"

Another dude, kinda weird with red hair, Craig or Greg, a mid-year transfer from a school across town, let go a hyena-howl of laughter. It uncorked a reservoir of mania surfing through the class; I felt it worming into my own bloodstream—the glowing eyes of the phones, the sweaty mess of Mr. F, the pathetic spectacle he was making of himself . . . Every student, all ten bodies wired to twenty pairs of eyes, physically *leaned* toward our teacher as though he was a magnet and our skulls were packed full of iron shavings—

My teeth ground together because of the drugs, it *had* to be the drugs and *Christ*, that weed was mounting a comeback.

Mr. F bleated. A sick cow. Everyone howled at how impossibly stupid he sounded, even me. He staggered around his desk, down the aisle separating me and Triny. The back of his head lolled between his shoulder blades as he seemed ready to pass out on his feet—

I reached for him. I only wanted to stop him from smashing his face on the floor, yet I was conscious of the phones crawling over me—*Way to cancel yourself, Carpenter!*—and God help me but I didn't *want* to touch him, not at all—

He recovered on his own, but not before my fingertips brushed the wax-pale nape of his neck. I jerked my hand back, wiping it on my pants as Mr. F stumbled to the supply closet where the beat-up classroom copies of *Hamlet* and *Lord of the Flies* were shelved. Abby giggled savagely as Foster's hip crunched into Brian Ashworth's desk—

Foster threw open the supply closet door—and flinched as though expecting something to launch out at him. But there was nothing but static-y darkness in that closet.

Wait, *was there?*

It had to be my high spiking. There was no other explanation.

Pests. That's what my mom called the whispery, thread-legged house centipedes that infested our trailer during the spring rains.

They'd slither out of the drains to sidewinder under the doors and windows, rust-colored and alien, lying perfectly still on the floor or a wall. Their bodies were revoltingly hollow; you could settle a Kleenex over them and when you took it off, they'd be all crumpled, their legs detached. For weeks, I'd find them in the grossest places: on the rim of my drinking cup or stuck to the ceiling above my bed.

That's what the weed was telling me lurked in the supply room's congested dark. One of those rust-colored centipedes, a *pest* . . .

Except huge. Its million-skillion legs not thread-thin but thick as extension cords, hairless as a rat's tail, wavering in the light trailing in from the classroom. A pest so big it was impossible to tell if it was rising from the floor or descending from the ceiling.

"I'm *sorry!*" Mr. F screeched into the closet.

Slamming the door, he fled the classroom.

"That dude is *so* fucking canceled," Craig-or-Greg said, breaking the silence.

Brian stuck his head out the door. "He's a vapor trail, man." Shaking his head, wide-eyed. "Mr. Foster, shit, man. Bro's life is *over.*"

Nobody disputed that. Nobody spoke at all. Everyone was pinned to their phone: rewatching footage and quickly uploading it to their social channels.

Try Not to Laugh Challenge: Perv-O Teacher Freaks Out!

I recovered the sheet of foolscap from where it had fallen under Smita's desk. It wasn't in Mr. F's handwriting, whose penmanship I'd recognize from my returned assignments. The three *i*'s in *initiator* were dotted with little hearts.

My attention shifted back to the supply closet. Nudging Harry with my elbow, I said:

"Did you see anything in there?"

Harry said: "Like what?"

I went to Mr. F's desk. A skull-shaped paperweight sat there; Mr. F had used it for that "Alas, poor Yorick" speech during our Shakespeare section. My hand closed over it.

"Stealing your disgraced teacher's shit," Logan noted approvingly. "I like where your head's at, Margaret."

Paperweight gripped in my hand, I took a step toward the supply room door.

I wasn't going to use the doorknob—something told me I didn't want to get that close. No, I was going to chuck the skull right through the door's frosted glass, which to my spiraling mind was the most effective way to let the light in.

A hand snared me from behind. Harry's fingers, manacling my wrist.

"Jesus, Mags. What are you doing?"

"Let *go*."

"Take it from Bad Harry, okay? Destruction of school property will get you expelled."

"Support a woman's right to choose violence, Cook," Brian said.

For a heartbeat my arm stayed tense. The high continued to tail through my synapses, making everything too hot, clapping iron bands over my chest.

Relenting, I set the paperweight back on the desk.

"*Booooooooo*," said Brian.

"I posted it on YouTube," Logan announced. "Logan-underscore-The-underscore-Unboxer. Check it out."

As the rest of the class sank down over their phones, I spoke the name.

"Serena."

When nobody acknowledged me, I pressed on.

"The girl who—y'know, who Mr. Foster . . ."

"Sexually assaulted," said Triny, her gaze rising from her Xperia. "Say it, Margaret."

"Yeah, okay, assaulted. Who is she?"

Ethan made a face like: *Why are you asking us?* "She's in our class."

"Margaret hasn't *been* in class for like forever, idiot," Abby told him.

Ethan slouched, gnawing on a pen cap. "What, I track her movements?"

"Serena's new," Triny told me. "She showed up late in the semester, same as this guy"—cocking her thumb at Craig-or-Greg.

"I've been here four months," he said.

"Seriously?" Triny's voice held genuine amazement.

What I saw on their faces wasn't exactly unease. More as though they'd been asked to recall someone who'd sat in their midst, only to discover nobody had really been there at all.

"She's *hot*," Logan said.

Brian, Ethan, and Craig-or-Greg laughed. Harry didn't.

"That's it?" I said. "That's all you've got—she's hot?"

Logan squirmed in his seat. "Sorry. I'm sure she's got other meaningful qualities."

Serena. Who the hell?

Pivoting on my toe, I marched out the door.

SEVENTEEN
11:53 a.m.

Harry caught up with me halfway down the hall.

"Mags, hey!"

He grabbed my sweatshirt. I spun, planted both hands on his chest, and shoved him as hard as I could.

"Why'd you have to get me so high, dude?"

I shoved him again. He bounced off the lockers.

"Did I?" Touching one finger to his chin, he feigned deep thought.

"Did I tie you up and blow smoke down your throat? I seem to recall you did that yourself."

Turning away, I stalked down the hallway. "Whatever."

"Okay, so now what?" Harry said, catching up and loping along at my heels.

"How long does this weed take to wear off?"

"Maybe not long?" he said hopefully. "How do you feel?"

"Feel? I'm scared, Harry. None of that, with Foster, none of it felt—"

Real, was the word that fit. What went down in Foster's room felt more like a play, or one of those little frozen scenes we'd made in eighth-grade English inside a shoebox . . . a diorama, with the tiny Plasticine and toilet-paper-tube figures coming gruesomely to life.

"Where are you going?"

"The office, Harr."

"*Stoned*?"

I made it down to the office minutes before the lunchtime bell. Ms. Crimsen occupied her usual perch at her high-banked desk shielding her from the student rabble. Tall and thin with an iron-gray updo, she'd always sort of terrified me.

"Margaret Carpenter." Ms. Crimsen didn't greet students so much as identify them. "And Harry Cook. Are you two all right?"

It was imperative that I behave not-stoned. But Ms. Crimsen had seen so many burnouts parade through this office that she could spot a fucked-up student blindfolded.

"It's Mr. Foster . . . something just happened up in his class."

I gave Ms. Crimsen the main bullet points. Foster's confession, how he'd run out of class.

She frowned. "All right, that's definitely . . . Did you see where Mr. Foster went?"

"By the time Brian Ashworth checked the hall, he was gone."

Ms. Crimsen's expression flattened out. Wires and wheels spun behind her eyes. Bustling to the back of the office, she checked the window overlooking the parking lot.

"His car's not there," she said, returning.

"Okay, is Principal McKinney—?"

"Both the principal and vice principal are at a professional development seminar," she told me. "Who else is in your class?"

I listed off the names of the other students. Ms. Crimsen copied them down on a Post-it.

"And the student who—" Ms. Crimsen tried to put it delicately. "Who Mr. Foster . . ."

"Serena. I don't know her last name, but she's in Mr. Foster's class."

Ms. Crimsen said, "There's only one Serena in this school. Serena Kennedy, the—"

"Drama instructor," I finished for her. "Yeah, that's what I thought."

Ms. Crimson pressed the intercom button. "Mr. Foster, if you're on the school premises, come to the office. Mr. Foster, to the office."

Letting her thumb off the intercom, she said: "Serena *who?*"

"Triny Goodhue said she was new?"

Harry said: "She's, like, yea tall?" Holding his palm flat against his chin.

Harr knows who she is. Something scuttled through me at the realization.

Ms. Crimsen walked to an olive-green file cabinet. Opening the middle drawer, she removed a folder labeled GR12 ENROLLMENT 2018. Bringing it back with her, she wetted her pointer finger with a sponge in a dish and started flipping through the file.

Her fingers moved in a practiced blur, pinning each sheet under the thumb of her opposite hand, *flip, flip, flip, flip, flip, flip* . . .

She stopped. Her eyes tunneled. Pulling a sheet out, she set in on top of the folder.

I saw the name—first name only, no last.

Serena.

Ms. Crimsen glanced up, saw me looking, and flipped the sheet over.

"Eyes to yourself, Ms. Carpenter."

But I'd already seen the handwriting on the file, and it looked an awful lot like Mr. Foster's. Had *Mr. Foster* filled out an enrollment sheet for this girl?

I'd never met her, meaning she could only have been at Northfield for as long as I'd been away.

A phone *ping*ed somewhere in the office. I spotted two eleventh graders using the photocopier near the teachers' lounge. One had her phone out; the two of them hunched over it, a pair of leering goblins. The shorter of them laughed while her eyes ballooned in noxious delight.

Mrs. Langtree, a tenth-grade math teacher, hurried past the girls and into the lounge. Her own phone was held above her head. "Have any of you seen this yet?"

The clock above the school crest read 11:59. One minute until the noontime bell. Phones would come out. Notification alerts would chirp. And everyone would see. *Everyone.*

Ms. Crimsen's finger stabbed the intercom button.

"Triny Goodhue, Ethan Collins, Smita Acharya"—rattling off every student in Foster's class—"make your way to the office. To the *office*, please."

The bell shrilled. Students emptied out of the classrooms and into the hallways.

"I'd like you both to stick nearby," Ms. Crimsen said. "This looks like another rather serious situation in a semester that's been heavy on serious situations."

Ms. Crimsen marched toward the teachers' lounge, but halfway there she started to wobble as if something had gone screwy with her inner ear.

EIGHTEEN

12:01 p.m.

The cafeteria was filling as Harry and I pushed through the doors.

To me, the caf always had the feeling of a Saharan waterhole after the rains came down. The biggest and bitchiest predators drank and bathed first; the gentler of us, the zebras and antelopes and anteaters, waited our turn to drink the alphas' dirty water.

"I'm gonna get some tots," Harry said, making a beeline for the steam trays. "Want anything?"

"Nah."

Mr. Archer, the A/V technician, was setting up a microphone on a portable stage erected in front of the windows overlooking the football field. A table with trophies and plaques sat next to the mic; Coach Murray must be giving out the athletic awards today.

Another banner, even bigger than the one in the hall, hung behind the stage:

**STARS SHINE BRIGHTEST ON THE DARKEST DAYS!
NEVER GIVE UP HOPE!**

Golden stars arced over the top of the slogan, each one inset with one of the missing boys' faces. Three stars, not four.

I scanned for a familiar face. No Dennis Weeks, not one soul from the Auto Shop crew. Phones were out, videos playing. Foster's meltdown rang out around the cafeteria to a chorus of scornful laughter.

"Foster's got that total rapist look," I heard someone say.

I took a seat at the end of a table occupied by a mixed bag of eleventh graders and two seniors, skaters named Sebastian Quinn and Owen Watson.

"Hey, Owe."

He pushed his hair out of his face. "Hey, Maggie."

"Weird question: You ever met this new girl, Serena?"

Owen shared a look with Sebastian, whose phone was out; I'd interrupted them in the middle of watching Foster's video.

"I heard the name," Owen admitted.

"You ever talk to her?"

". . . unh-uh."

Owen turned his back to me: *This conversation's over.*

"Did you see her hanging out with anyone?" I persisted. "Owen? Hey, *Owe.*"

He faced me again, his lip twisted in hostility. "Like *no,* okay?"

The Exclusives made their entrance. Glenda Curtis leading chest-first, Wanda Hollis—who may as well be scattering rose petals—and finally Miranda Lancaster dressed in black widow's weeds.

It wasn't exactly a hush that fell over the cafeteria, but the oxygen molecules seemed to gather toward the trio, leaving the rest of us breathless. It pissed me off—our unthinking impulse to worship—but my own head turned, too, didn't it?

Their table could seat twelve but never sat more than Miranda, Glenda, Wanda, and whichever token member—the Token Trans Person; the Token Fat Girl—they were idly toying with. Only Will Stinson and Chad Dearborn (who'd dated Miranda in eleventh grade, before they'd settled into the roles of platonic co-enablers) were regularly permitted to sit at the Exclusives' table.

Our school still remembered the only student who'd taken a seat at that table uninvited.

Claire Hudson. A flaming redhead who'd showed up from Prince Edward Island with a don't-give-two-fucks attitude. Her first week she'd walked up to the Exclusives' table, sat down, offered Miranda a tater tot . . . and after what seemed an eternity, Miranda *took it.*

For the next month, the two were inseparable. In the halls, at lunch, in Miranda's powder-blue Lexus: Claire in the front seat, Wanda and Glenda stuck in the back. Claire had ascended Northfield's hierarchy in record time—but she didn't act the part, y'know? You got the feeling she thought the Exclusives and everything they stood for were sort of stupid.

Then the rumor hit. The one that went Claire Hudson had fucked a dog.

Miranda started it, of course. She never admitted to it. The rumor was believed because those who spread it enforced belief—if not by everyone, then enough to tip the scales.

A dog's penis forms a knot inside the vagina, did you know that?

This was the most calculated angle of the rumor: that whiff of the scientific.

She's lucky she didn't get pregnant and barf out a redheaded beagle mutant.

Claire tried to kill herself, I heard. That people would believe she'd done anything so cartoonishly depraved without any kind of proof . . . Anyway, her family moved back out East and Miranda carried on as if nothing had happened, because for her, barely anything had. No different than squashing a fly on a windowpane.

Harry found me. He pushed his basket of tots over. I bit into one, chewed, tossed the stub back in the basket.

"So, you knew Serena?"

He crossed his arms and rested his chin on his forearms, staring straight ahead. "Knew? Mmmph. Knew *of.*"

"You have a pretty good idea how tall she is."

"You got me. We're best buds because I estimated her height."

"Okay, so nothing else?"

His head cranked sideways, cheek resting on his forearms. "She wasn't part of my social circle, so, yeah, *no?*"

His apathy pissed me off. Did nobody want to talk about this girl?

Up on the collapsible stage, Mr. Archer had finished tweaking the mic. He dismounted the stairs, leaving the platform empty.

When I stood, Harry said, "Mags?" When I started toward the stage, his voice went up a few octaves: "*Mags?*"

I walked between the tables until I was at the stage. Miranda's eyes rose from her phone to meet mine for a puzzled instant as I went up the steps.

Somehow, I found myself behind the mic. An energy crackled in the walls, or maybe just inside me: a taste of voltage in my molars.

I flicked on the microphone. A squeal of feedback.

"Hey, I—" My voice fled from the speaker, hitting the walls and rebounding back. "Sorry . . ." I tried to adjust the volume, failed, gave up. "I don't want to bother you. Just a question. About this new girl, Serena?"

As soon as the name came out of my mouth, I swear the sodium-vapor lamps dimmed. A new atmosphere descended on the caf. The feel of a storm lowering over the landscape, bringing with it sizzles of spoke lightning.

"Sing us a sea shanty!" a sleepy-eyed eleventh grader hollered. Someone let go a frightened, inane laugh at that.

The soul-sick realization came that this wasn't the drugs, not anymore; I was operating within the confines of cold reality, and the hum to the air—that was real, too. I felt something watching me from impossible vantages: from the knots in the popcorn ceiling, from the knobs of the speaker dials . . . that same yellowy, ancient gaze from my dream that morning—that presence under the dead boys, animating them from the guts of the earth.

"For fuck's sake." I could feel big, ugly balls of sweat rolling down my face. "Serena, *anyone*?"

"Don't you speak her name!"

That was Triny Goodhue, standing at the main doors. Her face was mottled red, her eyes knitted into unpretty little slits.

"Nobody gave you that *right*, Margaret!"

Phones were out now, trained on me. Only a half dozen at first, but within the next few heartbeats, many more joined them.

"Not shaming anyone, I'm just asking." I struggled to keep my voice from fraying.

Once, when I was a girl, my father had overtightened the brakes on my bike. I'd gotten up a good head of steam before squeezing the lever and flipping over the front tire, gravity gone haywire as the gravel rushed forward to meet my face. I felt like that now: a plaything of forces which I'd had under control only seconds ago, my equilibrium swimming.

"The student in Mr. Foster's class. The one"—why not just say it?—"he's talking about in the video everyone's watching *right now*."

"Foster's a fucking *rapist*!"

The voice shot out from the assembly, weirdly feral.

"I support her!"

A girl stood near the back. A ninth grader with a dark bob. The boy beside her wore a grease-stiffened denim jacket, open to the navel, with a flesh-colored shirt underneath. His face was a milky-smooth blank.

"*I* believe her!"

The feeling came of being walked through the steps of a ritual, and at the end lurked my own self-destruction. My fellow students would solemnly bear witness as I put my head through the noose, kicked the chair away, and hung myself in front of them as a public amusement.

Despising them for this, my anger curdled. I stabbed my finger at the banner.

"Three stars! *One, two, three!* Chad, Will, Allan, right? Where is Charity's star? Where were you all when Charity—?" But I couldn't make myself say it. "Why didn't you believe *her*? You hypocrites can all fuck right off!"

They invaded the cafeteria then—on God, I swear they did. The missing boys. Three pairs of blackened eyes peering from paper-skull faces, three mouths moving without making a sound. They levitated above the student body in a chorus, fueling the free-floating anxiety that had been swelling inside Northfield ever since they'd gone missing.

Why bother planning for the future, the black-eyed boys whispered, *when even the popular kids can disappear off the face of the earth, never to be heard from again?*

"Yes, Margaret, and where were you?"

Miranda Lancaster was eyeballing me, dressed in all her regal splendor. She didn't need a microphone. Her voice carried over her worshippers with a royal projection.

"Charity needed you, didn't she? So where were *you*, Margaret?"

The instinct to crab-scuttle off the stage swarmed me, but I managed to hold my ground.

"*We've* all been right here." Miranda swept her arm over her congregation. "We've pulled together"—her perfect chest hitched and tears, maybe even *real ones*, shone in her eyes—"while prioritizing healing. All you want to do is *trigger* us. Who are you to judge?"

"No . . . th-that's not true," I stammered. "You never cared about her!"

Faces in the crowd became carnivorous, backlit by their phones. The face of a woman in a hairnet—one of the nameless lunch ladies—swam in the vapor rising from the steam trays, teeth bared in a rictus.

"Nobody knows exactly *what* happened that night at the party," Miranda said to her rapt audience, everyone's heads bobbing away like toys. "You're saying Charity didn't consent? Or are you . . . are you *actually* slut-shaming Charity, your closest friend—is that what this is?"

"Charity didn't want *that*," I said, reaching into a deep well of loathing for this girl who'd bullied many of us since the second grade. "You *know* that, Miranda, you evil fucking hag."

A good-hearted meathead named Dave Cooper took to his feet. "Why doesn't everyone just calm the eff down—"

"*Rape APOLOGIST!*" Triny screamed with such force that the tendons bulged on her neck.

Dave sat down ponderously, his face stunned and bloodless.

Anyone ever tell you about a backdraft, Maggie?

My uncle Art was a volunteer fireman. *In an enclosed space—say, a room with a shut door,* he'd once told me, *a fire will dip low, almost-but-not-quite out. It'll feed on every scrap of oxygen it can find, starving but still very much alive. That's when a fire's deadliest, if you come along and open that door without knowing what's inside.*

A backdraft had been gathering inside this school, hadn't it? All the nights spent peering out bedroom windows into a darkness the streetlamps couldn't reach, all the fake smiles masking stark fright, the sheer unknowability of what had become of four souls who'd walked these very halls—gone now, evaporated, ghosted, eaten by something too horrible to name . . . and right now, those dangerous fumes were coiling under my feet. The air was condensing as it sucked to my skin, suffocatingly tight.

And just like a fire, all that rage needed was a spark.

My eyes found Harry. He'd slunk down the aisle and was now standing at the side of the stage, a few feet away from me.

"Who knows if those guys are even missing?"

I spoke these words calmly, clearly. Harry looked up at me, his eyes pleading: *Mags, oh no, please don't go there.*

My lips pulled into a gruesome party-spoiling smile as I prepared to give voice to the unspeakable thing that must never, ever be said.

"Maybe they're, ohh, I don't know . . . *DEAD.*"

NINETEEN

12:17 p.m.

"YOU DIRTY BITCH!"

It was as though the cafeteria floor had been replaced with a metal grate, same as in a Skinner box, and someone had rammed five hundred volts through the grid.

A projectile sailed through the air and hit my chest with a wet slap. It slid down my shirt, leaving a red smear.

A hamburger patty slathered in ketchup.

A Coke slammed on the stage apron; the can spanged off my knee, spurting foam, sending a spasm of pain jangling up to my crotch.

Harry hopped onstage as another can zipped at me as fast as a chucked baseball—he batted it aside almost casually, wincing as it glanced off his knuckles.

"Back door!" he shouted. *"Now!"*

I hopped off the stage as the entire student body lunged at me, an organism with a single-brained purpose. A juice box hit the back of my head and exploded; fruit punch dribbled down my neck.

Everyone was screaming at me. I heard *"Enabler!"*; I heard *"Victim blamer!"*; one hysterical, triumphant voice shrieked: *"Cuuuuuuunt!"*

Casting a glance back, I expected to see the whole cafeteria rushing at me, but the true number was much fewer. Alexa Meeber, Fiona DeLois, Connor Jensen, Ross Dempsey, a half-dozen more. Simone Lang, swinging her majorette's baton like a scythe.

Mr. Archer stepped into the aisle to stem the stampede. Simone caught him in a glancing blow with her baton and Mr. Archer folded awkwardly, heels rattling on the floor.

The rear exit door was made of glass, matching the windows. I'd almost reached it when a can of Fanta zipped over my shoulder, hitting the door hard enough to put a snarl of cracks in the pane. A hot hum baked my back as my fellow students closed the distance; I pictured Triny Goodhue gripping a plastic spoon, grinning savagely as she got ready to scoop my eyes out.

Harry broke ahead of me by a half step, shouldering the door open. There was a knife in his hand now. A brass-notched Buck. The sight of it—and the way Harry held it low at his hips, ready to stab with it—told me how insane this had gotten.

I tripped through the door, skidding on the concrete quadrangle. I scrambled up to see Harry slam the door just as the surge smashed into it.

"Block!" he yelled. "The *block*!"

Behind him, like lizards in some hellish terrarium, the faces of our fellow students were jammed against the door and windows, flattened and pushed out of shape.

"BLOCK!"

I dragged over the cinder block Dickie O'Reilly used as a door wedge. Harry was barely holding the door shut against the tide bashing against it.

"Wedge it under!"

I did as he said. The base of the door gritted against the block, but the door stayed shut. Danny Lombardi, youth pastor and leader of the school prayer circle, was squished against the door—his skin, pink as a hot dog, squeaked on the freshly Windexed glass. I waited for that glass to splinter, for his body to pour onto the tarmac; I pictured Danny's skin as proofing dough, the razor-sharp jags carving his arms and legs with the finesse of a deli slicer.

Harry and I dashed past the fire exit and the smokehole to the back parking lot. Harry still had his knife out. Digging into his pocket, he flipped me his keys.

"Get it started!"

He checked up, waiting for anyone who might be giving chase. Unlocking the car door, I climbed in. There were two keys on Harry's fob—*house and car, house and car*, my mind rabbited—and of course I chose the wrong one, jamming the house key into the lock cylinder for what must have been *easily* ten seconds.

"Shit, shit, shit—"

Glancing through the windshield, I saw that niner with the blank moon-face come around the corner of the school. He was clutching a metal water bottle. Shrieking, he hurled it. The bottle rainbowed over Harry's head and struck the Geo's hood with a clang.

Harry took a step toward the little shit, cutting the air with his Buck. The kid screeched and fled back inside the school.

I thumbed the correct key into the ignition and twisted. The Geo fired up on the first stroke. I scrambled into the passenger seat as Harry slung himself behind the wheel, dropped the transmission into drive, and hit the gas.

The Geo's tires made a scalded-cat shriek as Harry swung wide around the lot. A half dozen students poured into the smokehole. Whatever they were screaming was drowned out by the burr of the tires and the hammering of the four-banger, but their faces under the shadowy overhang were twisted into masks of hate.

Harry barely avoided colliding with the dumpsters; he got the Metro under control and took the exit onto Mary Street, zipping past rows of tract housing until we met a main road.

TWENTY

12:27 p.m.

"Holy fuck holy fuck holy *fuck*—"

I couldn't stop shaking. The panic wouldn't leave, this feeling that some part of me was suffocating.

"We're okay," Harry said, eyeballing the rearview mirror. "Nobody's following us."

We drove past Korean groceries and coin-op laundromats and dive bars with smoked-out windows. I got my shakes under control.

"I think they were going to—"

"Kill me, Harr? Yeah, think so."

Clouds moved across the sky in restless patterns. One threw its shadow over the car as Harry braked at a stop sign. Even that gauzy shade was enough to set my shivers off again.

"Where to?"

"Let's just drive around, Harr, okay?"

In a minute or two we'd reach a stoplight. Swinging left would lead us down Summerset, past a gas station and a doughnut shop to the grape fields and orchards marking the city's border. A right would lead across the bridge, over a long plummet ending in the Twelve Mile Creek, on into downtown.

The police station was downtown. Corner of Church and Agnew. We'd be taking the right.

I touched Harry's shoulder. "Thanks, man. That was insane."

He shrugged. *No biggie.*

We hit the stoplight. "Take a right."

He flicked the blinker. "Downtown? Why there?"

"We're just driving, aren't we?"

"So why not left, then?" Tucking his hair behind his ears. "If we're just driving."

I stared at him until he eased his foot off the brake and made the right. We hadn't gone five hundred yards before the iPhone went off in my pocket.

It went off a bunch of times. *Pikachu! Pikachu! Pikachu!* Harry nodded at my jeans.

"You want to check that?"

"Nope."

The Metro swung around a corner, the river gorge coming into view under the cloud cover. We drove past the barber college: *Five Bucks Gets You a Tight Fade!*

The phone rang in my pocket. That hadn't happened before. My resolve crumbled. I dragged it out.

UNIDENTIFIED CALLER.

Five rings . . . six . . . seven . . .

My thumb touched the green button. The hiss of an open connection: little pops and crackles, the sound of water moving under a shelf of Arctic ice.

Click.

A barrage of texts followed. *Pikachu! Pikachu! Pikachu! Pikachu!*

With the phone open, my eyes couldn't help but scan them.

TURN AROUND

PLEASE

UR GOING THE WRONG WAY

I pocketed the phone, teeth clenched. "Keep going."

Harry drove over the bridge connecting Western Hill to downtown. Chain-link fence rose in fifteen-foot curvatures over the walk-ways down each side. They were supposed to discourage people from making the three-hundred-foot leap into the Twelve Mile Creek. A decade ago, a middle-aged man walked out of his office at the Bank of Montreal on King Street, climbed onto the rail at the midpoint of the bridge, and leapt. He'd been stealing money from clients—*embezzling*, was the word I'd learned. He had a family, a home in the suburbs. A boy from school, Ethan Garrow, had been fishing for steelhead with his father in the shadows of the bridge when the banker jumped. His body detonated twenty feet from their boat. *He was* whistling, Ethan had told an assembly of schoolyard listeners. *A bomb dropping from the sky instead of a person. His tie, this red string, was whipping up from his neck. When he hit the water, it wasn't what you'd expect, a huge belly flop sound.* Ethan's face had been stricken, as if he didn't know why he was telling us this. *It was natural. The flap of a heron's wings. I ended up getting some of him on me, but I didn't know until later. Stuck to my jacket sleeve. I think it was part of his eye.*

For years afterward, every single time I crossed the bridge I'd think of that man, but sometimes instead of him falling it was me, my red tie riffling at my neck with the note of a flag flapping in a high wind.

As Harry and I crossed it now, I found myself thinking of a day a few years after that man jumped. A summer day on the bank of the Twelve Mile, nowhere near the bridge. Plum and I had been explor-ing, no real agenda. I'd turned over a rock in the swift-running water. A flash of emerald blue. A crayfish, recently molted.

The sight had brought the memory of that suicidal banker galloping back. I figured the police frogmen wouldn't have found his body. Maybe only enough to scatter inside a coffin and say: *Here lies the body of Ernie the Embezzler.* The rest would have dropped to the river bottom to be picked at by sunfish, by the water cockroaches the kids called toe-biters, and by crayfish.

The crayfish I'd found that afternoon was a female. Under her tail sat a clutch of pearly egg sacs. *That's so sick*, I'd said to Plum.

A hundred or a thousand children. The idea grossed me out. But a crayfish didn't think that way. A mama crayfish's eggs hatched, and her kiddos went skittering all over her, crawling on her legs and pincers, up her eyestalks to run around the naked globes of her eyes . . .

The phone rang again. Reluctantly, I pulled it out.

UNIDENTIFIED CALLER.

It didn't matter who this was—the police station was five minutes away, and nothing would stop us from going there . . . but maybe they'd say something I'd be able to tell the cops. Something that would help their investigation.

"What?" I said, answering.

"*Hello, Margaret.*"

The velvetiness of that voice shot battery acid through my veins.

"Who is this?"

Mocking laughter. "*Oh, come on. You know.*"

It wasn't Plum, I was sure of that much. But Plum had sent me the phone, hadn't she?

"*Pull over so we can talk.*"

Which was when it struck me—the dull clanging of a bell—that there was only one person on earth who it *could* be.

"I'm hanging up now, Serena. It's you, isn't it?"

Her laughter filled the interior. "*Aren't you a Clever Clyde. Are you upset about Mr. Foster? He's a very bad man.*" A simpering purr. "*Taking advantage of poor girls.*"

"Keep driving, Harr."

"*You know I've got Charity, don't you?*"

That possibility had never dawned on me. I'd never imagined their paths crossing—wait, how *had* they crossed? The timelines didn't line up. I'd already figured out that Plum must've gone missing by the time Serena showed up at Northfield, so how—?

"*She's tied to a chair in another room,*" Serena continued off my silence. "*Now, how would you like me to go into there and snip off Charity's big toe?*"

Oh Jesus Christ.

"*Maybe all the toes on her right foot, hmm?*"

"Don't—"

"*How about I saw off the whole fucking leg?*"

I said: "Pull over."

Harry slid into a spot on Saint Paul Street, across from the pool hall. Static crackled down the phone line.

"*That's better. Now. You're a smart girl, Margaret. A thinker. Charity's told me all about you. But the worst thing you can do right now is think.*"

My hand crept to my throat, pulse thwacking under my fingertips. This person must have kidnapped Charity. That's the only halfway logical answer.

"*If you go to the police, if you tell* anyone, *nobody will ever see Charity again.*"

The world lurched on a hidden pivot-point; I saw something in its dark gears, pale as gaslight with a bugfuck-crazy face.

"Don't hurt her, please."

"*Then don't make me hurt her. This is all working out so well. Charity's been very accommodating. Who else could have sent those texts? Ninety-nine ninjas. She wants* you *to see, okay? To* know. *You can believe me or not, but she wants everything to be clear to you. Much more than I do, honestly. So. All you need to do is exactly as I tell you. You won't be hurt, I promise. I have nothing against you, Margaret, or against Harry.*"

"Why did you take Charity? What do you have against her?"

"*Nothing,*" she said after a pause. "*We're all on the same team.*"

Two dudes slouched out of the pool hall onto the sidewalk. Guts too big, shirts too small, drinking bottles of Blue. I tried to focus on their exposed navels, but my heart was slamming hard enough to send black dots stuttering across my eyes.

"*I've got some more things to show you today, Margaret.*"

"Whatever you want. Just don't do anything to her."

"*I'm surprised you care.*"

"What do you mean?"

"*She told me about the letter, you know. What dirty snoopers best friends can be, huh? She found it in your desk drawer, tucked under some ribbons and shit.*"

The university acceptance letter. So Plum knew. And if she'd discovered that letter, she'd have suspected—correctly—that Mr. Foster had a role in me getting into that school.

"*How do you think Charity and I found each other, hmmm? She knew she'd need a new best friend once you'd abandoned her.*"

"No," I almost shrieked. "It's not like that, she *knows* that—"

I was talking to a dead connection.

Robotically, I dropped the phone in the cup holder. With that same mechanized movement I let my body fold in half, head dipping between my thighs. I let out a piercing wail.

"Mags, oh Mags, *hey* . . ."

I screamed so hard that the windows trembled. It felt good. A dam bursting. Harry's hand rested between my shoulder blades—it was too warm, a fleshy hot-water bottle—but I was too tired to fight it.

When my jag was over, I straightened up. I pulled the sun visor down and surveyed my splotchy face in the mirror.

"I'm okay."

Harry looked unconvinced. "You sure?"

He settled his fingertips on my tear-wet cheek.

"You're a good friend, Mags."

"If you really knew me, you wouldn't say that."

Harry leaned in. I breathed in his wild scent, hot sparks and something unnameable.

He kissed me.

Harry broke the kiss quickly. His eyes were darker somehow, dark and honest and a little worried.

A whistle from the sidewalk. The pool hall inbreeders were staring at us. One had his hands cupped in front of his chest in the idiot's universal sign language for boobs.

"Show us some skin!"

I flipped them the bird. The two of them hooted. Setting the car in gear, Harry pulled away. My heartbeat was in my lips, the pressure of his kiss tattooed on them.

"That was wrong, but I'd wanted to do it all day."

"No, it's okay," I told him. "It was nice. Just . . ."

He blew a lock of hair out of his eye. "Bad timing."

My thoughts settled into an uneasy rhythm. *Serena*. A girl whose name alone could set off a high-school riot. A girl whose school record had been falsified by the same teacher who'd confessed to crossing a scandalous line with her. A girl nobody knew a thing about aside from the blatantly obvious—*she's hot*—who'd drifted through Northfield's halls, a ghost.

Plum, I really wish you'd stayed gone.

The thought skated across my mind before I could stop it. Plum and me had been knit from the cradle. I'd seen the wonder in her eyes when she found a woolly caterpillar on an oak tree, the joy when it went inching up her index finger. We'd learned to ride bikes and bait a hook together. There was the time the two of us pulled an all-nighter in sixth grade, fueled on Fun Dip and Skittles, crashing head-to-foot as dawn's light climbed the escarpment.

Plum was helixed to my memories so tightly it was as if we shared a common heart. But something had happened to her, hadn't it? I felt this more strongly with each passing minute. Something bad that I couldn't name, let alone face.

So yes, I wished that she'd stayed gone. I didn't want her to be hurt or tortured, to feel any pain at all. More that she'd just evaporate painlessly and stay away for good this time. I couldn't fix what I'd done to her. What we *all* had done. The past was inflexible that way. It stubbornly resisted alteration. But if she wasn't around, then at least I could begin the hard work of recontextualizing our past, erasing the worst bits, reframing things in an effort to remember them how I needed to, and forgive myself just a little. I could go back to accepting that Plum really was gone (and I already had in the most honest chambers of my heart), and oh god what a piece of shit I am, what a bad friend, a bad person, a fucking ghoul—

Pikachu!

PART II
AFTERNOON

ONE
12:29 p.m.

The helicopter touched down thirty-two kilometers southwest of St. Catharines, Ontario. A late-model Escalade and a 2014 Chevy Malibu the color of dirty milk waited on the airstrip.

Rudyard watched, briefcase in hand, as his armored black trunk was transferred from the helicopter's freight hold into the back of the Escalade.

The trunk was roughly the size of a wild animal trap that a wilderness outfit might use to snare a juvenile brown bear. But rather than common metal bars, its exterior was crafted from ballistic aluminum, the kind common to fighter jets. Titanium rivets bristled down its every seam.

After it had been stashed safely in the Escalade, Rudyard consulted the readout panel on the trunk's exterior. He dialed up the concentrated oxygen mixture by 13 percent. It had been a long trip, and the pressure changes were no doubt distressing to its occupant.

Rudyard set his cheek on the trunk. "You're doing wonderfully, darling. You're being so brave."

He walked to the Malibu. Setting the briefcase on its hood, he popped the latches. Inside sat matchboxes. Three Torches paraffin-coated matches. An African brand, bankrupted three decades ago. He'd scoured the vintage market to find a case of them at an estate sale in Lagos.

He ran his fingertips over the rows of matchboxes. He could've been peering into a box of chocolates, except he didn't have a legend to tell him which one held the nougat, the caramel, the cloying cherry.

Selecting a box at random, he slipped it into his breast pocket. He shut the case, thumbed the latches, and set it in the back seat.

He settled behind the wheel. Jameson occupied the passenger seat. Their associate Roy would be driving the Escalade.

Rudyard swung the Malibu across the airstrip. When was the last time he'd actually *driven* a car? The feel of the faux-leather wheel was pleasant under his fingers.

A memory pierced his calm: his sister Elizabeth twisting the key in the ignition of that Jeep Willys as the silken rip-curling note of the ants darkened the air—

Rudyard packed the memory away for the time being. He pulled onto the road bordering the airfield. Roy followed him in the Escalade.

Rudyard could have marshaled a larger task force. There could be a flotilla of Escalades flanking him instead of just one, packed with Blackwater types. But it was imperative to keep everything small. No sense in riling the natives. If the three of them did their jobs right and got a bit lucky, they could be gone without anyone in this yokel-filled burg being any the wiser.

"In and out," Rudyard whispered to himself, "just like sex."

"What's that?" Jameson, the obsequious little worm, intruded.

"Nothing. Never mind. Have we made progress on the best friend?"

Jameson cleared his throat. "She's not at home."

"You're joking. She's a fucking houseplant. When's the last time she *left* her house?"

"She doesn't. She's been a virtual shut-in since the subject's disappearance."

Irritated, Rudyard eyeballed the sky. The helicopter dogged them in the holding pattern he'd requested. The dire fact hovered inside the Malibu. Project Athena could come apart today. More than two decades' worth of strife and toil, all down the shitter.

Rather than dwell on that, Rudy let his mind drift back to that day in Africa when the siafu ants made a meal of everything in their path, including his beloved sister.

As Elizabeth had collapsed onto the hood of the Jeep, consumed in a matter of heartbeats by those ants—her head surfacing from the spume, a stiff sprig of red hair bobbing at the back of her head like a dandelion in the wind—ten-year-old Rudyard staggered away from the advancing tide, his limbs gnawed bloody and his mind in shock. The storage bunker represented his only hope.

It had been dug behind the barracks. Eight feet deep, its shelves lined with tinned food. A steel trapdoor covered the entrance, with a glass porthole so you could check the interior before going down: snakes, spiders, and millipedes often clung to the earthen walls, waiting for anything that might blunder within striking range.

Rudyard had no time to make sure the bunker was safe, and anyway, getting bitten by an adder and dying with his neck puffed up purple as an eggplant seemed a better end than what the ants offered. Throwing the trapdoor open, he'd tripped down the steps. The purr of the ant colony was monolithic at his heels: the scrape of a trillion rusty razor blades.

Shortly after slamming the door shut on top of him, the ants steamrolled over it. They covered the porthole so thickly that the sunlight cut out, no different than if a lead blanket had been thrown across it.

The smell of the ants invaded the dark air: partly peppery, partly adrenal. He could hear them moving across the trapdoor at a dusty boil. He wondered—his heart almost stopped at the prospect— if they'd be heavy enough to cave the bunker's door in? It seemed impossible, but above him, the ants would now be corralled between the cliff faces; if they'd risen to his knees before, the tide would surely be much higher now that they were hemmed in. Some might try to scale the cliffs to the flatland topping them; the rest may eventually skitter back into the jungle, but right now they were a huge brown wave crashing against the shore: he pictured the ants stacked ten, twelve, fifteen feet high right on top of the bunker.

What did a single ant weigh? Surely no more than a raindrop. But trillions upon trillions would weigh the equivalent of a monsoon. The door's hinges issued a dull groan, a sound that made Rudyard's stomach cramp in terror.

Groping over the shelves, he located a lantern. Further investigation led to a box of matches: Three Torches brand, paraffin-coated. Getting the match to strike along the strip required an epic force of will. When it caught, he was able to get the lantern's wick lit.

He surveyed his prison. Potted beef and tinned peas glinted back at him. He set the lantern on the oiled dirt floor, spotting the side-winding of a millipede under a shelf. The lantern's light belled all around him, trapped within the small space—the bunker was shallow, the door only a foot above his head . . .

A shiny trickle was racing down the dirt walls, braiding through the torn root ends.

Ants. They were inside. Not a lot, not yet, but a steady stream.

Rudyard began to kill them. Coldly at first, but as his fear whet to a keener edge, the slaughter became frenzied. He stomped them, squished them, pulped them under his skinned thumbs. The ants clung to his socks and sleeves and bootlaces, biting viciously wherever they encountered bare skin. The stench of them mixed with the gasoline he'd poured on himself and the leaden smell of his own blood.

He noticed some ants—one in every thirty—were bigger than their mates: the size of his extended pinkie. These ones clung to him most relentlessly, taking the biggest gouges. As the agony intensified, his eyes fled back to the shelves . . . he spied a canister of pale-gray lard.

There was no way on earth he could unscrew that lid. His hands were incapable of fine motor skills. He lifted the glass, its weight slipping dangerously in his grip, and brought it down on the floor. It shattered. Scooping lard in both hands, he smeared it over him—it went on over his clothes and bare skin in a suffocating layer.

Once again, the gods of luck smiled upon him. The ants got gummed in the lard, sticking in it as if in heavy sap. His body browned with them, thickened with them, until he looked as if he'd been deep-fried.

Grasping a tin of potted meat in each hand, he used them to crush the ants into the floor and against the walls. The ants stuck to the ends of his fingers like cockleburs, feasting on tiny rags of skin.

You'll never drag me back to your lair, whole or in pieces, Rudyard thought as blood pooled in his boots. *I'll kill every one of you, swear to God, even if you finish me as I'm trying.*

Systematically, Rudyard crushed the remaining ants. Their bodies were incredibly durable. He imagined squishing tiny tanks. He smashed them into the bunker walls, but the dirt would give and their semi-impacted bodies would crawl loose again, legs snapped off but their pincers still working. He was woozy with blood loss—could a person get dizzy from *skin* loss? He ground his teeth on the ants that crawled past his lips, chewing on nasty little balls of tinfoil. Pinching the ants in half with his fingernails worked best, beheading them, but his fingers were so badly bitten that they didn't have a whole lot of nail left.

They've eaten my fingernails, he thought dreamily. *Eaten my nails, lah-dee-dah-dee-dum.*

Time bent out of true, minutes scalloping into hours. He waged deadly war with the ants, his focus such that he barely noticed when they began to clear out of the campsite. They departed the porthole in brown chains, and suddenly Rudyard was squinting up into the sunlight.

After steeling his nerves, he heaved the bunker door up. The camp and clearing lay empty—no, not merely empty. More as if some cleansing agent more powerful than hydrochloric acid had washed over it.

The ants had consumed any organic matter they'd come across, from the hemp ropes anchoring the barracks to the contents of the pots of lip balm some of his father's men used, right down to the stubbed ends of the cigars Carl Leiningen had smoked in the shadow of the cliffs. *Everything* had been eaten, leaving the camp in a lunar desolation. The only things moving were the ants themselves.

They remained, in their hundreds of thousands. Many of them were dead, crushed or suffocated under the weight of their own colony. They popped and crackled under Rudyard's boots as he staggered across the camp. The lard on his body began to brown and melt in the sun; the lard-gummed ants sluiced down his legs and off his boots as wax does off a guttering candle. The ones still clinging to him had become anemic. If they were still biting him, Rudyard couldn't feel it; his nerves were peeled so bare he couldn't even register the warmth of the sun on his skin.

The ants had eaten the upholstery and stuffing off the Jeep Willys. The struts of the chairs pronged up from the chassis in steel fangs. He couldn't see anything resembling the remains of his sister, but Carl Leiningen would later locate a clean-picked human rib cage wedged in the abandoned den of some bat-eared foxes a mile west of camp.

His sister's skeleton must have been borne along by the colony like flotsam in a river's current until there was nothing left to strip, then cast carelessly aside.

Over the coming years, Rudyard would consult entomological and historical records to chart the ant colony's progress once it had deserted the camp. The ants that didn't scale the cliffs had backtracked to a river on the eastern edge of the veldt. The colony was marching five miles wide by that point, razing and consuming all life in a clinical path of destruction. But the river ran swift and whitecapped over three-hundred yards wide from shore to shore. Most of the ants got swept away trying to cross it, carried downstream in a smothering rug that must have resembled an oil slick, all the way to where the river met the ocean ten miles south. A great deal of the colony was washed out to sea, but they would have remained a lethal water hazard: ants were of course buoyant, and any dolphin or whale who'd tried to breach through the carpet of their bodies would have been fortunate to survive.

But the river didn't claim all the ants. They were, much as Rudyard, survivors. They trooped down the banks to a man-made bridge. Crossing it, they regrouped on the far shore and continued their march, still voluminous enough to tear through the farms of several game herders on the eastern foliage line of the mesa. The farmers could do nothing but find high ground and watch their crops and herds fall under the voracious horde.

After several days the colony fractured, the separate divisions moving underground to build new nests. And with that, the great *Dorylus* ant migration came to an end.

Rudyard's father and his crew had been several miles north of the ants' path that fateful day. Apart from a few random bites from wayward drones—and a distant foaming hiss over the hillsides—the men had no clue what was happening. So when Rudyard's father returned to find his son a bloody mess, his face and hands and chest shredded by the ants—and much worse, the report that his only daughter was completely gone, *eaten*, not even her bones left—

Rudyard had been airlifted to a hospital in Johannesburg with catastrophic injuries. His heart stopped beating on the helicopter, but the shock paddles rallied him. At the hospital he was sedated, transfused, and sent back to the States as soon as he was well enough to make the trip.

At Cedars-Sinai, Rudyard's medical team informed his father that his son lacked sufficient "usable skin" for comprehensive grafts. They'd set about repairing the damage done by the ants—who'd left so many bites as to be uncountable—using skin harvested from his calves, buttocks, and wherever the ants had bitten least aggressively. Despite the team's best efforts, Rudyard's body would forever bear a pockmarked look, the lion's share of his skin dimpled in the manner of a golf ball.

The scars faded over time so that, looking at his face today, you'd think he must've been one of those lushly zitty teenagers. A real crater face. Rudyard didn't mind.

Beyond the physical rehabilitation, the medical team suggested Rudyard undergo intensive therapy. His shrink had been a solemn, vaguely Germanic man named Kreutz. He sat sphinxlike, pen poised over his pad, while his young patient spoke. Yet words were scarce; Rudy's time in the bunker had stamped a preternatural secrecy upon his character. It was a trait that would come in handy as a businessperson.

Now, there were a great many things Rudyard *could* have told Kreutz. Things that would have gotten his pen scribbling away to beat the band, oh my yes.

Rudyard could've told Kreutz how he'd started to see ants *everywhere*. They weren't real, but the problem was his brain couldn't quite accept that. He'd see them go tiptoeing across the ceiling, scuttling in the grout of his shower tiles, massing in every shadow—and the world was *full* of shadows. Rudyard had never noticed that before.

At night, lying in bed, the thinnest pressure of his sheets made

it feel as if ants were crawling all over him. They weren't biting—
though he wasn't certain he'd feel it even if they were, seeing as sensation had yet to return to a great deal of his skin. The ants had eaten
his nerve endings, *lad-dee-dah*, what kidders . . .

Rudy could have told Kreutz that the ants in his bed wanted to
make him their hill. If he lay there motionless, they'd go traipsing inside him, funneling up his nostrils and ears and even, he supposed, up
his sexual apparatus—because ants really didn't care, did they? They
only wanted someplace warm and dark where their queen could lay
her eggs.

Lying in bed with such thoughts, he'd have to get up and take a
scalding shower. Rudyard took a lot of hot showers. His skin shone
piglet pink for a few years, until he got the urge under control.

He also might've told Kreutz how he saw a *specific* ant. One the
size of a human being.

At first, he'd glimpsed it at the farthest edge of his sight line. It
would remain at that distance, emitting a queer zippering whisper.
But over time, this curious ant drew nearer. He'd catch it riding the
glass elevator in his father's corporate tower, ascending with people
in their suits and pencil skirts, all of whom stood oblivious to its presence in the carriage with them.

Before long, the enormous ant was in his house. He'd spy its
blobby shadow stretching around the corner at the end of the hall,
the inquisitive weaving of its antennae peeking around the trim.

Yoo-hoo, Rudy. Here I am.

It disturbed Rudyard to discover that the ant spoke in the voice
of his dead sister.

He was thirteen years old the first time the ant appeared in his
bedroom. It sat on the wooden rocking chair on the far side of his
room. Rudyard reared up in bed. *What do you want?* The ant only
rocked silently—except not in total silence, because an ant that size
was actually quite loud, a loudness composed of many small sounds:

the velvety gnash of its mandibles, the rubbery flex of its antennae, the tin-can pops of its carapace . . .

Since then, he'd seen the ant often. Its behavior was never overtly threatening. It merely observed him. The closest the ant had ever drawn to Rudyard had been in his private car: He'd stirred from a light doze to find it on the seat beside him in midtown traffic, the perfume of its body gothic and musty in the back seat.

What upset Rudyard was that he couldn't *control* the ant. The bastard came and went as it pleased. He'd tried to reduce it, not in size but in splendor. Tried to imagine it wearing a monocle or a smoking jacket, or without its arrogant fucking head—if he could make it comical, he could dominate it. But the ant resisted all such efforts. It was just *there*, his erstwhile unwanted companion.

After a while, Rudyard simply accepted it.

He could tell Kreutz worse things, if he'd felt like it. Much worse than the big quiet ant.

The same year as the ant first appeared in his bedroom, Rudy had come across something behind a service shack on his father's estate. The gardeners had strung yellow tape up, which had alerted him to its presence. On that afternoon, alone (as was often the case), Rudyard slid under the tape. It took no time at all to locate the cause of concern.

A massive crumbling mound of dirt.

A thrum shot through Rudyard. That hill belonged to a colony of fire ants.

Taking off his trousers, his shirt, his socks and underpants, he folded them neatly on the ground. By that point, he was hiccupping—a bodily response to the act his mind had settled around, and the fact he was helpless to resist going through with it.

Stark naked, he stepped to the hill. His toe flirted curiously with the grainy dirt . . .

His leg pistoned back. He kicked the hill as hard as he could.

His foot punched in like a hoe blade and came out teeming with ants. They poured out of their hill. Workers and drones in their thousands, alerted by a signal from their queen.

Rudyard didn't run. He let the ants climb him.

The first bite was a watery reminder of the siafus'. Still, it triggered a sensory response that would rule the remainder of Rudyard's life. The pain—the *memory* of that pain, engraved in his skin and mind—opened a doorway, and past it, shimmering in ethereal light, waited his sister.

Elizabeth. As real as if she were still alive, her smell and her smile, the brush of her hair against his face. Rudyard was back with her again as the ants rose up his body; his pain receptors brought her into an all-consuming clarity.

As his legs and chest vanished under a crimson boil of the ants, Rudyard began to cry. At the joy of meeting his sister again, yes, but also the horror of how broken he must be for this to be the pathway. His weakness sickened him, made him feel so vulnerable and alone.

In time, he staggered away. He brushed the ants off, killing and crushing as many as he could. Locating the hose behind the gardener's shed, he washed the rest of them off with cold water. His body was inflamed, swollen, leaking blood from ten thousand places.

He snuck back into the house buck naked and retreated to his room. He didn't think anyone had seen him, but one of the maids never looked at him the same after that day.

So yes, he didn't tell Kreutz about his adventure with the fire ant hill, or the modified version he would settle on in the coming years . . . the ritual and its peregrinations.

Most of all, he'd not told steely-eyed Kreutz—had told not a soul until the time was ripe—about the idea that had come to him in the hours he'd been locked underground in the bunker, battling for his life.

Down there, his mind had bent toward the possibility of something better . . . a truer, more durable, more aesthetically pleasing form of life.

While waging war with the merciless ants, an image had brightened the corridors of Rudyard's brain: a creature of neither one phylum nor the other, neither human nor *other*. A hybrid creation that hummed along his subconscious like a blistering-hot wire.

If Rudyard had been more than the weak, fleshy thing Mother Nature had dictated humans must be—if Elizabeth had been, too—none of that day's horror would have touched them, would it? They would have survived, because at a genetic level they'd have had a foot in each camp: both human and other.

What shape would this new iteration take? Rudyard's brain would conjure many over his adolescence.

Two strands entwined in a genomic embrace . . . a fun-house assortment of body parts that bathed him in an alkaline sweat: sculpted mantis limbs with serrate spurs that ended in delicate feminine hands—human organs encased in the ribbed, dusky, impenetrable carapace of a cockroach.

The commanding mind of such new geometries would be human, too, not insectile. Educated and wise, not predatorially instinctive.

The best of two worlds.

Rudyard carried these imaginings far from his childhood bedroom. Carried them through his first billion, past his second and third and fourth. He carried them to where his wealth far outstripped his father's—who Rudyard refused to talk to, right up to the old bastard's deathbed.

But there came a point when Rudyard had to confront the two questions buried in his lurid sense-memories, which were:

Is such a creature even possible? and *Does the world need this?*

As to the first, there remained much doubt. On a chromosomal level, using the modern alchemies of DNA strand recombination, could a team of genetic sorcerers create this *other* of his imaginings—could it step from his mind and take a seat at the table of reality?

Rudyard had spent many hours contemplating this question in the penthouse of his corporate skyscraper, staring down fifty-seven stories to the sidewalk where others of his species scuttled about. From that high up, pedestrians had the look of ants, no different than the two encased in transparent polyethylene blocks on his desk.

A pair of siafu ants, his old nemeses.

The first block held a common siafu drone with its anvil-shaped head and mammoth pincers, the same ones that had left scars all across Rudyard's body.

The second block was host to a siafu queen. Her abdomen was a regal barrel swollen with her stillborn brood: children she'd never bear, frozen in Lexan as she now was.

Even at that time, Rudyard had accumulated the bankroll to mount a serious attempt. He was obscenely rich. And he'd discovered that attaining a certain level of wealth entitled you to operate as a law unto oneself. Whatever rules applied to the masses could be over-stepped or ignored like so much piffle. All Rudyard needed to do was make money no object. He must keep the team small and the plan secret. Third, and most key, he mustn't get caught.

As to the second question—*Does the world need this?*—at the outset, it had dogged him ever so slightly. He couldn't see any utility to such a creation, frankly. Deep-mining operations? Terraforming on distant planets where the atmosphere was mostly methane, cold enough to snap human bones upon exposure?

Did the world—this one, or any conceivable future world—*need* this thing he was hell-bent on creating? If not, did he possess the unbridled ego to father something that had no place in any sane architecture, a creature God or Nature never intended?

TWO

12:49 p.m.

Now, sitting behind the wheel of the Malibu in the current year of our lord, 2018—following decades of deflating setbacks, grotesque breaches of scientific ethics, billions in development and millions in hush-money payouts—the only question that mattered to Rudyard Crate was:

Will one of my beautiful babies finally work?

The answer to that may lie within the boundaries of the town he was driving through.

Rudyard pulled the Malibu up to a stoplight. His pinkie finger tapped the wheel in a metronome's rhythm. The finger itself was a sawed-off stub: the ants had taken the tip as their prize.

Across the intersection, gardeners tended the hedges of the local golf club. They were manicured to look like duffer paraphernalia: balls and club bags and . . . what the hell was that one supposed to be, one of those idiotic dwarf golf pencils?

Golf. Christ. What a colossal waste of human effort.

But Rudyard knew that club surely represented the last bastion of his own breed. The private golf club, sad haunt of the Old Rich White Guy. Every last boardroom goblin and lizard king. Of course, the woke mob would happily see all such places razed to the ground, but what would they put there instead? Ethically sourced hemp warehouses? Gay and Lesbian Alliance community gardens?

Hah-hah, that's *not going to happen,* Rudyard thought merrily. *Oh heavens no. And why not? Because we old white devils are extraordinarily hard to kill. Dug in like ticks, we are, safe amid the gearwork, and tugging the strings, as always.*

The stoplight turned green. Rudyard trod on the accelerator.

He took one hand off the wheel and dipped into his breast pocket to locate the Three Torches matchbox.

When Jameson saw it, he blanched.

Rudyard balanced the matchbox on his thigh while unfastening the top button of his shirt. Picking the box back up, he settled it next to his throat and thumbed it open.

The roach was a Pennsylvania wood specimen. Not his favorite— that would be the Madagascar hissing—but Pennsylvanians were hearty travelers. It crawled out of the box and perched on his collar.

Rudyard coaxed it with one fingertip until it fell down the V-front of his shirt.

The pitter-patter of the roach made Rudyard's skin tighten deliciously. This was his Ritual. Well, *one* of them.

He made sure to never practice the Ritual on exposed skin. Still, over the years he'd managed to erase a great deal of the work done by his childhood surgeons. Sometimes the Ritual got out of hand, but he had a very good doctor who made discreet house calls. Rudyard didn't sleep with many women, but if so, he went with pros, stony-eyed leathernecks who'd seen it all. Still, most of them turned their heads when his clothes came off.

He enjoyed letting an aggressive insect loose under his shirt before stepping into high-leverage takeover bids. A bug with a fruity detonation of a sting that charted at Level Two on Schmidt's Pain Index. A trap-jaw ant, an assassin bug. A personal dare to himself, to not only outmuscle a hostile opponent, but to do so while a venomous insect turned his belly into a pinboard. He'd tolerate the assault for as long as possible before adjusting his shirt, diplomatically squishing the thing.

Was his fixation unnatural by today's prudish standards? *Duh.* But in the future, that might change.

The roach made a visible impression against Rudy's shirt as he drove. The fabric popped with its explorations. As it went tripping along his hip, Rudyard was able to think straighter.

Jameson, meanwhile, looked ill. Fuck him. Fuck him sky-high.

"We should have seen all of this coming," he snapped. "The subject has completely breached containment."

"We've been monitoring it, same as always," Jameson mumbled, ever the ninny. The urge to slap him was almost irresistible.

"What about the tracking implant?"

"The subject must have found a way to get it out."

"Wasn't it pretty much tagged to its brain stem?"

Jameson nodded glumly.

"There must have been a trigger to set off this new behavior," said Rudyard. "A chemical modification, some hitch in the signal. Goddamn it, Jameson. This was the time to be the *most* vigilant."

While ants had marked the start of Rudy's obsession, his focus had since enlarged. Project Athena's had, too. There were now many phenotypes in his subjects' genetic stew: roach, locust, honeybee, assassin bug, convolvulus hawk moth, tent worm caterpillar . . .

And wasp. Most of all and most prized, wasp.

Each subject in Project Athena was a Pandora's box of tetchy chromosomes. But the box was fated to open, eventually—that consequence had been hardwired into the package from conception.

And the likelihood of that box springing open was astronomically higher during times of dynamic bodily or neurological change.

Like basically, the entirety of human teenage-hood.

Rudyard lifted one hand off the wheel to check his watch. He remained hopeful he could get this under control.

"Coventry knew the risks," he said evenly. "We all did, right from the start."

"Coventry knew," Jameson repeated like a fucking mynah bird.

Rudyard pulled into a nondescript facility in a warehouse block on the southern scrim of town. The drive from the airstrip had shaved off thirty precious minutes. The Escalade flanked in behind the Malibu.

Rudyard stepped out of the vehicle. The hem of his shirt came untucked. The roach fell out and went skittering across the tarmac.

The most honest words Rudyard Crate had ever spoken weren't to his father, Kreutz, any of his business cronies, or even his sister. He'd spoken them to a sad-eyed, vaguely bullet-headed lady of the evening in a Lac-Brome cathouse. She took no offense at his deformities, which had disarmed him; she'd looked right at his naked figure, *all* of him, bold as brass. Her casual acceptance caused him to say:

How do I get back to that place where the world made sense? That time when I felt loved and understood by at least one person? If the key is dipped in poison, well, so what? I seek entry, anyway. I'm human.

The whore patted his arm consolingly. *Désolé, monsieur, je ne parle pas anglais.*

Facing his facility, suspecting that horrors may lurk within, Rudyard drew a breath. Roy stepped to his side. Jameson lingered behind them, a bad smell in a cheap shirt.

At the sunlit edge of the building, a bulbous shadow stretched across the pavement.

Hello, baby brother.

A pair of bobbing antennae topped the shadow.

What fun we will have. Oh, what fun indeed.

THREE

12:52 p.m.

Tell me, Cherry.

Tell me everything.

Tell me why you kept that acceptance letter a secret.

Tell me why you didn't let me know you were leaving.

Plum's disembodied voice. Pushing, needling, guilting.

Tell me why you weren't there when I needed you most.

Harry's Geo motored down Martindale Road, approaching the southern shore of the lake. We were tracking toward a red inverted teardrop on Google Maps. The address was the last text the iPhone had sent, over half an hour ago now.

After receiving it, Harry had driven us out of downtown, up Ontario Street and across the 406 highway, past a maze of big-box stores and the new hospital, until the buildings thinned into orchards and fields. Grapevines now enclosed us on both sides, the stake-lines running through dry caliche to the bottom of the escarpment. No sounds dented the air apart from the random, desolate report of a crow-cannon.

Tell me when you started hating me.

I thought: *Stop it, Plum. That's not fair. Why don't you tell* me, *okay? About Serena?*

Sullen silence from that inner voice now.

How did you two meet? How did you get twisted up with this psycho?

Was I even right about that? I'd never heard Plum's voice on the phone, only Serena's. Maybe Serena was lying. Maybe she didn't have Plum at all.

Nothing made sense, but there wasn't enough time to get my feet set because everything was moving too fast—and that felt purposeful, too: whoever was behind this didn't want to give me time to catch my breath, to think.

Lake Ontario shone goldenly through the shore pines. We'd entered the old-wealth part of town. The deep lots stretching to the shore were estates, not plain old houses. My gaze touched the side-view mirror, half expecting to see a police car's cherries flashing behind us. Soon some beef-bellied deputy would come swaggering up to the driver's side, his eyes shielded behind polarized lenses.

You two poor shits want to tell me what you're doing in rich-person territory?

Sometimes I had to remind myself that, technically, *I* was rich now. But I'd never felt rich, not for one minute of my life.

"Is that it?"

Harry pointed at a graveled laneway leading off the main road. A real estate sign was dug into the freshly turned earth.

ON THE MARKET SOON / PRIVATE SHOWINGS
BY APPOINTMENT

I checked the address—four brass numerals screwed into the gatepost—against the Google Maps pin. "1009 Lakewood, yeah."

Harry swung down the path. No gate, only that gatepost. A pair of hedges threw shadows over the car; the hedges seemed to narrow the deeper we drove down them.

"Who lives here?"

Harry shook his head: *no clue.* Gravel spat under the tires as he inched the Geo around the left-side hedgerow, which gave way to a grassy land-sweep behind a house.

Harry killed the engine. We sat staring at the place. It was twice the size of my new house in Executive Acres, probably twenty times the size of my Hallmark at Woody Knot. But it wasn't just the size. The gray brick, leaded glass windows, the copper shingles that were oxidized to a wintery green . . . it had the look of something that had been here forever, and always would be.

We got out. There were no cars in the drive. Nothing moved behind the house's un-curtained windows. An arctic desolation pumped out of the place.

My sweatshirt crackled. The ketchup from that tossed cafeteria patty had hardened.

"Hey, Harr, could you . . . ?"

He studiously looked somewhere else as I peeled the shirt off and put it back on inside-out. The tacky ketchup felt gross on my stomach, but at least—

The phone went off in my pocket. I hauled it out and saw the text.

33098

The back door sat under the leafy shade thrown by some beech trees. Their buds stuck to the treads of my sneakers as I walked to the entry. If we went inside—and I can't imagine we were expected to do anything else—that'd be breaking and entering, right? Not that I cared all that much. If the cops showed up, well, good.

The mailbox was shaped like a mouth. Naked pink gums, huge white teeth.

TELLER was stamped on its front. One cavity-black letter per tooth.

Allan's house. Shit, his father was a dentist, wasn't he? . . . no, a *denturist*. I'd caught that fact in one of the news articles. *Teller's father, a local denturist* . . . the realization that this was the home of Allan Teller, currently missing, sent ice-footed spiders scurrying up my back.

A property lockbox was fastened round the door handle.

I punched the five numbers in the text on the keypad. 3-3-0-9-8.

When I hit 8, the lockbox issued a mechanized whirr. The face of the lockbox came loose. A key rested inside.

I removed it. Slotted it into the dead bolt. Past the door's window, a long hallway trailed off into the dim. That queasy feeling of unchecked momentum hit me again—the sense of my heels skidding on an endless carpet of banana peels.

Placing his hand over mine, Harry applied the smallest pressure. The lock snapped open with a dull *thuck*.

"Now we're *both* guilty of a B-and-E," he said. "Co-conspirators."

Harry twisted the knob. The door swung inward. The smell that wafted out was stale and uninhabited, reminding me of a room at a run-down motel.

We stepped inside. The floorboards were waxed to a glossy shine. Harry bent to pick the beech buds off his shoes.

"It's such a nice house," he whispered sheepishly.

The door levered shut behind us. My heart jackrabbited, its rhythm—*ba-dah, badda-dah, ba-DAH*—putting me even more on edge.

That stale smell and thin coat of dust on the light fixtures told me nobody had been in here for a while. I wasn't scared of someone coming down from upstairs: the halls and landings held the silence of a grave. The dream that had woken me this morning rolled back: Allan Teller, Chad Dearborn, and Will Stinson crawling from a bubble in the earth with their blobfish heads, burial suits clinging to their chests in wet-newspaper tatters.

Harry and I padded down the hall, past a heavy door that lay partially open. Beyond it, I could see a room with an antique wooden desk hemmed by walls covered in—

"Are those *teeth*?" Harry whispered.

Yes, they were. Disembodied sets of teeth. Teeth without mouths. Perfect pearly white dentures, hundreds of them, mounted on the walls like hunting trophies.

I didn't know Allan Teller's parents. Never met them or had any reason to. Still, I'd vaguely hated them, based on the shithead son they'd raised. But I felt bad for them now, standing in their house. The house they must've decided to sell because of the memories it held. Bad ones, sure—every house had those—but there had to be good ones, too. The idea that they couldn't stand to be within these walls anymore, that their lives had been so unseated by the mystery of their child's disappearance . . . yeah, nobody deserved that.

Pikachu!

HIGHSCHOOLDICKS.wav

I touched the play button. Plum's voice filled the house.

"Allan, Will, and Chad. Those three felt like an inevitable part of the high-school experience, didn't they?"

Ahead of us, the hallway opened into the tile-and-chrome oasis of a large country-style kitchen. Copper pots dangled from the ceiling on hooks, sparkling in the sun that streamed in through the bay window.

"Remember Grease? That movie's ancient, but the types are ageless. Travolta, the cool rebel. Olivia Newton-John, the virgin pom-pommer. Nerds and gearheads and jocks, greasers and skids and ice-queen bitches . . . It's all the same, no matter how far back you go, probably to caveman days. Go to the basement, Cherr. Allan's room is down there."

My eyes met Harry's. The basement was the last place I wanted to investigate. But I'd be lying if I said curiosity hadn't started to grip me. Maybe it was the fact I was alone in someone else's house, but that feeling of intrusion, of peering into somebody's private spaces, was intoxicating.

We backtracked to the basement door. When I opened it, I swore I caught an uncanny inhale as if something down there had drawn an awakening breath.

"They were the same old dicks," Plum said as Harry and I crept down the stairs. *"Everyone fit to a role, same as the pieces on a chessboard. Take Chad. The king. God! He had that way of holding your attention . . . and if he put the full force of his personality on you, you felt like the only star in the sky."*

How would you even know, Plum? Chad Dearborn barely knew you existed . . . unless you had your own secret life, one you'd never told me about.

The stairs dead-ended at a wall. I could make out a pool table across the basement. Sunlight shafted through ground-level casement windows, picking up dust tumbling in the air.

A bedroom doorway was visible on the other side of the pool table. That room held a more congested darkness than the rest of the basement. Yellow police tape carved an X over it.

Until seeing that tape, I'd allowed myself to believe that Allan, Chad, and Will were only missing. But that yellow X spoke to a darker truth. It said they were *gone*.

I swung my hips around the pool table. The bedroom door hung halfway open. Through the crack, I could see a plastic-y gleam. The floor was covered in a clear sheet.

"Will, oh now he was the sexy knight. The Exclusives had the same version, you know, the Vacant Hot Bitch. God, it's sad how much attention I paid to the people I hated."

Harry ran his fingers up the edge of the police tape, stretching it just enough to fit himself through into Allan's bedroom.

"Allan Teller was the court jester. And he was the biggest shit, wasn't he, because he was the most dispensable. Allan realized how close he was to being one of us—no, worse, because we'd smother him to death if he fell to our level without the safety blanket of the cool kids. So he had to constantly prove his worth by being the meanest asshole on earth."

I followed Harry under the tape. The plastic sheet laid over the bedroom carpet crinkled under our sneakers. When Harry tried the light switch, nothing happened.

We stood in the mulchy light. It seemed to be a regular boy's room, not that I'd been in many. The bleached-out *Star Wars* cover and a frayed, rope-legged stuffed animal that Allan must've shoved into a drawer whenever friends came over.

A balsawood galleon sat on the desk, beside a few squeezed-out tubes of model glue; a yellow evidence card rested on the ship, marked A-13. Other cards were stuck atop the board games on the overhead shelf, next to a clay mug I recognized from fourth-grade pottery class. Allan and I had sat next to each other that afternoon, glazing our mugs in rapt concentration.

Farther down the shelf, a red light blinked. A Wi-Fi cam was partially hidden behind a Wing Gundam model. In the room's stillness, I could hear its servos whirring.

Serena? It had to be. I was pretty sure she'd been watching all day. In the furnace room, for sure. Had there been a camera in Mr. F's class, too? Even if I'd missed it, I bet there was.

"Teller was a master of the put-down, wasn't he? The nicknames. The needling cruelties. He pointed out the flaws in everyone else in the hope that nobody took note of his own."

"Mags."

I turned to see Harry pointing to the bed.

". . . prancing like a fool to earn a little pat on the head from Chad or Biebs," Plum went on. *"But under the surface, he was nothing but a scared little boy."*

I took two steps to the bedside. The plastic crackled, setting my teeth on edge. A set of handcuffs was snapped around the bedpost. Evidence card A-1.

A *bloody* set of cuffs. Blood and hardened peels of what could only be human skin.

There was blood on the carpet, too, under the plastic. A dried puddle around the bedpost that the handcuffs dangled from—

"I'll tell you a secret, Cherr: Allan was terrified of the monster in his closet."

My eyes tracked to the walk-in closet.

The blood trail led in there. A rusty ribbon under the sheet.

I didn't want to push through the closet's saloon doors into that cryptlike darkness. The possibility roused a childish fear in me, the one I'd once felt looking at the hazard symbol on the canister of

Drano: that skeletal hand reaching into a black pot. As a girl I'd been certain it wouldn't just be my hand that got eaten, either—no, my whole body would melt if I so much as *touched* that deadly Drano, leaving a pile of bones.

"*The monster used to visit little Allan Teller at night. He could hear it in there, scratching at the door.*"

An image floated through my mind: Allan shivering in bed, his *Star Wars* blanket pulled up to his chin as that scratching drifted out of his closet. The sound of a rat's claws scraping at a headstone.

"*Time passed, and Allan thought the monster was gone. He stopped believing in it. His family moved to another, bigger house . . . this house. But guess what? The monster followed him. Monsters do that, you know. They never lose your scent.*"

Harry was creeping toward the closet.

"*And this time, all his cool new friends and all of Mommy and Daddy's money couldn't stop that monster from getting in.*"

I grabbed his wrist. "Stop."

It took me a few tries to pause the .wav file. My thumb was shaking.

"What are we even doing?"

"She wants us to see," Harry said, nodding to the phone. "Whoever's on the other end of that. And if we don't . . ."

The blood trail thickened across the carpet the closer it got to the closet. I pictured Allan Teller getting dragged by . . . by . . .

But my brain refused to define it. All I could see was Allan digging his feet into the carpet, his mouth open in a silent scream as he was winched relentlessly inside that closet.

Harry prodded the closet's old-timey batwing doors open, holding his hand straight out from his chest. The darkness inside seemed too large for the space that contained it. Watery light came in from the window at the end, looking into the backyard.

We took a few steps inside. Darkness sucked to my skin. Allan's shirts and sweaters rustled as my shoulder touched them. And oh god, the *smell*. A lingering odor, not of blood but something much older. Something alien that didn't belong to humankind at all.

I could make out scratch marks on the exterior face of the closet window. Long, milky grazes, as though an animal had been running its claws across the pane out in the backyard . . . or something else. Some grinning horror hunched down at the dirt line, scraping and scraping while Allan shivered in his bed.

Little pig, little pig, let me in.

I thumbed the .wav back on.

"*After what happened at the Burning Van, I found Allan. Just wanted to talk, you know? Maybe even say I was sorry . . . And you know what he told me, Cherr? I'm not giving you a fucking cent. He thought I was gonna hustle him to keep it quiet. But he was the one who filmed it. He's the one who put it out into the world for everyone to see, and laugh at me.*"

Plum's voice danced in the grayish air. Harry was behind me, but his presence felt hostile now: part of me expected him to block my escape, trapping me in the closet with . . .

The monster, my mind yammered. *The-monster-the-monster-the—*

My eyes rose to the shelves below the drop ceiling, stocked with *Star Trek* Mega Bloks sets and *D&D* manuals, remnants of Allan's nerdy old life he couldn't bear to toss away—

Something skittered across the ceiling, hidden above the panels.

I went stiff, waiting for the ceiling tiles to cave in and send Allan's body jangling down into the closet: Allan Teller dead-but-not-*really*-dead, still foully alive somehow, his face swollen with noxious gas that made it purple and shiny as a broken ankle, and his eye sockets, those obliterated pits, the closet filling with the stench of a desecrated grave while horsehair worms twisted in Allan's hair, his mouth hinging open in a sick leer: "*I hid, Beefster!*"—hissing through vocal cords gone thin as a balding tire, the sinews showing through his rotted throat—"*I hid from the monster! Let me show you where!*"— his bony fingers scrabbling toward my face while his eyes, crunched from their sockets, went tether-balling on his cheeks.

"Mags, it's only mice," Harry said. "This is a country house, and all the money in the world can't get rid of the mice."

Plum's voice bled back in over the crash of my heart.

"*—can't keep the monster away, Cherr. It's coming. All it has to do is find a way in . . . scratch, scratch, scratch . . . but what if it wasn't a monster looking to be let in? What if it was just, I don't know, change? We all change, Cherr. That night at Burning Van, I sure did.*"

From somewhere inside the closet came a muffled *ping!*

"*And Allan, he needed a change too. That's all the monster was offering . . . and to be honest, how awesome would that be?*"

The .wav ended.

That *ping!* came a second time. Then a third and fourth: *ping! ping!*

Breath held, I pushed aside a bunch of what-a-handsome-young-man suits to reveal the back wall of the closet.

A fifth *ping!* The sound was coming from under the floor.

Harry knelt beside me. His fingers found the edge of the carpet and pulled it up.

Ping! Louder now.

Running his fingernails along the edge of a floor plank, Harry peeled a loose board up.

We peered into what must've been Allan's hidey-hole . . . a vial of Percocet with GAIL TELLER written on the label. A pack of Black Cat fireworks so old they probably wouldn't go off. And an iPhone. Exact same model as the one I'd been sent.

Back in the bedroom, I switched it on. Its password-protection feature had been shut off. The phone opened right up when I thumb-swiped the screen.

Ping!

The Wi-Fi cam swiveled. Serena must've been watching us right this minute.

The iPhone held seven new texts in the Message app. I scrolled to the final conversation string, between Allan and an unidentified caller.

Come

> no

Come

> no please

> please stop

> hear you outside

> my window

> please stop

> go away

COME NOW

> nooooo not fair

> oh please

> i don't want to anymore im sick i need to rest go to the hospital see a doctor

LET'S GO TO THE FURNACE ROOM

> please

> but

> *my parents have money*
>
> *anything you want*

DICKIE O'REILLY GAVE ME THE KEY

> *i love you*
>
> *need you*
>
> *whore*
>
> *bitch*
>
> *cunt*
>
> *please leave me alone*
>
> *don't leave*
>
> *love me*

COME FOR YOUR TREAT

> *love you sorry so sorry*

The final texts on the thread—the seven that had come in over the last few minutes, making the *ping*s that helped Harry locate the phone's hiding place, read:

and he

DID come, Margaret

over

and over

and over

and over

> and over

Reading that made the handcuffs on the bedpost even more sinister.

I pictured Allan Teller stirring in the dead of night to catch sight of someone—no, some*thing*—hunched outside his closet window. I saw this from Allan's perspective, lying in bed with his wrist cuffed to the post. Something coiled and sleek, made of famished angles with a face etched in cold moonlight. The metallic rake of nails on the glass and a smell, too, the alkaline whiff of a peeled-open battery.

Come to me.

I'd assumed Allan must have shackled himself to the bed to stop the monster in the closet from dragging him away to its lair.

But what if Allan handcuffed himself to the post to stop himself from *going with* the monster?

What if he'd torn the flesh off his own hand, peeling it right through the handcuffs' unforgiving steel ring, to join that monster on a midnight ramble?

FOUR

1:08 p.m.

What had Subject Six learned about itself?

That was the question Rudyard asked himself, entering the Control Center. *If* the subject had somehow discovered the project she'd been a part of since conception—*if* she'd already self-actualized, learning to harness the abilities her metamorphosis conferred—and *if* she'd found her way to the Control Center and learned Coventry's role . . . well, that didn't bode well for anyone.

Nobody more so than Coventry.

Rudyard, Jameson, and Roy let themselves in through a bomb-proof black metal door leading in from the parking lot. They went down an antiseptically white hallway to the control room.

Rudyard was surprised at how orderly it all appeared. He'd often heard it said that no life-form on earth enjoyed breaking stuff more than phylum *Terrorus teenagerum*. Yet there was no evidence of that. The filing cabinets were shut, the computer screens unbroken.

A sheet of paper was lying on the motherboard, ragged down one edge where it had been ripped from an old journal.

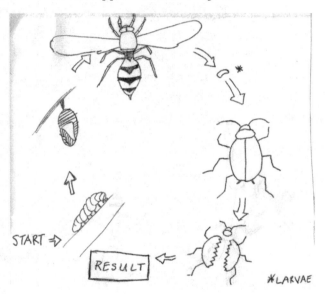

Rudyard had drawn it himself. Cartoonish, yes, simplistic also, but it stated his goal. It had sprung from conversations between Jameson, Coventry, and himself. Their task at the time had been finalizing Subject Six's gene makeup. The three of them had been twenty years younger then, fewer gray hairs and troubled nights sleeping. The air had crackled with the electricity of their wild ambitions.

We cannot birth a life-form of the kind you've envisioned, Coventry had told him. *Even using an artificial womb—not that the science is there yet—it wouldn't cohere. What you need, Rudy, is a parthenogenic or motherless birth. Athena crawling out of Zeus's forehead. A goddess who emerges dressed in full battle regalia. The subject has to give birth to itself, in a sense. The spliced genome gets attached to the DNA helix. A trigger set to fire at the time of first maturation is harnessed to the whole works.*

Roy had retrieved Coventry's cell phone from under the main console. He gave it to Rudyard. Coventry's Contacts list was barren. But of course it would be. Julian Coventry was a man unknown to anyone, likely even himself. He had few friends, no family, nothing that passed as a life outside of his job. This cipherlike nature, as well as his willingness to share Rudyard's unwholesome ambition, had made him an ideal candidate for the position.

Rudyard read the phone's most recent text string.

JULIAN DARLING

LET ME IN

i cant

dont make

me

please

DON'T MAKE ME WAIT LOVER

yes

ok

love

The text had been sent at 11:15 p.m., two nights ago. This coincided with the last time Coventry had made contact with home base. The red flag being when Coventry missed his second daily check-in—based on that, Rudyard had begun to assemble his team.

"Check the security footage, Mr. Roy."

While Roy called it up, Rudyard's attention was drawn back to the doodle. Something had been written on the other side. He flipped it over.

I KNOW EVERYTHING DADDY

"Mr. Crate."

Roy had located a half-minute of footage from a few nights ago, from the camera recoding the sole entry door. He forwarded it to 11:21 p.m. The black-and-white image was made hazy by condensation inside the lens housing, but Rudyard could see—

There. The briefest flash. A shape passing underneath the lamp and through the door, which shut soundly with its passage.

"Fast-forward."

Roy did so. At 1:17 a.m. the door opened again to permit the same shape to exit back out into the night.

"I can check the rest, but it will take time," Roy told him.

"Don't bother. That was Subject Six."

"What if it came back?" Fear laced Jameson's voice. "She could still be here."

And yet, Rudyard didn't think so. The final reckoning would be at a place and at a time of Subject Six's choosing. Not now, not here.

Flanked by Jameson and Roy, Rudyard passed down a well-lit hallway to the glassed-in Observation Cell. Panes of glass—one-way and two-way mirrors—looked in from opposite walls onto a white-tiled room.

Subject Six had been brought here once a year. Its Minder would take it out for a birthday meal—though it was not Subject Six's true birthday, seeing as technically things grown in test tubes didn't have those. During the meal, it would become sleepy. It would then be transferred here. For most of the test, the subject remained unconscious, except for a brief physical acuity assessment—during which it would scream and strain against its bindings. Its first such ordeal left raw wheals on its ankles and wrists. The following year, Coventry made sure the straps were padded. It was a necessary agony, as the subject's anatomical structure had to be assessed. Its digestive processes and, in time, reproductive capacity were also examined—and that particular milestone had been severely delayed in Subject Six's case.

The diagnoses were sent to Rudyard, as were those of the five other subjects seeded within North America.

After the tests were completed, Subject Six would wake up at home. Its memories would be foggy and unremarkable.

Another of those dang birthday nightmares, the subject's Minder was instructed to say. *Do you feel better now?*

Rudyard peered into the Observation Cell. Words had been scrawled on the wall, though they weren't nearly as neat as the ones on the back of his old doodle. But then, the ones in the cell had been written in the imperfect ink of blood.

THE GIFT ALL THE BOYS WANT TO CHASE

That particular phrasing—*all the boys*—nagged at Rudyard.

Among insects, the boys didn't make out too well. With animals, males were often the alpha. Consider the radiant peacock and the homely peahen. But with insects such as the male preying mantis, which got decapitated during intercourse with the larger and more ferocious female—her mate still pumping in his seed as she devoured his head . . . well, that was how the cookie crumbled.

And in the whole of that kingdom, all ten million species, only five honored queens.

Ants, bees, termites, the plain tiger butterfly—

And wasps.

Those were the five species Rudyard and his team had explored, right down to the links of their protein chains. Genes punched out and shoehorned in, spliced, added to, and subtracted from. The end result was a helix that to any molecular biologist might summon thoughts of Dante's rings of hell.

Six subjects. Six queens.

Four had misfired. Not quite sequentially, but not too far off. First, they had lost One, followed by Four, Two, and finally Three last year. Subject Five remained alive, technically.

That left Six. Who, remarkably, had been the team's biggest swing of all.

Rudyard continued past the Observation Cell, on down the hallway to the final door. The Observer's Room. It could be accessed through a solid metal door that now lay closed.

Twisting the knob, Rudyard toed it open—and at once, his head was aswarm. His hands went up in a warding-off gesture that was worthless against the intrusion of the fingers that were suddenly inside his skull—oh god, skeletal fingers rummaging and digging into his *brain*—

A pair of hands secured his head. Fingers slipped behind his ears, thumbing tabs in place. Rudy could only stand, inert as a toy in a tickle trunk, as his brain patterns began to sluggishly resume themselves.

Rudyard fingered the disc behind his ear. Roy had put it there. They were Jameson's invention, designed to counteract the pheromone signals that at least one of the subjects, Five, had displayed upon maturation.

Pheromones were commonplace in the insect kingdom. Chemicals produced by the endocrine glands by which insects could communicate with one another, or affect communal behavior. Many insect species employed them. During mating, or as a warning, or as a trace left behind on a particularly rich food source.

But queens used them most often, and pheromones produced by queens were unquestionably the strongest.

There was no more profound method of control in Earth's biosphere—encompassing all living organisms: flora, fauna, animal, down to the bacterial—than insect queen pheromones. A fire ant queen will hardwire her alates, her winged fertile male and female offspring, with a pheromone controller compelling them to take flight from the nest *en masse*, spreading her royal genes over a five-hundred-meter radius. This would be the equivalent control distance of several states, in human terms. The alates' queen is also sending them on a suicide mission, as every one of them will perish after fulfilling their monarch's order.

In honeybees and wasps, pheromones drive the life and function of the colony. The queen regulates all aspects of communal harmony using primer pheromones capable of modifying her brood on a physiological and behavioral level. Both wasp and bee queens secrete the powerful "queen signal," also known as the queen mandibular pheromone, QMP. Queens force-feed it to her drones and attendants, who then disseminate it throughout the colony. Once it is delivered, every subject is filled with a sense of belonging to—being *owned by*—their queen.

This service is as instinctive as it is benign: The queen is central to the health of the colony, so in the interest of maintaining homeostasis, she employs pheromones. A wasp nest or beehive with a dead queen devolves into chaos, filth, anarchy, and collapse.

Rudyard had once tried to explain this phenomenon to a disinterested dinner date.

The closest human equivalent would be hypnotism. I went to a hypnotist's show once, just to see. He got them barking like dogs, clucking like hens, taking their clothes off when he told them the room was getting intolerably hot, to the point they were set to strip their underwear off. But that's not even close, really, to the power a queen exerts. Just imagine: A queen bee can sterilize a worker without touching them. The next day she can make them fertile again. Drones will die in the tens of thousands to protect their queen.

Struck by the apathy of his conversational partner—he couldn't even remember her face, only the soapy, goatlike cast of her eyes—he'd probed deeper.

The more cunningly predatory orders of the insect kingdom—parasitic roaches, ambrosia beetles, hunter wasps—use pheromones to transfix their quarry. Has anyone ever told you about the jewel wasp queen? No? Oh, you're in for a treat. A jewel wasp is the most beautiful insect you'll ever lay eyes on. It's every color in the rainbow, constantly shifting, concentrated into a form no bigger than a blob of lead. She can exert pheromone control over a common cricket so powerful that it'll happily allow her to lay an egg in its abdomen. The larvae hatches, consuming that cricket for nourishment. The jewel wasp's control is so total that the cricket will go about its business with over three-quarters of its body eaten away! Can you picture it? The poor thing staggering around with the wasp larva protruding from its backside, larger than the cricket by then, piggybacking and devouring it until only an exoskeletal husk is left? I'd like to see any hypnotist pull that off!

Had there been a second date? He couldn't recall.

The pheromones secreted by Subject Five were adequately managed with Jameson's suppressor discs. But the brute force of Subject Six's—which, Rudyard noted with no small degree of concern, must only be a hint of their true strength, as they'd been diminishing inside the Observer's Room for hours if not days . . . they were another order of magnitude entirely.

He turned his attention back to the Observer's Cell. Roy had pulled its door shut.

There's nothing in there, Rudy. Except there was, wasn't there? Something brooding, tensed, fangs drawn, waiting to lash out.

He twisted the knob, toed the door open, and danced away.

Nothing moved. Roy reached inside, flicking the light switch.

The room was austere under the halogens. Rudyard took note of three items immediately.

One: a laptop set on a collapsible table.

Two: something in a chair next to the table, draped in a white sheet.

Three: in the corner. Old, tarnished. An army surplus footlocker.

Rudyard stepped inside the Observer's Room. Silence, but for the barest breath. For a moment it seemed to be coming from under the sheet, but no, it came from the vent.

"That's—" Jameson's hand rose, one quaking finger pointing at the sheet.

"We're all aware," Rudyard said.

A red light blinked in the face of an egg-shaped device socked in a high corner of the room. Rudyard motioned Roy to check it out.

"Nanny cam," Roy reported. "Remote access. Motion activated."

So, the subject knows we're here.

"Are we in any immediate danger?" he asked Roy.

After a considering pause, Roy shook his head. "But it's watching us."

Subject Six had clearly gone to a great deal of effort to set the *mise-en-scène*. He could tell without having to be instructed that there was a sequence he was meant to follow.

WATCH ME was written on a slip of paper laid atop the laptop.

FIVE

1:22 p.m.

I barreled out of Allan Teller's house into the afternoon sunlight. As soon as my sneakers touched the grass, I screamed so hard that black spots burst in front of my eyes.

My heart was beating too fast, the hummingbird rhythm of it droning in my ears, and I got scared, a different kind than in the closet, the fear that my heart was going to explode and then I couldn't hear anything, not a single note, and my knees gave out as I crumpled to the ground.

Harry sat cross-legged in front of me. His hands encircled my wrists.

"It's okay, Mags. Just breathe."

Gathering his feet under him, Harry said: "I'm going to do something my mom used to do when I got scared, okay?"

Placing the tip of his index finger on the grass, he dragged it along the ground.

"I'm drawing a circle," he said. "I'm closing us inside it."

He passed behind me, appearing again, his finger meeting his original starting point.

"We're safe in this circle," he said, sitting across from me. "It won't last forever, but for now, everything that's happening outside the circle can't touch us."

Amazingly, it helped. I could see a dome around us, a membrane thin as a soap bubble. The day's events could only rush around us like water around a boulder, leaving us dry.

"Harry, what the hell are we going to do?"

His face held a frank openness. "I honestly don't know."

"I think Allan's dead. I didn't actually believe that until just now."

After a pause, a shallow nod. "He could be, yeah."

This morning I'd woken up thinking my best friend was probably dead too. Then I was given proof she was alive, in the form of the iPhone. Then the furnace room, Mr. F's confession, the cafeteria riot, then I'm in Allan Teller's bedroom staring at a bloody set of handcuffs . . .

The iPhone went off in my pocket.

Pikachu!

Hauling it out, I heaved it as far as I could. It went end-over-end to land on the grass near Harry's car.

"Do you think we can catch up?"

I said: "What do you mean, Harry?"

"I mean, this has all been planned," he said. "I couldn't even *start* to put something like this together. But no plan is perfect, right? So, how do we fuck up the perfect plan? What even *is* fucking it up?" He shifted uneasily. "If we fuck up by not doing what we're told . . . well, that could mean that Charity—"

"Dies. Gets killed."

He nodded grimly. "Right. And this other person, Serena, she gets away with it. And if she also had something to do with Allan Teller and the other two, she gets away with that, too."

"I guess."

"So how do we stop that? Stop Charity from getting hurt and stop Serena from—"

"Who even *is* Serena? Why does she want to punish everyone?"

Harry gave me that frank look again. "I can see why *Charity* might want to punish everyone."

"Including us?"

Now Harry tilted his head: *Come on, Mags. Let's be honest here.*

"Why did I get the same text you did this morning, guiding me to meet up with you?" He pushed out a hard breath. "Fact is, I'm not nearly smart enough to know why, Mags. But let's play this out. Two big possibilities. One—and this is the dark part—is Charity blames you and me for not being there for her that night at Burning Van. This is revenge, pure and simple."

"Revenge."

"The second is nicer. Charity wants me here *for* you. She knew today was going to be a rough ride and didn't want you to face it alone." His expression changed. "Or we get dark again, right? And in that universe, I'm here because I won't be able to help myself."

I felt my brow beetle. "Help yourself how?"

He held his palms out. "Mags, you even have a name for it. Bad Harry."

Last fall, the carnival came to Port Dalhousie. Four of us had gone: me and Plum, Harry, and Dennis Weeks. The rides had been erected along the beach, bordering the pier. The air was blowing cool off the lake when we showed up after dark. I loved the carnival best at night; it felt alive, even dangerous, the colors streaking kaleidoscopically, and somewhere—gathering out of thin air—I always half expected a tent to appear: red-and-white pinstriped, set at the rear of the fairgrounds in a permanent shadow. From inside it came archaic music, voices, laughter with a sharp edge, while outside, a barker in a seersucker suit with silver teeth stood on a soapbox, straight out of that old Ray Bradbury story, inviting us to step right up, step right up, and taste an experience best served raw.

There had been that same tension in the air that night. It nestled amid the smell of corn dogs and wet hay, the shrieks of children and the gnashing of gears from the rides that always felt one torn belt or slipped gear away from flying to pieces—as if a carny, after putting them together, looked down at the loose collection of screws and fasteners in his palm and thought: *Eh, probably extras.*

Harry and I had ridden the Rainbow together. Its riders sat on a wide, flat platform that cycled up and down, round and round in a circle. The Rainbow's seats were worn, the seat belts frayed, and its momentum crushed us together. I was laughing, Harry too, his breath cinnamon from the Dentyne he was chewing. When we got off, my hair was wild. I'd lost one of the clips I'd used to pin my hair back.

We noticed it under the Rainbow. An inch-long wink of curved blue metal.

Harry said: *I'll get it.*

Before I could say anything—before I could even suspect his intent—he'd slung himself over the metal guardrail. The Rainbow was in motion, the riders shrieking as it carried them upward on its trajectory. The operator's sleepy eyes widened in shock as Harry dodged across the concrete and into the ride's downward path.

The Rainbow came down in a lethal sweep, its platform cutting the air like a guillotine blade, and Harry's hair rose from his skull with its downdraft, as if he'd touched a Tesla ball, while the ride hammered down on its long, pale armature, the pendulum of a doomsday clock tolling midnight, close enough that I'd swear it scraped each knob of Harry's spine. I waited for him to be knocked skyward, carried up and up, his broken silhouette framed against the harvest moon—

Then there Harry was, safe on the other side. He held up the prize he'd risked his life for: a ten-cent hairclip, one of a hundred plucked from the careless pile in my nightstand. Then he was off, sprinting away from fairground security.

Seeing him in full flight—the staggering, fiery lunacy that was Harry Cook—was to observe a shooting star: remote and unknowable. Nothing I did, or his parents, or this world in all its beauty and love would alter the dreadful precision of his trajectory.

A line from that Bradbury book had come to me: *Where does thunder go when it dies?*

So yeah, I understood why Serena might want Harry along. No matter how bad things got, no matter how dangerous or dead-end, Bad Harry would wade on in.

"I wonder if I should go," he said. "It's like, you *know* me. I'm full of broken things. I—"

"Don't go, Harry. Please, don't leave me."

He hung his head. "Okay, for now. But if you tell me to, I will."

The phone went off a few more times by Harry's car.

"That was definitely Plum's voice on the .wav file," I said. "She *knows* all this stuff. About Allan, the closet, the phone under the floor. That means she's involved."

"Or else she's being used. Fed information," Harry offered. "Told what to say by Serena."

When the phone went off a fourth time, Harry mimed opening a doorknob.

"I'm stepping out of the bubble, but I'm coming right back."

He walked over to his car.

"Harry, don't get it. I'm not ready yet."

But he already had the phone. He came back. Shut the invisible door behind him.

"Plans come apart, right?" He placed the phone on the grass between us. "Even the best-laid ones. What if we just keep going along for now and let it fall apart on its own?"

"Oh, Harr."

"There was that stuff at school, right? Foster's class, the caf. Like, this can't stay a secret forever. For all we know the cops are on it now. So, we go along, okay? We let everyone catch up. Start tracking cell phones, the Wi-Fi cameras. Give it a few hours. Maybe the cops break down the door of wherever Charity's at right now and rescue her." He tapped the phone. "All we've got to do, Mags, is let this perfect plan fail."

"And not get ourselves killed."

"Right. And that."

I picked up the phone. Hateful fucking thing. *Let the plan fail.* I kind of liked it. It asked the universe to fix things, not me.

I thumb-swiped the phone. An address, the same one, had been sent four times.

I wondered why it had taken this long.

SIX

1:34 p.m.

Faced with the three items in the Observation Cell—the laptop, the footlocker, and the thing draped in the sheet—it was the sheet that commanded Rudyard's immediate attention.

A human being lay under it, clearly. Coventry, almost certainly. But the top looked very *off.* As if someone had placed a misshapen crown on Coventry's head.

The sheet was saturated with blood. It had dried to a glaze that sucked tight to Coventry's face, denting into his howling mouth.

For a king, his crown . . .

Crossing the room, Rudyard settled his hand atop the footlocker. He caught no sense of movement from within. Satisfied, he returned to the computer.

WATCH ME

Rudyard opened it. The screen brightened. A file had been centered on the desktop.

A_HARD_RIDE.mov

Rudyard double-clicked it.

The video opened austerely, on this very room. The vantage was farther back than where he presently stood. A camera positioned in the open doorway.

In it, Coventry sat in a wooden chair, naked as the day he was born.

He was lashed to the chair: his ankles taped to the legs, wrists fastened behind his back. His underwear lay in a loose ravel around one of his shins, his chest and legs slick with perspiration. Rudyard could tell by the oily gleam at Coventry's armpits and swollen nipples that it had to be the syrupy, reeking sort—flop sweat, fear sweat—which would've perfumed the air with a cathouse tang.

But Coventry didn't look fearful, did he? Or *yes*, he did: His eyes bulged from their sockets, but that terror was also infused with an unspeakable note of longing.

His erection was as much as Coventry could summon from the equipment God had given him. It rose from a thatch of graying hairs, the tip whanging off his belly button. A fleshy doorstopper. His hips bucked, his sweat-slick buttocks elevating from the chair and coming down with a meaty *smack, smack, smack . . .*

Rudyard had known Julian Coventry nearly half his life. He was a quiet man who showed little interest in anything outside of what could be observed in test tubes. But Rudyard was looking at a crazed, underfed minotaur waiting to be let free from his cage to grope as many maidens as he could lay his cloven hooves on.

"*Naughty boy.*"

The voice came from off camera.

Coventry pushed himself up, arching on the balls of his feet, legs bowing grotesquely as he pumped his hips—offering himself to that voice. To the unknowable body that issued it.

"*I'm so hungry, daddy.*" A baby-doll simper. "*Will you feed me?*"

"Yes," Coventry breathed, his head whipsawing side to side as white curd foamed at the sides of his mouth. "Yes, *YES*—"

"*Yes*, daughter," the voice commanded.

"Yes, daughter!" Coventry yelped. "Yes, my daughter, feed you, only you . . ."

"You're my dirty daddy, aren't you?"

This was met with an inarticulate screech from Coventry.

"Are you man enough to feed my little baby?"

When she appeared, it was as a darkening at the left-hand side of the screen. The unfurling of some uncanny cloth without shape or definition, a sail tugged by a playful breeze . . . but within it moved something as solid as naked bone, hard and durable and watchful.

A concerto of feelings hummed along Rudyard's nerve endings, but none stronger than joy, and a frank arousal that made him light-headed.

My god. We've done it.

The darkness resolved into the slender outline of a young woman. She wore a flowing outfit, overlapping silks that billowed around her frame as she stalked toward Coventry, whose eyes rolled as madly as a cow trapped in a burning shed.

The subject drifted behind Coventry. The silks settled, draping Coventry's head and mantling his shoulders.

"I'm gonna find aaaall my dirty daddies. We're gonna have so much FUN."

Something began to happen then. A disturbance centered on Coventry's skull. Impossible to tell what; the light in the room had gone thin, and the movement of the subject's body was obscured by those scarves. Rudyard could barely perceive the unsettling and perhaps insane lines of his creation's body.

But there were sounds, oh yes.

Glutinous sucking noises. Some kind of blubbery inhale, or the moist parting of lips. The cartilaginous *pop* of a drumstick torn off a rotisserie chicken.

"That's right, daddy. Let the poison out."

Up until that point, Coventry had been making the coos of a toothless infant. But those gave way to a soul-stripping scream.

THE QUEEN — 151

"Subject Six has gone feral," Jameson said. "Completely off the reservation."

The shape lifted away from Coventry, retreating. The man was left sitting there. He looked quite a bit different now.

His jawbone had been wrenched off to one side, the bone ripped free of its socket. The bottom of his face hung slack, the edges of his mouth torn open as if to permit the passage of something that couldn't have fit otherwise.

Coventry's face was frozen in a look of either stark wonderment or inhuman terror; weird that those two expressions could be so alike.

"*I'll see you soon, daddies.*"

The clip ended.

Rudyard had to physically disengage himself from the screen—forcing his head to twist to one side, the act requiring an immense force of will. He slapped the laptop screen closed.

Naturally, his attention fell upon the sheet.

"We don't need to see."

Roy spoke these words, and it came as no small shock to Rudyard. Roy had seen things. *Fixed* things for Rudyard over the years, though none as serious as what they now faced.

"The scene is clean, relatively," Roy clarified. "No need to dirty things up."

Ah. So it was a simple matter of tidiness. But Rudyard had no intention of not looking.

The sheet hugged Coventry's head under its weight of blood, forming a stiff, concave bowl. The material was sagging *into* Coventry's skull.

Tweezing the cloth in his fingers, Rudyard pulled. The sheet made a gluey sound as it came away.

"Oh god," whimpered Jameson.

The skin of Coventry's legs was pale, but the rest of him was painted in a crack-glaze of blood. His face was a crimson mask; even his teeth—Coventry had always been vain about his teeth—were stained red. His expression was locked somewhere between horror and a kind of crazed glee; his cheeks and throat were flecked with curds that resembled dried oatmeal but were in fact rags of his own high-functioning brain.

Years ago, Rudyard had attended the funeral of a worker who'd died in one of Rudy's processing plants. The man had been fitting huge aluminum pipes and, in some million-to-one calamity, gotten his head wedged between two five-ton pipes just as they'd scissored together. The pipes had snipped off the top of the man's head as neatly as toenail cutters, shearing right through his safety helmet. Rudyard had attended his funeral as a public-facing act. Staring down at the stranger in his coffin, he'd been startled to see the man had been laid to rest wearing a gangster fedora; the undertaker had cut the brim away at the back so that the man's head could rest flush on the red satin pillow.

This memory came to Rudyard, looking at Coventry. That worker's head may've looked something like this under that fedora. Although not nearly so messy.

If the top of Coventry's skull resembled anything at all, it was an exploded trick cigar: a confusion of stiff, spear-like shreds of mortified flesh gummed to slivers of gleaming bone; his head was like a present that had been unwrapped from inside its own box by an indiscriminate child who'd thrown bits of paper every which way.

"When the queen reaches the stage of sexual maturity, she becomes"—Jameson swallowed with effort—"quite industrious in her mating."

Breath held, Rudyard stared into the yawning abyss in Coventry's head. The overhead light shone down, partially illuminating the empty vault inside the body. A note seemed to drift up out of it: the lonely whistle of a boy lost in a cave. The opening was large enough for Rudyard to jam his hand into it, past the wadded tube sock of Coventry's throat and into his torso, which Rudyard was certain he'd find empty, too, the organs pancaked to the sides, burst under some ungodly pressure . . . the only thing that stopped Rudyard from doing so was the concern that something might still lurk within Coventry, tucked out of sight inside his caverned shell.

From inside the room came the rising strains of Mussorgsky's "Night on Bald Mountain."

Kneeling beside his luckless employee, Rudyard spotted an iPhone taped to the back of the chair. A Post-it Note was stuck to one wooden slat.

ANSWER ME

Without overthinking it—swept up in this grand game—Rudyard did just that.

"*Daddy.*"

"Yes, darling," Rudyard replied pleasantly.

A satisfied exhale, somehow sexual in its longing. "*Would you like to see, daddy?*"

"See what, sweetheart?" His heart beat a high-hat tempo against his rib cage.

"*Your grandchild.*"

"Oh, am I a grandfather now?"

"*They're all unique. Like snowflakes. Even I can't control what shape they'll take . . . but this one was too hungry.*" A dry tsk. "*Go on, daddy. Look.*"

Click.

Rudyard put the phone in his pocket and faced the final element of the room's diorama.

As he knelt to unsnap the footlocker's clasps, he was reminded of Victor Frankenstein, Shelley's doomed antihero. When Victor first beheld his creation, his heart quailed and he'd run from his laboratory in fright. If he'd only had the strength to face what he'd made, to *kill* it—his creation had been weak as a kitten then—all the downstream horror could've been averted.

A man must face his creation. He cannot shrink from that duty.

The clasps popped. Rudyard lifted the footlocker's lid.

What lay inside was the size of two bread loaves stapled end to end. It was wrapped in a pink blanket. A baby rattle sat in the footlocker, beside a lock of coarse hair tied up in blue yarn.

Rudyard cradled the bundle. His fingers sunk into it with a dry crackle, as if punching into stale pastry. He lifted it. The parcel held an ungainly top-heavy weight.

He turned it over.

The fear he felt looking into its face was the most reasonable fear of all: that of authoring something outside the realm of the sensible world. His will had driven this thing into existence, however briefly . . . and the life he'd breathed into it was patently insane.

The thing's face (*Was that a face?*) was a confusion of parts that should never fit together: part proboscis, part dimple, part leather, part thresher. It weighed no more than a toaster, but it felt dangerous—he had only to look at Coventry to be assured of that.

A pacifier had been sunk in the little abortion's mouthparts, which stretched across the unnameable canvas of its face. The plastic nubbin had been bitten off between the gnashing gears of its teeth, which now lay frozen as dead machinery.

This is not the grandchild I wanted, Rudyard had to admit. *Though it is perhaps the grandchild I've earned.*

"Is it me," he said, "or does it look a little like Coventry?"

He held it up to the other two. Jameson's face went gray. Well, grayer.

"Something about the eyes, isn't it?"

Wait, did this little shaver even *have* eyes? More a pair of burrowed, seized pits. Rudyard laid it back in its makeshift cradle and shut the lid.

"Th-that is *nothing* like we forecasted!" Jameson nattered imbecilically. "It's well out of whack with every hybridization forecast we've ever run—"

Crossing the room swiftly, Rudyard slapped him. He'd wanted to do it all damn day. Not a skull-rocker, just a good centering smack. Rudyard then cupped Jameson's cheeks and planted a kiss on his lips.

"Jameson—*Jameson*, don't you see? This is incredible. Beyond anything we could have dreamed. My god, Subject Six is *fertile*."

Without another word, Rudyard left Jameson and Roy where they stood. He stalked down the hall, past his old friend the Ant—it stood gleaming in a storage closet, chittering among the mop bucket and toilet paper rolls . . . *Ignore it, Rudy. Don't let it spoil the mood.*

He passed down the hall and out to the parking lot. He was behind the wheel of the Malibu by the time Jameson got in, whereupon he obsequiously ignored the industry under Rudyard's shirt.

In celebration, Rudy had opened another Three Torches matchbox. A darkling beetle this time. Very nice, very juicy. Darklings could sting, but pain was a reminder he was alive.

"The trailer park," he said with a spank of his hands. "Tally-ho! Let's hop to it!"

SEVEN

1:36 p.m.

The tires of Harry's Geo hit the shale leading into the park. We passed under the rusted archway with WOODY KNOT spelled out in wood-log lettering—the *Y* and *K* hung cockeyed, making the sign read more like WOOD NOT.

We passed the superintendent's office, the double ice chest, and the row of vending machines.

Pikachu!

> You know which trailer.

We'd come straight from Allan Teller's house. The drive had passed in silence. I'd spent it thinking about this day a year or so ago. Me, Plum, and the bridge.

There were two bridges, actually. Upper and lower, spanning a narrow point in the Niagara River. The lower one was only half a bridge. That being the old bridge, partially demolished decades ago. But each end still stood: two stubbed tongues jutting from either side of the river. The new suspension bridge arched a hundred yards above the old one, carrying cars and trucks toward the big city.

On summer afternoons, local teens would gather on our side of the tongue. We'd lay out beach towels, drink in the sun. Someone would have music, maybe a few beers or something fun to smoke. Every so often, someone would lope to the end of the tongue, the tricky edge where snarled rebar poked through the concrete, and jump.

It was a thirty-foot plunge to water so deep it often ran black. Surfacing, they'd almost always kick for the closest shore, *our* shore, the shore marking the limits of our small city.

But infrequently, someone would try to pocket the toll.

That was our nickname for it. The new suspension bridge—the one whose shadow fell across the stubbed tongue we'd colonize—that bridge had a fare, okay? Three bucks one way, or a pack of ten tokens for twenty-five bucks.

For us, *pocket the toll* meant swimming for the far shore. And that was a real dare.

The first person I saw do it was Colin Murphy. Lean and supple as an otter. The current toyed with him, carrying him three hundred yards downriver and nearly out of sight . . . but we all saw him crawl out and raise his arms like a triumphant boxer.

Others had tried, only to quickly retreat to our safe shore. Astoundingly, Harry had never bothered. *Don't know how to swim, Mags.* Nobody had drowned that I knew of. But nobody had tried to pocket the toll a second time, either.

The day I pocketed the toll, the sun had sat a few degrees shy of blistering, the leaves starting to pinken on the maples layering the river. I could say I didn't know why I'd done it, but that would be a lie. Fact was, I'd been planning on it the whole summer in an idle, not-looking-at-it-directly kind of way.

Cherr? Plum said the moment I stood up.

I walked to the edge of the bridge in my one-piece bathing suit, dark as cobra scales. I was a confident swimmer, learning in the Twelve Mile Creek running along Woody Knot. I'd jumped before, twice in fact. But both times I'd swum for our shore.

My toes curled over the broken ledge of the bridge. Vertigo swarmed me.

From behind came the whispering groundswell that preceded someone making the leap.

She's gonna do it. Margaret's gonna jump.

I remember knowing why I was doing it, too, almost as if I were a character in a novel. To me, by then, poems and stories had become a bit like the engines Harry fixated over: I was interested in seeing how their parts meshed, and just starting to understand how writers might perform their magic, which led to me wondering: Could *I weave that magic myself someday?*

But if there was a premeditated top layer of my thoughts, what actually made me jump was more primitive. I think sometimes your blood asks you a question. One that forces you to put yourself at risk for something you really need—a thing so important that the rest of your life hinges on it, and the penalty of not going for it means you'll live half the life you could have.

The plunge was swift, the chill shocking. Surfacing, the immediate impulse was to kick for the near shore. But my hips pivoted as I began to carve my way toward the distant landfall, digging into the water with my arms.

The river clutched me in its current; I swallowed iron-cold water and went under with the sick feeling I was going to die, die for nothing at all, and the frogmen would have to drag my waterlogged corpse out of the river, my eyes plucked out by the crayfish just like Ernie the Embezzler . . .

I harnessed my breath, found a seam in the current, and dug as hard as I could. When I dragged myself onto the far shore, the bridge was only a dark sliver against the gorge. When I knocked the water out of my ears, I heard cheers drifting downriver to me.

Sometimes I think I pocketed the toll for Plum as much as for myself. I already knew, right? I hadn't applied to that writing program yet, hadn't gotten accepted, but still, it was in my heart to at least attempt to do something big, or if not that, then at least meaningful to me. And I no longer felt that could be accomplished within the city I grew up in. I'd been laying the seeds for my departure without coming right out and saying it. Leaving a trail of breadcrumbs so that when the inevitable happened, Plum could say: *In retrospect, she gave me fair warning*, and maybe that would hurt us both a little less.

All Plum ever said to me about the jump was: "Next time take the stupid bridge. I'll give you the token." Then she'd hugged me so hard that it stole the breath out of me.

Presently, Harry guided the Geo down the gravel-lined lanes of Woody Knot. Nothing looked much different than it had when I'd lived here. Most units displayed pride of ownership. A postage-stamp flower garden here, a shaded veranda there. One resident had let ivy grow over most of his trailer in the style of an old English country manor. I'd liked living here more than in Executive Acres. The residents looked out for one another. I'd always felt safe.

Harry slowed down as we eased around Cherry Close, then onto the neighboring laneway. It wasn't hard to spot Plum's trailer. The graffiti shone like a beacon.

GRIFTER SLUT

The letters were faded—someone, probably the park superintendent, Earl Tangs, had tried to strip the spray paint off with thinner. But the solution had peeled the base paint off, too, leaving the unit looking like it had been sandblasted.

The words were still visible under the slant of the afternoon sun.

CRAZY LYING WHORE

The graffiti job had been a midnight quickie, for sure. The letters sloppy and scared. Could've been Allan Teller. Him and Chad and Will creeping into the park in their upscale rides with a few spray cans of Day-Glo orange.

Harry pulled up in front of Charity's trailer and killed the engine.

"Hey, remember when Allan told you he'd be surprised if Santa even came to the trailer park, seeing as double-wides don't have chimneys for him to slide down?"

Back in ninth grade, yeah, I remembered. None of us believed in Santa by then. It'd just been one of the mean-spirited things Allan had taken to saying around that time.

Harry grinned. "Remember what you said to him?"

"Not really."

"That you were surprised his mom didn't sew up the pee-flaps on his underwear, seeing as—"

"His dick was an innie," I said, nodding as it came back.

"And his piss dribbled out his butthole," Harry finished. "That shut the dumbshit up." He patted my knee. "Let's hope Allan's not dead, because man, I'll sure miss you shutting him up."

While we spoke, nothing had moved behind the unit's cheese-cloth drapes. Dread sat heavy in my stomach—actually, more like my hip pocket, where the iPhone lurked.

On cue, its nauseating ringtone shrilled.

Pikachu!

> Go.

Pikachu!

> Don't make me ask twice.

We got out under the broiling sun. The trailer park had a desolate feel, as if the residents had been hoovered up in a passing UFO. Trees mounted the escarpment past trailers whose roofs were studded with rusted satellite dishes. A dog barked somewhere, the only sound apart from the far-off boom of a crow-cannon.

I faced the trailer Plum shared with her mother, Estelle. It was the most indifferently tended unit in the park. It was jacked up too high on the right or too low on the left—either way, the floor had a permanent tilt so that every round object, marbles and Superballs, Skittles and desiccated blueberries, all ended up under the captain's bench at the far end of the trailer.

Did I kinda hate Estelle for never fixing that? For not caring if it pulled her daughter to one side of the bed so she always woke up squashed against the wall? Yeah, a smidge.

I mounted the three swaybacked steps to the porch. My knuckles rattled the screen door.

"Estelle?"

I opened the screen and set my ear to the inner door. Past the cheap pressboard, I could hear the purr of an oscillating fan.

I tried the knob. It turned without effort. The door fell open.

Sunlight crowded through the entry. Everything looked as it always had. The ancient Wedgewood gas range and particleboard partitions, that one cupboard above the sink hanging on a busted hinge. The mingled smells of fryer grease and sour wallpaper paste.

But the La-Z-Boy recliner was empty.

You could usually find Estelle parked in it during the daylight hours, working on a bottomless glass of rum-cola. Plum mixed Estelle's drinks for her on weekends and after school, altering the percentage of rum to Coke as the day wore on.

It's like a morphine drip, she'd say. *Gotta get the dosage right.*

For a while, Estelle tried to get me to call her "Mom Number Two," but I just couldn't, because to be honest I thought she was a fairly shitty Mom Number One.

Harry came in behind me. The fan swept back and forth, rustling the pages of Estelle's *People* magazines. I shut it off.

A digital recorder sat on the kitchen table.

PLAY ME was written on a sheet of yellow foolscap next to it.

I picked up the recorder. With the fan off, the silence was oppressive, apart from the distant drip of the bathroom faucet—but then: *vhrr . . . vhrr.*

Another egg-shaped Wi-Fi cam. This one sat on the countertop, ever watchful, making sure Harry and I stuck to the assignment.

I pressed the play button.

"Hello, Margaret."

Not Plum this time. That was Estelle's voice.

"It's time to come clean, okay? And hey, I'm sorry you got sucked into all this."

My eyes drifted into the bedroom. Through the folding accordion door, I saw a battered Samsonite on the mattress. Flung open, clothes scattered around. It looked as if Estelle had been interrupted while trying to take an emergency vacation.

"*So, here it is. When the man gave Charity to me seventeen years ago, he showed me this video about monkeys.*"

And with that, the madness intensified.

"*A bunch of scientists took some rhesus monkeys away from their mothers as infants, yeah? Predictably, the babies went pretty much insane, until the scientists put a . . . guess you'd call it a surrogate mother in their cage? A mother made of ropes and stuffing with a little hole with a rubber nipple poking out that the baby monkeys could suck at for milk. It wasn't their real mom, but the babies were damn well fooled. You see where this is going, Margaret?*"

"No," I said mulishly.

"*I was thirty-three. My shitty-ass boyfriend had snaked my house out from under me and left me with other debts besides. This stranger found me out of the clear blue. Made an offer . . . Lord forgive me. He had this baby. Beautiful baby girl. All I had to do was raise her like she was my own, and not tell a soul. That was the deal. He'd pay me for it, too. Plus a big balloon payment when my hitch was done. And when he put that baby in my arms, I melted. We were two lost souls, y'know? It wouldn't be a problem. I'd make a good home for her. I—*"

A whisper in the background, someplace behind Estelle. That was when I realized Estelle couldn't have been recording this on her own. Someone must have been there with her.

Estelle said: "*I'm getting to that. I'll tell her every—*"

A drilling shriek.

"*I'll tell her! I will! Oh god oh Jesus please stop that please oh pleaaaaasssse—!*"

Estelle tore in a ragged breath and went on in a voice that had gone soggy with terror.

"*The man asked me to report any . . . behaviors. That was the word he used. Behaviors. There was only one time I ever did. That incident with the Trent boy. You remember that, Margaret? The game Charity played with him? She called it Spider.*"

Nelson Trent used to live over on Peach Crescent. Plum and I didn't hang out with him much. Nelson was mealy, unimaginative, had bad breath. Up until the moment Estelle brought him up, I'd forgotten all about chicken-chested Nelson Trent.

Charity had gone with Nelson underneath an abandoned trailer a quarter mile into the scrub around Woody Knot. Sometimes, if a tenant pulled up stakes and abandoned their unit, Earl Tangs hauled them out there. Made for this kind of ghost town out in the poplars.

As I'd heard it, Plum had peeled back a flap of plywood that skirted that abandoned unit. She and Nelson crawled under the trailer, all alone. Later on, someone heard screaming and ran out there to find Nelson tied up like a Christmas turkey under the trailer, ropes knotting his arms and legs. He'd been naked. Charity was latched onto Nelson in a way nobody around the Knot wanted to talk much about.

Plum never told me what happened with her and Nelson, either. Had I avoided asking, or let myself believe it was just two kids playing doctor? The Trents moved away soon after.

A few years afterward, me and Plum had been walking home near dark. We came upon those derelict trailers rusting in the scrub. The trailer she and Nelson had gone under was still there. The plywood had been nailed back over, but Plum set her fingers to it. It ripped loose with the splinter of decayed wood.

"Want to see what me and Nelson did, Cherr?" Plum remarked, her face pinpricked with sweat. "I can show you, if you'd like."

The flap yawned open. I remember that now, too. And how under the trailer it was dark as a wolf's den. For a flash, I'd pictured us under there. The dirt alive with worms and beetles, Plum's body long and angled and pale.

"I won't hurt you. You trust me, right?"

I trusted her, but we were kids. Even back then I knew that kids could get carried away with their games.

"It's getting dark, Plum. My mom's waiting for me."

Plum had seemed genuinely relieved to be told no. "Okay, yeah, totally."

"*After the Nelson Trent thing,*" Estelle went on, "*the man took Charity away. She came back no worse for wear. And she never did nothing like that again.*"

That background whisper returned. It scraped along the low bass of the tape, scaly and reptilian: "*Tell Margaret what they told you, mommy.*"

Estelle's throat clicked. "*You're gonna kill me, aren't you? You never were gonna let me go, you liar.*" To this, I caught no answer. "*After she disappeared, the man called and said if she ever came around again, I shouldn't go anywhere with her. I had to stay out in the open where people could see me. Couldn't let her take me anyplace quiet or out of sight.*"

I heard Estelle shift. I got the sense of her shoulders squaring the way a prisoner's would when facing the firing squad. If she had epaulets, I imagine she'd have turned them down.

"*This is not your fault, Margaret, okay? And not Charity's, either. In a pretty generous light, it's not even mine. How often do we know the gears that turn our lives? Do we really even want to peek inside that gearbox?*"

"*Now, you better get about doing whatever business you're set on,*" she said, this time to whoever was with her. "*I had bingo tonight, but the girls'll get on without me . . . Oh, and one last thing, Margaret. Don't let this weird cunt take you into the dark. Don't let her do to you what—*"

Estelle's words got cut off in a scream. The sound went up to a yawling nonsensical whine that broke at last into a hysterical giggle, as if Estelle found it unbelievable that this kind of pain could exist.

Click.

In the shock that followed, the only sound was the *vhrr* of the

Wi-Fi cam. My head cranked to it. I pictured my face swollen in the camera's fish-eye lens as the predatory presence on the other end observed me.

Pikachu!

> She's not dead.

Pikachu!

> Not yet anyway.

Pikachu!

> The lazy boy

Pikachu!

> move it

Harry read the texts over my shoulder. "You want me to?"

Before I could answer, he set his shoulder to the recliner. It moved frictionlessly on account of the linoleum floor and the throw rug it sat on. The rug scraped over some irregularity I couldn't see . . .

The edges of the tired linoleum curled up along the length of a slit sawed into the floor. There were three slits in total, marking three sides of a square.

A door?

EIGHT
1:48 p.m.

Vhrr-vhrr-vh—
Pikachu!

> Open it

Harry knelt, fingers creeping into one of those slits. The flap of floor came up, reminding me of the hinged lid on a jewelry box.

Blackened puffs of pink insulation clung to the bottom of the flap, drawing my gaze to the darkness beneath the floor, so much like where Plum had taken Nelson Trent to play Spider.

A hole had been dug into the earth under the unit. It was about the size of a manhole. Chunks of mildewed concrete littered the ground surrounding it.

Harry said: "Look."

A rope was tied to a stake at the rim of the hole.

Pikachu!

> Go

I typed:

> no

The cam whirred.

Pikachu!

> I may trick u, Margaret. but I wont kill u.

Pikachu!

> U will be safe swear to god

I typed:

> dont believe u

Pikachu!

> Can't u see yet? You are the witness.

Pikachu!

> My trusted set of eyes.

Pikachu!

If i kill the writer, who's left to tell the story?

Pikachu!

Harry, u go first. Go, Harry. Good boy, Harry.

"The fuck's that supposed to mean?" Harry screwed the toe of his sneaker into the linoleum. "She's not the boss of me."

Fungoid air curled out of the hole in the earth, its coldness running up my pant leg—

From someplace down there came a voice.

"Please . . . *please* . . ."

It sounded impossibly far away, but not so far as to stop my skin from knotting.

Harry said: "It's her. Charity's mom."

"We don't know that."

". . . *please* . . ."

Oh, fuck me. *Was* it Estelle? Sure as hell sounded like her.

"I'll go look."

"You wouldn't fucking *dare*." The idea that he'd go down there filled me with formless dread. "Harr, no."

"So, we're just going to leave her down there?"

"Let the cops go down, okay, with sniffer dogs and shotguns and—*Jesus Christ!*"

I watched him hop down through the trapdoor in the trailer floor. When he looked up, his eyes were grave but faraway, as though he were attuned to a voice coming from a great distance.

Activating the flashlight on his Motorola, he trained it down the hole in the earth. "I think it's a pipe. The hole's dug into the top of it."

That voice again, the same persistent plea: ". . . *please*."

"Don't go," I said. "Let's just *think* for a sec, okay?"

Pikachu!

Both of u or else.

Gripping the rope, Harry levered himself into the pipe. My mind dodged down dark corridors, trying to find a solution, something that would make him stay. *Harry, I love you!*

I nearly said it, too. Then there he went, down and down. His jeans rasped against the rope. He vanished, and seconds later I caught a gentle splash.

"It's a pipe, all right." His voice rose up. "Big cement one. Some water in here, too."

Finally came the note of his footsteps, ever lighter, as he set off.

"I'll be back, Mags."

Asshole. Bad Harry. Fucking stupid asshole.

I could leave him down there, couldn't I? Run outside and scream my ass off. Earl Tangs would be around someplace, I bet. I could tell him about the hole and—

My eyes snapped to the drop ceiling. Every trailer had one of those: a two-foot-wide gap between the ceiling and roof. A spot to store Christmas decorations, boxes of receipts, drugs, a carton of counterfeit smokes, anything you—

It came again, more declaratively this time: movement above the water-stained gypsum panels. It wasn't *loud*, but deliberate. As if whatever was up there wanted me to hear it.

Where was it coming from? I'd caught it first over by the door, but the second time it felt a lot closer: above the kitchen table, crossing the ceiling. Closing the gap toward me.

A third time. A harsh, tickling scrape, almost right overhead.

Nothing's up there, my mind jackrabbited. *It's just shitty air circulating like it always does in vents full of mouse shit and spiders' webs.*

I waited for the ceiling panels to crack under some unthinkable pressure. For something to drop down in a hail of gypsum. My overheated brain summoned a body as thick as a trash can and horridly long, a tube that spanned that gap above the ceiling from the door to the table—it hadn't been moving *forward* at all; its body had simply *unkinked* like a hose filling with water . . . I pictured a ribbed, milky *something* that had crawled out of that pipe running under the trailer park: a muscular ribbon that had slithered up into the drop-ceiling and solidified there, the way a molted insect does: its carapace air-hardening with a dry crinkle, a dozen pairs of wet boots drying over a heating grate.

It was there now, congealed to a leathery sheen, orienting on me with whatever apparatus it had in place of eyes. I could hear it breathing. The consumptive snaffle of a sick Saint Bernard—or a creature that breathed through its skin, a million mouths puckering along its thickened torso.

My heels stuttered backward. The floor disappeared.

My arms pinwheeled madly as it dawned, too late—

You backed up into the trapdoor!

—and fell as if I'd been pushed out a window, my tailbone slamming into the square sawed into the floor; splinters needling into me as I dropped again, the mucky stench of whatever was below me rising up, god no, my hands grasping uselessly as my sneakers hit the edge of the second hole and held for the briefest instant, toes scuffling at the slick edge until the bottom dropped again, even faster, and I was plummeting into darkness—

My hands caught hold of the rope. A velvety hiss as it burned across my palms.

I came down hard. My ankle twisted, sending a shotgun blast of agony up to my knee. Letting out a soundless scream, I hobbled to one side of the pipe.

The light from the trailer shone down through the hole. I spotted the phone and crept over to it. Those footsteps told me my ankle wasn't broken, at least. The note of pain it radiated was sharp, but I couldn't feel the ends of any bones grinding.

Closing my fingers over the phone, I pulled it across the brown algae that furred the base of the pipe. It was working, its screen uncracked.

"... *please* ..."

The sticky darkness inside the pipe dug into my eyeballs. I took a hesitant step. My ankle creaked inside my sneaker, but after a few more steps I discovered that so long as I distributed my weight evenly it wasn't too bad.

This was the storm drain, wasn't it?

I indistinctly recalled hearing that one ran under Woody Knot, but in all my childhood explorations I'd never found it, and no wonder. Who'd want to explore a dank cement tube that washed rainwater out to Twelve Mile Creek?

But if the pipe's purpose was to transport rainwater to the creek, that meant there had to be an exit, right?

I couldn't hear Harry. Couldn't see the pinprick of his cell phone's light ahead of me. I crept forward. Estelle's trailer—and the thing lurking in its drop ceiling—receded. The darkness thickened.

My sneaker sank into an obliging softness; it compressed under my foot, the flesh of a waterlogged corpse. Gagging, pain arrowing from ankle to kneecap, I shook the phone until the light came on.

A patch of luminous, frilled, lushly belled toadstools sprouted from the floor. That's what my foot had mushed into.

I pulled my sneaker out, shook off the gelatinous goo, and trained the phone deeper into the pipe. You could drive a car down it. My breath echoed in my ears. Darkness pressed at my spine. An itchy, dispossessing kind that felt too much as if I'd been nailed inside a cement casket.

Estelle's voice came from someplace ahead. "... *please* ..."

NINE
1:57 p.m.

I moved toward Estelle's voice, avoiding the trench of water running down the middle of the pipe. I told myself that sunlight and birdsong were only twelve feet above my head, but some shitty self-defeating voice kept saying: *Wrong!* In my mind, I was now at the bottom of the ocean. A deep trench with a million pounds of pressure per square inch pushing down. Tension built behind my eyeballs; soon they'd burst, no different than grapes in a wine press.

". . . *please.*"

Gritty gray fungus colonized the circumference of the pipe. It hung pelt-like in spots, thick as fatback, looking as if it would be right at home on long-dead carcasses. The slabs were alive with beetles and sludge-worms and other unknown crawlies; they twisted in and out of its moist shag. It dangled overhead in soggy stalactites; a few of them hung so heavily that it reminded me of those cloth tongues in car washes that slobber soap suds on your pickup.

As I ducked under an especially long one, something rappelled from its edge to go skittering around my neckline. I batted at it with a gag of horror as it raced down my hand and plummeted off my fingernail.

I kept going, sweeping the phone's light from one side of the pipe to the other—

—passing a face white as a corpse a few feet away.

I'd never screamed like that before. A trapped hiss that shot between my clenched teeth so hard that it left my throat scoured raw, but I barely made a sound.

It was Harry. He'd been standing there in the dark.

He whispered: "My phone died. I didn't know where I was."

"Next time, we stay together," I whispered back.

We moved deeper into the pipe. It was getting harder to force one foot in front of the other. It had nothing to do with the pain in my ankle. It was more some innate safety feature in my mind resisting forward progress; each step now required a distinct command: *left foot, right foot . . . left, right, come on, keep going.*

The phone's charge hung at 85 percent, but still, the fear that the damp might crawl inside its casing and short the battery out . . . if the light went out and I was left down here with the skitter of bugs and the velvet lick of the fungus-tongues . . .

The phone's light settled on a chair.

A common orange plastic chair. The kind you could find in Northfield's cafeteria, or any other high school in the city.

The phone illuminated two more. Three chairs in total, set in a rough circle in the pipe where the fungus had been hacked away.

I inched closer. At the base of the chairs lay wet scraps of what I knew had to be clothing: upscale jeans and T-shirts, Banana Republic or Patagonia. The moss was colonizing them already, reducing them to mulch.

I shone the light on the neck-hole of a T-shirt that had once been white. The blood on it had been leached away to a pinkish tinge . . . blood and the residue of something else that reminded me of the Tang-colored syrup that drooled out of my blisters when I'd caught poison ivy, a substance I'd never known a human body could produce.

Harry patted the pockets of a pair of moldering jeans. He found a wallet.

I didn't want to be the custodian of whatever knowledge lay inside that wallet—didn't want to know the truth that everyone in this town was holding out hope against.

Harry opened it. Pulled a card out. A Northfield High student card.

We stared at Chad Dearborn's face. That switchblade grin.

My hand clapped over my mouth as the fact hit me with a flat concussive force. The missing boys must have been taken—snatched from their beds, maybe—and brought to this dripping hell under the trailer park . . . to endure what, exactly? I couldn't stand those guys. I'd hated what they'd stood for, hated the student body's instinctive urge to hold them up as avatars of some unearned exceptionalism. But as the realization seeped into me—*they're dead, in a way I can't even begin to guess at*—it was as if I'd been propelled ahead to a future time; in it, I saw an older me, wiser and more broken, watching a movie from my youth. In that movie I'd see Chad Dearborn and Will Stinson and Allan Teller more clearly as boys—stupid ones, but also just that, *boys*—innocent of most of the crimes I'd secretly convicted them of.

"*. . . please . . . oh please . . .*"

Moving around the chairs, Harry and I edged toward that voice. I was gripped by an anaesthetized calm, the final stages of carbon monoxide poisoning.

A note reverberateed out of the darkness, prickling the hairs on my neck.

The fungus grew sparser. The pipe's concrete showed through it again. The water channeling down the center thinned to a trickle. I swept the phone in a tight arc, just wide enough to see what lay directly ahead of—

Something was on the tunnel wall. A piece of hard candy stuck to the concrete.

With the faintest shimmer, it was gone.

A new smell hit me. Not the greenish perfume of the fungus or a clean rainwater smell that could mean we were approaching a storm grate. This was a leaden, rotty stench that made my gorge rise.

The light fell on six spray-painted words.

ALL EYEZ REPORT TO THE QUEEN

I tracked the phone over the pipe until the beam illuminated the space ahead of us.

The world lurched on a trick axis as I beheld death.

I'd seen things that may've been touched by death, sure. But for the first time in my life, I was looking at a dead body.

"*. . . please oh god please . . .*"

That wasn't Estelle's voice. The tinny, canned quality of it was so obvious now. It echoed off the walls, lifeless and unfeeling, the voice of a robot.

It couldn't belong to Estelle.

Estelle had no head.

She sat in a chair whose legs were balanced precariously on the outer swell of the pipe's curved basin. A wooden kitchen chair from her own trailer. At first, my mind couldn't reconcile the shape in that chair with a human body, or anything that had ever drawn breath. All my eyes processed was an *object*. A soggy, slashed-open sack of birdseed.

Her body sat erect, legs spread and her hands flat on her thighs. Estelle was naked—that may've been the worst part—her skin torn in hairline fissures down her rib cage. Her stomach, no, her entire *torso*, looked wattled: a balloon that had been inflated until it nearly ruptured before someone let the air back out.

Twin coins winked in the backs of her hands. Nail heads. Huge six-inch deck nails—*railroad spikes*, my father would call them—had been driven through the backs of Estelle's hands, on through her thighs, pinning her to the chair like a butterfly in a specimen case. Her legs were frozen in rigor mortis, split open in a sickening come-on.

Fancy a ride courtesy of Mom Number Two, Maggie?

Estelle's voice—the one in my head—bubbled out of the

hardened, depthless hole in the stump of her neck . . . but it wasn't even a stump, was it? Her entire neck had been obliterated, nothing left but a sagging collar, a tube sock with the elastic all worn-out. The remains of her upper spine and skull were scattered around the chair or mantling her shoulders; they shone in the phone's light, shards of shattered crockery.

One eye, wrinkly as a raisin, stared forlornly from where it had landed in the crook of her elbow.

Hop on the baloney pony, darlin'. Twenty bucks a ride. Half price on Fridays.

I gathered in the elements of Estelle's corpse—the sunken state of her chest, her breasts two flat pouches that looked as if they'd been eaten away from the inside, the hole above her clavicles that seemed not only deep and dark but somehow *empty*.

It registered that something must have come *out* of Estelle.

Something that had grown inside her like . . . like a . . .

That was where everything slipped into a dreamscape; this feeling that I'd stepped into one of those paintings where eyeballs stare from the brim of a man's top hat, or staircases with no end or beginning climbed endlessly into a cotton-candy-pink sky.

That sound was back now too. That buzzing, swarming note.

Ten feet from Estelle's body, suspended from a length of wire knotted to a grommet screwed into the upper swell of the tunnel, was . . .

"That's meat," Harry said, spotting it too.

A hunk of meat on a hook. What may once have been a fat rump roast, but now the meat was wadded up like the folds of those Asian dogs, what are they called . . . Shar-Peis.

A cheap plastic end table, the kind that sat on a lot of porches around the Knot, was positioned under the meat. Field flowers and red-stemmed weeds were looped around its legs. A glass jar half-full of some dark substance sat on it.

A piece of white hockey tape was stuck to the glass. Two words were written on it.

DRINK ME

Shapes were busy inside the jar, harvesting that sludge.

"...*please*...*please*..."

The buzz rose over Estelle's recorded voice, becoming a wall of sound, as if whatever was making it was wired to some subtle volume knob previously set to a quiet purr and now cranked up full blast.

Thumb-swiping the iPhone, I accessed its settings.

OPTIONS > FLASHLIGHT BRIGHTNESS

Training the phone ahead of me, I dialed the slider up to maximum.

My backward step was involuntary. What I was looking at was so unbelievably *wrong*.

A beehive? It couldn't be. Bees are orderly creatures. What I saw was chaotic. No gleam of honey. This was a *nest*.

A nest that choked the entire pipe.

It looked nothing like the wasp nests that plagued the trailer park during the low summer days—the ones that appeared in the crotches of the elms shading the communal picnic tables, or the ones that grew flat and unseen behind the siding of trailers and took two or three well-placed bug-bombs to get rid of.

This one was composed of carbuncled slabs that looked less like the usual papery stuff and more durable, somehow metallic. Wasps teemed in its numberless crannies and cliffs in their tens of thousands, building in their industrious, menacing way. Thin tubes extended from the flat slabs, meeting a secondary construction that covered the pipe's walls to a thickness of three or four feet. The tubes were so sheer that I could see bean-shaped larvae wriggling through them. The whole structure we'd stumbled upon appeared alien, as if it had crash-landed from another planet.

Worried that the phone's light might attract them, I dialed the brightness back down. But they seemed disinterested in me, focusing instead on the chunk of hanging meat . . . tearing off bits, it appeared, to ferry back to their home. None of them touched Estelle's body. It would seem they actively avoided it, as if judging it unclean or unworthy.

One of the wasps landed on the rim of the jar. It was bigger than any wasp I'd laid eyes on. My bladder tightened and I thought I'd piss myself—I may have, too, if not for the fear that the smell might attract them.

In the center of the nest sat a corkscrewing emptiness with the look of a funnel spider's web. The whole thing had to be the size of ten thousand ordinary nests.

When I looked over at Harry, his mouth was hinged open, eyes bulging. His eyes were on Estelle.

I followed his gaze. The light came around with the motion of my head, hitting Estelle with the intensity of twin high beams boring down an unlit country road.

Her chest. Her stomach.

It *moved*.

It wasn't the final breath pushed from her lungs or the last shudder of her heart. Both of those had occurred hours if not days ago.

Something *inside her*. That's what had moved.

All I'd noted was the subtlest shift. A fist balling up under a heavy blanket.

The phone jittered. I could barely hold it straight.

Next, Harry and I saw something roil past the ragged hole where Estelle's head had once sat. *Oh Jesus, it's still in there.*

Whatever it could be—the *something* inside Estelle, the thing that had been there the whole time we'd been standing here, the thing that must have made its way out of her before crawling back inside her cooling remains . . .

I waited for it to reveal itself. For many long, jointed appendages to spread themselves from Estelle's neck hole like the naked struts of an umbrella, hooking into her mortified flesh . . . for something to ease itself out of her corpse with the lithe flexibility of a contortionist from a box.

The wasps made a revving-bandsaw sound as they rose in a shimmer.

My feet came unglued. Harry and I backed away. A wasp droned past my ear with the burr of a slow-moving bullet. Another snagged in the cuff of my jeans, buzzing angrily.

"Don't breathe," I squeaked at Harry.

A wasp slammed into Harry's bare arm. He smacked it once, twice, three times until it fell. He stamped on it as we continued to retreat down the pipe.

In the phone's light, I could see Harry's arm. Oh shit, he'd been stung. The stinger was stuck in his skin; he pulled it, the barb clinging on, his flesh tenting until it finally popped free, releasing a broth of blood and foam.

My lungs were shrieking for air. But the wasps were relenting—the air wasn't so thick with them. Harry had started to stumble, though, his sneakers dragging. A glazed cast had come into his eyes. I had his elbow, guiding him. We'd have to keep going down the pipe, past Estelle's trailer and whatever was up there . . . but oh, Harry was not good. *Very* not good. His neck was inflating.

"Come on, Harr," I urged. "Just a little—"

A form loomed out of the darkness. White as a snow-covered field, moving toward us with the crinkle of plastic.

A hazmat suit? No, a *beekeeper's* suit. Some kind of heavy-duty version, with thick leather uppers and ballistic nylon panels. A man's face was framed in its Lexan face shield.

"Come on, go!"

He slung Harry's arm over his shoulder and hoisted him into a fireman's carry. The rope was there; light filtered down from Estelle's trailer. I squinted up to see a second man framed in the concrete ring.

"Thank goodness you're okay," he called down. "Let's get you out of there."

TEN

2:07 p.m.

Harry managed to haul himself up the rope with a lot of help from the man in the beekeeper's suit. He helped me up, too, until I could grab the hand of the second guy.

I climbed through the trapdoor in the trailer floor to find Harry lying down, his head under the kitchen table. His skin was rashed in gooseflesh. The sting was an inflamed anthill.

"What happened to him?" said the first of the two men in Estelle's trailer.

"Something stung him!"

I'd barely gotten the words out before Harry started seizing, his teeth clenched tight as his head rat-a-tatted on the linoleum. Foam emitted from the sides of his mouth, and a stupid, drifty horror washed over me because, oh god, was Harry going to *die* right now?

"Help him!"

The first man slammed the trapdoor shut, dousing the buzz from the pipe. The second man—thin and pale as a corpse—bent over Harry.

"It's a reaction," he said, trying to find Harry's pulse while his skull whanged off the floor. "How many times did he get stung?"

"Only the one time, I swear!"

The second man knelt beside the first. I'd never seen either of them before. They didn't live around here, I'd bet my life on that—the second guy's boots might be scuffed and his jeans off-the-rack, but he carried himself like a rich dude.

The guy unbuttoned Harry's jeans and yanked them down to his ankles.

I saw Harry's tighty-whiteys and nearly looked away, but I had to see what the man was searching for—more stings—but thankfully there weren't any.

"What happened down there?"

"There's a nest. A huge nest, and—"

And a woman named Estelle. But not really Estelle anymore. Not really a person at all.

The first man pulled a small black kit from his back pocket. In it were several needles, preloaded. He uncapped one as the second man straddled Harry's chest, pinning his shoulders down. Harry strained, hips bucking, the back of his skull pistoning off the floor.

The needle went into the big vein in his throat. Harry went stiff, then relaxed.

"His pulse is galloping, but it's strong," the dead-looking guy said. "He had an event, along the lines of a febrile seizure, I'd say, though he's too old for those."

"We need to get out of here," I said. "Get Harry and get out."

The second man pushed off Harry. He wiped his hands on his jeans, as if he'd touched something unpleasant. "Have you been stung too?"

"No, I—" I ran my hands down my arms, horrified that a wasp might be drowsing under my sleeves. "But I heard something. Before. Up in the ceiling."

"*This* ceiling?"

"Yeah."

Grabbing the broom, the man walked the length of the kitchen, popping the handle into each ceiling tile. They lifted easily; some grit sifted down. Nothing was lurking above them.

"I think we're good. Let's get your friend settled."

Cradling Harry under the arms, the men carried him over to the sofa and yanked his jeans back up. I settled my forehead on his chest and felt the racing of his heart through my skin. For a second there, I'd swear his soul had lifted out of his body and gone flapping around the trailer like a fat confused moth. *Please, Harry. Please, just be okay.*

"Margaret, we need to talk."

The shape of my name in this stranger's mouth felt a bit like going downstairs in the middle of the night, your brain still half-asleep, and missing a step in the dark: that horrible weightless lurch that was as if the bottom had dropped out of the world.

"Who are you?" I said thickly. "Wait, are you the cops?"

"I'm afraid not. We hail from the world of private enterprise."

The man sat at the table, his elbows braced near the recorder. PLAY ME. Had they listened to it? What would it mean to them?

"You can call me Rudy if you'd like. That gentleman there is Jameson. The one down below us is Roy."

Rudy's eyes, green with the thinnest band of gold ringing the irises, studied me with an intensity that made it feel as though bugs were scurrying across my face.

"What else is down there? You said a nest. Anything else?"

"How do you know my name?"

Rudy only stared at me.

"There are chairs," I said, unnerved. "And clothes. And an . . . um, Estelle." I found myself choking up. "She was—"

"The Minder," Rudy said over his shoulder to Jameson before turning back to me. "She's not alive, is she?"

"You *know* Estelle?"

"We know Estelle. We know Charity. We know you."

Standing there with these strangers, I had the sense of being on an archaeological dig in the desert. I'd unearthed the tip of a fossilized bone and just by looking I knew it must belong to something that had died millions of years ago, its petrified remains spreading out beneath me, a puzzle aching to be solved . . . except I'm scared—terrified beyond all reason, in fact—that it's *not* a dinosaur; it's something much more ancient, something that doesn't belong there, and if I keep digging (and oh god, I *want* to keep digging), I'll uncover it, and the moment I really see what I've found, I'll go screechingly insane.

"I'm going to call the police," I croaked.

Rudy winced. "You *could*, but I don't think that's the best idea."

Rudy spread his hands on the tabletop. "The police are the natural choice, aren't they? Whenever something bad happens, you call them. And if we did so now, I'm certain they would do everything in their power to understand what's going on here."

Rudy smiled at me in a way I'm guessing he meant to be gracious, even fatherly, but only made me feel like a mouse getting batted around by a nasty old barn cat.

"The police, now what would they do? Cordon off this trailer. Likely the whole park. They'd perform an investigation, call in a forensics team, the FBI—wait, it'd be the Mounties up here, yes?—the military, and eventually experts. They'd be baffled, I assure you. As for you, Margaret, they'd take you down to the station and ask you all sorts of questions. And what answer would you likely give to each and every one of those questions?"

"I don't know," I said.

"Sure, because how *could* you? None of their questions will get them any closer to a solution, not nearly quick enough. By the time the authorities get any kind of grip, it'll be too late. For us, for you, for your friend Charity. So *that*, my dear, is why we won't be calling the cops."

Behind him on the countertop, the Wi-Fi cam came alive. Someone was watching us.

"What would you do if I called the cops anyway?"

Yeah, what if I did? Just pulled out the iPhone and dialed 9-1-1. What would this weird bastard do?

"Or I could walk out that door and start screaming my guts out."

I could, couldn't I? Rudy was wiry-looking, but old. Jameson may possibly be made of papier-mâché. I wasn't any kind of brawler, but I was scared and desperate—those being pretty much the only emotions I'd experienced since waking up this morning. I felt pretty confident I could get my ass out of this trailer.

"I'm not going to lift a finger," said Rudy. "But before *you* try anything, let me tell you a story."

He kicked back in his chair, hands knitted behind his head. "It's about a serial killer in the 1970s. I know, right? *Grim!* But bear with me, it's instructive in our present impasse. The Yellow Dog Killer, as the news media called him. He broke into houses at night. He preferred families. He liked that risk. The Yellow Dog was a scrap of a man, one-hundred-forty pounds soaking wet. But he knew the clockwork of his victim's hearts."

Rudy's tone was folksy. The voice of a natural-born storyteller.

"What he did was, he put his gun on the man. Told him if he did as he was told, his family would be fine. They're being robbed, that's all. But everyone had to be tied up. He needed assurance that nobody will run or call the police."

Rudy folded his arms, tongue clucking. "Now you see, *that* was the last moment of true choice. Even if that husband only had a nail file or his own bare hands, he'd look back with such regret and think: *I should have tried to kill him.* Even if he'd wound up dead himself. Even if his *wife* got killed, or his wife and one of his children. At least that meant there would be survivors. But in every one of the Yellow Dog's home invasions, the husband never did. *People* don't, as they get lulled into the ridiculous belief that if they go along, play nicely and be agreeable, this maniac will do as he promised. They think that the longer they can persist without having to make a real choice, that life-and-death one, things might somehow, magically, just . . . work out."

Rudy shook his head. *The folly,* that headshake conveyed. *Ah, the folly of mankind.*

"The husband tied up his wife and his kids, then the Yellow Dog had him put his hands behind his back. Soon their ankles were pulled tight to their wrists, backs bowed, trussed up like Christmas geese. Then, predictably, the Yellow Dog killed them. One by one he killed them all."

Standing up, Rudy crossed to the fridge. He opened it and pulled out a carton of milk. Gave it a sniff, checked the expiration date, poured some into a jelly jar. He sat back down, passed the jar over to me, and took a slug straight from the carton. He smacked his lips and let go a theatrical *Ahhhh.*

"He used guitar wire," Rudy went on. "Went in through the eyeballs. It wasn't always clear, the order of dispatch—kids first, wife first, kid-wife-kid—but the hubby always went last. He had to watch." He wiped his milk mustache away. "So, why am I telling you this?"

Rudy stood once again. Went to the trapdoor and lifted it just in time for the guy in the beekeeper's suit to rise out of the ground. He did so eerily, a man riding an elevator. The buzz followed him up. Rudy swung the trapdoor shut. A heartbeat later something pelted the underside. *Plik!* Then another. *Plik!*

The new man went into Estelle's bedroom. I could hear him in there, getting out of his beekeeper's gear.

"The preceding collection of moments represented your best chance, Margaret," Rudy said, retaking his seat at the table. "While I was rambling on about the Yellow Dog, you could have knocked Jameson down—let's face it, he's no obstacle—run outside and screamed your lungs out, just as you'd threatened. Most times you only get a narrow aperture, and once you lose the opportunity, it's gone for good." He winked. "But here's the thing: Even when people *know* it's their moment, they fail to grab for it anyway."

Leaning across the table, Rudy erased the distance between us. His eyeballs ticked, the corneas seeming to move counterclockwise with audible *snips* as they rotated against the grain.

"As I said, *I* don't intend to do anything. But that man in the bedroom, he will. It's pretty much all he's ever done. He has a terrible knack for it. So, if you run now, he'll follow. He won't harm a hair on your head, I promise. But anyone who comes to help you, he will kill."

The man—*Roy*, wasn't that the name Rudy had given?—stepped out of the bedroom. He was shirtless, the beekeeper's outfit hanging down his thighs. His torso was sweaty, flushed, the muscles organized in squarish blocks. His eyes were two tiny TVs broadcasting snow.

"Do you believe me, Margaret?"

". . . yes. I believe you."

Rudy said: "Anyone you know at this park, the people you've grown up with . . . people you like, people you don't—whoever that is, they'll be dead before they can even think to call for help. And that fact holds whether you bolt for it now, or start shrieking like a harpy when we take you and Harry out to our cars."

"Your cars? Where are you taking us?"

"I can't say just yet." He glanced at the Wi-Fi cam. "I'm not the conductor of today's orchestra. The point is—and please, trust me on this if you don't believe another word out of my mouth—my associate will kill anyone who interferes, and for my purposes, that means anyone who even *approaches* us. That outcome will be on you, because if nobody bothers us, nobody has to die. Understood?"

"Yes."

"You don't have to die either. Or Harry here. Or us, I egotistically hope. *Nobody* else has to die, so long as we don't call attention to ourselves. We can just do what needs to be done, disband, and go our separate ways. A merry band of thieves."

I thought: *This fucker would've made an excellent serial killer.*

Roy exited the bedroom, fully dressed now. He was holding a glass cylinder. A specimen jar.

One of those wasps was inside it. Roy set the jar on the table.

Under the trailer's light, it was nearly an inch long, with a jellied eyeless head that hinged on the sprocket of its body; instead of the standard black-and-yellow markings, its abdomen was a fleshy white olive-shape, with thickly bristled legs.

The wasp flung itself around its prison, whining like an angry little drill. Tipping over, the jar rolled toward the edge of the table—

Rudy caught the jar as it fell. He held it up between his thumb and forefinger. I could see that the wasp's stinger was barbed. A fishhook. Venom jetted from it, foaming on the glass.

"There's a whole bunch down there," Roy said. "And the nest . . ."

"What about the nest?" Rudy asked.

"Looks like there's a chunk missing."

"You'll have to explain that."

A shrug from Roy. "Long straight edge down the right side. The wasps are building it back over, but it looks like a chunk's been hacked away."

"You're sure?"

"No. A lot of activity down there. Wasn't sure the suit was gonna hold up."

"And the Minder?"

"She's there. What's left of her. Same as Coventry."

Pikachu!

The phone vibrated in my pocket. I shifted, the phone digging into my hip. The Wi-Fi camera *brrr*ed as its lens aperture widened.

"Someone calling you?" Rudy said.

Pikachu!

That wasn't my phone this time. His eyes never leaving mine, Rudy reached into his back pocket. He pulled out an iPhone. Same color, dusty rose.

"Go on," he coaxed. "Let's see yours."

With some reluctance, I laid mine on the table.

"Ahh, now look at that. A matching pair."

So, she'd sent us both phones? Plum, or Serena, or . . . that meant she knew these guys. I remembered what Plum said on that first .wav audio file Harry and I listened to, sitting on the bus bench this morning.

. . . *this story I'm a part of—that I've* been *part of for a long time, it turns out . . .*

"What's happening?" I asked Rudy. "What the hell did you guys do?"

"You wouldn't believe me if I told you, Margaret."

My phone rang.

"Answer it," ordered Rudy. "On speaker."

I thumbed the phone open. Pressed the green call button.

"*Daddy.*"

Serena's voice.

"Yes, dear," Rudy replied, a quaver leaching into his voice.

"*If you do anything, if you hurt them in any way, I'll kill myself.*"

"Put that thought away, darling, please."

"*I'll do it, daddy. You know I will, just for spite. And all your work, all these years, will be for nothing.*"

"Why would I hurt anyone? Just tell me what you want."

"*Margaret, you can't stop now. You know where to go. It's the only place left. How is Harry?*"

I said: "He's been stung."

"*I can see that. How many times?*"

"Just once."

A pause. "*He'll wake up in an hour or so. He'll be okay.*"

You promise?"

"*Yes, I promise. Go on, now. And daddy? I'm watching.*"

The line went dead. Rudy said: "Your friend Charity cares about you a great deal."

"That's not Charity. That was Serena. The girl who's with Charity. Kidnapped her or whatever."

"Right," he said after a lengthy pause. "Serena. Of course." He nodded to Roy. "Get the boy. Out to the cars."

ELEVEN
2:18 p.m.

Jameson and Roy carried Harry out of the trailer. From someplace east, over the sawtooth ridge of the escarpment, came the mutter of thunder.

Two vehicles were parked outside the Hallmark. The Chevy Malibu didn't look out of place. The Escalade sure as hell did. Roy got into the black SUV while Jameson tucked himself behind the Malibu's wheel. Rudy got into Harry's Geo. He instructed me to sit in the front seat; Harry was in the back, dozing as contently as a cat in a sunbeam.

We drove out of the park. The Escalade sharked behind us in the side-view mirror. Roy's long shape sat behind the wheel.

As we rounded out of Woody Knot, I spotted Janey Colson out front of her unit. She sat on a lawn chair with her freshly painted toenails—I could tell by the wads of Kleenex jammed between each toe—propped on a cinder block. Pink rayon shorts and a crop top, a midafternoon tallboy of Busch. You'd see all that and figure she'd be reading a supermarket tabloid, the ones with lurid headlines—*Skin Divers Discover Mermaid Cemetery!*—but Janey had a copy of Richard Powers's *The Overstory* open across her lap.

Janey didn't look up from her book. Good. Better she didn't spot me. But seeing her dragged a long-lost memory across my mind.

Back in second grade, our class put on a play. *Give a Hoot, Don't Pollute!* Chad Dearborn played Hootie the Owl. Miranda Lancaster was the Forest Princess. Allan Teller played the villainous Litterer. I'd worn a white bodysuit adorned with clumps of pillow stuffing as Cloud #2. Plum had been encased inside an industrial cardboard tube for the role of Sad Tree. A hole had been cut in it for Plum's face.

Phew, it's so sweaty in there, she'd told me after rehearsals, *and hard to stay balanced.*

The evening of the play, before a packed house at Mother Teresa Elementary, the Litterer had—*accidentally*, as Allan Teller later swore up and down—bumped into the Sad Tree. Plum had toppled over and gone rolling across the stage with her legs kicking helplessly, past the Forest Princess, who let out a squeal, bouncing down the stage steps until she'd come to rest against Miss Florence's spinet piano.

In the hush that ensued, pierced only by the muffled moan of Plum stuck inside her tree, someone laughed. It wasn't the laugh of a child, either.

Who the fuck was that? In the shadows of the footlights, there was Estelle. Her face mottled in fury, throat puffy as a bullfrog. She'd come with Janey Colson, whose son Rutger had played Busy Beaver. Estelle shoved herself to the end of the row, slapping knees—*Move your goddamn legs!*—into the aisle.

Which one of you shits laughed? When nobody spoke up, Estelle spat: *One of you ritzy pricks, dollars to doughnuts.*

Reaching her daughter, Estelle tried to pull Plum upright, but there was nothing to grab onto; may as well try to lift a fallen log. *Get off your ass and give me a hand!* she shouted at Miss Florence, who'd sat rooted behind the piano.

The play went on without its Sad Tree. After the ovation, I'd spied Estelle and Plum sitting by the fire exit. Tears tracked through the woody-brown stage makeup on Plum's face while Estelle huddled over her, rubbing her back. *Everything falls over eventually, baby. Even the biggest, strongest trees.*

That was the woman whose body lay in the storm drain under the trailer park. Naked and nailed to a chair, head gone. Ah god, Estelle.

What was going to happen to her? The simple matter of her body? Would it be found and buried? Who'd go to her funeral?

Rudy pulled the Geo to the T-section of the main road. "Which way?"

"Left."

Rudy smiled. He had capped teeth, but his face was pocked all over with deep digging divots; the June sunlight made his face look younger somehow, the face of someone who long ago had gone through an ordeal that had repatterned his whole world.

He turned, not bothering with the blinker. Clouds chased themselves across the horizon-line. Knife-winged kites lifted from the power lines; they dodged and barrel-rolled over the cherry orchards, through heat waves that radiated in sluggish squiggles above the trees.

We passed Don Carlo's Hot Tub Emporium. A battalion of inflatable tube-men wobbled and flapped past the chain-link fence. An involuntary shiver gripped me.

"What's the matter?" Rudy asked, but I could tell he didn't really care.

I didn't answer. But it was those tubes. I hated those fucking things.

It had happened the same year as the school play. Plum and me had been screwing around in the bushland bordering the cherry orchards.

We'd lost track of time. It was only when the night-sprinklers snapped on that it dawned on us that we'd gotten lost.

We held hands, walking the rutted clay between the cherry trees. Darkness descended quickly, an axe-stroke coming down. We blundered out of the orchard into the scrub, a thicket of brambles that tore at our Giant Tiger T-shirts and made predatory stabs at our eyes. I'd caught a riffling note from someplace. A thousand tiny sails bellying to the breeze.

The thicket gave way to a field of knee-high grass. Ahead of us, a distance I couldn't judge, highlighted against a moon that bled its light across the ground, stood a group of famished giants.

They rose from the earth like fairy-tale beanstalks. That riffling sound—*they* were making it. They weaved and fluttered and then wilted, leaning down as if to lunge at us . . . they had no faces; no features; massive, flabby worms; fat, pale, laughing wax worms—

I screamed. Plum joined me, but her scream quit out before mine.

They're those tubes, Cherr. Those blow-up tubes. We're at the hot tub place.

Later that night, after the owner—the man himself, Don Carlo—heard our screams and found us in the scrub east of his emporium; once I was back home, after a stern admonishment from Mom and Dad to never be out past dark again, then tucked safely in bed, the specter of those things crept back. And when they did I was scared all over again, because the realization came that it wasn't the tube-men that frightened me.

It was what had been *inside* them.

This impression had been fuzzy then, and it had become ungrippable now. I'm too old, my mind can't capture the illogical horror of it anymore. But in those clipping heartbeats, as the sharp blades of grass sawed against my bare skin and the moon shed its light across the flat and somehow lunar expanse, I'd felt something *in* those tubes.

Nothing that possessed a physical body. More an awareness that had traveled an impossible distance—one measured in the lifetimes of stars—to be there, then, for Plum and me to stumble upon. Why it chose to fill some gaudy ripstop nylon tubes at a hot tub store, I couldn't possibly guess. But the fear sprung from that, too: the randomness of it. Whatever it was, it wore those tubes as a skin. It had no definition or form without them.

I pictured these tubes detaching from their blowers, snapping their guywires, and pulling free of their air-hoses to drift across the cherry orchard. Their nylon skins brushed against leaves that withered at their touch. I saw them floating into the park, borne on an unfelt wind, until they were clustered above the roof of my trailer, *bump-bump*, *bump-bump*, a clutch of balloons in a clown's white-gloved hand . . . any moment now they would rupture, their unclean insides hissing out, invading my bedroom through the window. It would enter me next, filling me in a way I couldn't even comprehend.

That night roared back at me, and with it the sense that Plum and I had been earmarked. More and more, I felt myself being engraved into a living moment in history—of fickle fate's hand manacling my wrist and forcing me to bear witness to events that historians would inscribe in the record books.

Why me?

Why anyone? Estelle's voice. *Why me, why you? Just accept it, darling, or you'll wind up down here in the drain with Mom Number Two.*

Rudy took us west, into the sparkling sunlight. We were headed to the last place on earth I wanted to go. But you could only run from the piper for so long.

Sooner or later, everyone had to pay what they owe.

TWELVE
2:30 p.m.

This one knows more than she's letting on.

Rudyard Crate sat behind the wheel of the unconscious boy's shit-bucket, driving west toward the lake. Margaret eyed him from the passenger seat, her plump little head full of questions.

Rudyard wished he was able to crack her skull apart and go rummaging through her thoughts—the secrets and desires and data twisting away behind her eyes, lithe as centipedes—plucking out the valuable ones. After that, he could unbuckle her seat belt, open the door, and push her out of the moving car like so much damp laundry.

The Minder was dead. Dead in a drain. Same state as Coventry, according to Roy. Grim way to go. But they all knew how this could end—well, maybe not the Minder, she'd never been given the full picture, but her role hadn't required that.

Could he find fault with Subject Six's behavior? No, not really. Its reaction to what it had discovered could be considered a touch, well, *overboard*, at least by human standards. But it didn't have to hold itself to those, now did it?

His subject had discovered its existence was a grotesque lie. That would set the most even-keeled mind screeching off-kilter, wouldn't it? No wonder it was a bit upset at all this.

Reaching across the armrest, Rudyard patted Margaret's knee.

"Everything is going to be ay-okay."

Yet another grotesque lie! Rudyard had no belief—zero, zilch, nada—that everything would be okay. Far from it. The chance that *anything* might be okay, after all was said and done, now sat between slim and none, and, as the old saying went, slim just left town.

But he had Margaret now. That seemed vital. Something, some-one, Subject Six cared about—or *had*, at least. Rudyard wondered just how compromised the subject's mental faculties had now become. Its neural pathways could be radically altered; its brain could have new *parts*. Not runnels and sulci and gyri, the typical human apparatus, but elements grafted in from a different phylum. How those parts meshed, *if* they meshed, was the big question. With the other subjects, they hadn't. With the other subjects, *ho-ho*, the living motors of their brains had once or twice ejected from their mandibular mouthparts or from the sockets of their new and much more complex eyes in the manner of spray-foam insulation.

Heartbreaking, but no man of action could allow himself to dwell on his failures.

He had Margaret, and he had her phone. He could take it at any time—snatch it out of her pocket this very minute and smash her head into the window if she tried to get smart . . . but he'd been warned about that. Subject Six had eyes on them. Right now, he felt secure in a blind spot, but it wouldn't do to have Margaret all busted-up the next time they encountered one of the subject's cleverly placed little cameras. No, he'd let her keep the phone. Let her maintain some illusion of control.

The inescapable fact was that *nobody* had control of this. Not even Subject Six. What he'd seen back at the Minder's trailer told him as much. This was like grappling blindfolded with an octopus. He was at a severe disadvantage. His quarry knew the terrain and had already set a well-thought-out plan in motion. But to what end?

Rudyard had no earthly clue. And that was quite thrilling to him.

Subject Six—formerly known to its classmates as Charity Atwater—was Project Athena's last viable prospect. Rudyard had seeded a half dozen, all females. Over the years he'd watched in abject impotence as four of them failed and expired. All except Five and Six, and large doubts existed as to Five's ultimate viability.

Rudyard had elected to let five of his six subjects be reared outside a lab setting. In the wild, as it were. He'd let each have what they believed to be a family and a home. Allowed them to be free—within limits—to pursue friendship and human connection. After all, they *were* human . . . partially. The ticking clocks in their DNA helixes would in time erase a great deal of that humanity, but Rudyard's spirit of fair play insisted that they be permitted to pursue lives of quiet normalcy, with all the joys and heartaches that girlhood held in store.

His first subject, One, had been raised in captivity, in a facility set in the lofty pines of coastal California. Rudyard had hoped its life might be akin to killer whales born in a tank: If it had no inkling that a vast ocean existed, how could it miss it? But dammit to hell if One hadn't figured out his ruse; though it had persisted in mulish igno-rance into puberty, the monstrousness of its existence had ultimately dawned. Then, during the early morning hours on its fourteenth birthday, Subject One had unceremoniously melted.

The other five subjects had been released to their Minders as in-fants. Of those, three failed to flower profitably.

As a preteen, Three slaughtered a homeless man under a freeway overpass and had done something to his skin—made some kind of cape out of it. It had been found dashing around in the shadows of the overpass before dawn, cars zipping overhead, with the thick, tacky pelt of the man's skin flapping at its heels. It had been laughing like hell.

Rudyard was able to bottle the incident up, and Three had been remanded to the custody of its Minder. Later that summer, Three vanished. A reconnaissance team led by Roy found it burrowed in-side a hollow log in the marsh of a nearby nature area. When the team dragged it thrashing from the swamp, they'd seen evidence of uptake: the subject's flesh was replaced in areas with a knobby car-apace, but in other spots was as soft as a waterlogged apple. During the struggle, Three's body split open with shocking ease, releas-ing a mess of undeveloped organ-sacs. The subject had evidently screamed bloody blue murder, its face more or less unchanged—that of a girl. Then it died.

For years, Subject Two held promise. Although it had been committed to a sanitarium at the age of eight—it was given a private room where it was often found in a "nest" of shredded clothes and bedding—it outgrew this phase and was returned to its Minder. But sadly, Two triggered before puberty hit. It fashioned one of its nests in a bedroom closet. Its Minder was alerted by the strong smell coming from behind the door. Rudyard and Roy arrived in time to witness its emergence. Torsional and articulated and quite beautiful in its way. It slumped from the closet in a drift of shredded linens and rose, blinking stupidly . . . then it caught sight of itself in the antique cheval mirror (a gift from none other than Rudy himself) and began to scream. Its barbed limbs, smooth as the shell of a leatherback turtle, smashed the mirror. It wheeled around the room, a pair of teardrop-shaped wings fluttering against its back, gummed to its exposed spine-bone with afterbirth. Two kept murmuring *"Whuuu mmma iiii"* over and over. It was hopelessly insane—or if not, then unthinking on any usable level—and flung itself on the carpet like a Victorian heroine, screaming on and on, except it couldn't *really* scream, not a human sound anyway, because its mouth wasn't a mouth anymore, it was a tapered tube of cartilage and gristle and the sound that came out of it, pushed by the strange new bellows of its lungs, was the ear-splitting hum of an enormous fly.

It rolled over and over, ripping gobbets of mealy skin off its arms and legs, repeating that same clipped murmur, which Rudy later realized had been a question:

What am I?

Two was quietly removed for study. It perished during transport.

The less said about Subject Four, the better. Suffice it to say, its surrogate mother's womb had emulsified during the birthing process. Things had gone downhill from there.

That Subject Six was still alive counted as a minor miracle. Coventry had described Six's gene sequencing as "unstable, unharmonized, and prone to abrupt deterioration." Of all his subjects, Six was Rudyard's biggest swing.

But if it *cohered*, oh what a mighty, mighty dinger Six would be. He'd have socked one right out of the park—*BLAMMO!*

He glanced over at Margaret, sunk sullenly in her seat. Lord knows this must all come as a shock. To have passed your childhood in the bosom company of a creature that was, at its root essence, inhuman. How strange must that be? Not much different, Rudy guessed, than hearing the news that your one-time best friend had climbed a belltower with a rifle and started picking off innocent joggers.

How could I not have *seen* that? How could I have shared my innermost feelings and vulnerabilities with this incubus who'd gone parading around inside a human skin?

At this, Rudyard's thoughts returned in their unrelenting way to Elizabeth. To his sister staggering onto the hood of the Jeep on that long-ago day, shrugging that seething coat of ants off—her eyes wide, her eyelids eaten back by a thousand hungry little mouths. That image, and the command written within it, graven upon his brain:

Find me again, Rudy. Bring me back, make me whole, restore me to life.

Even then, he'd known it to be impossible. You cannot raise the dead. But when he thought of monsters now—of how a person can be *made* monstrous—he found it could happen two ways. You could be born with that monster inside you, twisting against your DNA helix and the soft walls of your brain, waiting to manifest, as in Subject Six's case . . . or that monster could needle into you via circumstance, couldn't it? You could become a plaything of your own history.

A shadow darkened the back seat. Rudy's breath caught.

Gripping the rearview mirror, he angled it until the glass revealed the bulbous outline of his old nemesis. The Ant sat behind him. Its feelers cut the air like whips. Its scent hung thick in the car, barbed and vinegary.

He tipped an imaginary hat, chauffeur-style. "Evening, sir. Where to?"

This provoked a reaction out of the vegetable in the passenger seat.

"Why are you like this?" Margaret asked. "You must have some serious trauma."

Little girl, you have no idea.

THIRTEEN
2:40 p.m.

As he pulled Harry's Geo into the graveled bulb bordering the grape fields, I kept trying to figure out who this guy, Rudy, reminded me of. Then it hit me.

Casey Hogarth.

Nobody had seen Casey in years, thank god, but back in elementary school he used to moon around the fringe of the schoolyard eating bugs. He didn't even try to make much of a secret of it. I think Casey *liked* people to watch as he stuffed whatever he'd found under the rock garden into his mouth. Sightless beetles, earwigs, the pupating cicadas he'd dig from the turf and mash up between his teeth as if they were flabby grains of rice . . . *moonbugs.* Wasn't that what Casey called them? *Moonbugs taste dandy, yummy as candy.*

Adult or kid, he creeped everybody out. Our teacher Miss Fairchild cringed when she spotted brown bits—the feelers and legs of insects—in the cracks of Casey's teeth. I sat in front of Casey in Miss Fairchild's class. His piebald eyes rested on the back of my neck. I took to wearing my hair down.

The rumor went that when Casey was twelve, he crushed three of his mother's sleeping pills into his babysitter's Coca-Cola. When she fell asleep, Casey pulled her panties down, snipped off a thatch of her pubic hair, and ate it. After that incident, Casey got sent someplace up north. Nobody heard from him again.

That Casey Hogarth vibe radiated off Rudy. Same sense of calculated vacancy. If I pushed my hands into his chest, they'd sink right through Rudy's skin and inside he'd be all hollow, hollow and cold, a frigid breeze cycling around his ribs.

"Is this it?" he asked me. "The right spot?"

"Yeah. Through the field and down."

I checked on Harry in the back seat. Still sleeping. His chest rose and fell evenly.

The Malibu and Escalade pulled in behind us. Rudy got out of the car and clapped his hands—*lovely day for a walk!*

Pikachu!

My phone this time.

> You know where to go.

The grapes—wine grapes, not juice grapes—ran in green barbwire snarls down rows staked into the caliche. In the early June haze, insects shimmered over the vines. The grapes were just starting to bud, filling the air with a damp, sugary smell. Past them, down the far end of the rows, the land dipped into a hollow that ran flat to the shore of the lake.

That was where the party had been held. Where we'd all gathered that night.

At Burning Van.

Rudy paced, his nose to the air. "So," he said, "why here, Margaret?"

From the edge of the parking gravel, something rose with a barely audible purr. It hovered over the plastic tarpaulins laid down over a half-acre to keep the soil moisturized.

Pikachu!

Not my phone this time. Rudyard pulled his out, read something, then lifted his eyes to the sky. "She's watching us," he said, waving at the hovering drone.

Pikachu!

Go alone. Just you. They won't follow.

Rudy said: "We'll keep your friend Harry company."

As I set off down the rows, it was with that feeling a soldier might get walking the field where he and his platoon had fought long ago, in the mud and the crud and the blood—Harry's father, if he'd been forced back to that spot where he'd put one in that poor Iraqi's eye . . .

The vines closed behind me. Bugs hazed over the stake lines. The land breasted in a grassy hillock, sloping down into an open patch scattered with sun-bleached pallets, abandoned blankets stiffened by the rain, a shit-ton of bottles and cans. Past a thin run of malnourished trees that fringed the clearing, the afternoon sun sparkled off the lake.

That night wept up from my memory, seeming to come from the ground below me: that adrenal perfume in the air, that brew of excitement and rage and sex that was never allowed to come out in the classrooms of Northfield High . . .

. . . and the mocking laughter that had transformed into something else, much more primal, when Plum had crawled out of—

The van.

It sat in moody isolation at the farthest edge of the clearing. A blackened hulk whose angles swallowed the sunlight.

Pikachu!

I want you inside it.

Jesus Christ. *Please*, no.

It rolled back to me then, on a sickening wave. The memory of that night. That party. Of Burning Van.

BURNING VAN

As the legend went:

One night many years ago, a Northfield High senior named Dustin Rebello got drunk on his mom's Boone Farm zinfandel and hopped in the E-Series Econoline van that his father, the manager at Buns Master Bakery, used to make his deliveries. Dustin's given intent was to drive to his girlfriend's house, one Elizabeth Fortson, and tell her they ought to get married immediately; once she said yes, Dustin's further intent had been to get a quickie wedding at the Little Blue Drive-Thru Chapel in Niagara Falls.

But Dustin Rebello never made it to Elizabeth Fortson's house that night, because a minute or so from his own front door, Dustin had lost control of the van, which had gone charging through the grape fields, snapping stakes and tearing vines, over the lip of the berm and down into the lowlands, where it slammed into a maple tree. Dustin slumped from behind the wheel, miraculously unhurt, and staggered away before the van's gas line ruptured, sending his father's property up in a crumpling fireball.

For reasons lost to the mists of time, the van was never towed away. It was a total write-off, gutted down to the pins, so it probably wasn't worth the towage fee as scrap. It squatted at the edge of the clearing years after it had wrecked, the layer of char preventing it from rusting too badly. Long after Dustin Rebello graduated and moved out of town—without Elizabeth Fortson, who married a minor-league hockey player named Dougie Barnes—the van remained.

It became a beacon to Northfield's student body. It was Burning Van.

That was the name given to the parties held down in the valley. A goof on Burning Man, the festival in Black Rock Desert, Nevada, where trust-funders in welding goggles bodysurfed to Diplo like a bunch of *Fury Road* rejects.

I'd been to a couple of Burning Vans. There was an informal understanding. If the skids called dibs on it for a night, it was standard for the other cliques to stay away. That kept the parties small. It kept the cops from breaking them up, too.

But on the fateful night in question, borders got breached. That night, Burning Van hosted a rager the likes of which Northfield had never seen, not in my era.

It grew online: Slack, Discord, group message threads, Twitter DMs . . . word of it spread as a digital fungus.

Before the party, Plum and I split half a bottle of vodka while sitting on the bleachers at Grapeview School. Plum had hooked the bottle from Estelle's war chest. Grapeview sat halfway between Executive Acres and Woody Knot. Since I'd moved, this had become our informal meeting spot—it was as if, by silent decree, we'd begun meeting on neutral territory.

We'd passed the bottle back and forth, taking sips chased with swigs from a jug of Lipton's Iced Tea. High school was coming to an end. For me, new and still-secret horizons beckoned. A university on the other end of the country. Fresh connections and challenges, people who shared my interests and who might end up rivals, friends, even lovers. Sometimes it would hit me—*I'm leaving soon, I'm starting a whole new life*—and the mix of fear and anticipation made me light-headed.

By the time we'd arrived at Burning Van, Plum and I were pretty much shit-faced. Watching Estelle work through her endless afternoon rum-cola, sinking into her La-Z-Boy as though her spine had gone to jelly, was enough to convince us that booze wasn't any kind of pathway to victory. But that night, the liquor acted as camouflage and confidence, all sewed up in one.

There's an energy to a party, isn't there? A force that can be felt along the sensitive areas of your skin as soon as you step over its threshold: through the doorway, down the basement stairs, into the circle of firelight . . . that party's core, its furious place.

Burning Van was pure chaotic electricity. My hair just about stood on end, as if I'd touched a Tesla ball. Five kegs were lined up on a patch of flattened duckweed, sunk in plastic trash cans packed with ice. Ten bucks for a Solo cup, all you could guzzle. Most guys were drinking from the kegs, and plenty of girls, too—but blackberry White Claw was a popular choice, and swigs were being taken from bottles of Fireball and Southern Comfort surfing around the party, which ranged over the valley under the constellations to the lakeshore.

A portable generator was hooked to a JBL PartyBox speaker; when Fetty Wap's "Trap Queen" hit the mid-song break, those clubbing bass notes echoed off the hillside and made the entire valley throb, *lub-lub-dub-dub*, the heartbeat of a buried giant.

The voice of the student body mingled with the music: hysterical laughter and screams and howls soaring up into the blackness above the massive central bonfire. Someone had stolen a scarecrow from one of the nearby fields and strung it to a stripped pine tree—it towered ten feet above the fire, a sentinel with shiny button eyes and a porkpie hat. It was just starting to smoke, the flames rising high enough to set its stuffing at the ignition point.

Pockets of partiers extended out from the bonfire, bits of space junk orbiting an asteroid. In my half-smashed state I spotted Miranda

Lancaster and Glenda Curtis with the Exclusives and Exclusive-Adjacents: the whole pack of them was wobbling, totally lit, in the same pair of platform buckle-heels.

Conversations sparked all around me and Plum, this constant crosscutting babble:

"You're telling me that some shithead fish walked out of the water a trillion years ago and now we're gonna have to get a job and pay rent 'n' shit? Fuck evolution!"

"Advertising execs are all, like: What do teens like? Is it memes? Memes about goblins? Dolphins? Is it pisslords? We need to sell more yogurt here!"

"—buncha fake-ass *biiiii-ya-tches!*—"

It was around then that I set eyes on the van. It sat where it always had, where Dustin Rebello had crashed it: its hood accordioned around the trunk of a maple that had been nearly sawed in half, the tree's upper branches folded down over the van's roof. Someone had lit a much smaller fire near the van, although nobody was sitting by it.

One of the van's rear doors was cracked ajar. I remember that. The door, and that yawning cubbyhole of darkness inside that the firelight couldn't touch.

In one of the party's outer rings, Plum and I found the Auto Shop crew. Harry was there. The firelight danced off his teeth—I remember that vividly, too, and the sudden weight of Plum on my arm. I stroked her hair. "You okay?"

"So long as I'm with you." Then, with quiet desperation: "Don't leave me, okay? I don't quite feel myself tonight."

"Okay, Plummy. I'm with you."

But it was Plum who'd disappeared. Admittedly, I was out of it—in addition to the booze, Norm Conradi had some gummies, and I'd taken one with Harry—and the next time I reached for Plum, my hand found only air. She'd left our little Auto Shop circle.

"Shit," I said once I'd realized it. "Plum's gone. I have to go look for her."

Harry said: "I'll come with."

By then, the party had mutated. It levitated on the edge of pandemonium. Someone had brought glass—dozens of thin panes the size of bathroom tiles—and the jocks and meatheads were smashing them with their fists or bare skulls, howling as blood leaked out of their hands and foreheads.

"Hey," Harry—*Bad Harry*—said. "I might enjoy that."

"Plum, remember?"

We passed two shirtless boys kissing in the shadows of the peach trees; I was pretty sure one was the Northfield Pumas' quarterback, Billy Beck. More anonymous bodies bobbed in the lake under the moonlight.

As we searched for Plum, Harry and I engaged in a highly serious debate: What hurt worse, getting kicked in the balls or the vagina?

"Has to be the nuts," Harry said. "They're just *hanging* there, defenseless!"

"Boy or girl, it is an incredibly no-fun experience," I told him.

"Yeah, but have *you* ever taken a proper boot down there? Not to brag, but I've taken a lot of nut shots."

"What's that I hear in your voice, Harr? Is it *pride*?"

Harry popped a pair of phantom lapels. "My old boys are steel-belted, I'll have you know. Plus, your junk is, like, *inside* you, isn't it?"

"Are you telling me you don't know where a girl's junk is?"

"No, I-I don't," he blubbered theatrically. "My parents . . . society . . . nobody's ever taught me where your hidden junk *is*!"

I let myself collapse against his chest, but only long enough to feel the wild beat of his heart under his T-shirt.

As much as we looked, we couldn't find Plum. We asked around, scoured the beach calling her name, but nobody had seen her, and she never answered us.

At some point, somehow, accidentally-on-purpose, Harry and I were alone.

We'd found ourselves sitting along the ridgeline, overlooking the cauldron of Burning Van. We must've told ourselves it was the best place to keep an eye out for Plum, but from where we sat everyone looked pretty much the same.

Harry said: "You're so fucking cool."

"No I'm not." I swatted him. "Go away."

"Yes, you are, you are, you really are," he said, nodding and shaking his head at the same time. "And you're so pretty. Like, *so* pretty."

He brushed dander off my cheek. Was there even any dander there? His hand lingered.

"You play it all whatever, who gives a shit, but you *want* stuff. And, uh, it's hard to want stuff, sometimes, if you think you wanting it is going to hurt somebody else, right?"

Struck dumb by how neatly he'd read me, I didn't say a word.

"Like, the crazy things I'm driven to do, they don't just hurt me. I *know* that, but that doesn't stop me wanting them." His hand came away from my cheek. I wished he'd left it there. "There's this crab, okay?"

"A crab, okay, please go on," I said, studying him closely.

"I saw it on YouTube. This crab, it grows to the size of its enclosure. A small tank, the crab stays small. But the bigger the tank, the bigger the crab gets. And I thought of you."

"You saw a crab and thought of me. How sweet."

"Stop it. What I mean is, some people grow past the spaces that once held them. And you can't feel bad about that, okay?"

"Who says I'd feel bad?"

He gave me an enraging, oh-so-knowing look. "I *see* you, Margaret Carpenter."

Which was when Harry Cook kissed me.

Does it ever happen quite how we picture it? For me, it happened on a rolling hillside near Lake Ontario under a star-freckled sky. I can't say there was anything bad about that. I was a lot drunk and a little stoned. And that felt okay, too.

Later, days after the party and after Plum had vanished, I wished like hell I could've sat on my old bed in the double-wide with my best friend and told her how it had gone with Harry. The truth? *Weird.* Fumbling, clumsy, not knowing where to put our fingers or tongues, guided by a bunch of scenes we'd seen in movies—*the two lovers kiss rapturously in the rain!*—but it wasn't nearly so tidy as that.

Spittle. There was a lot of it. Our first kisses were sloppy as two Dobermans; I think I might have licked his cheek by accident, then I'd started to laugh: these hysterical giggles that reminded me of being tickled as a kid, that helpless loss of control, your nervous system overwhelmed from tiptoes to the roots of your hair, so the only way you could deal with it was to laugh like a maniac.

Harry's hands migrated under my shirt, but I kept pushing them down, not because it didn't feel nice, but because if my shirt rucked up he'd be able to see my stomach. All of a sudden I was highly aware of the parts of my body that felt imperfect—my knobby knees, my tummy—but I didn't want it to stop, so I let my fingers roam between his legs and Harry's breath came in funny pops and he said, "Is this okay?" and my thought at the time was: *It's too early to say one way or the other,* so I made a soft note that was neither yes or no, and Harry stopped as if he needed permission, so I grabbed his shirt and rolled on top of him, straddling his hips. Harry let out a shocked grunt as I put my hands on his shoulders for balance and my fingers accidentally slipped around his throat for a second. Then I got scared because maybe Bad Harry was going to ask me to choke him, strangle him, until his face went purple, but Harry didn't ask me for that, thank god, so I kissed him—really *kissed* him—and his hands gripped my waist and we switched positions, and suddenly my jeans were rumpled around my ankles, and Harry's head hung in a halo of starlight above me, and next he was in me.

In that flickering heartbeat I felt something move between us, a secret language only we shared, as some part of me reached into him, that innermost part, the vulnerable center he kept stashed away from the world . . . but right then, and maybe only then and ever, he allowed me to touch that part of him and he touched mine, too. But that connection was an overbright starburst—you're trying to hold on to the tail of a comet as it arcs across the heavens, hugging our planet's gravitational curve for a few seconds before it's gone and you'll never see it again, not in your whole lifetime, and what you do feel is galvanic and quickly fading, a touch of fairy dust that trickles through your fingers until all you're left with is its taste on your tongue, the taste of longing—of being allowed near something transformative just long enough to feel its power, and for us humans, for our brief life cycles, if that's all we get, well, at least it's something.

Harry collapsed onto me. He whispered "I hope I love you" into the crook of my neck. I could have been confused, even angry—you *hope?*— but I understood: You want your first time to be with someone you love, right? But neither of us knew the real shape of it, so all we had was hope.

We lay on the grass, breathless and dazed. I was amazed at how fast the whole thing had happened, this act I'd fantasized about a million times in a million different ways, with Harry but with all sorts of different and impossible partners, too, and that it was now a closed book and we couldn't ever go back . . . some experiences, maybe most of the important ones, are doorways you can't step through again. I'd never see Harry in that dizzy-diamond way I'd held him in just minutes ago, a viewpoint that seemed instantly childish after the physical act, the grunts and awkwardness and bleachy odor of it—and I could see from Harry's eyes that I now rested the same way with him, too. We'd stolen something from each other. I didn't know what to make of it then, and I still don't to this day.

Somewhere in the distant seethe of the party, a note of commotion bristled. Something live-wire, dangerous, and dangerously inviting.

Harry and I stood. As I rucked my jeans up, the dread came that Harry had, had, had *finished* inside me.

My future came unzipped: I saw us outside a double-wide in Woody Knot, Harry balding with a bandanna tucked in his back pocket, me with my graying hair done up in a bun, frowning as our teenaged sons, *triplets*, raced around the yard whacking each other with Wiffle bats.

"Harry, did you—?"

"Unh-uh, don't think so. But we should make sure."

Early the next morning, we'd meet outside the Shoppers on Main Street. Harry would go inside and come out with a Plan B kit. We'd walk to Tim Horton's, sitting beside the fake fireplace with our knees touching. I'd thumb the pink button out of its blister pack and put it between my lips—looking at Harry, contemplating, as I think he was, what it might mean to have a child together—before swallowing the pill with a gulp of bottled water.

But well before that, we'd move down the hillside into Burning Van, a pair of hounds on the hunt, following a note that chimed in our bloodstream.

A group had gathered at the charred van. Harry and I moved toward a point of collision.

Reaching it, we saw what we saw.

FOURTEEN
2:46 p.m.

The memory of that night was fresh in my mind as I stood on the precipice of the hill, staring at the remains of Burning Van.

The phone was still in my hands, its last unthinkable order shining on the screen.

> I want you inside it.

Even as my brain cried *No, don't do it, you don't have to,* my feet carried me down the rise toward the van. I wished then that Dustin Rebello had never lived . . . but I wondered if that would've made a difference, really? If fate wanted you in its crosshairs, it could reshape space and time to put you where it wanted.

My sneakers hit the clearing. My foot came down on an empty can of White Claw, sending a spikewire of pain up my ankle.

Pikachu!

I didn't look at the phone. Kept walking. Through a gap in the trees, the lake ran glassy-green.

Pikachu!

Pikachu!

I checked the screen ten feet from the van.

You need to go IN

Shivers gripped me, my skin knotting behind my elbows and knees.

Its the only way to feel what your friend felt

Pikachu!

THATNIGHT.wav

Sunlight petaled off the roof of the van. A hard metallic sheen. The wind rose to a brief whine, flurrying the cockleburs around the van's bare rims—from inside came a dry rustle, the sound of dead leaves pulled across oxidized metal.

Everything felt very far away now. The cars, Harry, Rudy. Something could lunge out of that van. I pictured the doors bursting open as something flew out at me, pulling me into its dark guts before I could gather a breath to scream.

My fingers curled around the edge of one door. It pried open with a rusty screech. There was nothing inside except a few worn blankets.

I crawled in. The ancient fire had burned the seats down to struts and springs. The steering wheel and dash had melted into black taffy, but the smell of fire had been erased by hundreds of rainfalls. What remained was the tang of shaved metal and something else, less a smell than a lingering aura that made my brain go a bit buggy.

I lay on the floor. My head on bare metal, looking up at the van's ceiling.

I pressed play on the .wav file.

"Don't leave me, Cherr. I don't quite feel myself tonight. Remember when I said that?"

Shutting my eyes, I let Plum's side of the story wash over me.

"I felt so strange that night. Wasn't a bad feeling. I can only describe it as a new power gunning through me. A switch had been thrown, I think, letting me feed off some bigger power grid. A source that had been there for a long time, but I'd never had access to it until then.

"I was looking for something at that party, Cherr . . . not love. I wanted to feel a body on mine. Guess that makes me a slut. Just like everybody said after. A grifting slut." Her voice dropped. *"You need to know this, Cherr, okay? I heard a voice. It was coming from under my skin. Kind of muttering along my veins. Ohhh, and that night—it was so, so strong. I couldn't control it, but I didn't want to.*

"Can I just tell you how shocked I was when Will Stinson sat beside me at the lake that night? I'd wandered off from you and the Auto Shop crew . . . but the voice never left, so I can't say I was ever alone. I could tell how surprised Will was, too. Like, he didn't want to be next to me, but he couldn't help himself . . . you'd have thought his skeleton wanted to claw out of his skin." Soft laughter. *"He took my hand and said he never noticed how beautiful I was. That the moonlight brought out the green of my eyes."* An embarrassed snort. *"Can you believe that, Cherr? The handsomest boy in school. He didn't even know I was alive!*

"That's when it hit me—those were the things I'd always wished a boy would say to me. Those exact words, about the moon and my eyes. They came out of Will's mouth, but I could tell that speaking them terrified him so badly that he nearly wet his pants. It came to me that I must have made Will speak those words. I couldn't tell how, but it hadn't taken much effort at all. I'd just, like, thought them at Will, and he said them."

The wind blew through the van door, circuiting around my ankles. Plum's voice could have been a message sent across the cosmos from another galaxy, crackly from its journey between the stars.

"We walked from the lake to the van, holding hands. There was nobody around; everyone was at the bonfire, where that scarecrow had started to burn. Will left me and wandered over to Chad and Allan Teller. He pointed at me.

And I'm telling you that I wanted them, Cherr. Will and Chad, I mean. Allan was just there. So all I did was, I thought my desire at them. Feelers pushed out of my eyes and fingertips, picking across the grass, slipping up their legs and coiling around their ankles. Pulling them to me."

Another laugh, but this time it was cold.

"I climbed inside the van. The voice was mumbling behind my ribs: spiky balls bashing around, new knowledge that I knew I shouldn't touch. Will crawled in with me. He was hot, feverish, grinning like the devil. And we . . . made love. Oh, Cherr, it was exactly how I'd imagined. Will was so gentle. You'd never believe the tenderness in him. His fingertips danced along my hips, timid little moths. His lips at my ear whispering how much he adored me, worshipped me, only wanted to be with me and to please me, forever and ever . . .

"But there was a strangeness, too. I have to be honest, Cherr. As much as I don't want to ruin the memory of my perfect first time . . . there was a pane of glass in the van, okay? Running right down the middle. The pane was dark. Tinted. And something was happening on the other side.

"A mirror image. I could see two other people. I know that's impossible, but . . . every so often a bar of moonlight would stream through the busted windshield and reveal them to me. They looked like . . . well, like me and Will. On the other side of the glass. And those two"—her breath came out in an angry hiss—*"were just plain fucking, okay? It was ugly. And gross. The couple through the glass didn't touch each other the way Will and I did. They were sweaty and naked and weird. It looked more like fighting, or like they were trying to eat one another.*

"And ooooooh, I just hated it. Those two ruined everything and it made me so, so mad. I wanted to smash my fist through the glass and grab them both and make them stop, be quiet, squish their heads together until their bones went all funny . . ."

Plum's voice scaled down. The rage bled out of it.

"But they weren't really there, Cherr. Only me and Will. And like I said, it was perfect.

"After Will, Chad came in. A muggy sex-smell hung in the van—it made me ashamed because I knew I was partly the cause of it. When I grabbed for Chad, he pushed my hand away, like he was sickened by me. So, I just thought at him: You love me, Chad, you silly goose. I'm all you've ever wanted. *Chad's eyes changed. He went all gooey. He was helpless as a lamb! It was even better the second time. I didn't think it could be, but I surprised myself. Chad was surprised, too. And if that dark glass returned, and if the couple on the other side did things I didn't like—screeching so loud the pane rattled or flinging themselves around like dumb little birds . . . it was easy to ignore now. I focused on me. My experience, my joy. I deserved that, didn't I?"*

Was it then that an undertone bubbled into Plum's voice? Something as gaseous and corrupted as a body washed up on a lonely shoreline.

"Chad started to cry. He was so happy, you see. By the end, Chad was screaming. Anyone listening outside may have thought I was the one doing that. But no, it was him.

"After Chad left, Allan slimed inside with me. By then I was mostly full. Still, all I had to think was: Come here, you goofy bitch. *Next, Allan was shivering in my arms. It was over fast. Allan shrieked when his milk dribbled out. I thought it would be fun to make him eat it. But I just made him leave and lay in the van, alone. Uncontrolled voltages raced in my bloodstream. The voice pushed against the bones of my face, expanding into my eyes. I could feel a little blood, too, tacky between my legs. But it didn't hurt.*

"Nothing hurt anymore.

"And out by the bonfire, as that scarecrow burned, those three boys were busy changing history. Because it wouldn't fit, would it? The narrative that two of the coolest boys in school, plus Allan Teller, fucked a poor trailer-park girl in a bombed-out van. What would Miranda Lancaster say? Miranda, who'd dated Chad Dearborn for most of junior year? So, you need to understand—Cherry, you need to know—*that the story changed to fit the need."*

The rumor had been perfect in its simplicity. The best rumors usually were. It leveraged how high school had always worked—the way we thought it was *supposed* to work, at some ingrained level—against a threat to its unbending hierarchy.

"*The story became that I'd taken them into the van one by one. I laid out some bullshit story about needing money. I had to get out of town. Maybe I'd stolen someone's drugs, maybe I'd got myself pregnant. They were rich. Come on, just a few hundred bucks. What was that to them? If they gave it to me, it was over. If they didn't, I'd tell everyone at the party I'd had sex with them in the van.*"

The rumor had been sharpened to a slaughterhouse edge by the time I heard it. By then, Plum *was* pregnant, *had* stolen drugs, and had no choice but to jet out of town—and if the guys didn't give her money, she was going to tell everybody she'd been *raped* in the van.

"*It's amazing, isn't it? How easy it is to get people to believe something totally untrue. And it* worked, *because why wouldn't it? They were cool and rich and* special, *and I was . . . I was me. Why would they risk their social standing by having sex with someone they barely recognized, even if we'd passed each other in the halls a thousand times?*

"*And who was going to defend me, after I came out of the van looking the way I did? You can't change the past—whatever version people come to believe in—once it gets a chance to plant roots. Well, anyway . . . they can believe whatever they want. They'll know the real story soon enough.*"

Her laugh was the charmless cackle of a witch.

"*And I'll always have my three little boys. Remember Lennie from* Of Mice and Men? *We read that in Mr. Foster's class. Lennie loved his bunnies, didn't he? I love my boys in the same way. Love them so much that I may just break their stupid fucking necks.*"

The .wav ran silently for twenty seconds. Just the low cycling of Plum's breath.

"*I saw* you, *Cherr. That night, outside the van. I saw* you *watching me.*"

By the time the file cut out, my chest had gone clammy with sweat.

FIFTEEN
2:58 p.m.

. . . I saw you, Cherr.

After dragging myself off the floor of the van, I slouched out onto the valley. My head throbbed; I felt dizzy and sick.

As kids, Plum and I found a Ouija board up in the drop ceiling of my Hallmark trailer. Our eyes shone, as if we'd found covenant gold. We took it out to the woods, where we went with anything illicit: Dad's *Dirty Little Limericks* book, Mom's issues of *Cosmo* with their "10 Ways to Drive a Man Wild" articles. We balanced the board on a stump and put our fingers on the planchette. I waited for Plum's eyes to roll back in her skull, her mouth to hinge open like a ventriloquist's dummy, and an ancient voice to fill the shadows under the trees.

That didn't happen. Nothing had. But the scabrous, demonic voice I'd been waiting to hear that long-ago afternoon had finally reached my ears.

It was Plum's voice at the end of that .wav file.

I may just break their stupid fucking necks.

I walked up the hill, back through the grape field. The stuttering *zzz-zzz* overhead was either a dragonfly or the drone dogging me. The phone lay silent in my pocket. I was struggling to get a grip on Plum's version of that night's events. The sorrow I felt for not being there for her sat against the new impression that she actually hadn't needed any help.

I made Will say those words.

I just took him.

The cars came into view. I hung back, scanning for a dog walker, jogger, *anyone* . . . but I'd just get those innocent bystanders killed, wouldn't I? Roy would execute them.

When I got back, Harry had regained consciousness. He stood

218 — NICK CUTTER

unsteadily between Rudy and Roy. As I stepped from the field, he broke away from them and met me.

"Are you okay?" I asked.

"Better," he said, jerking his head at the men. "They told me I passed out. The sting?"

"Yeah."

Harry gave me a look that I interpreted as: *These guys—should I trust them?* I shook my head. *No.*

"Are *you* okay, Mags?"

Even if he'd just woken up, Harry knew exactly where we were. So, he also knew where I must've come back from. "I'll be okay."

"Children, come to teacher," Rudy called.

I had no intention of telling Rudy what I'd heard down in the van. Silence was my ally. Information—what I knew, what they didn't— was my friend. What else was keeping me and Harry alive, other than the watchful eye of that drone?

"Care to give us a report?" Rudy asked.

I didn't say anything.

"What did you see, Margaret? What did you hear?"

I stared at him with wordless hostility. The drone hovered over the parking lot.

"Can that thing hear us?" Rudy asked Roy.

"Not sure," said Roy.

Rudy rested his hands on his hips. "You think I'm the enemy. Fine. In a way, you're right. But in a more important way, I'm the only one who can prevent this from escalating to DEFCON 1. If we don't share what we know, we're all cooked."

My look said: *You go first.*

"I can show you something," he said finally. "An explanation of sorts. But if we cross that bridge, we can't go back. I want you to think hard before we—"

Pikachu!

Pikachu!

Our phones went off at the same time. Rudy hauled his out first.

"It's a video," he said.

The same link popped up on my phone. A vid posted by the You-Tube account @AXS_PRODCO.

Oh shit—Allan Xavier Teller.

DON'T TRUST THE GRIFTER FREAK!

I wanted to snatch Rudy's phone and smash it.

Pikachu!

> Watch it.

Pikachu!

> Daddy and Margaret

Pikachu!

> together, just you two

Rudy cocked one eyebrow. "We'd better do as we're told. Coming, Margaret?"

The piper. Sooner or later, everyone paid what they owed.

"Mags?" Harry said as I walked with Rudy toward the Escalade.

"It's okay," I said without looking back. "I deserve this."

I settled into the front passenger seat of the SUV. Rudy started the motor and swung the vehicle in a backward arc. I could see the top of what appeared to be a box behind the rear bench seat: jet black, issuing a muted hiss. When Rudy put the Escalade into drive and pulled down the lane, the box slid backward a few inches and struck the rear window.

Rudy didn't travel far. Only to the closest cutoff, a few hundred yards from the road. It was dead quiet out here in field country. Nobody was going to interrupt us.

He parked. Pulled out his phone.

"Would you like to tell me anything before we . . . ?"

I knew what he'd see. The clip everyone at Northfield had seen after Burning Van. The video that went zipping around school on a viral wire, *pinging* on phones and being mainlined into a thousand greedy eyeballs.

Before Rudy hit the link, I had that same feeling I'd had that night, shivering in my bed, imagining the tube-men *bump-bump*ing above the roof of our trailer. The dire sense of something demonic coming home to roost.

SIXTEEN
3:09 p.m.

Laughter.

That's how the clip started. No light, no color, just a black screen and the hyena-ish laughter of teenage boys.

Next, an unfocused image filled the screen of Rudy's iPhone. The perspective swung until the camera centered on its subject:

The van, as black as a million midnights rolled together.

"*We find the freak in its native habitat,*" a boy's voice intoned, then giggled hysterically.

The perspective swung to frame Allan Teller, Will Stinson, and Chad Dearborn, standing at a watchful distance from the van. Their skin shone corpse-white, their eyes over-adrenalized and weird.

They'd filmed this after what happened inside the van with Plum. They must have, and that much would be obvious once she emerged.

"*Wait, ooooo, she's coming out.*"

That was Will. He sounded terrified.

The van door creaked. Darkness hung inside, and when Plum crawled out of it, the boys let out a collective hiss.

She exited the van all crabbed over, a crone hauling herself from a hut of sticks.

"Oh, Six," Rudy whispered. Those pitted divots on his cheeks and forehead shone, pricked with sweat. "I understand it all now."

The camera swung away, almost as if Allan couldn't handle the sight of Plum. As the angle listed, the camera caught a glimpse of Will tilted back on his heels: the posture of someone standing too close to an explosion.

Plum *glowed.* Not that radiant glow that romance writers claim a woman gets after her first time. This was how historians say the bomb victims in the fallout zone of Hiroshima looked, the ones who weren't incinerated by the blast but died of massive radiation poisoning days or weeks later. The sick plutonium illumination of their skin.

Sitting there in the Escalade rewatching the video, I was hit with the same memory I'd had that night at Burning Van.

Sixth grade. Mr. Godfrey's homeroom class. I'd felt sick most of that morning. This roiling churn in my stomach. Plum and I sat next to each other, as we'd done since the first grade. As the pain sank past my stomach and into my hips, I raised my hand. *I need to use the bathroom.*

I'd made it into a stall and by the time I sat down on the toilet, a dark patch had begun to spread across my jeans. Shame swamped me. At first, I was sure I'd peed myself. But when I unbuttoned my jeans and pulled them down, there was blood. A lot of blood.

I'd goggled at the red on my thighs, soaking my underpants. The initial fear that I must be bleeding to death quickly faded. I knew what this was, but I didn't know what to do about it. I just sat there and wept.

The stall door opened. Plum eased inside with me. I was shocked, vulnerable, didn't want anyone to see me like this. But Plum was calm. *It's your period*, she said.

I know that, but what do I do now?

Plum gathered a handful of toilet tissue off the roll. We were a couple of inexperienced surgeons trying to staunch a wound with cheap one-ply TP. Plum was fascinated by the change in me: the blood, the flush of my skin. My embarrassment intensified. *What am I gonna do?* Neither of us had a sweatshirt to knot around my waist in the hopes of hiding the stain.

We switch jeans, Plum said, no big deal. *You wear mine.*

Did I really understand the gift she was offering? Did I allow myself to think about it all that much before I accepted it? There in that stall, so close that our skin touched at fiery contact points, we both pulled off our pants. Charity's jeans were a bit bigger, but they fit.

She pulled my panties on, my cooling blood tacky against her thighs. Squirmed into my jeans. When she'd gotten them on, she smiled.

There, Cherry. All better, right?

Before we stepped out into the hall, I said: *You're just gonna come back to class with me?* Plum shook her head. *I'll walk home.*

Home was five miles away. We got bused in from Woody Knot.

Tell Mr. Godfrey I'm still in the bathroom, okay? They'll call Mom, but I'll be home before anyone misses me.

Okay, was all I'd said. *I'll tell him.* Plum touched my wrist shyly. Then she ducked out. I went back to class. When Charity didn't come back, Mr. Godfrey went to the office. I played dumb.

Charity walked all the way home that afternoon, mostly through the greenbelt and orchards, but sometimes along the roadside. She wore my bloody jeans. The next time I saw them, they'd been washed spotless and dried in the trailer park's coin-op machines. Plum handed them to me neatly folded.

That memory passed through me as I sat beside Rudy watching the video.

THE QUEEN — 223

On the phone's screen, we saw Plum hobble away from the van. Drawing herself up to her full height, she pointed one finger. The view panned to show she'd singled out Will Stinson.

"You," she breathed off-screen. "Are *mine*."

Will laughed—no, he *tittered*, a startled birdlike note.

"*Mine*." Jabbing her finger at Chad next. Finally, her arm came around until she was pointing directly at the camera. "*MINE*."

The view panned again to show the distant bonfire, whose light was joined by many smaller pinpricks. They looked like fireflies, but I knew that wasn't it.

They were phones. Dozens of them.

The student body had been alerted in that subliminal way—a prickle in the inner ear, the hairs quilling at the napes of our necks—that something devilish was afoot. Everyone had gathered, phones out, lenses trained on the hilarious shambling hag who'd tottered out of the van to make a spectacle of herself.

"Skinny bitches," Plum lisped. "Skinny bitches, gonna eat some skinny bitches . . . skinny bitches"—her words gained the cadence of a chant—"skinny bitches, skinny bitches, gonna *eat* some skinny bitches."

Laughter wept from the phone in Rudy's hand. It wasn't just Will and Chad and Allan; the whole valley swelled with feverish, frenzied laughter that tiptoed on the edge of screaming, as if the onlookers were watching someone douse themselves in kerosene and tease a lit match down the hem of their blouse . . . because that's what Plum was doing, wasn't it? Symbolically setting fire to herself with this unforgivable act of exhibitionism: making herself seen by all for the first time in her life, only to be torn apart in mockery.

The footage took on a syrupy pace, the laughter going sludgy as the angle panned the crowd. It moved past Miranda and Triny and Cody Evans, past Dennis Weeks and the Auto Shoppers, who all watched.

Oh god, I thought. *Oh please, no . . .*

I wanted to snatch the phone out of Rudy's hands before he saw it but—*but*—

There. Me. Margaret June Carpenter. Standing amid the crowd. My face broadcasting the same horror as everyone else.

The shot froze on me for a damning moment. Just another face in the mob.

The video sped back up. The perspective swung back to Plum. By then she was stalking toward the camera, her skull shot forward on her neck, a creature of the hunt.

"*—BITCHES! SKINNY BITCHES, GONNA EAT AAAAALL YOU SKINNY BITCHES!*"

Hunchbacked, she rushed at Chad, Will, and Allan. The boys let out a unified scream—despite whatever story they may have spread over the coming days, they were frightened out of their wits right then—and scattered.

The final image captured Plum veering into the woods, running down the lakeside.

SEVENTEEN
3:17 p.m.

In the silence, something moved inside the Escalade.

A sound coming from the black box in the back. Something had stirred, stretching its limbs within the box's confines.

"Tell me what happened," Rudy said, tapping the phone. "After all this."

That night, once my inertia broke, Harry and I had searched for Plum. We'd traced her path into the woods. No luck. The party was still going by the time we rounded back to the bonfire. I'd hunted around for Chad, Will, and Allan—they'd done something awful, I knew it—but by then, they'd disappeared, too.

Everyone, and I mean *everyone*, at Burning Van was watching some version of the video. Only one version ever got posted publicly, but nearly everyone left with a piece of Charity on their phones. Of her crabbing out of the van, her body hooked and predatory. Hissing about skinny bitches. She looked . . . Christ, a monster.

When I showed up at Woody Knot the next morning, an hour after swallowing the Plan B pill, Estelle told me Charity hadn't come home. *She will when she's ready,* she said. I'd gone to school, one of my last days before retreating to my room. Allan, meanwhile, had posted the video, and by midafternoon everybody at Northfield—freshman to senior, the teachers, Dickie O'Reilly and the custodial crew—had seen it. Next came the mash-ups and remixes and GIFs. Those were easier to laugh at. But the original footage, captured at those weird drunken angles—no, I honestly don't think anyone found it funny at all.

Most of those who watched the video couldn't have picked Charity out of a police lineup. Yet suddenly she was the most known student at school. When the video crossed the online threshold into other schools, she became the most known person in town.

Known is problematic. Known isn't beloved, it isn't respected, it isn't admired. It can be the most dehumanizing thing of all, becoming known.

The video, along with Charity's ongoing absence, fueled the rumor. Those boys couldn't have planned it any better. Charity wasn't around to give her side of the story. After twenty-four hours, the rumor—shaped by Miranda and the Exclusives—set in concrete and hardened into truth.

That Saturday morning, I'd found Plum on the swing set at Woody Knot. The same one we used to play on as girls, giving each other under-dogs. I took the swing next to her.

I should have been there for you, Plum.

It's not your fault.

Yes, it is. Really, it is. I promised to watch over you.

I told you it's okay, didn't I?

Those fuckers . . . they raped you, didn't they?

There are things you feel skin-deep and things you feel heart-deep, but the most profound things are soul-deep. I knew Plum had lost her virginity in that soul-deep way. Worse, I knew it had happened at the same time I'd lost my own with Harry. She'd never have gone into that van understanding what was coming. Maybe she'd simply done the same thing a billion girls our age had done: allowed ourselves to believe the guy of our dreams (or some collective dream) really liked us, seeing us for who we truly were.

Did you tell Estelle?

Huh, right. And what's she going to do?

Let's go to the cops, then. They can do a rape kit.

Cherr, that's not what happened. I knew what I was doing.

I know that's what you believe. But Plum, I'm *saying you were raped.*

No. I'm sorry if I'm letting you down.

I moved my swing across, wrapping my arm around her. *Plummy, no, that's not it at all. I just . . . I don't want them to get away with it.*

Reporting it as a crime would put so much weight on her. But if she didn't, that rumor may come to define her.

What was she wearing?

How drunk was she?

Did she ask for money?

They're good boys.

She has no proof.

She's lying.

The boys said she asked for money.

She's looking for a payday. *They* always do.

She wants to wreck those boys' bright futures.

She's a fucking crazy trailer-park bitch.

We're changing, Cherr, she said. *All of us, so fast it's hard to think straight.*

She shrunk in the swing, almost as if she expected me to laugh at her for speaking those words. Her reaction made me feel like the worst friend.

A new future's coming. For you and me both, Plum.

Oh Cherr, come on. You'll go to college, won't you? You're going to be a writer. Settling her head on my shoulder. *I'll pick up a book in the store and see your photo on the back and say: I knew her. We grew up together. I don't know* who *I'll say that to, but I'll say it.*

You're going to do great things, too.

You don't have to say that.

I'm so sorry I wasn't there for you, okay? But we can fix this.

You can't fix what's already in the past. But you know what? You'll write about me one day. One way or another, you'll remember me.

Why had that sounded so threatening, even then?

People slip away from each other, Cherry, even soulmates.

Her defeated shrug carried down my spine. The heat of her body was unbearable.

That doesn't have to happen with us, Plum. I really don't want *that to happen.*

Me neither. But it will.

We'd swung in silence. The clouds chased themselves across the escarpment.

A few days later, she was gone.

And now, here we are.

Rudy said: "You don't want to tell me what happened, hmm? Acceptable. I don't think it matters. What I watched was sufficient." He pointed one finger up: *a-ha!* "Would you like me to show you something?" He answered himself. "No, I don't think you would. But I believe I'm going to show you anyway."

EIGHTEEN
3:26 p.m.

Rudy popped the trunk release. "Hop out."

By the time I met him at the rear of the Escalade, the trunk had risen. I could see the black box now. It had the look of a toy box for a militarily inclined boy.

"Let me be perfectly frank about something, Margaret. I'm a rich man," he said. "*Stupid* rich." He spoke the following as if the notion had only occurred to him: "Some people shouldn't have money. They only get up to mischief with it. But the universe . . ." A bemused shrug. "The universe doesn't seem to operate on sane principles, does it?"

From his pocket, he produced a sleek, glossy oval. He pushed one of the buttons on it.

The black box extended from the Escalade on a set of rails, stopping once the back of the box had passed the edge of the trunk. With a motorized whine, it lowered to the gravel.

The box was made of a material I'd never seen before. A computerized readout on one side displayed what were obviously vital signs. Pulse rate, blood oxygen level.

"I wish I'd seen that video before now," he said. "If I had, there's a chance—perhaps only a small one—that this could've gone differently."

The sun collected in long rails down the box's angles. In the slack emptiness of Rudy's face, I saw Casey Hogarth again—Casey, taking my sleeve on the playground and leading me to the outskirts where the chain-link met, kneeling, pushing aside dead leaves to show me the head of Annie Reynolds's doll. Molly the Dolly, which had gone missing when Annie brought her to class for show and share earlier that week; Annie so heartbroken that Miss Fairchild organized a search party, our class hunting the classroom and playground for Molly, but nobody could find her—but there she was, Molly's head anyway, under the moldering leaf-litter; her eyes had been punched out and bugs had made a home inside the plastic, centipedes and juvenile beetles twisting in Molly's sockets. *Do you think she sees what they see?* Casey asked me, his liverish lips wet with spittle. *Can Molly see through the centipedes' eyes, you think?*

"What really happened to Charity?"

"You could say she's not herself anymore," said Rudy. "Not the girl you grew up with. That's for sure."

The *cree* of late-molt crickets rose in the sultry air. Rudy pushed a second button on his control.

Following a series of interior clicks, the top of the box rose. Tendrils of supercooled air ribboned from inside. Metallic strands connected the lid of the box to its base; those strands lengthened, filling the widening gap in a diamond grid.

Something was hunched behind that alloyed spiderweb. The impression I got was shadowy, but what I perceived was not in any way normal.

"It's okay, darling," Rudy said. "Come say hello."

A shape crooked into sight above the lip of the box. A stuttering and somehow mechanical movement.

A bulbous, craggy rock. A rock made of flesh.

That's a head, *Margaret.*

Something was alive in there. Stashed inside that box.

Massive eyes dominated the top half of that head: a pair of bulging disco balls—they were faceted, I noted with quiet horror. The thousand-odd flat panes making up each eye spat back the sun. Its mouth was not a mouth at all but a tube of milky cartilage open at one end in a funnel. The funnel projected below its eyes, bent and mangled as a stubbed cigarette. The rest of its head was bald, though tufts of hair clung stubbornly here and there.

One tuft was cinched in a pretty red ribbon.

The thing in the box had a pair of petite, horrifyingly human ears.

"She's rather skittish," I heard Rudy say. "She doesn't meet new people. You should stand back. That's ballistic tungsten netting. Strongest metal on earth, but why test it?"

The smell drifting out of the box was dusty and acrid, but there was something unidentifiable in it, too—something that came out of the thing's pores in a living mist. It was making gasps and clatters, sounds you might hear if you put your ear up to the face of an old clock to hear the tick of its brass gears.

Rudy's face was inscribed with pride. "Can you say hello to the nice girl, Five?"

The thing shrieked. The entire box rattled, rocking forward on its cleats. In a second it would topple over and hit the ground, and the unloved toy inside would—

"The light hurts your eyes, doesn't it?" Rudy soothed the thing. To me: "Five's eyes are phototropic. A trait she shares with the death's-head moth."

The crown of its head was covered in raised veins. The misaligned plates of bone pulsed, ready to come apart and reveal whatever strangeness filled its skull.

"You play with Dolly," Rudy said sweetly. "That always makes you happy."

A stirring in the guts of the trunk, where the rest of the creature's ungodly body must be stuffed out of sight. The head of a plastic doll rose into view. Its eyes had been punched out, its mouth caved in as if it had been melted with battery acid. Molly the Dolly. The diamond facets of the creature's eyes circled in helpless spirals of madness—

"*Urgh burk aa eee.*"

These sounds bubbled out of the ulcerated tube in its face. The flaps of skin sputtered, leaking dog-slobbery ooze.

Rudy grabbed my elbow. "Step away from her, *now.*"

The thing shrieked again—"*Urgh burk aaa eee!*"—and the thunderclap of understanding hit me:

Don't look at me.

That's what it was shrieking at us.

DON'T LOOK AT ME.

The next instant, something slammed into me. Not physically, but psychically. Fingers seized my brain and pulled.

I jerked out of Rudy's grip as a hysterical inner voice screamed, *No, don't, Christ NO*—as I found myself wanting *to hug* the thing.

Movement. The clipped beating of wings. Something stabbed through the metallic netting. The flickering impression of a pole, but translucent, more an endless icicle coming at my face—

Rudy grabbed my collar and yanked. The icicle jabbed through the space where my skull had been the instant before, *shiz-shiz-shiz*, the needle on a sewing machine.

The box's lid lowered. As soon as the automatic locks engaged, my head cleared. Rudy's thumb covered the button of his remote control.

He got off me. I sat up, dazed. Gravel shards were stuck to my cheek. Rudy brushed them off gently. He sat cross-legged facing me. Braced his palms on his knees.

"So. You have questions."

I couldn't scream. I sat on the ground, legs splayed, completely without feeling.

"W-what is that . . . ?"

"Something I've created. I've been working on her for quite a long time."

"*Why?*" No other question seemed nearly as important.

"Because it didn't exist," he said simply. "Now it does. And I should admit that Five isn't an only child. She is one of six. Sextuplets. *Sisters.* You know one of them."

I shut my eyes. Don't say it. Don't speak another word. *Please.*

"Subject Six. But you know her by another name."

No, no, no, *no-no-no-no-NO*

"Charity Atwater."

I opened my eyes. Rudy's face radiated sick good cheer.

"The woman you knew as Charity's mother didn't give birth to her. She was hired by me. An eighteen-year hitch of improvisational theater, playing the role of Mom. But Charity Atwater has no mother. She only has fathers."

He fiddled with his remote control. Motors whirred. The box began to lift off the ground.

"You're lying," I said as the box retracted back inside the Escalade.

The SUV's trunk lowered soundlessly. Rudy patted my knee.

"The organism you've known since childhood." He spoke slowly, patiently. "Who you grew up with and who presented for all the world as a girl. She *was* a girl. But she's so much more than that. Subject Six is a conceptual hybrid life-form, sprung from the mind of man. As was Five. As were One, Two, Four, and Three, may the Lord rest and keep them."

He scooched closer. Gravel rasped against his thighs.

"Can I be nakedly honest with you?"

Rudy shivered in the June sunshine. You'd almost think that the weight of whatever monstrous machinery he'd set in motion was crushing him into dust.

"Do you believe it's possible to get trapped in a moment? You're probably too young to accept that, but before today's done, you'll see what I mean. I got trapped a long time ago, as a boy. I won't bore you with the specifics, but that day"—his hands came together, fingers spread and tips touching—"a bubble formed. A bubble of time. I got stuck inside it. When that happens, you watch this other version of yourself—the *you* you could've been if that moment hadn't snared you—walking away into a future you'll never touch.

"Charity was born that day, too, if only in my subconscious. So was that young lady in there"—a nod to the Escalade—"and her sisters. They're all the result of me getting trapped. I never quite managed to pull myself clear of that day."

"Did you ever try all that hard?"

As impossible as Rudy's truth was, it settled in my chest with the thud of authenticity. Everything I'd seen today, leading up to the box, pushed me to accept it.

"The quarry we're now chasing," Rudy went on, "is akin to Five, but of a greater and more complex magnitude. If Six *worked*, and yes, I believe she did, and is now aware of what she is, as is evidently the case, and has been planning this caper for some time, having surrendered none of her intellectual ability during her ascension to a higher order of life, learning how to harness the gifts that come with it . . . that would make her a stunningly able predator."

He was talking about Plum, who refused to skewer worms on a fishhook and cupped spiders, carrying them out of her trailer so Estelle didn't squish them.

"That night, Margaret, at this party," said Rudy. "Having now watched that video, I can tell you that's where Six's transformation began. It's not worth our time to explain more than to say that each of my subjects requires a trigger—an event that encourages the chromosomal cascade and exalts them from what they are to what they'll become. That party, those boys—the ones filming her, whose moony faces I saw when the camera angle shifted . . . Charity had sex with them, didn't she?"

"They raped her."

Rudy laughed, a high honk that made my skin crawl.

"Oh no! No, no, no, *NO!* If they went into that van with her, *she* dictated the terms of engagement. She pulled them in, did as she fancied, and marked them so she could find them later and make them fully hers."

Marked them. I pictured Plum in the valley, lit by the distant glow of the bonfire, pointing to each of the boys in turn.

Mine, mine, MINE.

"Charity went missing not long after that party, didn't she?"

"Yeah," I said finally. "She didn't come home after the party. But she did eventually, sticking around for a day or two. Then she was gone for good."

"And you haven't seen her since."

"No."

"And those young gentlemen, what happened to them?"

"They went missing."

"Charity first, then the boys?"

I nodded.

"You know, it's stunning," he said. "For all the billions I've spent, all the investment and legwork put into monitoring my subjects' development, until now I had no clue how she'd gone missing." He clucked his tongue. "Leave it to teenagers to keep their world a secret from the adults, hmm? The most clamlike band on earth, you lot."

"You're the enemy," I said, not meaning Rudy specifically, but adults. No adult could be fully trusted, even the ones we kind of liked.

"Well, I'll tell you this," said Rudy. "I wouldn't want to be in those boys' shoes."

He stood up. "I need to move. Helps organize my thoughts. Come on, hup-hup."

NINETEEN

3:39 p.m.

A genuine curiosity now gripped me. If my childhood friend's existence had been a grotesque charade—a wealthy man's experiment, a fact hidden from her all her life—then . . .

"What *is* she? Charity, Six, whatever you'd like to call her."

"Blue-skying it?" Rudy held out his hand. "A queen, Margaret."

He helped me to my feet. The field hung still in the late-afternoon sun. High above us, a jet left its contrail across a postcard-blue sky.

"A queen."

"That's right. A queen my team and I manifested."

We faced the grape fields. The vines stretched out to a vanishing point my eyes couldn't define.

"When an insect queen reaches sexual maturity," Rudy went on, "she steps into a vast range of abilities. If Six is now truly a queen herself, she's in possession of powers not of our species. You felt the most impressive of them. That *pull* toward my trunk. Toward Five."

"I couldn't help myself."

"Five's pheromones are responsible. Insect queens use them as controllers. Of my subjects, only Five has that power—and now, her sister."

"But why does it work on us?" I said stupidly. "We're not bugs."

"Five evolved the ability post-transformation. Some adaptive hitch must make the pheromones she produces work on you and me."

He held up one finger. "And I have every reason to believe that Six's abilities far outstrip Five's."

The sun beat down on my neck. Sweat soaked into my jeans. I noted the bulge of the remote control. Rudy had tucked it into the smaller pocket—the watch pocket, my dad called it—of his jeans. The fob stuck out an inch, a leather tongue.

"There is a substance only queens produce. Queen mandibular pheromone. Though it varies slightly between wasp and bee and ant, it's the same base element."

Rudy kicked a clod of clay. Potato bugs went scurrying across the parched earth.

"On Earth, only three compounds have ever been adjudged scientifically unclassifiable—that is to say, their chemical and molecular makeup is resistant to cataloging in all known tables or strata. One is the material found inside the Ensisheim meteorite, which struck the earth in 1492. Two, an organism dredged up in a trawler's longline from a trench over an abyssal fault in the Adriatic Sea; it burst apart from over-pressurization, so nobody ever knew what it was, or if there were others like it. The final unclassifiable compound is QMP—queen mandibular pheromone."

Rudy bent, plucking up one of the scuttling potato bugs. He dropped it down his shirt.

"Most pheromones are transmitted through the air," he went on, no biggie. "But QMP is secreted as a fatty compound by emergent queens. Once it's been transferred into a mate, the queen can command it from great distances, ordering it to seek pollinating buds, to attack, to retreat. She directs thousands of mates simultaneously, as a conductor does the strings and brass of her orchestra."

Rudy's words made me feel as though I'd been pumped full of Freon, the refrigerant gas inside discontinued fridges.

"We've been studying QMP for a century and are no closer to understanding how it works. Humans secrete pheromones, yes, in our piss and shit and vaginal walls and glands, but they're a watery reflection of the insect world. If Six can produce her own version of QMP . . . imagine, Margaret—being able to make someone do anything you want from miles away? An invisible leash that gives you unquestionable authority over another human being. In the insect kingdom, or ah, *queen*dom, it's *de rigueur*. In our species, it would be the most criminal abuse of power imaginable. But what if the one who wields it doesn't bend to human notions of empathy or morality? What," he said after an introspective pause, "if its only desire is vengeance?"

"If she's got that kind of evil superpower . . . how do I know she's not commanding *you*?"

Rudy smiled. "I guess we don't. And that goes double for this Serena person. The voice on the phone. I've been thinking about her, too," he said. "Come on. We should get back."

Down the road, the other cars were specks against the spruce trees. Five's pheromones lingered on my skin, a million fishhooks tied to invisible lines waiting to be yanked.

"Oh, get in," Rudy snapped. "She can't touch you from inside her home. It's airtight."

Reluctantly, I sat back in the Escalade. My eyes drifted to Rudy's pocket. The fob was still sticking out.

"*Serena*, as she calls herself," Rudy said, starting the SUV up. "One thing you must've noticed with Five is that"—he chose his next words carefully—"she's not really fit for public appearances, is she? She'd give children a fright, that's for sure."

He reversed, swinging the Escalade around. "Six may be in the same boat. No longer human enough to walk among us. So, she could've selected a stand-in. Someone to do her public-facing business who's under her control, attached to Six on an unbreakable psychic wire."

"So, what . . . Serena's, like, her Renfield?"

Rudy slapped the wheel. "Hah! *Yes*, precisely that! Her Renfield."

"Where could she have found someone to do that?"

"Another school in town? Even a runaway, someone she plucked up off the streets. Believe me, she wouldn't be starved for choice."

As the Escalade moved back down the road, as the specks resolved into the shapes of human beings, one question nagged at me.

"You said there were six of these sisters. Did you raise them all in trailer parks and . . . y'know, poorer communities?"

"You really want me to answer?"

Subject Five thumped inside her box, some kind of insectile Morse code. I couldn't root the image of Five's ears out of my head. . . . the tiny divots in the lobes where they'd been pierced at a strip-mall J&CO, same as any other girl.

"Yes," Rudy said finally. "All of them poor white trash. I was surprised how eagerly my offer was accepted by their Minders. I ended up paying a lot less than I'd been willing to. Then again, when you're dealing with people who've never had much of anything, I suppose a little bit of something feels like a lot."

TWENTY
4:02 p.m.

Margaret, I told myself, *once this Escalade stops, after you and this psycho get out, you've got to do something.*

A feeling had been gathering. That of a convicted man being led to the hangman's noose. Or a witch to the pyre. If I didn't at least try to escape, it was over. These men had no vested interest in whether I lived or died. And Serena, she sure as hell didn't care.

I was a cog. Dispensable. Harry, too. Seeing as I had no idea when I'd stop being useful—maybe I'd hit that point already—there was no way to tell when or if Rudy's lapdog might nestle his pistol against the back of my skull and pull the trigger.

Now or never. Now or never. A chant in my head. *Now or never.*

The Escalade rolled to a stop. I took note of the placement of the other vehicles. The Malibu's nose faced the grape field. Jameson would have its keys. Rudy had the Escalade's keys.

But the keys to Harry's Geo were still in the car. Rudy had left them hanging from the ignition cylinder when he'd gotten out.

I stepped from the Escalade with a plan. A stupid one, probably, that could get me and everybody here killed. If it didn't work, Roy might put that bullet in my brain. He'd put one in Harry's head for good measure, because what value was he on his own?

My pulse beat in my throat as I rounded the Escalade's bumper. Harry sat on the hood of his Geo; he looked okay, his eyes clearer. I sent an unvoiced plea across the humid air: *Please, Harr, be ready.*

I fell into lockstep with Rudy as he joined me around the driver's side. I wouldn't say he registered the threat, but Roy—Roy, with his raven's eyes—might have. There was no time. To think, to debate. I had one chance. It wouldn't come again.

—now or never now or never now or never now now NOW NOW NOW

Casually, almost as if I was pointing to something—*Hey, look!*—I let my arm stretch toward Rudy. He turned, brow wrinkling, as my fingers dipped to his hips. *Does he think I'm gonna give his dick a honk?* This nonsensical thought zipped through my brain while my thumb and pointer tweezed the fob in his watch pocket.

With the gentlest tug, the remote control was free. As a first-time pickpocket, I couldn't have done any better.

Roy reacted instantly. Dropping his head, he sprinted right at me. His android-like approach made me fumble the control; it slipped out of my fingers, hit the gravel.

Shit, shit, *shit*—

I dropped to the ground, scrabbling for the fob—a shadow fell over me as somebody, Rudy it must've been, tackled me, throwing me forward with a bone-rattling jolt.

Before I fell, though, I scooped up the control and lofted it in a high arc, over Roy, who leapt to snare it—the control sailed twenty feet, high and true, landing exactly where I'd aimed:

Right in Harry's hands.

"Push the buttons!" I screamed. "*All* of them!"

Bad Harry understood the assignment, bless him.

TWENTY-ONE
4:03 p.m.

Fhook.

That was the sound the Escalade's trunk made when it opened. The one I heard, anyway, lying face down on the gravel.

Hiiiiii-zzzzhiiim.

That was the sound of Five's box riding those polished rails out of the SUV's trunk, lowering to the ground.

"That was a stunningly bad idea, Margaret," said Rudy.

Vapor ribboned from the box as its lid rose, that tungsten netting stretching taught—

From inside came a shattering scream that lifted the starlings off the power lines.

Five smashed into the lid. Its metal buckled, rivets squealing at its stress points.

Pulling my knees under me, I made a dash for Harry's Geo. Rudy's fingers snagged my belt loop, my sneakers slapping cartoon-ishly on the gravel for a few steps before I wrenched free.

"Five," I heard him cajole. "Darling, there's no need to—"

I cranked my head back to see Five slam the lid so hard that the box lifted off the ground and went cartwheeling backward. It struck the Escalade and bounced, landing on its side.

Harry was already behind the wheel. I raced around the Geo's hood as he cranked the key in the ignition; the motor coughed and grinded.

Oh, you shitty little beater you. We spent hours in Auto Shop, doting on you, so don't you dare *not start now.*

The next time Five hurled herself at the lid, the tungsten netting broke cleanly; the strands snapped, settling softly on the gravel.

Through the Geo's windshield, I watched Subject Five emerge from the box.

If a scrap of disbelief remained about the madness Rudy and his team had brought to life, it was erased when that body uncrimped piece by piece and limb by limb.

In the hot haze of that June afternoon, Five looked as if she could've stepped through a dimensional gate from another planet that our strongest telescopes couldn't mark on a stellar map. Every part of her was achingly familiar, and yet none of them belonged. She expanded out of her box, contours swelling as if pumped full of dense chemical compounds—*no, a tube-man,* I thought, *an inflatable tube-man hooked to an air compressor.* She stretched, a child waking from some endless dream.

"What is that?" Harry said, knocked into a state of shock as he cranked the key. "Oh, Mags, what am I looking at?"

Five's body was lean and dry, with the fissured wrinkling of an elephant's trunk; her limbs were translucent sickles and her hands massive, the size of dinner plates, bent at impossible angles against the pipestems of her wrists. She was encased in an armored exoskeleton at certain junctures—plates the thickness of an old man's fingernails—and for the stuttering heartbeat that I held her in my field of vision, I knew Five's skin would be as cold to the touch as frosted lead.

When she leaped, she did so as a grasshopper might. Those

late-summer ones as long as your thumb that hardly seem to move at all when they jump—more a muscular arrow being launched. She went twenty feet into the air, limbs outflung against the canvas of sky, coming down in front of Jameson. A chilly snap bled past the windows. A bone sheared through Five's carapace, a greenstick fracture that shone deliriously white in the sunshine: the insect part of her had made that leap, but the parts that were still human hadn't been able to withstand the impact of coming back to earth.

Jameson's hands went up. They clapped together in prayer. Five's sickle limbs whickered.

Jameson's face slid clean off. It detached from his hairline to the underside of his chin, exposing the inner makings of his head. It would have looked no different had he jammed his face into cheese wire.

The pop of the Geo's solenoid cylinder covered the pissing sound of Jameson's skull evacuating its blood, but I could see it needling out of his cleaved sinus cavities in pressurized jets, the purple stump of his tongue. His brain slid from the shelf of bone above his brow, bumping down his shirt until he was cupping it in his palms, cradling his final dying thoughts. He collapsed to his knees, a boy in church, gagging on the liquor of his halved eyeballs—

The Geo's engine caught. Harry dropped the transmission into drive and stood on the gas pedal, fighting the wheel as the tires flirted with the gully, gravel spitting as the car clung to the road.

A glassy *pop*. A hole appeared in the windshield, two inches below the rearview mirror. I stared back between the seats at the second hole in the back window and past it, saw Roy balanced on the hood of the Malibu with a long-bore rifle. I ducked as a second round slammed into the Geo, juddering the chassis as Harry pulled alongside the Escalade, the SUV's flank snapping off the Geo's side-view mirror as we shot past and into the open road—

I dared another glance back and saw, in the boil of dust left by the Geo's tires, that Roy had turned his attention to Five. She was scrambling into the grapevines, trying to escape, and I hoped to hell she did, but Roy had his rifle on her, tracking her against the green canopy of the vines—lastly I saw Rudy, his face impassive as he watched us go, maybe smiling, but by then we were too far away to know for sure.

TWENTY-TWO
4:29 p.m.

"We go to the police."

Minutes had passed since our escape. I kept checking the rear window, but so far nobody had given chase. Harry made a series of turns, down one side road and onto another, past orchards and fruit stands, a serpentine route that ought to prevent us from being followed.

"Take Martingrove," I said. "It connects to St. Stevens, and we can take it all the way into downtown."

Taking one hand off the wheel, Harry stuck his finger in the hole in the windshield.

"That guy actually tried to kill us," said Harry, awestruck.

He put both hands back on the wheel.

"You heard what I said, Harr?"

"Huh?"

"Martingrove to St. Stevens."

"The cops aren't going to help us." He shook his head. "My cousin Bobby, he got the shit kicked out of him by a few of Niagara Regional's finest. Police brutality. He wasn't even doing nothing, just walking through a vacant lot with a bottle of beer. They started hassling him, shoving him around." Hunching over the wheel. "What are they gonna say when we walk in talking about all this? They're gonna say we're on drugs. They're gonna—"

"I don't care," I said. "That's for them to figure out."

Would the police believe us? Not immediately, no. Fine. Let them think I was nuts.

"You think they know where we live?" said Harry. "Those guys?"

"How should I know?"

"Well, I don't like that. What if they—I mean, what if they go to our houses? Do you think they'd kill our parents?"

The thought had never crossed my mind. "Why would they?"

"How should *I* know? They would've killed us. They're fucking psychopaths."

"Please, Harr. Just drive."

We were nearing the cutoff. A left off First Street would lead us to Martingrove. Ten minutes later we'd be at the police HQ on the corner of Church and Carlisle, next to city hall. Maybe they'd wrap us in a blanket and give us a cup of something hot to drink, like the heroes at the end of action flicks. If this was too big for the local cops, they could call the army. Or the Justice League, or who-the-fuck-ever.

We reached the turn. Harry flicked the blinker. He slowed down . . . then sped up again, blowing past the intersection.

"Harr?"

His eyes were fixed on the road. "I know a shortcut."

We both knew there was no quicker way downtown. Passing the turnoff meant we were heading out to the country again. Nothing but farmsteads and fields.

"Turn back." My voice held a quaver. "Hey. *Turn back.* There's no shortcut."

He whistled tunelessly through the gap in his front teeth. "The police won't help us. They never do."

"Harr . . . ? What are you—"

No. Oh god.

"Look at me, Harry. Right now."

When he glanced over—oh, the wretched cast of his eyes—the day's events replayed themselves at a new refraction.

In this light, I saw Harry pushing past me when I hesitated at the furnace room door. I watched him locate the hiding place for the phone in Allan Teller's closet, as if he'd been told exactly where to look.

And in this light, I could see someone in the shadows behind him, someone who'd been with him from the start, controlling Harry with the ease of a ventriloquist's dummy.

All day. Right from the start. That gentle hand in my tailbone prodding me deeper into these discoveries. Harry Cook.

All Eyez Report to the Queen.

"How long, Harry? How long has Charity been—"

"She's *not* Charity." The skin rippled up his throat. "The two of them look nothing alike." He let out a shuddery breath. "She found me maybe a week after Burning Van. Charity had already gone missing, and you," he said, "weren't around anymore. *She* was. But not so much as something you could see. More like a taste." He licked his lips. "You wouldn't understand. Once I got some, I couldn't control myself."

I'll always have my precious boys. . . . I love them so much I might just snap their fucking necks.

"Pull over, Harry. Right now."

"I can't do that."

"Yes you can. Please. It's not too late. Pull over. Let me out."

"You'll be okay. Really. She doesn't want to hurt you."

"Are *you* saying that, Harr? Or her?"

He sucked at his lip. I wondered if that line, the one separating her (*it?*) from Harry, had gotten so fuzzy he couldn't see it anymore. What would it be like to surrender yourself so fully? Maybe it was a joyful release. The pure joy of letting go.

"Oh god. Please don't do this. You don't *have* to."

"That's the thing, Mags." His hands tightened on the wheel, rubber squeaking between his palms. "I don't have a choice. She's in my *head*."

"Is she in there now?"

"She's never not there."

"If you can fight her just long enough to—"

"You were so brave today." Tears stood in his eyes. "I'm so sorry. About all the deception and trickery and just, y'know, being a sneaky piece of shit."

"You can make it up to me, then. Pull over."

He gritted his teeth. Sweat collected along his hairline, rolling down his cheeks. I'd swear he was trying to fight whatever held him in its thrall . . .

At last, he shook his head. "Sorry. I just can't."

The sight of Harry under the power jack in Auto Shop came back. The interplay of light and shadow halving his face, saintlike to beast-like. Bad Harry, who'd surrender his life for a ten-cent hair clip.

We entered grape country again. The vines climbed the rises in emerald stripes to the foothills of the escarpment. I'd forgotten how beautiful the little part of the world I'd grown up in could be. You get so used to its wonders that they fail to penetrate.

The impulse came to fling the door open and hurl myself out. At this speed I'd go rag-dolling across the concrete. Would I unravel like a bloody ball of yarn? The urge passed.

We drove past two Dominican field hands riding ten-speeds in the breakdown lane. They wore parkas despite the late-afternoon heat. One of them waved at us.

TWENTY-THREE
5:01 p.m.

When we pulled into the potholed parking area under the shadow of Processing Shed 1, a sense of déjà vu hit me.

Lark Hill Farms. The three cavernous processing sheds. Nicknamed the Sweat Box, the Squasher, and Old Reeky.

The first, where endless crates of apples, pears, plums, and apricots—the produce grown on Lark Hill's acreages—were washed of pesticide dust and graded. The second, where the crop yield was pressed in massive industrial juicers. The third, where the fruit that didn't make the grade sat and rotted down to compost.

I'd busted my ass in all three of them, and in the neighboring orchards. Lark Hill was the first summer job for a lot of local kids. The farm hired workers as young as fourteen, paying us piecemeal as pickers: five bucks a crate for apples, pears, plums, apricots. After the school year ended, the familiar refrain from parents—especially the poorer families—was:

Get on your bike, ride over to the Lark, earn yourself a few bucks.

Plum and I spent two summers out in these orchards or stuck in the sheds. Twelve hours, nine-to-nine, combing the low-hanging branches and filling green twenty-gallon crates in the stultifying heat. Bitten by mosquitos and horseflies and stung by the wasps who built their nests underground in the trees' root systems.

At the end of each shift, our hands red and itchy from fruit fuzz, the owner, "Big" Ed Hill, paid us in cash out of a steel lockbox. He'd chintz you if he could. Ed didn't pay for half crates, or even three-quarters. Near the end of the day, Plum and I would dump our apricots into a single crate so one of us could claim it. On the bike ride home, we'd split the five bucks.

Harry parked in the rutted lot. I got out, thinking of Ed Hill. His belly round as a pumpkin with no butt to speak of, the seat of his fruit-spattered jeans hanging like a sail in a dead wind—we used to joke that his ass must've migrated to his gut. Ed's knurled fingers counting bills out of his lockbox. *You sure it was eight crates today, missy? That's a hefty number.* If you told him to go check with the foreman, Ed's eyes would get shrewish. *Oh, you can bet I will. If I find out you fibbed, that's you out on your ear.*

Lark Hill had since gone belly-up. Ed Hill had bolted town, no forwarding address. The sheds lay motionless. The orchards had gone unpicked for many seasons. If you caught yourself downwind of Lark Hill come late August, the stench of rotted fruit was enough to send you staggering.

"This way," Harry said, nodding me along.

I trailed him toward Shed 2. A gust of wind whistled down the rusted eaves, making the sound of a skeletal pair of lips blowing through a steel flute. Bits of abandoned machinery—the tractor with three flat tires, the cherry picker with its boom and basket hanging like a deformed, palsied arm—had been left to disintegrate in the shed's long shadow.

A man had died in this shed. Died, been horribly mutilated, depended which story you chose to believe. The rumor went that a Cuban field hand had gotten sucked into one of the industrial juicing mills. The spindles caught hold of his loose sleeve and corkscrewed it, along with the young man's arms, into its armatures. Depending on which version of the rumor you heard, his arms were torqued apart into thick rags, the flesh sucked off the bones from the shoulders on down, or else they simply exploded into red mist under the unforgiving drive of the mill.

Some people said Ed Hill and one of his foremen buried the Cuban's corpse out in the back forty. Others said Ed dumped the guy at the ER and drove off. Either way, Ed Hill vanished soon after, leaving his orchards and the contents of the shotgun shack he lived in untouched.

According to my father, the rumors were bullshit.

Ed Hill was a drunk, a chiseler, a poor gambler, a welsher on his debts. A truly disgusting combination! I'm guessing some men came a-calling for the money he owed, and Ed pulled a scamper. That, Margaret my love, is the long and short of Mr. Ed Hill, may we never see his kind again.

My dad's version was a lot less fun, so the rumors of the buried field hand persisted.

Harry walked me past a stack of fruit crates; the sun cast bars through their plastic hexagons, imprinting its pattern on his face. The high-sided tin wall of the shed reflected the day's heat.

Harry toed the door open. The shed stretched out in the dim. The machinery still stood. Four juicing units. Hunched metallic monsters seized with disuse, no electricity running to them . . . yet I couldn't shake the feeling that one of them would spring to life, its corroded teeth grinding away.

You best step lively, missy. Big Ed's voice. *One of these babies could suck you right in, just like that Cuban I had to bury.*

Harry and I entered the cavernous space. The wind blew along the corrugated roof, rattling loose rivets—a racing, skittering noise that sounded a bit too much like footsteps.

"This is as far as I can go," Harry said. "I'm sorry again . . . but look, she won't hurt you, okay? She promised."

"What's her promise worth?"

My voice startled a pigeon from the roof girders. When Harry didn't answer, I brushed past him.

The cement pathway narrowed between the juicers. I inhaled the vinegary smell of the ancient fruit stuck to their tines, decaying in the dark hearts of the units.

A line appeared underfoot. Bright yellow, recently spray-painted on the floor.

I followed it. My footsteps echoed. Harry's presence dwindled until the sense came that he'd evaporated, no more substantial than steam off a hot bath.

The shadow of the largest juicing unit fell over me. I heard sly, ferreting movement inside its shell of silent metal: mice or rats or—

I spun on my heels. A rash of shock-sweat broke out down my spine.

Footsteps. I'd heard them, I swear it. A ghostly secondary set a few paces behind me. But nobody was there.

It's that rascally Cuban, I tell ya.

Big Ed again, his voice crawling with worms.

He's come back looking for his arms. Maybe he'll take yours, fibber!

For one terrorized beat I caught the *clop-clop* of work boots. I waited for that field hand to appear around the gun-metal flank of the juicer. A young man whose face had gone blotchy with decay, a winter coat sucked to his chest—*so cold*, his voice as colorless as the unmarked grave Ed Hill had stuffed him into. *So cold here, lady, not like home*—the coat's material brown with dried blood as he staggers toward me, maggots burrowing in his hair, his eyebrows squinching in frustration because he's trying to grab me but can't on account of his arms being torn off: a pair of gummy, festering stumps projecting from the shoulders of his coat—

The line. The yellow line. *Focus, Margaret.* I followed it around the unit to where it terminated at a storage shed within the larger building.

I opened the shed door. The walls were hung with spare parts. Cogs, flywheels, sprockets, and lode-springs, all on hooks.

But that wasn't what my eyes caught. In glancing, yes, but the biggest part of me—the part responsible for the instinctive revulsion that shuddered through me—was focused on what lay on the floor.

A large woolen *something*. It had been wrapped in Christmas icicle lights, dazzlingly white. It resembled a moldy sleeping bag you'd find in an attic . . . or a milkweed pod, the kind Plum and I used to squeeze until they burst to release their sticky juice.

I drew closer. The sac or pod was tapered at both ends. Its exterior was a papery, woolen white. I didn't want to touch it. But when I did—I couldn't help myself—it crackled under my fingertips. Recoiling, I wiped my hands on my jeans.

In the glare of the icicles I saw a slit running the length of it, end to end. A stretched, lipless mouth.

With that same disembodied helplessness, I watched my hands reach into that sunken cleft. That crackle again, particles coming loose as my fingers curled under those lips—it was sturdier than it looked, an inner flex of cartilage—my mouth puckering as my fingers sank deeper, the tips brushing something inside: a smooth soapy contour that made me gag, but I was past caring. I had to see.

The lips gave way as I pried them apart, the woolen layer warm and feverish against my palms until it sprang open, a mouth yawning wide and I understood, too late, that this thing had already been opened.

It wasn't a sleeping bag or a milkweed pod. This was a cocoon. It cracked open like a sarcophagus, releasing the trapped scent of its occupant—Irish Spring soap, Plum's brand, eternally on sale at Price Chopper.

TWENTY-FOUR
5:16 p.m.

Disbelief hit me, but it passed quickly, just as when a lake wave slaps you without warning: the initial shock, that alkaline burn in the sinuses, then everything's flat again.

Her face stared up from its final resting spot inside that shell.

It's me, Cherr.

She was naked. Her arms tucked to her chest and her feet pointed

252 — NICK CUTTER
down. She rocked inside her cradle, as weightless as a pile of goose feathers.

down. She rocked inside her cradle, as weightless as a pile of goose feathers.

I screamed. Deafeningly loud. Then my jaw snapped shut.

Her eyes were gone. Two pits rimmed by her eyelids. Her mouth hung open in a stupid gawp. Her teeth and gums and tongue. Gone. At first it seemed a trick of the light, but no: just her lips were left and those had gone wrinkled, as lips must look after months underground.

The three holes in her face reminded me of a bowling ball.

My fingertips moved across her cheek, the bridge of her nose, up her forehead until they were in the coarse strands of her hair . . .

. . . they sank into a depression. A cleft in her scalp. Her *skull*.

Withdrawing my fingers, I turned the body over. I thought it might get tangled in the icicle lights, but it was so dehydrated that it rolled frictionlessly. You'd think it had been coated in rosin.

I spied another pair of lips running from the base of her spine to the top of her head—the skin rising in jagged peaks down the length of that massive spinal wound. I understood that nothing could be inside anymore. Her leg holes were just that: *holes*. Whatever had come out of her had taken everything with it, leaving an emptiness where Plum had once been.

This was different than Estelle. It was worse.

It was as though—my mind screamed this possibility at me—a *new* face had grown behind Charity's. A face that had developed slowly, its features establishing themselves . . . and then that face had detached, pulling away with a throaty suck as a second inner head split the back of Plum's skull open to let this updated version emerge.

The new version had the old version's eyes. It had kept those.

"The caterpillar goes in."

THE QUEEN — 253

TWENTY-FIVE
5:18 p.m.

The voice was in the shed with me.

"The butterfly comes out."

When she emerged from behind sacks of fertilizer stacked where the tin walls met, the sight conjured such a feeling of sickness that it was all I could do to not scream. I stuffed the heel of my palm into my mouth, mashing my lips, shoving the sound back.

In the shed's incurious light, the girl—naked, same as Plum in her cocoon—looked nothing like Charity. Plum's body had been solid, dense, practical. This one seemed not to occupy the space she was in but be cut from it somehow; the atoms surrounding her vibrated into microscopic explosions.

She slid around the fertilizer sacks, presenting herself. She was candlewax-pale, the kind of skinny a degree shy of malnourished, except there was an obvious strength collected at her shoulders and hips—I couldn't see the jut of her ribs, but that was because she didn't have those: her torso was cylindrical, banded, dipping to a smooth vacancy between her legs.

A pair of nubbins projected from her back, Vee-ing from either side of her throat. *Wings.* The stubs, anyway. Either they'd never quite grown in or else she'd clipped them to appear more like us.

If so, it hadn't helped. Yes, this thing had two arms and two legs and a head; it had the same coral-blue eyes as Plum and a nose with the same pert upturn, but when it smiled, revulsion barreled through me. It wasn't anything human.

I took a step back as it—*she*—came at me in eerie mincing steps. She could've been moving on a million legs, centipede legs that feathered over the floor.

She's going to eat me; after all this, that's all I was to her: a meal—

She stopped next to the cocoon.

Gripping the lips of the ragged wound running down Plum's spine, this other thing—Plum 2.0—pulled it open.

I whispered: "No. Please, don't."

I stared, unable to wrench my eyes away. The fatigued flesh of Plum's caverned corpse creaked as the trench in its back widened.

Still grinning, the other one slid inside Plum's remains. The note of legs slithering down vacant leg holes. A dead-leaf rustle as this thing tucked itself inside its old host.

When it was done, she turned—inside Plum's body, she turned—to peer out at me from behind my friend's empty face.

"Whenever I can't sleep, I climb back inside. It feels so much of home."

Those bright blue eyes staring from Plum's sockets.

I never knew what happened after that. I rocked on my heels, chin tucked, blinking sluggishly like a cow smashed between the eyes with a poleaxe. I let it happen—at this point, I was so happy to just let go. I blacked out and—

TWENTY-SIX

—came to in Harry's car.

"Take it easy. I'm not going to hurt you."

My eyelids came unglued. My head throbbed like a rotten tooth. We were on Grapeview Road—on my left, McIvor's Fruit Stand flashed past in the paling sunshine.

She sat behind the wheel. Dressed now. A long black evening gown with a high throat and black gloves with holes cut in the knuckles, same as a race car driver. She could pass for human if you didn't know. High voltage crackled through the wires of her unearthly body.

I cleared my throat and asked, conversationally: "So, how long since you . . . ?"

Hatched.

"Were born? That happened a few days after you last saw Charity. On the swing set, remember? After that, Charity made her way to Lark Hill. She found a quiet, safe place."

So that would make it roughly a month by now.

"And so it's been you, then? The girl people have been seeing around school?"

A nod. "Serena. It's a nice name, isn't it?"

The creature who'd named itself Serena smiled. Her teeth were straight and white, but each one was worried down to a point.

"You took those guys. Chad and Allan and—"

"*Took?*" She *tsk*ed. "They came with me."

A shiver went through me. "The way the rats were happy to follow the Pied Piper."

"Wasn't it kids who followed him?"

"How much of Charity is still in there?"

"All of her? None of her? Hard to say. I can still feel her. A radio station that comes into range from time to time. Or the buzz of a confused bee in a rain barrel." She looked at me momentarily, lips pursed. "How else could I know all that stuff on the recordings? I can even summon her voice if I need to."

She demonstrated: "See, Cherr? Don't I sound just like her? It's like there's one wheel, and sometimes I'll let her drive. But mostly it's me." Serena's jaw flexed, uncommon bones moving under her skin. "Whenever I want, it's me."

I checked the side-view mirror. A white delivery van drove behind us. I could make out Harry behind the wheel.

"Why him? Of everyone at Northfield, why Harry?"

"That was Charity's choice. She wanted him. And your English teacher, too. You shouldn't be all that surprised, Margaret. Your best friend had jealousies, same as anyone."

More puzzle pieces slotted into place. Mr. Foster, for pushing me toward that writing program. Harry, for being with me at Burning Van.

The men responsible for pulling me and Plum apart.

"You petty fucking bitch."

Serena laughed gaily. "A bitch indeed. Petty, pretty, and oh so tricky."

"Where are you taking me?" I asked tiredly.

"You'll see. It's not far now."

"Your creator's still hunting for you, you know. He's insane, by the way."

"Oh, I know. He'll be meeting us there."

"As soon as you stop, I'm going to get out and walk away." I rooted myself against the seat. "You can sic Harry on me, I don't care."

She patted my knee. "Turn that frown upside down!" Setting one finger on my chin, she applied pressure until I was facing her. "You know I can make you, right?"

Next, something sideswiped me. The feel of being smacked in the face with a cold, wet rag.

Touch me.

The command filled my head. It ran straight down my arm. Then my hand was creeping across the seat-rest, my fingers running over her shoulder and down her back to fondle something attached to her spine, flabby and pulsating, a clutch of overgrown kidney beans—

The pull relented. I snatched my hand back.

"Now, I promise never to do that again." Serena favored me with a sharkish grin. "It's an invasion I'd rather avoid . . . plus, Charity already did it to you once, didn't she? Her very first time. That was an accident, though. She felt bad about it."

"What are you talking about?"

"She was just getting a sense of her powers, Margaret. Come on, you remember."

That last evening in my trailer. Me and Plum, alone. After our day at the lake, sun-drugged, tweezing sunburned skin off each other's shoulder blades. I'd woken up sweaty and tingling; Plum had fallen asleep tucked against me so tightly that our skin peeled apart like a huge Band-Aid when I broke away from her.

I'd undressed without waking Plum. Got in the shower. The bathroom door slid open on its accordion hinges. She stepped into the stall with me.

We'd seen each other naked before. In locker rooms, at the run-down waterpark off Highway 403 when the slide sucked our bathing suits up the cracks of our asses, in our own bedrooms where we traded tops and jeans, unashamed. But never in my Hallmark trailer shower, narrow as the hull of a surface-to-air missile.

Plum, hey—a trace of alarm in my voice, but her fingers, wet with water, touched the swell of my hip. A charge fled into my bones, into every skin cell.

Tell me. Plum's voice in my head. The leaden toll of a cathedral bell.

Tell me you want me. Tell me you would do anything for me. Tell me you'll never hurt me and never leave me.

Her voice was on me, *in* me.

TELL ME

The sensation was that of a dam bursting, the release of a pent-up passion that had been simmering for years. I'd wanted Charity forever, hadn't I? Her touch, her body, the softness of her lips. All I wanted was to please her and make her feel safe.

She set her fingers under my throat, the tips resting on the rounded knobs where my bones met; her other hand moved downwards, not making contact with my skin but achingly close. A warning went off in my head: *This isn't right, I don't really want this.* But a stronger voice overrode this protest: *Of course you do, silly. It's what you've always wanted. Me, only and ever me.*

Our lips not touching, not quite, but the heat between them sent needles radiating along my jaw, down into my belly—my hands no longer wholly part of me, my brain bobbing like an apple in a bucket as I pressed my body into hers—

It was Plum who reared back, her eyes wide and traumatized. Her spine hit the shower wall as she mumbled, *I didn't—oh, Cherr, oh no,* and stumbled out, leaving me standing there.

I found her curled up on the bed, weeping.

What's the matter? Why did you leave?

She gathered the bedsheets, wringing them in her hands. *You didn't want that, did you? You don't like me that way.*

Plum was right—I'd never experienced that specific longing for her. But how else could I explain what came over me? A raging desire I hadn't felt for anyone, not once in my life.

I'm sorry, Cherr. I don't know why I did it. Don't know how I did it.

I liked it, I told her, though I wasn't sure that was truthful. *Don't worry, I won't tell anyone. I mean, if that's what you're worried about.*

The look she gave me held a great deal of fondness, but also—was I wrong?—a note of cold loathing. *I wasn't worried at all.*

Let's just go back to sleep, okay? Which is what we'd done, on opposite sides of my bed.

"I wasn't born yet, not that night," Serena said, her voice pulling me back. "But *she* sure remembers. She feels guilty." A roll of her eyes. "On and on and on, blah blah. Like, shut *up*."

We cut down a service road. The architecture of downtown

St. Catharines lay flat and sun-dogged in the middle distance. Serena slowed. The van sped up. Harry passed us in the opposite lane. He was all dressed up, crisp black suit coat and tie.

The van settled in ahead of us, brake lights reddening. Serena dogged the van to an intersection on the corner of Glenlake and Fairview. When the van turned right, she followed.

I pulled out the iPhone and checked the time.

TWENTY-SEVEN
5:58 p.m.

The parking lot of the St. Catharines Golf and Hunt Club was stuffed to capacity. Until Harry's Geo rolled in, there wasn't a single shitbox to be found. The cheapest ride was probably an Acura ILX, and that could've belonged to the kitchen staff.

Serena pulled into one of the few empty spots at the back of the lot. Harry drove the van down the service road, passing a sign that read LOADING BAY.

Something big must be going down. A gala, a soirée, whatever rich people called them. By now almost everyone was inside. I spotted a few stragglers by the entrance dressed in cocktail finery, their tuxes and furs.

Serena produced her own iPhone from the folds of her dress. The *whoosh* of a text being sent.

"Daddy has to know where the party's happening. He'll be here in two shakes."

"What do you have planned?" I asked, not really wanting to know.

She winked. Her eyelid went *pip!*, the sound of a can of soda being popped. "You're the writer, Margaret. You should know how these stories end."

"What kind of story is this?"

"Oh, the best kind. The one where the poverty-stricken rise up and do what they always do every fifty years or so. All throughout history."

She opened the door and stepped out. Sunk her head down to peer in at me.

"They eat the rich."

She shut the door. I opened mine and got out. Our faces met across the roof.

"I really should have figured this out before now, shouldn't I?"

For the first time, Serena's smile appeared genuine. "I'm honestly shocked it all came together so perfectly. I can't believe it worked."

She crossed her arms on the Geo's roof, chin balanced on her wrists. "To answer your question, yes, for a smart person you were astonishingly clueless today. I mean, *really* dumb."

"Thanks."

"No, thank *you*."

I nodded at the club. "I'm not going with you. Unless you make me."

Serena pushed off the roof and began walking toward the doors. The lot lights popped on against the gloaming dusk.

"I promised to only do that once," she called back. "But where else are you going to go?"

"Home. To bed, to sleep. When I wake up, I guess I'll find out what you did."

"Oh poo. That's no fun." She turned, arms crossed and elbows cupped. "Listen, if you come, I'll give you the chance to save one or two of the shitheads in there. They don't all have to die. But if you've had too long a day, well . . ."

She flounced off toward the club. This time she didn't look back.

They don't all have to die.

Frosted lights sparkled on the mulberry trees banding the lane leading to the club's doors. Buttery light poured through the windows.

The closest I'd ever come to this place was when Plum and I used to ride our bikes down the highway and see the members scurrying after their balls in checkered pants.

The stragglers had gone inside. A security guard was posted at the entry. The cuffs of my jeans were splattered with storm drain muck, my sweatshirt on inside-out and reeking of adrenal sweat. No way was that guy letting me inside.

But as Serena approached the doors, the guard staggered backward; he fell hard against the wall, slumped like a drunk on a month-long bender. His eyes were rolled back in his skull, white as Ping-Pong balls, by the time I walked past.

TWENTY-EIGHT
6:04 p.m.

Inside the club's ballroom, a reception was in full swing. None of the faces were familiar—wait, there was Leo Zlatar, who everyone knew to call when they got hit by a car—but if they could afford the club's membership fee, they must represent the most monied families in our city.

Everyone was dressed in suits and flowy dresses. Jewels dripped at wrists and necklines. A woman in a white evening dress sat behind a grand piano tinkling a muted version of Taylor Swift's "Cornelia Street."

A potted tree sat on a stage set against the bay windows overlooking the putting green. The tree had been trimmed into three prongs. A trident. A banner aproning the stage read, in big tinselly letters:

THE LIVING MEMORIAL—A CELEBRATION OF HOPE

This was for the missing boys, wasn't it? A money-grab or fundraiser or just, I don't know, whatever wealthy people do to keep their spirits soaring.

I was spotted immediately. Same as in a horror movie, when a living person tried to blend in among a crowd of rotting zombies. The guests' heads cranked in unison, their eyeballs sucking onto me.

"What are you doing here?"

Miranda Lancaster was stunning in a floor-length, form-fitting, low-key slutty dress that glittered over her curves.

"No, seriously." Her eyes cast around for someone to help. "How did you get in, Margaret? You can't be here—wait, no, *can you?*"

The gears were winding in Miranda's brain. She knew my family had come into money. Did that mean I'd gained entry to her world? The possibility clearly horrified her.

"Miranda, listen to me. We need to get everyone out."

"Oh, you'd like that, wouldn't you? This is not *about* Charity, okay?" She flapped her hands, upset. "I know you think that's unfair, but you couldn't be any more disrespectful, showing up here and trying to cause a scene."

I scanned the crowd for a reasonable face. Finding none, I snatched Miranda's wrist.

"Just you, then. Find anyone you care about, take them, and go."

"You're so *gross*," she hissed, twisting out of my grasp. I gave up, shouldering past her. Miranda let out a bleat of disgust.

I couldn't see Harry. He'd driven that van into the service entrance. Probably a rental, or stolen even. Except I guess Serena wouldn't need to steal anything, would she? She could just waltz into the nearest Hertz and walk out with the keys. She could walk in *anywhere* and walk out with *anything*—

Someone bumped into me.

"Mr. Foster?"

He broke into an idiot's grin. "Margaret, heeeey." Pawing at my sleeve. "You working on a new story? Got to keep those writing muscles sharp . . ."

He trailed off. His eyes were soaped windows. I could almost see the puppeteer's strings rising off his shoulders, elbows, the top of his skull.

"Come with me."

I'd save Mr. Foster. That's what I'd do. I don't know what use it would be, but maybe he could pass the rest of his days in a home, fussed over by good-natured nurses.

He let out a nervous giggle as I took his hand. "Where are we . . . ?"

"Don't worry, we're going someplace fun."

A few guests took note of us. Maybe they figured Mr. Foster was drunk—he had the soft, doltish look of one—and I was his mortified daughter. I'd guided him halfway toward the exit when he started to squirm.

"I, I—I can't." He shook his head, big childish sweeps. "Mommy wouldn't want me to."

"*Shshsh.* Mommy said it was okay. Mommy said you could leave."

"*NO!*"

Mr. Foster began to squeal, these air-cutting piglet noises. He pulled out of my grip and fell, sprawled on the ground. He wept messily, chest hitching and snot webbing from his nose.

"Mommy!" he shrieked. "*Mommy!*"

A woman in a lavender dress bent over him. "We're all upset," she soothed. "But chin up. Those boys need our hopes and prayers."

Right then, my attention was snatched by the sight of a black helicopter touching down in the middle of the putting green. The *thop* of its blades vibrated the bay windows. Quite a few guests took note, but none of them did anything—the air of the ballroom was oddly subdued, almost narcotic.

Rudy and Roy exited the helicopter, ducking in the rotor wash that snapped at their clothes. Roy was carrying a duffel bag. They moved toward the club, on around the caddy shack as the helicopter rose back into the sky.

Once the commotion died down, a man stepped onto the stage alongside that three-pronged shrub. The room turned solemnly toward him.

"Good evening, everyone. Most of you know me, but for those who don't, my name is Quinn Dearborn. I'm Chad's father. That's my wife, Sue-Ellen, down there."

A woman stood at the foot of the stage. She had the withered look of a mushroom forgotten at the back of the vegetable crisper.

"I want to thank the club for letting us use this annual gala occasion not to mourn, but to hope," Chad's father continued. "Hope is what's gotten us through these last few impossible weeks. A hope for the safe return of our sons." His voice warbled. "Our precious little boys."

The lights dimmed. A movie screen lowered behind the stage. "We Are Warriors" by Avril Lavigne started playing from somewhere.

A slideshow began. Photos of Chad and Will and Allan Teller. Riding trikes with tinsel ribbons knotted to the handlebars. Grinning gap-toothed at Disney World, a pair of mouse ears stuck on their heads.

A slip of light as the ballroom doors opened. Rudy and Roy ducked inside.

Something zipped past my face. In the dim it was hard to say where it was, but a bolt of fear shot through me at its familiar buzz—

TWENTY-NINE

6:11 p.m.

Put your eyes somewhere else, bitch, Rudyard thought, *or I'll pluck them out.*

The woman wore a cream taffeta evening gown, a getup that must pass for high fashion in this one-horse town. She was staring at him. The blood on him, specifically.

It was a medley of blood, actually. Some of it Jameson's—Rudy had gotten it on his pants when he'd hurdled Jameson's corpse where it lay in the gully. His expensive Harvard-educated brain cradled in his hands, his cleaved-open face forcefully ejecting his life's juices.

But the lion's share of the blood on Rudy belonged, sadly, to Subject Five.

He'd chased her into the grape field, shouting to Roy—*Don't shoot!*—and to his beloved Five—*Don't run, precious, nobody wants to hurt you!*—but Roy either hadn't heard him or had his own agenda, because Rudy could only watch as Five's head splintered against the backdrop of the vines, the sound of the bullet's impact muffled and damp.

By the time Rudyard reached her, a gassy smell had begun to weep out of her. Her carcass emitted cracks and pops as it cooled, sounds an old furnace makes when it stops pumping heat. Tiny blood-slicked creatures scuttled from the broken bowl of her skull, mites or aphids, parasites at any rate, the sight rousing the memory of his sister with ants tunneling into her pale blue eyes. He'd yearned to hold Five in his arms, but when he knelt to get closer, one of her limbs had scythed—her nerves firing a last senseless fusillade—nearly lopping his head off at the neck.

He'd slapped Roy for his transgression. The man took it stoically. They'd dragged Jameson's body out to join Five's and thrown a tarp over them both. Later—if there *was* a later—he'd have a team return to collect them.

Presently, Rudy scanned the ballroom. Everyone was staring with bovine fascination at the screen. The towheaded ragamuffins in the slideshow must be the missing boys. This shindig was for them, wasn't it? These clowns had no idea. If they knew, *really* knew, they wouldn't want those boys back. What would be returned to them now? Their parents would take one look at their sons and go stark blithering mad.

He had to hand it to his creation. Subject Six had set this up with laudable precision. Rudy had the distinct impression of being led down the kill chute, the iron bars waiting to clap around his neck for the bolt that would get driven through his temple. Still, he'd been in tighter spots. Ever since that day in the jungle, his life had been borrowed against fate.

And yet, the long odds energized him. He would secure his subject. He'd whisk her away to a safe spot. There he could explain her purpose, her value. He could express his love for her. And yes, study her.

Perhaps she was fertile. Perhaps she could make more just like her. Or slightly better.

If everyone in this room had to die to afford Rudy that chance— and he did mean every man jack of them, by fire or lead or his own furious hands—that should be considered a fair price to pay for scientific progress.

Roy sidled up. He unzipped the duffel bag. Inside, weaponry winked. Rudy stayed his loyal companion with a nod. *Not yet. Let's keep our powder dry.*

The ceiling. High, bowed, ambiguously cathedral.

Was something up there? Massing at the vent, clustered around its four-sided diffuser—their gathering drone pushing against the music—

THIRTY

6:16 p.m.

"What are you doing here?"

Harry, natty in his rental tux. I reached out and touched his cheek. He swatted my hand away. "She said she wouldn't force you to come. She *promised* me—"

"I followed her in," I said. "She said I could save some of them."

Some old guy shushed me. "Fuck off, dude," Harry said without looking at him. He had my elbow, steering me toward the exit. "You need to *go*, Mags. You can't be—oh shit."

I followed his gaze to the main doors. Which were now chained and locked shut with a padlock. Mr. Foster skulked away from them, his job done . . . and I could make out dark, darting atoms occupying the airspace he'd departed.

"Mags, you have to get out of here." Harry glanced around, a rat in a trap. "You don't want to be here for what's coming."

The slideshow kept playing. The song rose to its glittering crescendo.

"There's only one way out." He pointed to the left of the stage. "But that's—"

He went silent. The crowd shifted. Cattle in a field as a storm brewed over the hillside. A wire of tension fled across the dark space.

Screee . . . screeee . . . screeeeeee . . .

THIRTY-ONE
6:19 p.m.

A smell wafted through the ballroom. Rancid grease and something else, even worse—the gassy stink of a roach's lair.

Something zipped again past the nape of my neck. More, so many more, were flitting amid the guests. One woman flapped a distracted hand—a flash of gold trickling down her neckline—then another hand, another, all over the ballroom.

Screeee . . . screeee . . .

The music had stopped, but the slideshow continued to play. There was little Allan Teller with chocolate cake smeared adorably over his face . . .

Screeee . . .

That eye-watering noise was joined by others: a laughing hiss like the air squeezed out of a busted accordion . . .

When they finally appeared, it was with the logic of a bad dream—that's how it must have dawned on the gala guests as they saw the cart wheeled through the extra-wide kitchen door and into the ballroom.

On the screen: a prepubescent Will Stinson aiming a BB gun at the camera . . .

In the ballroom: two grotesque shapes propped on a long banquet cart.

A tablecloth draped the cart. In the center, between those jiggling shapes, sat what I swore was a $2.99 McCain Deep'n Delicious cake. Candles were jammed in it, throwing shadows against the heaps.

Screee . . .

What I saw resembled two enormous Jell-O molds, the ones from the '70s, stuffed with miniature marshmallows and canned fruit.

Serena was behind the banquet cart, pushing it. The cart's wonky wheel was making that *scree*. The cart wobbled, seesawing side to side with the gentle list of its bounty.

The woman nearest to me had gone pale as cream. Chad's father stood at the dais with his hands at his throat, his fingers crawling under the collar of his dress shirt.

The cart came to rest. Its cargo quivered. The kitchen door cracked open as something came jangling into the ballroom. It moved all bent-over, as if its bones had been broken and set badly; it skittered across the carpet, dragging its tangled anatomy to the side of the cart—

In the pin-drop silence, this one clambered onto the cart with the two Jell-O things. They looked human in the broadest brushstrokes. Arms too long or skinless, legs atrophied into their bulging, tortured mass—I could see feet sticking out at the bottom, toes wiggling—and heads nothing but famished skulls.

There were more of those airborne flickers now, too, but they seemed ignorable in comparison to what sat on the cart.

On the screen: the three missing boys, shirtless at the beach, grinning . . .

And on the cart sat what had become of Chad and Will and Allan.

Two of their bodies were monstrously overripe. Their dirt-caked flesh wept science-class globs. The third one, the one that could still move, had the appearance of bits of wood tied loosely with twine.

One of the bulbous things' faces had gone the speckly black of a decayed banana. Its eyes peered blindly from sockets, a pair of pearl onions. The other one was bald as an egg. Some unimaginable pressure had sucked everything back into its skull, as if its brain had been eaten away to let its face cave into the space where it had been.

The skeleton-y one scampered between the two jiggling lumps. Tending to them, licking and cooing in the voice of a rusted hinge.

"*Eeee-eeee-eeee*," it grated. "*Lovely so lovely so—*"

Someone in the crowd giggled: a high, skating note.

My gaze fled up to the ceiling. I could see them then.

The wasps.

Tens of thousands were up there. They were coming in through the air duct, spreading across the ceiling in dark strings.

Serena strode before the banquet cart. In each hand she held a lit Canada Day sparkler. She spun them in circles, wheeling in her evening dress, she was breathless, her chest heaving—

Positively *radiant*.

The wasps began to buzz down from the ceiling as Serena bowed to the crowd.

"Rejoice! Your prayers worked! Your missing boys have come back!"

THIRTY-TWO

6:23 p.m.

What happened over the next thirty seconds was impossible to describe in any sane way. For me, the action unfolded as a series of thumb-swipes on a Facebook page: a JPEG doomscroll of some unspeakable art installation.

In the first thumb-scroll, I started to run. But not toward the main doors. Not the fire exit, either. I remembered what Harry said. The direction he'd told me to run.

So I did. Straight at the banquet cart.

Directly at the missing boys.

I had to get past them, into the kitchen. You could say that decision saved me, if you want to call it that. It also happened to give me the best view of the fates of Will Stinson and Chad Dearborn.

I was closest to them when they—

In the second thumb-scroll, the wasps descended in a grainy cloud, attacking the guests. I collided with a man sporting a walrus mustache, wild fright in his eyes; he clutched at me and I spotted a wasp stuck on the side of his eye—a fat writhing jelly bean—and next his eye was full of blood, that quick, a squib exploding in his eyeball, and I spun off him, a running back eluding a tackler, sprinting as fast as my legs could carry me.

In the third thumb-scroll, Serena swung onto the banquet cart with an elegant sweep. Something was happening under her dress—it was as though her body was coming apart in savage sections—

The ballroom burst into hysterical shrieking and the mad crash of bodies. I trucked for that kitchen. That's where the loading bay should be. It was where Harry's van must be, too—the van he'd driven the boys in, no doubt, their bodies strapped down in the back . . . If the loading bay was there, and if the doors were unlocked, and if the van was idling with the keys in the ignition . . .

If, if, if.

Serena stood on the cart between the boys. In her hand: a glittering butcher knife. Amid the screams, she pushed one of the boys' heads casually to one side and plunged that knife into his neck.

The screams intensified; they had a childish quality, and I realized that at a certain pitch an adult's screams sound no different than a kid's. A few men had grabbed chairs, hurling them at the bay windows. The tempered glass just flexed with a *woww-woww* sound, flinging the chairs back at them.

With brutal casualness, Serena sawed the blade deep into one of the boys—I think it was Will—slitting his throat and carving down his sternum. It took no effort at all. She could've been cutting crustless bread.

Will opened up as if there were a trick zipper running from his throat to his groin. His skin came apart with the fatigued rubbery squeak of a beach ball ripped in half. His head and his caved-in face, they angled back as his skin *shrugged* down his shoulders, a velvet robe slipping off. His naked clavicles shone white as nautilus shells.

Will's body held its shape for an instant—whatever had been nesting inside him was the only thing providing any structure— before it collapsed, wadding up like sheets of soggy fleece. What came out of him was almost as big as its host; something soft and gelatinous that broke through the cleaved rib cage riding a stinking broth of putrefied tissue and impacted organs, liver and kidney and pancreas so dry that they hit the carpet and burst open, old logs spurting sawdust.

I beheld a creature soft in most places but hard in some. The gleam of exoskeleton or of exposed bone. It lay on the floor in its own afterbirth, squealing. The sense came that it didn't have long to live—that it had used up most of its energy in the effort of being born.

The Allan-Teller-thing tried to coax the horrible abortion up.

"Come, little one," I heard him hiss as he prodded the flabby, milky-eyed thing. "Don't disappoint Mother."

By then, most guests were crushed at the main doors. They shoved into them, ignoring the chains and lock, made stupid in their frenzy. A man in a herringbone jacket grabbed a woman by her hair and jerked her to the ground. Another one in a Mr. Peanut tuxedo was pulling himself up a thick gold curtain rope to reach a casement window—the wasps swarmed him, and the man fell screeching . . .

The Teller-thing saw me. Its skinless mouth stretched in a knowing leer.

Run, Beefster! its eyes cheered. *Run, you poor dumb bitch!*

One of the wasps touched on my forearm. It was the size of a thumb. I slapped it off with a cry of horror.

Serena watched me flash by. Her dress had torn down the front so that I could see—

(*fuck me oh fuck me*)

—that everything below her navel was not physically human.

Her sex parts were now *out*. Outside of her body. Her skin had folded down and open, these trapdoors of flesh that made me think of the numbered cubbies on the Advent calendars my mom used to buy around Christmastime—and from those cubbies sprung hard tubes with the sheen of bamboo. The tubes were sunk into Chad Dearborn's exposed spine, pumping and pumping. Serena's teeth skinned back from her lips in an inhuman grimace as Chad bucked under the strain, his head swinging as his eyes stared out of his ruined face.

When Chad tore in half, it was louder than with Will, and the sound was very human: a snapping crunch as his upper half separated from his lower in a vicious corkscrew and something sluiced out.

And this time, I saw everything. My brain couldn't censor it.

What Chad's body birthed was a fusion of human and insect about the size of a six-year-old boy, except not boyish at all. It writhed, a landlocked tadpole, between its host's legs.

Shouldering into the kitchen, I fell and went skidding across the tiles. My chest slammed the leg of a prep table and I nearly bit my tongue in half.

I hauled myself up, breath whinnying out of my mouth. The screams in the ballroom reached a lunatic pitch. The kitchen door was still swinging on its hinges as I stumbled back to it. Past the door, the guests' bodies resembled TV snow: balls of static bouncing randomly off one another in their panicked idiocy.

From within the throng came the crumpling *boom* of a shotgun. A man in a waxed hunting jacket flew back. There was Rudy, stomping through the ballroom with a twelve-gauge, stepping over a woman convulsing on the floor.

He was making his way toward the kitchen, his face contorting as he stalked through the wasps. The shotgun barked again. The wad-cutting round tore a woman in a flared midi-dress right in half. Her torso skipped across the carpet until it came to rest under a table.

Rudy strode determinedly forward, his legs starting to wobble—

THIRTY-THREE
6:24 p.m.

When the wasps stole the first eye, the left one, the loss arrived painlessly: a collection of pressure, tension, release. Rudy's rods and cones continued to broadcast, first in milk and then in mud, before the left side of his world went dark. Rudyard barely felt it.

He could still see *her*, though. Margaret. She'd made it into the kitchen. Hah. Clever lass. He'd join her there. They could hunker down and wait out the deluge. Play board games! *Haaaaa . . .* the wasps. Under his shirt now. Crawled in the vents between the buttons, the sneaky boogers. Up his legs, tickling him, *tee-hee*, but *oh!* How sharp their stings. A million Three Torches matchboxes stuffed with a million little deaths. Their venom had a narcotizing effect; a wintergreen cool spread over his skin.

Before the wasps made a home of his second eye, before blindness stormed in, he saw his precious subject. Six, oh Six! She was dancing in the Ant's embrace. The two of them dervishing about, kicking their heels; they performed an immaculate reverse fleckerl, the Ant dipping Six until her raven hair neatly swept the floor—and froze, both of them, staring right at him.

Everything then went black. Rudyard stumbled forward in the dark. He could have been crying or maybe he was laughing madly, impossible to tell because the wasps were in his ears, crowding down the canals and chewing into his eardrums.

—it hurts Elizabeth hurts so bad but Rudy did it your li'l Rudy your baby bro christ they're in my eyes Lizzie my brains oh heavens to betsy oh jesus i can feel them squirming is this how it felt when the ants loved you Lizzie your beautiful blue eyes the sun burning in each strand of your hair the stars Lizzie my queen did you ever think you'd get eaten alive by beauty Lizzie—

THIRTY-FOUR
6:26 p.m.

The kitchen door didn't have a dead bolt. *Shit.* I scanned for something to block it with. Rudy. The prick was still coming.

The kitchen was a silvery oasis. It took one heartbeat to itemize the flattop range, the hood exhausts, deep-basined sinks, shelving units, deep fryers and prep benches, an industrial washing machine and deep-freeze, a deli slicer and dough mixer, a side office marked

MANAGER, corkboards with menus push-pinned to them—*Monday Special: Beef Wellington*—pots and pans dangling on hooks.

None of it seemed especially helpful right now, *fuck*.

Setting my shoulder to the nearest prep table, I was dismayed to find it had been bolted to the floor. Blitzed on adrenaline as I was, I wasn't nearly strong enough to drag the stove or anything else over to bar the door—

Glancing back out the porthole, my dismay doubled: Rudy was almost there. His face shuddered under a blanket of wasps. He marched blindly, his shotgun having been dropped a few paces back. He clawed at his face, ripping wasps off in pulpy gobs.

—wait, the door *did* have locks, just not where my eyes had been focused. The bolts were on the top and bottom.

I slammed the top one home with my palm. Stomped the other one shut with my foot just as Rudy's face squashed against the porthole. Both his eyes had burst. His sight leaked down his cheeks in blood-veined streams. The rank stench of his body wafted under the door.

The buzz of those wasps prickled under the door, too. There was a gap big enough for them to squiggle under.

Rudy grinned at me. His mouth was crammed full of wasps. His knees gave out. He slipped down, out of sight. He must have come to rest right against the door, because the air coming under it cut way down. His body must be acting as a draft stopper.

But the wasps had a million ways to get in here.

I raced around the kitchen, pinpointing every grate, duct, vent, anything they might enter by. The hoods over the stove were covered by interwoven metal mesh. I set my fingers on it—

Pink!

Something hit the mesh from inside the vent. The wasps were already in there.

The one big air duct—probably the outtake fan—was grated. I

snapped its metal flaps shut. I'd have to cover it with something more durable ASAP, but for now I prayed it'd hold.

I returned to the door, scanning the ballroom. Although only a handful of minutes had passed since Serena appeared with the banquet cart, the room had gone still. The guests lay on the floor in tangled piles. Wasps hung everywhere. The densest swarms clustered at the main doors and the fire exit. In the dim pools of light, I thought I could see the sticklike thing that was once Allan Teller dodging over the floor, sniffing from pile to pile of guests.

Another face rose up into the porthole window. I staggered back.

Oh Harry, my poor Harry.

Wasps crawled in his hair. They tiptoed on his cheeks. He seemed past caring.

"The doooooo . . ." His mouth contorted. "The *doooo*—"

The door. The loading bay. Of course! The entire reason I'd locked myself in here.

It lay at the end of a narrow hall leading from the walk-in freezer and a deep-case fridge. As soon as I flipped on the lights to illuminate the hallway, my heart sank into my shoes.

The loading bay doors were chained shut.

A Master Lock was threaded through the chain, fastened tight.

Grabbing the door handles, I gave them a yank. The chain was strung so tight that I couldn't open the doors more than a half inch. A whiff of freshly cut grass from outside.

Setting my eye to the gap, I could make out the loading dock. Harry's van was backed up to its padded concrete lip, doors flung open.

"Help!" I screamed. "I'm in here!"

The golf course's ornamental gardens lay silent in the twilight.

Something smacked off the door.

The wasps. They were out there too. One of them tried to arrow through the door-gap, coming right at my eye—

I slammed the doors, severing the wasp in half. Its head fell to the floor, its gas-mask face staring at me as it *zizz*ed in a broken circle.

The iPhone. I snatched it out of my pocket. Dialed 9-1-1.

"Come on come on *come on* . . ."

"*Your call cannot be completed as dialed. Please check the number and dial again.*"

I tried again. Same message. Tried my parents' number. Same. 9-1-1 for a third time.

"*Your call cannot be completed as dialed—*"

Pikachu!

> Check the phone settings

When I did, I saw what she'd done.

Outgoing calls and data locked by owner. That sly bitch had set the Parental Controls.

All incoming data remained open and unlimited. Okay, good enough.

I hunted around the kitchen for a landline phone, finding one on the wall next to a clipboard hung on a nail. But when I lifted the receiver, I caught the hiss of a dead connection.

I let my legs give out and sank down on my ass.

Pikachu!

> Come watch.

Pikachu!

> You like to watch me, don't you, bestie? Especially when I act silly

I returned to the door with a handful of dish towels. I wadded them under the door, packed tight with the tip of a butter knife. Serena

278 — NICK CUTTER

seemed content with me being trapped. If she decided to change the game, well, she could force me to do whatever she wanted, digging her pheromone hooks into my brain.

But I didn't think she'd do that. She wanted me to bear witness.

I comforted myself with the hope that nothing could be as bad as what I'd already seen today. If I'd had the gift of foresight, I would've realized the stupidity of that.

No, the worst of it started once Rudy and the other guests began to rise.

PART III
THE NEST

THE ST. CATHARINES
GOLF AND HUNT CLUB

June 15, 10:05 p.m. – June 16, 11:04 p.m.

ONE
10:05 p.m.

The first one to get up was a woman.

She hauled herself off the ballroom carpet. She wore a sheer dark dress torn raggedly at the collar. I could see her bra strap and the wasp-stung tops of her breasts.

I watched out the porthole window as she tottered in a meandering circle, moaning, eyeless and confused.

Serena—

the Queen

—occupied one corner of the ballroom, perched on a rickety pile of chairs in the bloody light of the fire escape.

Descending the deadfall, she made her way toward the woman. Her offspring, the creatures that had spilled out of Will and Chad, had dragged themselves under a table by then. Their bodies made congested phlegmy noises; I pictured a pair of mucus-covered hearts beating fraily under the table. I thought they might be dying. I prayed that impression was right.

The Queen held out her arms to the woman, who collapsed into her embrace. The two of them sank beneath my line of sight, but I got the sense of spiny, kinked appendages unfurling from the Queen, jabbing into the woman.

By the time the Queen finished with her, another guest had tottered up. The woman in the ripped black dress crawled to a spot on the wall.

The second was the man in a herringbone jacket. His mouth hung slack, his lips swollen as sausage casings. The Allan-thing slunk from the shadows, grabbing the man around the legs and dragging him down to receive the Queen's gift.

That was when I turned away. Better to occupy myself with plans of escape. I scanned the windowless kitchen. Prep tables, deep-basined sinks, pots and pans . . . a walk-in cooler.

When I pulled the cooler's door open, I got hit by an icy blast of air. Boxes of frozen meat and fish sat on wire racks. There was a red plunger on the inside of the door, I guess in case you accidentally shut yourself in? I toyed with the idea of freezing myself to death. It wouldn't feel *good*, but better than the fate waiting out in the ballroom.

By the time I'd exited the freezer and returned to the porthole, more guests had risen. They shambled around in their bloodied evening wear, bumping into one another, some falling to lie on the floor with their legs bicycling uselessly. The wasps circled in moody patterns. Big gouges had been taken out of some tables, almost like bites from a cookie. The wasps must be chewing the wood into pulp to build their nest.

And yes, that's exactly what they were building, with frightening efficiency. The main doors were covered in a five-foot-thick layer of material resembling an oyster's shell. The bay windows had disappeared behind a gray nest.

Meanwhile, the Queen continued her coronation tour. One man held his wallet out to her—the plastic laminate tongue spilled from it, snapshots of his kids or grandkids or golf buddies. The guests fell into their queen's embrace; fell like children in their snapped heels and tasseled shoes, their heads fuzzy with wasps, these surreal Q-tips poking from their collars.

The worst part was that the guests obviously enjoyed it.

Once the deed was done, the wasps lifted from the guests. Their naked faces were left not so much swollen as knotted, these ancient goblins. They then found spots along the walls and sat with their legs splayed.

The Queen saved Rudy as a final morsel.

I was near the kitchen door when I felt his weight shift on the other side. I stood up to see him in the porthole, grinning in at me.

Rudy's tongue had pushed his mouth apart, a gristly turnip jutting between his lips. He gnawed at it, making glottal noises of strain, *glugh-glugh-glugh*, as his jaw muscles bulged; he bit straight through his own tongue, grunting in satisfaction as his teeth came together. His tongue fell, *splot*. Rudy's grin widened.

Next he began to moan, blood bubbling over his lips. Whether the sounds were ones of happiness or anticipation or horror or raving lunacy—who knew, and by then who even cared?

I think he might've been saying *Livvie. Livvie, Limme*, something, but his words were muffled by the tea towels under the door, plus it was hard to tell with his tongue gone.

The Queen met him at the kitchen door. She wanted me to get a good look. She presented herself to him—even though Rudy couldn't see her anymore with the yolk of his eyes crusted on his cheeks—but I think he must've sensed her, the way you can feel the heat off a stove element.

"Am I all you ever dreamed of?" I heard her ask.

"*Lum lub lub*," murmured Rudy, reaching for the object of his fascination. "*Lummy limmie limmie looooooo . . .*"

The Queen leaned in close, whispering into the overripe fruit hanging off the side of Rudy's head that had once been an unremarkable human ear.

Gripping his shoulders, the Queen guided Rudy to his knees.

Her fingers crowded into Rudy's mouth, wrists flexing as she pulled against his teeth, her head cocked inquisitively as she applied slow pressure, just enough to get the job done. The wintry fracture of Rudy's jawbone was loud in the cathedral silence.

When her fingers withdrew, Rudy's lower palate hung slack, tears streaming from the ducts of his eyeless eyes. The Queen cradled Rudy's skull while the fearsome parts of her lower extremities, those sharp tubes of cartilage, forced their way between his lips and into his head.

The snap of broken teeth was the sound of a three-hole punch going through a stack of paper. Her body began to move in gentle rhythm. Rudy thrashed, arms flapping, his skull flopping around. When she was done, she dragged him behind a table and dropped him. She seemed to have lost all interest.

I stared at the phone. The clock read 10:34 p.m. Time passes slowly in hell.

TWO
10:40 p.m.

Out in the ballroom, squares of light began to vibrate on the carpet. The guests' cell phones. What time was the gala supposed to end? How long before someone got worried? One of the guests' kids or the babysitter or *someone*. Surely they'd call the police?

Oh please, call the police.

I filled the biggest pot I could find with water in case the supply got cut off. I'd already found industrial-sized cans of peas and peaches in the walk-in pantry, corn and cocktail wieners and all sorts of shit. Enough food for months.

I returned to the loading bay, to those locked double doors, thinking—in the stupid headspace of any trapped creature—that they might have magically unchained themselves. I gripped the handles, rattled the chains. The sound had such a coffin-nail finality that it put me on the verge of tears.

A hum pulsed through the handles, tickling my palms.

Kneeling, I lifted the rubberized lip at the bottom of the left-side door. In the inch-high gap between the bottom of the door and the floor, I saw wasps: only a few right now, their wings whining in that congested space.

I let the flap fall shut. The rubber was thick, but if they kept coming—wasps in their thousands, their tens of thousands—would the combined weight of their bodies be enough to push that flap open?

I returned from the kitchen with a thirty-pound case of canned tomatoes, setting it down along the rubber lip.

When I went back to the kitchen door, I could see the Teller-thing moving between the tables, a jackal on a battlefield.

I sat on the floor, hugging my knees to my chest and rocking, rocking, rocking.

THREE
11:32 p.m.

I stopped rocking when the first responders showed up.

A dozen uniformed police officers. I saw them enter the ballroom through the porthole. They had no idea what they were stepping into. Really, how could they?

The wasps must've been dozy on the exterior of the club. Same as with the loading dock: you could see they were there, yeah, but not yet in unnatural numbers. The responders could've figured there was a big nest tucked away in the club's eaves, but not *this*.

It required a group of officers to crack apart the nest material grafted to the inside of the doors and heave them open. The wasps retreated as the officers struggled to get inside the ballroom. A pair of bolt cutters reached through the gap in the main doors to cut the chain.

I watched the first policemen step into the ballroom. The club's security lights streamed in from outside, shining off the shattered hunks of nest that hung like slabs of busted drywall. More officers stood on the outer walkway, inhaling what would be their final lung-fuls of air before following their fellow officers inside.

They strode in confidently, but their footsteps faltered. Their brains weren't making the necessary connections, not nearly fast enough. *Run*, I thought. *Turn, sprint, GO.* But their feet locked up, their faces a portrait of spellbound confusion.

The wasps swept down. The policemen's pistols popped off, slugs punching into the ceiling and walls and the guests slumped against them. Within seconds, they were running around in the same frenzied spirals as the guests. They were humans, after all, meat-sacks with badges pinned to their chests and oh, how rapidly their faces were writhing with wasps . . .

When the first wave of officers failed to exit the club—I could hear their walkie-talkies squelching out in the ballroom: *Copy, do you copy?*—a second wave was dispatched.

A larger unit this time, in full riot gear. They broke the door down with a tactical battering ram, fanning out with a precision that made me think this time it would be different. Maybe one of the doomed first-wave policemen had been wearing a body camera, giving this group a sense of what they were up against.

But no. The wasps found their way under the riot cops' face

shields and inside their armor. If anything, the struggle was even less spirited this time.

When I forced myself to look again, the Teller-thing was distributing the bodies of the second-wave cops around the ballroom. Once that was done, it closed the doors with a ghastly flourish: a groveling butler backing out of his master's chamber.

From then on, those doors stayed shut.

FOUR
SATURDAY
June 16, 12:17 a.m.

The night was endless.

I had two vantages into what was happening. The first was the porthole looking into the ballroom. The second was the TV news, which I could still access on the iPhone.

I'd spent some time scouring the kitchen. I'd found a toolbox in the manager's office. It held a set of hex wrenches, some saws including a hacksaw, a hammer, a carpet knife, vise grips, screwdrivers, duct tape, a few other items that might be of use. I'd also found a universal charger in the office's desk drawer.

By then, both waves of police had shambled up to receive the Queen's gift. I hadn't watched. I knew the drill. The next time I checked, the officers were along the walls with the guests. The Teller-thing scuttled around in the gloom, squealing away: *Eee-eee-eee.*

I hadn't heard a peep out of the things that had come out of Chad Dearborn and Will Stinson. But if I set my cheek flush to the door, I could see their outline at the farthest edge of the porthole. Were they dead? Had they ever been fully alive? Years ago Janey Colson, our old friend at Woody Knot, lost a child in utero. My mother spoke to her one summer night, the two of them sharing a cocktail on our porch while I'd eavesdropped at my window.

It's called gastroschisis, Janey said. *A birth defect. Um, his little insides, they came out through a hole to the side of his belly button. Incompatible with life, is what the doctor told me.*

I hoped the things that had come out of Chad and Will were incompatible with life. I prayed that nothing that came out of the Queen would thrive.

When the iPhone's battery started to flash, I plugged it into the charger. It worried me that the electricity could go out. Would the police cut the power? Could the wasps chew through the electrical cables?

Walking back to the loading bay doors, I clasped the handles. That hum from before was fainter. I slid the case of tomatoes away. Pulled on the handles until I caught a papery crackle through the quarter-inch gap.

The wasps had sealed the doors in.

Poking one finger through the gap, I scraped the fresh nest. My fingernail burred as if I was scratching corrugated cardboard. It pushed threateningly against the doors.

I pushed the tomatoes back in place. Muttered: "*Shit.*"

When I returned to the manager's office, the iPhone was at 37 percent. I sat by the outlet as it continued to charge, scrolling social media.

The first sign of public awareness came on Twitter. A tweet timestamped 11:54 p.m. last night.

Teacake @teacake80s ·
Anyone else notice all the cop cars parked outside the Golf Club? Looks like every cop in the city! Hey @NiagaraRegionalPolice you guys keeping something from us?

FIVE

1:31 a.m.

The *thop* of helicopter blades filled the sky above the club.

I went to the porthole. The beam of a searchlight shone through the atrium-style skylight in the ballroom ceiling, but by then the skylight was almost covered in the nest. You'd think the wasps knew it was best to keep prying eyes out.

A bullhorn-amplified voice called out, but the words were muffled by the nest. It didn't matter, anyway. There was nobody in the ballroom to appeal to. Only me in the kitchen—and the Teller-thing, likely incapable of coherent speech—and the Queen, who wasn't a conversationalist.

I kept up with news bulletins on the phone. By the time the local crews mobilized and began to show up on scene, the police had established a perimeter.

The club sat on the corner of Westchester and Willowdale, and from what I could see from the CHCH news simulcast, yellow sawhorses had now shut all traffic lanes. A camera panned over the club from the far side of a police barricade. The guests' cars were still in the lot. Thirty or so police cruisers, the entire NRP fleet I bet, were parked near the front entry with their cherries rotating. A pair of helicopters, one black and the other an orange-and-white search and rescue chopper, strafed the club's roof with their searchlights.

The air above the country club fizzed like the space above a freshly poured glass of Coke.

That had to be the wasps. So many of those nasty fuckers.

SIX

2:54 a.m.

I took breaks from the news to watch the ballroom out the porthole. The ceiling potlights glowed, as well as the fire exit sign, but faintly due to their netting of gray fibers. Their light was still enough to chart the fearsome evolution of the nest by.

The largest nest, which the wasps had built over the main doors, had the look of a ski chalet buried under an avalanche, only some idiot had opened the doors to let the snow inside—except instead of snow it was gasoline-rainbow nest material.

They couldn't just *keep* building, could they? Before long the entire ballroom would be packed in. The guests and police would be buried under the nest. God, was that their intention? To graft flesh and nest together, with humans stuck inside like candied cherries in a fruitcake?

The sheer size of the nest would rupture the power lines and plunge the club into darkness. I'd be stuck in the kitchen as the nest pushed against the door until the hinges snapped and it sagged open to let the nest roll in . . . the sly crackle of the nest expanding toward me in the dark, backing me into a corner and creeping over my toes, up my shins, over my fingertips as it gradually sucked me into it, making me a screaming part of it.

I hunkered by the stove, combing online newsfeeds. The incident had gone viral.

No, bigger than that. It was about to go full-blown nuclear.

SEVEN
4:06 a.m.

The army arrived a few minutes after 4:00 a.m. Tactical helicopters in the predawn sky. Olive-green military vehicles positioning themselves behind the sawhorses.

An early-morning jogger whose route took him across the third fairway posted a video to Twitter at 4:12.

The phone footage revealed the northern side of the ballroom: The high windows were smashed, the nest oozing out. The citizen journalist tried to get closer, but the buzz of wasps bled in on his recording—"Holy shit, they're huge!"—and he'd wisely fled the area.

That post was up only a few minutes before getting taken down, but what it showed unlocked one of the mysteries that had been nagging me.

Where had these wasps come from?

The old water tower. It rose from the oaks banding the western border of the golf course; in the evenings, I'd bet its shadow stretched over one of the fairways.

The tower had been around since before I was born. It had since been replaced by a new tower up the hill by the university, but the old eyesore had never been torn down. I didn't even understand how water towers worked until my dad explained them to me.

Water's stored up in the big bell. If we get a power outage or a drought, the city's water engineer releases a valve and gravity—or hydrostatic pressure, to use the ten-dollar word—anyway, the weight of the water itself will carry it down that cement column to refill the supply.

When I'd asked how much water was in a tower, he said: *Oh, tons and tons. When there's that much, they measure it not by volume, but by weight.*

On that jogger's video, in the dawn light peeking over the escarpment, I'd seen a haze over the old tower. The telltale sign of the wasps. And it clicked.

The wasp nest. The one down in the storm drain. Those orange cafeteria chairs, the wreckage of Estelle, and that nest.

I remembered Roy telling Rudy that a piece of it, a *chunk*, had been missing.

My mind summoned an image of Serena in the drain, carving

out a slab of the nest. Dragging it into a van. Driving to the old water tower, prizing the rusted entry grate open, and heaving the nest inside.

How long had the wasps been in there? Could they have filled the whole tower? Or had the nest simply furred its walls like mold? And then, when the time was right, all Serena had to do was release the valve to send those wasps into the water lines—lines that must still access the club, seeing as it'd been here forever, too.

My father's words came back. *Oh, tons and tons. When there's that much, they measure it not by volume, but by weight.*

Tons of wasps. Of *these* wasps. How many could that be? Billions, surely. *Trillions?*

EIGHT
6:54 a.m.

By 5:00 a.m., the country club was lead-segment, Canadian national news. At 5:14, a General Emergency Alert went out.

ST. CATHARINES GOLF AND HUNT CLUB UNDER
MILITARY AND MEDICAL QUARANTINE ORDER.
HIGH DANGER ZONE. INFECTION RISK.

The phones in the ballroom shrieked through the alert before going silent. In the pinprick glow of those phones, I saw none of the guests were moving . . . not their limbs, anyway. Their *chests?* Maybe.

Something was going on under their dresses and suits and riot gear.

At 6:48 a.m., the Public Health Agency declared the Golf and Hunt Club a Biosafety Hazard Site. From what I could tell, nobody—not the military, police, or infectious disease specialists—was allowed to approach. The situation was, as one newsman said, *fluid.*

Dozens of agencies showed up. The local stations were joined by crews from the nearby cities. Before long I'm sure the international delegates would arrive. The heavy hitters from south of the border and overseas, with more hurrying after them.

In the early morning light, I saw my prison on the CBC's morning news. The club was penned in. The roads closed. Military transports, police and fire and ambulances everywhere. Helicopters circling. When the news camera panned, I could make out a large group of onlookers well back of the official fray. More than a few of them had binoculars.

The club had taken on the look of a deranged sandcastle. The nest bulged from the shattered windows. The roof was overcast with wasps. They seemed disinterested in the human circus. They simply built and built. The southern flank of the country club was covered in their cragged nest. Before long, every inch of the club's architecture would be encased.

Nobody had a clue what was happening inside.

Well, except for Twitter.

QAnon @Qanon76 · 2m
Globalist parasites, Hollywood Elites, and Deep State operatives caught releasing bioweapon in sleepy Canadian town. #thegreatawakening #deepstateterror

Mother Jones @MotherJones · 1m
The Far-Right Militia's dangerous roots in southern Ontario, and what that may mean as this situation progresses. bit.ly/3euiC4g

Nobody knew I was inside. Or that, for all intents and purposes, I was the only survivor. I couldn't get any information out. The phone's outgoing data was locked. Wasn't sure it would have helped much anyway, except to help me feel less alone.

Did the world really need to see what was going on here? *I* had to watch, and even that felt like one set of eyeballs too many.

NINE

10:38 a.m.

The creaking noises forced me to return to the kitchen door. Through the porthole, I watched the guests and police get up in unison, as though waking to an alarm.

Their stomachs were rotund.

The Queen's subjects dragged themselves to the banquet cart that Will and Chad had once occupied. What was left of those two still sagged off the cart: a snapped jumble of limbs and skin and organ meat that shone in the shafts of sunlight piercing the concavities of the nest.

The guests were drooling. A pack of hungry infants.

"Oh no," I breathed. "Oh no don't do that *please* don't do that don't—"

Rudy crawled out from behind the stage scaffold . . . a massive chunk had been gouged out of his skull. His brain was visible, the curdled gray matter gummed with strands of sun-bleached hair. Rudy didn't let this hinder him from strapping on the ole feed-bag.

Everyone ate their fill. Chad's father was down on his knees, jostling shoulders with Rudy. Quinn Dearborn had a piece of his own son in his mouth, chewing with mechanical mindlessness. The air rang with grunts and yips and the crack of joints pulled from sockets.

The Queen watched from her throne with solemn satisfaction.

She'd been wrong. The poor didn't eat the rich.

The rich ate themselves.

I staggered away from the porthole and vomited. Hardly anything came up.

TEN
3:03 p.m.

201.

According to Fox News, that was the final tally of gala guests, catering staff, and police personnel who could be verified to be in the ballroom.

To that, I could add Rudy and Roy, who nobody outside would know about.

The names of me and Harry weren't likely to show up on any official recording. My folks may have filed a missing person report, but the cops had their hands full. Chad and Will and Allan weren't included in the tally, either. Or the Queen.

As the day bled into the afternoon, I was starting to get punchy. I hadn't slept in how long? Nearly thirty hours, best guess. Adrenaline was hitting me in eye-opening waves, but even sheer terror wasn't enough to keep the gears meshing.

But I *had to* stay up. The second I slipped to sleep, the wasps would find a way in.

I rested against the wall next to the kitchen door. My fingers flexed rhythmically on the hammer I'd scrounged from the toolbox.

Stay awake stay awake stay . . . my chin dipped to my chest—

I came to with a shriek. The wires had been cut for just a second, ushering in a heartbeat of pure blackness.

Fuck me. Not a healthy way to go about this survival game, Margaret.

When I peeked into the ballroom, everything was still except for the guests' chests. They expanded and contracted as if their lungs had tripled in size.

The wasps had stopped building, too. The ballroom air was clearer. Sunlight streamed from those funnels in the nest—the exit holes for the wasps, who I could see from the news coverage were continuing to build outside. The newscasts of CNN, NBC, CBC, ABC, CBS, FOX, OAN, BBC World, MSNBC, Al Jazeera, and dozens more broadcasted footage of the nest cobbling itself over the club's walls.

I tried to choke down a can of peaches, but the nectar was sweet, and it made me think of thinned honey, and honey made me think of bees, which made me think of wasps even though they didn't *make* honey, oh Jesus Chr—

I puked the peaches up. After scooping strings of bile out of my mouth, I drank some water from the pot. Then I had to pee.

I ended up taking a piss in the walk-in freezer, perched off a box of frozen fish fillets. No one would ever eat them, anyway. The frost-clad pipes clattered. They were doing the same out in the kitchen. The wasps. They were in the water lines. Now, my plumbing knowledge was for shit, but I figured the pipes must connect. That could mean they had gotten into the sewage lines, too. And the heating ducts, the vents, everywhere.

Perched on that box of fish, I bawled my eyes out.

Nothing to see here, folks, just a half-mad girl crying while she pees on some fish.

A certain clarity comes after a good cry. It's not lasting, it doesn't *fix* anything, but the edges sharpen a bit. A person can think more clearly.

Bladder empty, I paced a circuit of the kitchen: prep table to sink to fridge to freezer to the porthole . . . the briefest glance—mmm, *no*. Back to pacing.

The iPhone was plugged in near the sinks now. I caught an interview on ABC.

"I'm here with Dr. Robert Phailson, an entomologist from the local university. Our cameraman recently recovered one of the creatures. Some manner of wasp—is that right?"

The ABC reporter jammed his mic in the face of this Dr. Phailson.

"That appears to be the case," said Phailson, *"but I have never seen one even remotely like this. The wasp, order* Hymenoptera, *is among the most diverse phyla in the insect kingdom. They've been around since before the dinosaurs, unchanging. But* this *one . . ."*

The camera focused away from Phailson to zoom in on the wasp, which lay in a specimen tray.

"It stung our cameraman," the reporter said off-screen. *"Right through his leather glove. The effect of the sting was immediate and quite frightening."*

Phailson: *"He went into some manner of neurotoxic shock, yes?"*

"That's right, he passed out. Comatose for a full two hours. From a single sting. He's revived now, but in quarantine."

After both police delegations failed to exit the club, no further attempts had been made to get inside. The newsfeeds told me as much. But there were other ways to figure out what was going on in here. The newsfeeds told me that, too.

They used body-heat maps (*"What we're seeing in there is, by and large, not making any earthly sense,"* intoned the reporter from BBC), plus cell phone data groupings to gather a schematic of the ballroom. Not long after that report went live, the Teller-thing scampered around collecting the phones and tossing them into a pile. The Queen must be monitoring media developments, too, so—

THRACK!

Something smashed into the kitchen door. The wood splintered, dead bolts screaming as the door appeared to bulge inward.

A butcher knife in one hand, hammer in the other, I retreated to the walk-in freezer. If something came into the kitchen, I'd shut myself in. I already knew I couldn't lock the freezer from the inside,

298 – NICK CUTTER

but maybe whatever was out there wouldn't know how to open it, either—

—or wouldn't have human hands to work the handle.

I watched the kitchen door from the freezer. With a cold coiling note, something set its weight against it. The hinges squealed. Cement dust puffed from the countersunk screws.

That same thing began to crawl upward.

It slithered over the porthole. I saw it.

Big. Too big to comprehend. It covered the porthole yet felt as broad as the door itself. Its body was segmented into durable plates like the belly of a snake. The flex of its long muscles made those plates move.

The smell of it came through the splintered wood. Darkly oily, part soy sauce and part caked shit, but there was a fleshy undertone, too, something wholly human.

The adrenal, sour-sock smell of a teenage boy. And I knew then what it must be. One of the things that had come out of Will and Chad. They weren't nearly so dead as I'd prayed.

I saw its face. Oh, *oh*, its face.

It had its mother's face. Charity's face, except widened and flattened out like the blade of a shovel. A geometric patterning, bright yellow, curved elegantly from blind eyes as hard as hammered brass. Its mouth was monstrous, studded with niblet teeth that *screeched* over the glass—a face that broke my heart for the fact that something human still lived in it, an aspect both lonely and longing.

It kept going, up and up. Had to be nine or ten feet long—its upper half was now scaling the wall over the door. The plating gave way to a vein-strung sheath, a sheen of silverskin tight as naked gums and kinked, fleshy knots that made me think of the jumble of power cords in Northfield's computer lab.

The thing climbed on until I found myself staring at *a second* face, Charity's again, and finally at a pair of feelers tiptoeing across the glass.

The pressure relented. I could hear it above the door, clung to the wall, and it dawned on me that they had conjoined—the things that had come out of the boys.

They'd fastened their bodies to each other somehow, and those sounds I'd mistaken for their death throes had been them fusing together.

A few minutes later, the thing came away from the wall and eased down to the floor. I heard it slither off into the ballroom, clanking, a suit of armor full of goo.

ELEVEN
5:22 p.m.

Meadow, let me tell you something I learned the hard way: When it comes down to it, your friends will always let you down.

The voice, belonging to Tony Soprano, comes from the unlit manager's office. I could make him out in there: kicked back in the chair with his Gucci loafers up on the desk, legs crossed in a pair of olive slacks, chest hair *sproinging* from a camp-collar shirt.

You remember that, Mead. In the end, the only person you can really trust is you.

I stared at him, gape-jawed. Where did he come from? He looked so *real*. His permanence reinforced the belief I'd been chewing on for the last half hour or so: that going crazy might be a good thing, because at least I'd get a whole bunch of fun new friends.

"Gabagool," I croaked.

Tony uncrossed and recrossed his legs. The shoe-polish and gunpowder smell of him drifted out of the office.

What did you say, Mead?

"Gabagool," I repeated, giving it some real *Italia-issimo*. "Funny word, isn't it?"

Eesh, said Tony. *Pardon my French, Mead, but you sound like a retard.*

"That's inappropriate," I said, and unleashed a shrill titter.

Shaddap. You want to get out of here? You ought to melt the chain. Use that little torch.

The chef's butane torch. Where had I seen it? In the toolbox, right.

Hey, good idea, Tony.

I headed back to the loading bay doors with the torch. Switched it on and narrowed the flame to a blue point, training it on the chain. After a few minutes, the metal glowed red-hot, but the links wouldn't melt.

The torch ran out of gas. The chain cooled. It was unblemished. This wasn't going to work. "Shit idea, Tony," I said.

You got a real smart mouth on you, Meadow.

Back in the kitchen now. I flipped on the office lights hoping to see Tony, but he wasn't sitting behind the desk anymore.

"Tony?" No reply. "Hey, sorry I shit on your idea."

But Tony was gone. I found myself perilously close to tears.

I took his chair in the office. Unlocked the phone and thumb-swiped newsfeeds. The Royal Canadian Air Force had grounded a helicopter flying in restricted airspace near the club. When the press released the name of the helicopter's registered owner, Twitter lit up.

@toxicbanana
Rudyard Crate. Two words: integrity and honor. Businessman, scholar, philanthropist, humanitarian, disruptor, icon. I had the honor of doing Jagerbombs with him and Elon at Davos.

@BigBillJimmerson

If you look up the word scumbag in the dictionary, you'll find a picture of Jeffrey Epstein . . . but if you squint, you'll see Rudy Crate behind him with his dick stuck up Jeff's ass.

@GenTechDesign

Public Stock Exchange records show SysWell Dynamics, Crate's company, has invested heavily in genetic engineering start-ups, with a focus on genetic pest management.

Rudyard Crate, huh? I fired up his Wikipedia page. A billionaire at twenty-eight. Never married, no children. Nowhere did it mention: *Rudyard Crate has an unnatural fixation with insects, devoting many years and much of his fortune to the creation of some unholy surrogate bug-daughter.*

I surfed from Wikipedia back to the mainstream news outlets.

"Viewers, something frankly unimaginable is happening in the Canadian city of Saint Catharines, Ontario."

That was NBC's Lester Holt, staring gravely at the camera.

Les, you have no idea.

Another newsfeed showed that the zone around the club had become a maze of military portables. News crews had been pushed back to the land abutting the 406 Highway, but with their telephoto lenses they could still get footage of what was happening outside the club.

The citizen onlookers had been pushed even farther back. I found a YouTube live stream uploading from the end of the Geneva Street Bridge, half a kilometer from the club. It looked as if most of the city had gathered. The crowd choked both traffic lanes, strung all the way back to the intersection at St. Paul Street. Police had established a barrier at the midpoint of the bridge but were struggling to hold it. Nobody was trying to breach their barricade. But the sheer weight of fifteen or twenty thousand bodies, all perched on tiptoe angling for a better look, threatened to collapse the barricade.

Scanning the crowd, I saw familiar faces. Triny Goodhue. Simone Lang. Alexa Meeber. Danny Lombardi. Those two nameless ninth graders, Black Bob and Flesh-Colored Shirt. The students who'd chased me out of the cafeteria for daring to speak Serena's name. They stood at the bridge abutment, eyes blank as test patterns, straining toward the club—toward their queen—a pack of dogs on an invisible leash.

TWELVE
5:40 p.m.

Later that day, an anonymous Twitter account went live.

@ProjectAthenaTruths

Within an hour, it had gained over three million followers.

@ProjectAthenaTruths

Two decades ago I was hired onto a venture spearheaded by Rudyard Crate. Project Athena. Eighteen years ago, I quit.

@ProjectAthenaTruths

My specialty is genome editing. A knockout artist, ha ha. Inactivating or "knocking out" one or more precise genes from an organism's DNA sequence.

@ProjectAthenaTruths

Project Athena's scientists were siloed from one another. One hand must never know what the other was doing. Except those at the very top. A man named Jameson, who may still work for Crate. Another man named Fisher, who I know to be dead. Good riddance.

@ProjectAthenaTruths

Little girls. I discovered this in due time. Crate's idea. Little girls into Queens.

@ProjectAthenaTruths

It was a folly. An impossibility. To fundamentally alter the form, structure, utility, biology, the essential TRUTH of two obverse stratums of life. Insect and human.

@ProjectAthenaTruths

I took the money. God help me. I took it and signed the NDA. What real harm? If a billionaire wanted to play God—and if us so-called experts knew he was nothing but a fool pretending at godhood—why not let him?

@ProjectAthenaTruths

So I'd thought until today. Until I read this news and what it seems to augur.

@ProjectAthenaTruths

What follows is some of my own work. My small part of a project still in its infancy. The records I've kept all these years, smuggling them out of Crate's lab. They won't make sense to the layman. But to anyone with expertise in the field, they will chill the blood.

@ProjectAthenaTruths

God forgive me. God forgive us all. And may God rot Rudyard Crate.

As for the tweets that followed, the anonymous whistle-blower was right: Most of them didn't make sense. Diagrams, tables, graphs, readouts from diagnostic devices . . . but there were photos, too.

One was of a sprawling lab, an oasis of white tile and spotless chrome. Another of a wasp crawling out of a dead cockroach in a specimen tray. And a final photo captured Rudy Crate, grinning like a devil, surrounded by unsmiling men in lab coats.

I let the phone charge. Time passed in a manner I'd never experienced. I was carved out of it. The machinery of the hours and minutes became unstable. Time flowed forward, backward, it stood perfectly still. Eternity was right here in this kitchen. When I next caught my reflection, I expected my hair to be bone-white, my face trenched in wrinkles. Or I'd be a child again. Five years old, my clothes puddled around my arms and legs, sucking on my thumb.

The Queen brooded on her throne in a dark corner of the ballroom. She was eternal, too. She'd been here since before the dinosaurs. Back when they roamed the earth, she'd crawled under their plated hides to feed. Her face had graced cave paintings and woodcuts and oil portraits; she had been worshipped for centuries, churches and palaces and nests, oh so many nests, built in her honor.

She was the queen of all worlds, both the living and the dead. The hands on the clock bent to her. And I did, too.

THIRTEEN
7:01 p.m.

One of the guests stood up.

I watched him through the porthole. A man in a crushed-mulberry suit, the fabric stuck to his chest from the fluids leaking from his skin. The bottom buttons on his shirt had burst to let his stomach bulge through. It had the shiny, dilated appearance of a rotten pumpkin.

"Diversify!"

His voice rang out in the ballroom. His arm came up, his fingers forming a gun. His thumb-hammer came down. *Bang!*

"It's a bull market, baby!"

He strode over to the bar. His legs scissored, the walk of a toy soldier. As he moved, the bulge in his stomach . . . I watched it *migrate*.

The overstretched flesh of his belly flexed. His skin tore in threadlike fissures, blood pissing out in pressurized needles. Something relocated inside of him. His stomach deflated. The loose skin settled over his belt buckle in a wadded pouch. The man's eyes rolled in a mad delirium. He brought one arm down in a chopping motion.

"Don't let your cocks go soft now, boys. Limp-dicks finish last!"

His pants began to expand. The back of them, pushing the soggy vents of his suitcoat out. A gradual, deliberate inflation. I imagined a pair of lips blowing a humungous bubble in the seat of his slacks. Blood burbled over his waistband and went foaming down the backs of his thighs.

He'd reached the bar by then. He slapped one hand on the polished brass rail.

"Shotsa blurbee, blarboo!"

His pants split soundlessly. What drooled out resembled a huge dark teardrop. A blob of warm patching tar left behind by a road crew. It slid from the caverned grape-cluster between the man's legs onto the carpet.

Something else drooled out of him. A milky hangman's noose. His knotted intestines.

The man began to laugh. A baritone trumpeting full of false humor: *Hyah-hyah-hyah.* My father called it the "Businessman's laugh."

It's as fake as a three-dollar bill, Margaret. Never trust a man who's perfected his Businessman's laugh.

The creature on the carpet unfolded itself. A switchblade of gleaming meat. It had the look of something half-made. A cake pulled from the oven too early. Once it had unkinked, it started inching toward the man with the creeping wriggle of a maggot.

Reaching him, the thing crawled up the man's thigh. It clung to the back of his knee, a persistent nettle. The man's eyes tracked it helplessly. He kept on laughing. In fact, he was howling now—*HYAH-HYYYYYAAAAHH*—as blood frothed over his lips.

The thing anchored itself on the man's hips and began to . . . *nuzzle.* In short order that nuzzling created a hole in the man, below his ribs. The thing was trying to get back inside. Its lower half thrashed and flicked. The man screeched.

His legs gave out. He toppled over. His skull hit the footrail. The thing that had made its way halfway back into him ended up crushed underneath its host's body. The wet dark tongue of its tail flapped once or twice before going still.

Neither of them moved again.

A few minutes later, something slammed through the ballroom skylight and stuck in the carpet. A red light flashed on it. The wasps disabled it, but not before it recorded forty-three seconds of footage that would shortly explode on TVs and phone screens worldwide.

The device had been fitted with a 360-degree fiber-optic camera. It was never clear who'd deployed it. But at 7:34 p.m., those forty-three seconds showed up on Twitter, posted by another anonymous account: *@APublicTrust1010.*

The clip was only up for six minutes, but in that span it had been copied enough to prevent it ever being contained. What it showed—the ballroom and the nest and the guests lining the walls like dummies at Madame Tussauds, the stuff I'd been staring at for hours . . . you can imagine the panic it sparked.

This citizen journalism must have pushed the actual authorities to double their efforts, because over the next few hours the news came fast. In the name of national security, a joint task force—FBI, CIA, the military, cybersecurity experts, more—descended on Rudy's compound in the Santa Clara badlands. They busted down the doors of his lab and unlocked a bunch of computer files. There must've been a mole in the task force's personnel, because it wasn't long before some astonishing details began to leak out.

It was ABC's David Muir who first spoke her name.

"Charity Atwater. Eighteen years old, a student at the local Northfield High."

I was sucking water out of a kitchen pot at the time. I stopped, picked the phone up. My friend's face—the photo from her Facebook profile—was being broadcast on live television.

"In the files we've secured from SysWell Dynamics, Charity Atwater is identified by another moniker," Muir went on. *"Subject Six. She seems to have been . . . this information is coming to me live and it's hard to process what I'm receiving . . . but for now we can say she appears to be the object of an experiment having to do with genetic manipulation."*

The next time I checked the news crawl, a scientist named Carson Greevy was speaking to Dr. Sanjay Gupta on CNN.

INTERVIEW ON CNN'S *SANJAY GUPTA MD*
INTERVIEW SUBJECT: DR. CARSON GREEVY
AIR DATE: JUNE 16, 2018

GUPTA: For the benefit of our viewers, you are—

GREEVY: Chief geneticist at the Greenwell Institute, a scientific think tank based in Modesto, California.

GUPTA: And your specialization is in transgenesis, yes? Can you explain to our viewers what that is?

GREEVY: It's the process of introducing genes from one organism into the genome of another organism. Gene transference, if you will.

GUPTA: You haven't had a chance to go over the information coming out of SysWell Dynamics in any detail. But from what's been released so far, what can you tell us?

GREEVY: The most obvious fact is that whatever Rudyard Crate and his team were doing was blackly amoral. Their so-called "work" ignored every ethic of medicine and subject consent. All scientists work under an oath, much like the Geneva Convention. And from what I can see, Crate burned that oath to the ground and danced on the ashes.

GUPTA: What do you think was the point of it all?

GREEVY: . . . I really don't know *what* he was trying to do, honestly, and I don't think that matters. It involves the genetic manipulation of girls—as embryos initially, but progressing through their adolescence. How he got away with it for this many years—

GUPTA: So you think it's the result of some long-term project?

GREEVY: Possibly? As impossible as that is for me to believe.

GUPTA: Impossible how?

GREEVY: The *elements* Crate's team was working with,

the arrangements of gene plasms that exist antithetically to one another—it's inconceivable to me that they would splice or, ah, *cohere* in any rational form.

GUPTA: The reports we're getting don't sound rational.

GREEVY: That an embryo could survive with that inharmonious arrangement of cells, human and insect—and the possibility that said embryo could grow to an infant, then to a girl who may've passed as human . . . I apologize to your viewers, but I'm still trying to wrap my head around all this. Wildly simplified, it's like this: You can put a Ferrari engine in a Toyota Tercel. There's nothing stopping any imbecile from doing that. It would shred the gearbox and both car and engine would never work again, but it's not illegal, it's just stupid. What Crate somehow managed to do is, in a genetic sense . . . you have to understand, there's an *infinitely* better chance of a Tercel running on a Ferrari engine than whatever seems to have happened at the genetic level with that girl. The uptake and spread of that splicing impossibility is now manifesting itself at that golf club in Canada.

GUPTA: Do you have any idea of where it might be going? An endgame or . . . ?

GREEVY: I haven't the foggiest idea. It would depend on an endless number of variables. But—

GUPTA: Yes?

GREEVY: Whoever's in there now? The, uh, guests at
             that golf club event? I'm sorry to say this, but I
             can't see it ending well for them.

GUPTA: Should the military go in? Rescue them if
             possible?

GREEVY: I suspect it's too late. Insect larval-stage de-
             velopment happens very quickly. What takes
             a human nine months takes an insect a day,
             if not hours.

GUPTA: You're saying something may soon be *born* in
             there?

FOURTEEN
9:17 p.m.

. . . Then, from the ballroom, came a familiar voice.

"Mags."

"Harry?"

"You couldn't get out, could you?"

"She locked the loading doors."

"Oh."

His voice held no spark, and I thought: *He's dead already*. He didn't smell right—this close, his scent came through the splits in the door. I had to breathe through my mouth.

"My grandpa . . ."

"Harry?"

"Grandpa was sick," Harry went on, a windup toy with a few

cranks left in it. "Mom kept bugging me to record little pick-me-ups to him on her phone. She'd send them to him in the hospital. I never knew what to say, and it pissed Mom off. *You love Grandpa, don't you?* she'd say. *Well, Grandpa's had three operations. They've cut him open and taken things out, stuff that's been in there since he was born, but it's bad now, all rotten, and he's really sick and I wish you'd be more serious.* I remember thinking, I love Grandpa a whole lot, but also I'm ten. I don't know how this works. Sickness, death. But Mom, she had this idea of who I ought to be. The loving little grandson, and I . . . I just *wasn't*."

For a long while, all that registered was his labored breathing.

"That's what the world wants of us, too, y'know? To be something we can't be, some perfect kind of, of *character*. The thoughtful little boy you see in movies written by adults, who should know better. But I wasn't ready for that, not then and not now and so I guess not ever. Still, I would have been that for Mom if I could have, and for Grandpa, because I loved them. But this *world*? I don't owe it shit."

He went quiet. Even his breath went away. The life force of the death-defying Harry I'd known—the two faces of Harry Cook, yin and yang, grinning crookedly in the shadows under the Auto Shop power jack—was gone. He'd never film another stunt, but I think he'd earned the death he'd always seemed to crave. That bizarre, incomprehensible ending.

"Hey, Mags?"

"Yeah?"

"Do you think you ever loved me? Like, for real?"

"I don't know," I told him honestly. "We're pretty young. I don't have anything to compare it against."

"I appreciate your truthfulness. But it would be cool if you did love me. Even if you just said it and didn't mean it."

"Okay, Harry. I love you. Y'know, I guess I've loved you all along."

"Hey, cool." A trembling spark. "Thanks. Thanks a lot."

More silence, then: "Guess what? I saw him. Just now."

"Who?"

"Grandpa."

I squeezed my eyes shut. "Did he say anything?"

"He said, 'Shit happens, dude.'" I caught the smile in his voice. "Hey, Mags? This is going to get worse, but you're gonna come out okay, I think. You're so tough, you don't even know how—"

A shriek filled the ballroom. I shoved myself up to see the Queen's inhuman mouth stretching open as the Chad-and-Will-thing side-windered toward Harry. It sent a table flying; it reduced a chair to matchsticks.

Harry set his back against the door, fists up. The Queen's child plucked him off the ground. Harry let go a bright hysterical laugh as his body hurtled in a broken cartwheel, bouncing off the stage and knocking over the three-pointed shrub that had miraculously stood until then—

"*Bitch!*" I screamed so hard that spittle flecked the porthole. "You cheap-ass resentful petty fucking rat-assed *biiiiitttch!*"

The Queen sat on her throne, regal in her silence.

FIFTEEN

9:47 p.m.

Pikachu!

The phone.

> When did it go bad between us?

I came to fuzzily. After Harry's death (and I truly hoped he was dead, not lying on the stage with a broken back), I must have dozed off.

Pikachu!

Can you remember when?

I looked out the porthole. She watched me from what seemed a great distance, her throat bathed in the light of her phone.

I typed:

who am I talking to, Plum or Serena?

Pikachu!

Does it matter?

I guess it didn't. I thought for a bit, then wrote:

i wish we'd fought more often, plum. i think we were scared, right? that burden of being a best friend. to be one of those, you had to know your opposite's secretest heart. well, i couldn't know yours and you couldn't know mine. that heart was always changing. still is. i wasn't the same girl you met all those years ago. but you obviously weren't either, right?

I sent it. When no reply came, I typed some more.

why did i HAVE to know you that way? or you me? couldn't we still be friends accepting that there was a little dark spot within the other, a spot that was off limits to everyone, even ourselves? couldn't we have grown apart just a bit? staying the way we were . . . isn't that a kind of suffocation? i wanted us to be little old ladies on the porch of an old folks home. but if we got there it had to be us as our own people.

By the time I typed the last word, my thumbs were aching. I sent it.
Out in the ballroom: *ping!*
Pikachu!

> K thx

I texted:

> u bitch

The phone rang. I picked up.

"*Remember last summer, that party at the Knot?*"

It was Plum. I could tell. Something elemental in her voice.

"*Everybody was at the firepit, singing and carrying on. But you snuck off. Climbed the bluffs. I saw you up there. I watched you watching.*

"*I felt something off you that night. That ache, you know? The ache people feel. And isn't this the time in our lives when that ache's the strongest, because we don't understand it? It's not even a bad ache. An ache for understanding and connection and something to quench this crazy want, right? To be loved and to love back as hard as you possibly can. But mostly it's this desire to be* seen. *For who and what we are, simple as that. You know what I mean? Please say you know.*"

"Yeah, Plum," I told her. "I do."

"*When I think of you that night, I know I felt the same ache you were feeling, and that helps me draw the hope that I was at least a little bit like you. A little bit . . . you know. Because we shared that same ache.*" A long sigh. "*Ugh, I'm fucking this all up. I should've practiced it.*"

"No, no, I get it. I do."

"*I watched you in the moonlight over the bluffs and saw you as you really are. The timid wolf, the fawn with claws. That's how you really know someone, isn't it? You can only really see someone when they think nobody's watching. When they allow themselves to open up—and that's the, the, the um beauty of us, isn't it?*"

"That's our beauty, sure."

"*That may be your only* real *beauty though. You humans, I mean.*"

A slight alteration of her tone. Serena creeping in over her brain waves, maybe.

"You who are made of soft things, of disloyal and fickle things . . . but it's like, I saw you. Your music, Cherr, the notes of you moving through my own blood. I heard. And it was beautiful because it was you, which is all I wanted to say. You're gonna get there, y'know? If you don't, I'll never know, but you'll pocket the fare. You'll go, you'll leave, and you'll be great."

"You can get there too." Why was I even saying it?

"My life was never my own," she went on. *"All those hours we spent in our bedrooms talking about the people we might fall in love with or the places we'd go and the faith that our lives might someday match our dreams . . . Tell Me, right? But I was never going to get there."*

The breath coming down the line was now broken by a rhythmic snapping. The sound of blunted ends of bone grinding together.

"You're real to me," I whispered. "Real to the people who actually knew you."

"I'm going to miss you, Cherr. An awful lot. You have no idea how much."

"Don't say that."

"Miss you."

"Don't say that!" It came out of me as a shriek. The phone clattered to the floor as my hands went to my hair, yanking hard enough to rip strands out. *"Stop saying that!"*

I pictured how I must look to her: my sweaty pinkened face at the porthole, peering across the senseless horror of the ballroom. We may as well be on separate planets. In a lot of practical ways, we always had been.

"I do like that image, you know. You and me as old ladies."

"We can still get there."

"Sure we can."

"Can't we just go back to how things were?"

That got a real, honest-to-god laugh out of her.

"Oh, my Cherry-berry. Tell me, do you still love me?"

"I do, Plummy-wummy. Always have, always will."

"Who would have thought, huh? A couple girls from Woody Knot. We're gonna shock the world, aren't we?"

The *click* was on her end.

SIXTEEN
9:57 p.m.

The night had grown teeth by the time the guests began to gather.

The sunlight streaming through the nest's funnels had given way to starlight. By then a few more guests had gone the way of the man in the crushed-mulberry suit. Their corpses decorated the floor, rigor mortis creaking their bodies into ungodly poses. Their own miscarriages had evacuated from their skulls riding a pressurized geyser of afterbirth, flopping around until the Teller-thing finished them off.

The remaining guests stirred in the waxen light daubing the ballroom. They moved toward the throne, cradling the bloated gourds of their stomachs. There they sank to their knees, staring up at their queen in the chilly light of her altar.

I didn't want to be around for whatever came next. The kitchen trembled on the verge of collapse. The pipes were rattling nonstop. I'd found more rags, stuffing them into every drain-hole and up every faucet.

The cell phone signal was getting fainter, too. It toggled between two and three bars, with the odd heart-stopping dip to zero. The lights fritzed and popped. Was the nest putting too much pressure on the wires?

I had to get out of here.

But getting out through the ballroom was an impossibility. Both exits were sealed under at least fifteen feet of nest. The loading dock. That was it. The only way out.

Meadow, Meadow, listen, daughter of mine.

Tony. He was in the office again, hipshot against the filing cabinet, flipping a quarter. The light caught the coin as it traveled up, hit its apex, and came back into his hand.

Stop frowning. You'll get wrinkles. All you need to do, see, is get on that phone of yours and seek some expert advice. But don't call Christopher Moltisanti. He's an idiot.

Why hadn't I thought of that before? I mean, where did anyone turn if they needed an answer to one of life's vexing questions?

In YouTube's search box, I typed: *How to break a lock*

The first video was a bullseye.

HOW TO BREAK A PADLOCK WITH TWO NUT WRENCHES.

When I checked the toolbox, my hand closed on a full set of wrenches in a leather sleeve. I hurried to the loading dock doors with them. To that fucking miserable Master Lock.

According to the video, the trick was simple: All you had to do was wedge the heads of two wrenches inside the metal U of the padlock and squeeze the handles together until the shackle snapped.

On my first try, the wrenches fit through the metal U of the Master Lock nicely. When I squeezed the handles, I felt the tension, the bite—I squeezed harder, scissoring the wrenches—

The heads slipped off each other. The handles snapped on my fingers.

I tried a few more times, my desperation building, the blood flowing from my fingers making it harder to grip the wrenches. After the sixth failure, I dropped them and proceeded back to the kitchen, to Tony, looking for a fresh idea, anything that might—

Something zipped through the air behind me.

I ducked, stifling a screech as it passed overhead, close enough to lift strands of my hair. A blur of yellow and black droning past like an angry bullet.

A wasp.

SEVENTEEN
10:34 p.m.

And that should bring us back to the start, pretty much.

Back to that point where I stood transfixed at the porthole, watching that woman with her old-school beauty give birth to the Queen's love child.

"Bananas," I breathed, trying to push my mind toward a less horrifically absurd sight. "Bananas being peeled, that's all this is, that's all that's *all* . . ."

The occupant of the woman's body made its way out through her skull. One of its limbs, sharp and tubular and barbed as the poisoned fin of a stickleback, punched through the crown of her head; her hair pouffed upward, a wispy atom bomb detonating on her scalp.

The woman's head broke apart as the thing inside her, the *newborn*, destroyed her skull with brisk, declarative jabs. I pictured a DMV worker stamping forms: *whump, whump.*

That same process was playing out across the ballroom. Guests were toppling over under the top-heavy weight of the things struggling out of them; they came crawling out of wadded neck holes, ballooning grotesquely, tires pumped full of air.

They were the size of large dogs. Skinless, with carapaces shining at the collisions of their joints. They moved with the creeping slowness of chameleons. They gathered their hosts' bodies, dragging them to private spots in the ballroom. One of them passed near to the porthole, hauling a sack of skin in a sparkly cocktail dress—

The horrid thing stared in at me. Its face a waterlogged walnut. Its cheese-soft teeth fluttering in the loose hole of its mouth.

Oh hey, it's Miranda . . .

New Miranda Lancaster lugged Old Miranda slowly up the wall. It hung there like a hungry teardrop, consuming its own husk.

The kitchen lights went out.

Dead silence. The pipes rattled much louder in the dark.

They fluttered back on.

Once my heart stopped trying to claw out of my throat, I returned to the loading bay. The padlocked doors. Those two bloody wrenches.

I picked them up. They felt heavy as anvils. I gave the YouTube hack another try, but my hope was pissing away. I couldn't get enough *oomph* to bring the handles together, couldn't put enough tension on the shackle to snap it. My knuckles were shredded and my hands red as candy apples with blood—

I'm going to die here.

The fact hit me as less of a shock than I'd have figured.

There are knives in the kitchen. Lots of knives.

The voice didn't belong to Tony. It was simply a cold, pragmatic voice.

The freezer. You could cut yourself as deeply as you can and go in there. It wouldn't take long. It would be quick and pretty painless, I bet.

From the ballroom came a shattering roar.

I dashed back to see the Chad-and-Will-thing tossing tables and chairs around to clear a spot in the center of the room. It was frighteningly powerful now, a monstrosity of bone and armor and gristle. It began to smash at the underfloor, breaking jags of concrete free.

A few of the newborns skittered down off the walls. Their skin had already begun to harden; they moved more confidently. They gathered in the center of the ballroom and—

—were they digging a hole?

Hey, Meadow, move your ass, will you?

320 — NICK CUTTER

Tony sat behind the office desk.

Things are getting real hinky around here.

Tony's eyes had grown and spread, breaking from the contours of his face.

"Tony," I said, "you okay?"

Oh, y'know, Mead. His eyes. Huge and faceted. *I've been better.*

Back at the loading bay doors, I gripped the handles and pulled until the tendons stood out on my forearms and spittle foamed between my teeth. Defeated, I let go. In the red haze of my exertion, the handles looked different.

"Jesus. They're screwed to the door."

They were indeed. Four screws at each corner of the plates fixing the handles to the door.

"Oh my god, you stupid fucking idiot."

All I'd ever needed to do was *unscrew* those goddamn door handle plates.

I dashed to the kitchen, retrieved the toolbox, and raced back. It took thirty seconds with a Phillips-head screwdriver to loosen the screws in the bottom and top of one door handle—when the second screw released, the handle fell off the left-hand door, swinging on the chain.

I dug my fingers into the gap between the doors and cracked one of them open, alert for the wasps. The door released from the nest with a sucking crackle.

I faced a solid wall. The nest filled the doorframe from top to bottom.

I hunted through the toolbox. The wood saw seemed my best option, but when I tried to carve into the nest, the blade only bowed before snapping back straight with a metallic *whang.*

The hammer. I'd smash the nest apart.

I drove the claw end into the nest, tearing chunks free. Within seconds I was oiled in sweat. I could have been clobbering through sheets of compacted cardboard. Sticky black fluid was trapped between the layers of the nest; it dripped on my hands and face, thick as motor oil, and Lord did it *itch*. It was all I could do to keep the hammer gripped and keep bashing away, because all I wanted to do was scratch myself raw.

I hacked away a good two feet, down on my knees and working steadily to core a tunnel into the honeycombed sheets; a ragged overhang formed above my head as I carved deeper and deeper, crawling down the tunnel I'd made along the loading dock's floor. I kept waiting for my hacking to unearth the wasps. I was petrified that I'd carve into a pocket housing an egg chamber or a drones' workroom and they'd come whipping out at me, hundreds or thousands of them, stinging me to death in the claustrophobic swelter of my own escape hatch. But the only sign the wasps might be lurking was that syrup that dripped onto my hair and down my back, heavy as molasses.

Needing to keep an eye on the situation outside the kitchen—the tunnel was way too narrow to turn around in—I shimmied out backward and crept to the porthole.

The ballroom was nearly empty. The Queen stood on top of the hill of earth her offspring had dug up.

Pikachu!

I'm scared.

then don't go.

When my text arrived, her face lifted from her screen. She screamed at me. A sound of rage and fear and horror, but most of all, a scream of duty. It was Serena I was looking at, not Plum, and Serena's own programming had been set in a lab, and was irreversible.

When she descended into the hole, she did so with a stiff breed of pride. I watched until she finally sank out of sight, down, down into her unthinkable new home.

I returned to my own hole. Crawled back into the choking, womblike tunnel and got back to hacking. I took the wood saw with me. It worked better now that the teeth had something to bite on. I sawed through the nest and ripped chunks free with the claw end of the hammer, carving a path from memory—where I'd seen the van backed up at the loading dock . . .

. . . and I had to pray the wasps hadn't continued to build their nest *inside* the van.

The kitchen lights went out again. Darkness flooded down my tunnel.

My limbs seized. My breath drummed in my ears. The nest dripped its toxic discharge all around me, the iodine-y stench of it stinging my sinuses, the brittle sheets of the nest pinching in at my elbows.

I could now hear wasps in that darkness. They must be trapped in the layers, left behind like miners in a cave-in. The feathery beat of their onion-skin wings. They were crawling out of the nest, half-suffocated but not quite dead. They would fall on me in this claustrophobic kill-chute, slipping under my collar and worming in my hair—at any second I was going to scream any second now now NOW—

The lights rallied back. They flooded down the tunnel, much weaker now. I cast a glance back to the kitchen, tucking my head and looking between my legs down the ten or eleven feet of nest I'd carved away.

Nothing moved out there. Not that I could see. Not yet.

My tunnel continued to shrink. I could make more forward progress by hacking away less nest, but doing so meant the passage dwindled steadily; I was on my hands and knees, the nest raking my spine as I slashed and ripped—where was the van, where was that goddamned va—

The hammer's claw *whong*ed, sending a tuning-fork shiver through my chest. I dropped it and used my bare hands, now shriveled into reddened claws stuck with rags of wasp-fiber, to rip at the nest—

My fingertips gripped metal. I cleared its surface with the heel of my palm.

The van door.

Blitzed on adrenaline, I tore and tore until I located the door handle. The itch was by then a living part of me. I gave the handle a yank. The hinges squealed, but the door barely budged.

I pulled as hard as I could, venting a thin scream. But I couldn't reach my fingers inside the van. The nest was too dense. It was sealing the door shut.

Grabbing the hammer again, I slashed at the nest above me. Something hit my upturned face: A wriggling ball of cheese curds burst across the bridge of my nose. Plump wasp larvae stuck to my skin and wriggled down the neck-hole of my sweatshirt, fat as overcooked rice. Gagging, stifling the urge to scream, I snorted, *phoooooo!*, ejecting the larvae plugging my nostrils and then—*FUCK IT*—dug the hammer into the nest again, *again*, past caring now, let them come, wasps or larvae or Lord Beelzebub himself, I didn't give a shit, bring 'em on, Margaret June Carpenter ain't gonna die in this fucking nest.

After clearing six inches of wiggle room, I dropped the hammer and re-gripped the door. I was able to haul it open those six inches before it hit the nest. Shit. Another couple inches of clearance and I'd be able to squeeze through.

With the edge of the door held in both hands, I slid onto my back—larvae burst on the knobs of my spine—and braced my heels against the second door. I pried as hard as I could, using all my body weight to flatten the nest and give me those few precious inches I'd need to get inside. I pushed the door shut and yanked it open, smashing it into the nest. I got into a rhythm: *pop* goes the door, *crackle* goes the nest—a quarter inch of clearance—*pop* goes the door, *crackle*, another half inch, *pop, crackle, pop, crackle* . . .

When I cranked my head back to get a look at the kitchen, I couldn't see it: I'd carved the last few feet of the tunnel on a curve, the kitchen now bent out of sight. But the light flooding down the tunnel brightened and dimmed. The lights were fluxing with each power surge.

A buzz built in the upper part of the nest. The packed layers trembled over my head, torn edges fluttering.

I pulled even harder, but the nest resisted: I'd already compacted it to a density that felt rocklike, every molecule of air squeezed out, no different than snow piled up behind a shed door. But I was sweaty, my entire body slick and slippery; if I sucked in my stomach, I might be able to squirm through the gap sideways—

Something smashed into the kitchen door. I caught the unmistakable crunch of wood and the buckle of hinges from where I lay. Without needing to look, I knew that the door had been broken down.

Something was inside the kitchen.

Go, I thought. *Now. You have to get inside this van.*

I jammed the top of my skull between the doors, screwing the top of my head against the frame; the metal bit into my scalp and my next shove earned a painful *crunch* as my head *compressed*, I'd swear it did. My vision flooded with red and I wondered if I'd hemorrhaged, if my eyes were now bloody stoplights, but I kept driving forward—the doorframe gripped my ears, pulling the flaps down and pinning them to the sides of my head. There came a fibrous tearing sound that I figured must be my earlobe coming off my scalp, but oh well, what were ears anyway? Decorations, only decorations . . .

Next my jaw was locked tight, pinned in the vise of the doors, my head bathed in cool flames, and if I broke my jawbone, so be it. The human body was amazing, it could endure a whole lot and keep on trucking—

My head popped into the van. The pressurized black spiders raced off my face. I squeezed my shoulders through with my torso cranked sideways. My arms came through next.

Inside the van, the stench was that of corpses soaked in sugary Kool-Aid. The button on my jeans snagged on the frame and got pinned, the denim reefed up the crack of my ass—the button slipped into my navel and popped free.

I jerked my legs in, my kneecaps smashing the edge of the door and sending an electric jangle down to my heels—but I barely felt it because I was in, I was in, I was fucking *IN*.

I pulled my knees under me. My head was a swollen tomato, but nothing felt irreparably broken. The van was dead dark. Frail light came from the kitchen, trickling down the tunnel and through the cracked van door.

I could hear something out in the kitchen. The dry click and clitter of nails on the tiles. A mucousy suction as something hunted about with great interest.

I pulled the van door shut quietly. I pawed around in the dark, getting my bearings. What felt like burlap bags lay under me, sending up that unholy reek.

Breath held, head tucked, I hunched my way up to the front of the van. My fingers felt over the driver's seat, the steering wheel, down the transmission . . . the keys were still in the ignition. *Thank you, Harry.*

I sat behind the wheel. When I turned the key, the dome light snapped on. I flinched.

A skittering scrape came down the tunnel, loud enough to be heard through the van's shut doors. It was followed by a grunt, but one that could have been made by a massive roach—the air around me went concave, the oxygen sucked right out of it.

The nest covered the windshield. Wasps moved sluggishly within it. Maybe that meant they were still building, which could mean I was close to its outer perimeter.

I gave the key another twist. The engine ground but didn't catch.

Was the nest plugging the muffler? That meant even if the van *did* start, carbon monoxide would begin to fill the cab almost instantly. If I took more than a minute or two to break out of the nest, I'd pass out from the fumes and die in this shitty deathtrap.

I reefed the key a third time, telling myself not to mash the gas pedal and flood the engine. *Just goose it, Maggie, go tender on the gas . . .*

The air inside the van decompressed. My eardrums popped.

"*Shsihsihsssiisisssss . . .*"

I cranked my head back. By the dome light's glow I could see the van door was open. Something was out in the tunnel, right at the van's bumper.

By the light coming from the kitchen, I could perceive its jagged shadow. Something had crawled through the dripping layers of the nest to find me.

Screaming, I twisted the key. Forgetting my own warning, I stood on the gas pedal.

The door rattled open. A voice infiltrated the van, cold as the grave: "*Beefster!*"

The reedy scrape of Allan's nails on the van floor as he scrabbled toward me.

The engine caught with a coughing rumble. Still screaming, I jerked the transmission collar once, twice, three times—

The brake! Put your foot on the brake!

The Allan-thing's rawboned fingers scraped up the upholstery of the driver's seat and invaded my sight line—

I stomped on the brake. Dropped the transmission all the way down into D2.

Hit the gas.

The scalded-cat screech of the tires on the concrete floor of the loading bay and the stink of fried rubber rising up from under me— under *us*, me and the Allan-thing, its fingers now twining possessively in my hair.

"Fuck off!" Pinning the gas pedal to the floor. "Let me go, you fucking *creep*!"

The tires bit with a sudden jerk, throwing the van forward. The chassis shrieked. For a dreadful few seconds, I thought the axles would lock up and the van would go not one more inch—*the nest's solid*, my mind yammered; *it's fifty feet thick from the windshield to its end; you may as well drive through solid concrete*—but then the grille lurched forward another foot, the nest crumbling as Allan and I bashed around in the cab, Allan's thorny fingers gouging at me—

A squealing keen as the van shot forward, shedding plates of nest. It tore out into the night, my wide eyes following upward to the stars speckling the sky.

The van charged across an ornamental garden and slammed into a decorative marble fountain going twenty miles an hour.

My head dummied off the wheel. I had the sense of something flying past my shoulder to crunch the windshield.

I jerked the door handle and fell out, landing on the grass. The *smell* of grass, green and vivid and glorious. I rolled over with the wind knocked out of me—

"Don't move!"

I dragged myself up. The van's engine was still running with a heavy hack.

"On the ground!"

Chest burning, I took a step forward. So much *noise*. Generators powering a small city of military portables and comm tents. The world in all its glory thrumming in my eardrums—

"I won't tell you again! On your *knees*!"

Dizzy, kinda wanting to throw up, I thought: *You get on your knees, you shitheap—*

Dots. Red ones, all over my chest. I squinted down and snorted— *oh fuck.* My nose. Must've busted it on the steering wheel. Blood stained my shirt in a sloppy triangle.

"Identify yourself!" a voice said.

Laser sights. That's what those red dots on my chest must be. Some of the happy assholes at Woody Knot put them on their .22s, too, as if you'd need them to blow the ass off a possum.

I squinted at the lights. Past them, the dot-makers. I grinned, tasting blood in the gaps of my teeth. I felt sick but not scared. What was there ever to be scared of again?

"What are you gonna do, shoot me?"

"Identify yourself!"

"My name is Margaret June Carpenter. My father patented a cookie tray; you've probably used it, so yeah, you could say my family is a pretty big deal."

I burst out laughing. This all seemed deliciously funny.

Then the creature who had once been Allan Teller slumped out of the van's passenger-side door.

How the men with the laser-sights had missed him, I'll never know. That they chose to focus on the girl with the busted nose, now *that's* the mystery.

It dragged itself around the base of a tree pruned into a golf ball— right down to the dimples. It hauled the wreckage of itself over the grass, a blind crab up a beach. I saw now how feeble it was. The hair on the head of the thing that had been Bradley and Gail Teller's boy was bone white. Its eyes, too. It was as insane as anything you could ever imagine.

"*ake eeeee,*" it gobbled.

The flashlights lifted from its body as the men and women who'd held them recoiled in a bewilderment of horror.

"*ake eee eeeeeease . . .*"

Its fingernails skated on the cobblestones. It crawled toward me, a skeletal bug with its bones showing through at elbows and knees. It struck me that it had probably walked this same cobblestone path with its father, a golf bag slung over its shoulder.

"*Take eeee,*" it said, finding its voice at last. "*Take eee ith oooooooo . . .*"

It held one hand out toward me, pleadingly. Too late, I understood that it had never intended to kill me, whether on its own or in its queen's name.

I saw him then as the poor, tragic, underloved boy he may have always been.

"Oh, Allan buddy."

The thing had nearly reached my feet. Its fingers scrabbled at my sneakers. I knelt. Took its hand. So cold, the skin worn smooth to the bones.

". . . *pleeeease . . .*"

"Where can I take us, Allan?" I whispered, too low for anyone else to hear. "Can't you see that I'm lost, too?"

PART IV
EVER AFTER

The Daughters of Minerva:
Subject Six, Rudyard Crate,
and the Long Shadow of Project Athena

(as published in *Esquire* magazine)

by Chris Packer

Journalism is an act of personal erasure. The writer is subservient to the subject, whose voice they amplify using the tricks of their trade.

Hunter S. Thompson would disagree. George Plimpton and Tom Wolfe and Joan Didion, too. Those noteworthy exceptions aside, this gig is what it's always been.

In the unlikely event my byline means anything to you, the recognition may stem from my piece tackling the fallout of Amos Flesher's New Mexico compound, or the more recent but no less tragic outcome of the Falstaff Island incident on Prince Edward Island. Knowing my background, you'd logically suspect that was why I'd been selected to cover Project Athena.

Well, yes and no.

If you were to enter the doors of Northfield High School—not that you could anymore without special military dispensation—and walk past the main office where Deb Crimsen passed thirty-plus years as Head Secretary (a term no longer much in fashion), you'd find yourself at a wall of framed class photos.

The senior graduates since 1974, the year the school opened its doors.

Scanning past the seventies and eighties and early nineties, the shag haircuts and blowouts, the fat collars and mohair and spaghetti straps, running your finger along the dusty framing glass, you might pause on a nondescript student.

Fire-engine-red hair, round cheeks, staring with louche teenage apathy from the one-inch lozenge that hemmed his face.

Christopher Packer. Class of 1998.

You see, I went to Northfield. A son of the city. I don't live there anymore, haven't since the day I went away to college— in that way, and *only* that way, do I share a fleeting similarity with Margaret Carpenter.

I walked these halls. The tile hasn't been replaced since my day, and it's jarring to realize that the young men and women whose names the world is now familiar with walked the same flecked quartz my own Converse hi-tops covered nearly three decades ago.

Charity Atwater. Margaret Carpenter. Harry Cook. Chad Dearborn. Will Stinson. Mark Foster. Allan Teller. History has an uncanny way of not only retaining names but making them emblems of our grand human tragedy.

And at a given point, a person can reach a level of fame or notoriety where a singular name suffices.

Cher. Madonna. Adele. Oprah.

Serena.

This is her story. And Margaret Carpenter's. And that of Serena's creator-father.

Fair warning, reader: You'll find no answers here. Some mysteries are ungraspable. To dig too far into them is to find yourself in a hole no different than the one that spans out under the St. Catharines Golf and Hunt Club: a hole so deep, so dark, and so hostile to human life that it holds nothing but madness.

"They can all go fuck 'emselves."

So says Earl Tangs, superintendent (since terminated) of the Woody Knot trailer park. Tangs is a man of points. Sharp elbows, knobby knees, angular chin. And he's got his own point—albeit a self-serving one—about the townsfolk's reaction to his controversial business venture.

"They hate me. They curse and shame me. Some bastard stuck a steak knife in the tire of my bus!" His laugh is a whinnying bray. "Well, fuck 'em sideways. I've got a shed fulla spares."

He shows me his ad, the one adorning hundreds of telephone poles and community event corkboards within city limits. He's got a website, too, and books reservations from all over the world.

The Queen's Tour.

For one-hundred-and-fifty dollars, Earl Tangs will load you into a yellow school bus and show you the sights. His tour encompasses Northfield High, the Teller homestead, his old haunt of Woody Knot, a depressed valley in the grape fields where a burned-out van once lay, the St. Catharines Golf and Hunt Club, and a few other spots that in Tangs's opinion are of consequence.

"Sure, it's grim," Earl confesses. "But thousands of people go to Salem every year to celebrate women who got burned at the stake a few hundred years ago." He touches his upper lip to the tip of his nose, ruminatively. "People are all fucked-up."

I pony up Tangs's fee. A bit dear, sure, but an entrepreneur's got to strike while the iron's hot. The tour takes four hours. One ham sandwich, one bag of chips, and one beverage (Pepsi or Vernors ginger soda, no substitutions) included. On the day I go, the bus is half-full. A pair of German tourists, three women from Japan, a gaggle of Americans. Most have plans to visit Niagara Falls afterward, but a few came expressly to retrace Margaret Carpenter's and Harry Cook's path on that fateful day.

"Oh, I'm a huge fan," says Dierdre, a notary public who made the trip from Bakersfield. "There's just something about Charity's story, you know? It's so relatable."

In the nearly twelve months passing since the event, Charity Atwater has undergone a public transformation from villain to victim to avenging angel.

"Those boys got what they deserved," Dierdre says to me at a confessional hush. "Not as *bad* as they got it, but still."

When I ask if she includes Rudyard Crate in that category, she spits: "Why not? He's the biggest boy of all."

That question—how bad did those boys really get it?—is the subject of much conjecture. Apart from those forty-three seconds of footage recorded by a fiber-optic camera that have received a level of scrutiny previously reserved for the Zapruder film—that, and a few sketchy "eyewitness" reports later revealed as grifts— what happened in the ballroom during those early hours is largely unknown. The few scientific and military personnel tasked with investigating the aftermath have not spoken to the press.

Still, as with any significant event in human history, the rumor mill never stops churning.

"That's where Subject Six took Allan Teller, folks."

We're at Northfield High. A military barrier has been erected at the road leading to the parking lot; the football field, tennis courts, and quadrangle are off-limits. Earl Tangs pulls the bus up as close as he's allowed. The passengers crowd into the right-hand seats to get a better look. My old school seems grayer and more institutional than I remember. The wall is crumbling along the roof, as if the place is afflicted with structural leprosy.

"Down there in the furnace room." Earl has hooked up a speaker system with a CB radio mic; his voice fills the bus. "That's where she took Allan. She tore his little boys off down there." He stagily clears his throat. "His testes, to use the scientific term."

One of the German tourists runs the word *testes* through the translation software on her phone, nodding with her partner— *hmmm, ahh-hmmm.*

There is no verifiable report that Allan Teller was in fact mutilated in the furnace room. We will likely never know the exact fates of Teller, Chad Dearborn, Will Stinson, Harry Cook, Mark Foster, or the two-hundred-plus guests and policemen and anyone else at that fateful fundraiser. All we can determine is that, apart from Teller himself, they were all hosts to aberrant life-forms that may still exist, in some state or another, beneath the club's ballroom floor.

The children of Charity Atwater, Serena, whichever name you choose to apply.

The only one who might know more about these events is Margaret Carpenter, who spent an unthinkable amount of time in the club's kitchen. But Carpenter could give D. B. Cooper a few tips on how to keep a low profile. Nobody knows where she is, if she's mentally fit, or if she's even alive.

We *do* know that, after escaping the club, Margaret Carpenter and Allan Teller were taken to a facility unseated from known geography. We can surmise they were tested, assessed, observed. One suspects Allan Teller never left. His experience must have reduced him to something human in only its broadest terms. Through various leaks and loose lips, we now know about his bedroom. The handcuffs. We know about the storm drain under Estelle Atwater's trailer. How Serena must have bred the unnatural wasps down there, starting with common German wasps, feeding them her own blood. Worker insects ferried that blood back to the nest. The DNA cross-pollinated rapidly, the queens laying eggs with that new encoding to create a much different and far deadlier variant.

We also know that Teller and the other two boys must have spent an unspeakable period, weeks perhaps, in that storm drain with the wasps, the nest, and Serena. They, along with Estelle Atwater and a man identified as Julian Coventry—whose corpse was found in Rudyard Crate's observation suite off Welland Avenue, one of five such sites scattered across continental North America—were Serena's first attempts to breed new life.

"She made a drone out of him," Earl goes on. "It's common in the insect world. If a queen finds her offspring deficient, she gelds it to stop its weak gene plasm from getting passed on. I guess poor Allan Teller just didn't make the grade."

Give Earl this. He's done his homework.

The tour continues. A guy on the sidewalk sees us go by—Earl's emblazoned the tour's name across the flank (*The Original! Accept NO Substitutes!*), with a cartoon portrait of a wasp—and chucks a half-eaten Big Mac at the windshield. Direct hit. Earl switches on the wipers to clear away the mess. He flips the guy the bird and hi-ho, away we go.

The tour's final stop is at a grape field in the shadow of the emerald hills. We're in wine country now. The caliche and mineral deposits carried down from the escarpment form the area's unique terroir. When I set foot in the field almost a year after Margaret Carpenter and Rudyard Crate did that late-spring afternoon, the sounds are those I remember from growing up around here: the stirring of early-season crickets, the rattle of buds on the vines.

The van is gone. The valley floor has been scoured of all evidence. First by the police and forensic teams, then by a joint task force of the Public Health Agency of Canada and the Centers for Disease Control. The spot up the hill where the remains of two bodies were found under a tarp—one belonging to Franklin Jameson, a Harvard-educated geneticist and suspected lead researcher of Project Athena; the other of a human-insect hybrid the Project's records refer to as Subject Five—is unmarked.

The valley was closed for months, until it was clear there was nothing more to be gleaned from any investigation. After it opened back up, the disaster tourists descended.

The area has a scrubbed, parched look. Recently, thousands have come to collect bottle caps and glass shards and beer tabs. *Litter*. Anything Charity Atwater (or Margaret Carpenter, a distant second) may have touched or put their lips to.

In the spot where the ruined van sat, you'll find wreaths and flowers. Laminated handmade signs. Crosses and grave markers and candles guttered down to pools of wax.

RIP MY QUEEN

MAY YOU REIGN FOREVER

The boys have been forgotten. This shrine is for Charity.

Ultimately, this story isn't *about* the boys. They have since been recorded as the evil stepbrothers, reduced to obstacles our heroine was forced to overcome.

Despite their fundamental innocence—everything we've since learned about the van incident points to the fact that they didn't enter it willingly—I can't help but see them as bit players in a greater and more interesting tragedy.

Earl Tangs joins me as the others in the tour group hunt for anything that might bear the faintest trace of Subject Six's DNA, somehow clinging there despite the lashings of rain and wind and sun.

"You grew up around here, right?" When I nod, he says:

"Then you know this town doesn't treat all missing girls equal."

In the early nineties, two girls were killed by the serial killer John Hanover. A fifteen-year-old named Ellie Ballaster went missing in 1991. The next year, sixteen-year-old Dawn Hollins disappeared. If you lived around here back then—and I was in my late teens—you'd remember the dread that hung over the city. One afternoon I was at the rowing regatta down in Port Dalhousie when the police interrupted practice; they had everyone, coaches and rowers from every local school, drop our oars and hunt the bushes around the club. We didn't know it then, but we were looking for Dawn Hollins's remains.

Dawn Hollins was attractive. A talented volleyball player. She came from a good family. A family with money. She had her whole life ahead of her.

Ellie Ballaster was raised—I suspect Earl may've known her as a little girl—at Woody Knot, the trailer park referred to as *Would Not* by uppity locals, as in: *"Would Not" Live There on a Dare*. The same park Margaret and Charity grew up in.

John Hanover cut Ellie's body into sections, encased them in quick-dry cement, and sunk her in a quarry near the Morningstar Mill. Dawn's body was found in a culvert on the outskirts of Mississauga. These are the dry and horrible facts.

Reaction to their deaths differed. Everyone had a story about Dawn. Everyone had *known* her, had once had intimate conversations with her, spoke of her with such adoration. There was this parasitical attachment to a dead girl who could no longer say: *I have no clue who you are.*

Nobody knew Ellie, though. Nobody even bothered to pretend they had.

Earl nods to the signs and flowers.

"Good to see people making a fuss over a poor girl. Sad it

took all this." He pinches a gob of spit between his lips and lets it fly. "But it's mostly out-of-towners. The shitheels in this town would root for tuberculosis in a children's hospital."

———————

To gaze upon Rudyard Crate, one can't help but see a resemblance to the Roman emperor Tiberius.

There's something repulsive about the faces of sons of privilege. A watered-down version of the traits that made their forefathers such titans of commerce or art or faith. The granite chins become recessive, the noses turn flat and porcine, the eyes jitter in sockets like under-poached eggs.

Tiberius was earmarked for leadership of the Roman Empire from birth. In marble busts, his countenance—as captured by even the most forgiving sculptor—is mealy and oh-so punchable. The face of a census taker, a professional cat-sitter, a part-time DMV functionary.

Yet owing to his lineage, Tiberius was for a time the most powerful person on earth.

If you put the faces of Rudyard Crate and Tiberius side by side, you'll note the same narrow heads and close-set eyes. The same thin and miserly lips. Except there's something *more* in Crate. Those scars on his face. Ones you might mistake for a tragic case of childhood acne. The tungsten sheen in those gray, vaporous eyes evidencing an inner hardness.

If they'd had any inkling as to how it would all unfold, so many people—those unfortunate souls in the St. Catharines Golf and Hunt Club ballroom, their spouses and children, the students at Northfield High, Rudyard Crate's own doomed scientific advisors . . . they'd have prayed for the man to be like most other sons of privilege. Soft, ineffective, useless.

But tragically, Rudyard Crate was powerful enough, intelligent enough, and capable enough to engrave his uncanny desires into living flesh.

Carl Leiningen would only speak on the matter once, to a crowd of reporters gathered on the lawn of the Delamore Retirement Villas in the Meadowmont neighborhood of Chapel Hill, North Carolina.

Leiningen was eighty-eight years old when an orderly wheeled him onto the porch. He stood under his own steam on the shaded veranda. Stooped then, but there was a confident elegance to his gait, the sense of a body that still remembered the strength it had forfeited. He unfolded a slip of paper with crepey, liver-spotted hands and read directly from it.

"I won't rehash what went on that day in Africa all those years ago. Much news has already been made of it. The ants and all such. I'd worked for Augustus Crate for ten years. I knew Auggie to be a hard driver, not one to suffer fools, but mostly a fine and honest man. I was fond of his daughter, Elizabeth. I taught her how to drive stick shift at that jungle camp. Not well enough, as it should turn out. And yes, I knew Auggie's boy."

The throng of reporters, me included, waited. There were hundreds of us on the lawn that afternoon. You'd be forgiven for thinking it was an inauguration, a grand ribbon cutting.

"By the time we got back to the camp that day, the ants had cleared off. The tents had been devoured. Canvas, jute, ropes, everything. Only the metal eyelets were left, scattered on the ground like Oriental coins. To be at the site of such appetite is to step onto another planet. The sun still shines, you can breathe the air, but it feels alien. And Rudy, who was only ten—he looked alien, too."

Leiningen folded up the paper and stuck it in the pocket of his housecoat.

"That boy was black. Not that his skin had changed color, you understand; he appeared burned. As if he'd stepped from an inferno, still alive somehow. It was the ants. They were stuck to him, thick as midnight. He'd rubbed lard all over himself. Very clever. It saved his life. The ants couldn't bite through it, got gummed in it, suffocated. Only when we scraped that lard off did we realize how badly hurt he was. His skin was cratered. Deep pits and pools, some all the way down to the bone. He was more blood than boy."

Leiningen swooned, his bony shanks faltering. But when his orderly reached to prop him up, the old man shooed him off. He gathered himself for what was, to him, the most important part. The point he wanted the assembly to walk away with at the forefront of our minds.

"It was a remarkable act of resilience for him to survive. I always applauded the boy for that. Most of us—all of you lot out here—you'd be dead. Torn apart in a manner the human mind cannot truly conceive. He lost his sister. He never said so directly, but it's my guess that he watched her get eaten alive. They had a bond, those two. Perhaps not normal—" He stopped himself. "I never blamed him for being unable to outdistance what he went through that day. I blame him for the evil places that lack of distance took him to, yes. I'm a God-fearing man. And you better believe that Rudyard Crate consigned himself to the blazes of hell for what he did with those girls."

Leiningen then sank back down in his wheelchair. The speech had sapped what little strength he'd ventured outdoors holding. Chin tucked, eyes downcast, Carl Leiningen let the orderly take him back inside.

Perhaps not normal.

Of everything Leiningen said, these three words leave the most vexing tracery.

Of all the questions surrounding Project Athena, the simplest and most elemental is:

Why?

Why would a man pursue this path? In all of human history, has a man ever risked so much for so obscene a reward?

Other than Leiningen, there are no surviving witnesses to the event that so clearly reordered Rudyard Crate's world. He was ten years old. His sister, Elizabeth, sixteen.

Perhaps not normal.

The woman's name—the one she gives me—is Kiko. We meet at a chain coffee shop. When I arrive, I find her tucked away at a back table nursing a cup of herbal tea.

Kiko is thirty-one. There is an air of the corn-fed country girl about her. Long, rangy limbs. Coiled strength flowing from the joints. A gymnast's physique. Her eyes seem distant even when she's looking straight at you.

Of all the information trickling out about the raid of SysWell

Dynamics—some of it made public, much of it not—you'd need to be paying close attention to note the line item on page 9,870 of the 12,000-page FBI document, on which the million-plus items seized are scrupulously annotated.

Sculpture pieces (4). G. Beenhouer.

Gustaf Beenhouer is a Dutch artist. A disciple of H. R. Giger. Unlike his mentor, Beenhouer is little known. He subsists on commissions. It must've been a great boon when a multi-billionaire reached out with an unusual request.

The photos of Beenhouer's pieces came to me in the way such things do. A person who knows a person who knows a person. The images reveal what appear to be two hollow metallic sickles, over two feet long and tapering to blunt points. There are leather thongs on one end, with buckles. Also, what appears to be a chest-plate adorned with milky sacs.

"They were filled with petroleum jelly," Kiko tells me.

She goes on to detail her interactions with Crate. She would show up at his Del Mar estate in the evenings. There was a room in a sub-basement. Low, domed ceiling; honeycombed walls. Perhaps it mimicked an ant burrow. Or the queen's chamber in a wasp nest.

Kiko would take her clothes off. Strap Beenhouer's sculpted chest-piece to her torso, the sickles to her arms. The lights were low. She was instructed to approach in jerking, cantilevered movements. Her client would be on the floor, naked, wearing a thin coating of artificial hemolymph, or insect's blood.

"It smelled sweet," she says. "Caramelized sugar."

Kiko would guide the sickles over her client's body, eliciting squirms of delight. They didn't talk; insects don't, other than by passing wordless messages along the stems of their antennae. Kiko would rake the serrated edges of the sickles over her client's inner thighs.

When their encounters proved a regular thing, Crate commissioned Beenhouer to fashion a mask. I haven't seen the piece, but Kiko admits she had difficulty seeing out of it.

"The eyes were huge." Cupping her hands in front of her own eyes. "Two Christmas tree ornaments."

Kiko gives the impression that what Rudyard Crate asked of her may not have been out of line with the requests of her other clients. She knows what Crate had done with his six subjects, but the grace she displays toward him is seemingly depthless.

"People have their fetishes. I don't kink shame."

When the emperor Tiberius grew old and paranoid, he retired to a villa on the isle of Capri. There, the ancient historian Tacitus writes, he engaged in the most perverse manner of debauch. It is said that he enjoyed lounging in a pool, and trained boys as young as four years old to hold their breath, dip underwater, and "nibble" him. Tiberius called them his "little minnows."

I wonder if those who witnessed this turned the same generously blind eye as Kiko. If Tiberius's minders were seduced not by the allure of power but simply by the *power* of power.

I don't kink shame either. Still, the question nags.

Why?

Is it possible that Rudyard Crate spent two decades and billions of dollars, putting his company, his fortune, his reputation, his personal freedom, and his life at hazard—

—all for the shot to fuck a giant bug?

Earl's tour bus gets as close to the St. Catharines Golf and Hunt Club as possible without notarized permission from the Canadian Public Health Agency. Which is to say, not that close at all. The club is barricaded from all angles. The city's infrastructure has had to adjust to the new zoning requirements. Weeds and bracken twist across the golf course's once-pristine fairways.

We pull up at what's become the official overlook, a half-moon platform built on the hillside connecting St. Paul Street to the ancient basin of the Twelve Mile Creek. There, on the other side of the spaghetti-snarl of overpasses and detours—the highway is in the process of being rebuilt to bypass the kilometer-wide quarantine zone—you get a clean sight of the club.

Though not the structure itself. That's buried deep in the nest.

Even having seen it thousands of times on news videos and in photos, it's still stunning to behold. I suspect everyone settles on their own way of seeing. To me, especially at this distance and with the sun at its lowering ambit, turning the freeway into a river of fire, the nest looks like a child's sandcastle at the beach. The evening tide is coming in, sucking at the edges of the castle in approach of its erasure.

The overlook is busy today. Binoculars are bolted along the railing; a buck buys you two minutes of subpar magnification. I brought my own pair. Socking them to my eyes, I let my gaze travel over the vertiginous spires and gibbosities of the nest. Some rise a hundred feet up in scalloped stalagmites. Most are crumbling now, crooked as arthritic fingers. The building itself is under there somewhere. Biomass mapping shows the nest is eighty feet thick in places, with an average thickness of fifty. To be in the ballroom now would feel like being inside a bubble blown deep in the earth.

The site is a scientific landmark. Yet it's fast on its way to becoming a tourist trap. On our way down the stairs to the overlook, our group passes vendors selling shirts emblazoned with the slogans now associated with Serena, Rudyard Crate, and the event itself.

NOT ALL CINDERELLAS WEAR GOWNS

EFF AROUND AND FIND OUT, GENTLEMEN, with the smirking cartoon face of a half-girl, half-wasp hybrid.

One has a silk-screened name tag that reads: HI, I'M SUBJECT SEVEN. On the back: PROPERTY OF SYSWELL DYNAMICS.

"They got ones in Salem that read *We're the Granddaughters of the Witches You Couldn't Burn*," Earl says. "I bought one of them for my niece."

Amazing, how quickly this all went from being the biggest threat to humankind to something memorialized by overpriced novelty T-shirts.

As soon as it became clear that the events in the club didn't signal some kind of super-virus, the global panic cooled. The madness in that club was localized, incapable of any consequential spread. In fact, it couldn't go any farther than those strange wasps could fly. And within a week of Margaret Carpenter's escape, every one of them fell dead from the air. Some enterprising soul collected the ones that had dropped past the barrier; you can find them on the dark web, selling for tens of thousands.

Inside the club, the things that had come out of their human hosts continued to burrow under the ballroom.

An international bilateral coalition—the PCPH: Protectionist Coalition for Public Health—voted to leave the nest and its inhabitants alone. No death squad or extermination team was dispatched. In the interests of scientific progress, five pinhole cameras were remotely installed in the ballroom. A few drone units descended into the hole itself; these didn't last long, though, before being destroyed by unseen hands.

But those five cameras watched. After a Freedom of Information petition was passed, the world was able to watch, too, via a 24/7 internet feed. We're still watching to this day.

Live from St. Catharines, it's the Nest!

The cameras in the ballroom broadcast in monochrome grays. The view is akin to a shipwreck. Motionless, but your mind tells you that the stillness you're observing had once been alive with desperate screams and movement. All that's left now is an unpleasant stasis. The feel of some great horror frozen in time.

Webs of fiber crawl over the rubble. The nest forms in overlapping layers on the walls and ceiling. If you'd been tuned in to the feed for too long, sometimes you might see shapes slinking across those humpbacked slabs—but that could only be eye fatigue.

Things seemed to be going on under the floor, however. The cameras couldn't show it, but their speakers picked up sounds from down there.

Sometimes furtive. Sometimes hollow and echoing. Sometimes a note not unlike the crack of ice on a remote lake. Sometimes what could be a transmission received from deep space. The noises could infrequently reach a sonic register that creates a quiver in the inner ear so extreme that your hearing shorts out, akin to a fuse blowing.

The International Society of Audiologists now recommends against tuning in to the feed for prolonged periods.

The Global Psychology Alliance issued their own warning. In the early weeks of the feed, tens of millions addictively watched it. Not sleeping, not eating, not leaving their rooms. Reports came out of viewers starving to death. Of suicides and self-harm. The feed can have that effect.

The most sensational development captured on the feed occurred within a ten-hour span on October 15 of last year. That was when CAMs 3 and 4—trained on the center of the ballroom, specifically the mound of earth—picked up a mad scuttle at the brim of the hole. Shapes deposited ghostly encasements. Hundreds of them, collecting at the base of the rubble pile.

Anyone who'd come upon a shed snakeskin in the woods knew what those were.

Carapaces. Serena's offspring were molting. Entering the next phase of their life cycles.

She was down there somewhere, too. The subject of world-wide speculation.

Was she still alive? Had her brood revolted and slaughtered her?

What was she doing? What was she *thinking*? Our beloved, secretive Queen.

———————

Earl Tangs can't wrangle his tour bus past the guard's box defending Northfield High's parking lot. But I got lucky.

During my time in St. Catharines working on this story, Northfield's quarantine was lifted. The school was reclassified as a site of scientific interest. While not open to the public, it became possible to arrange a private visit.

The morning is bright, dew sparkling on the grass ringing the school's ornamental garden. My daughter is with me. She's accompanied me to my hometown while I work on this story—she *asked* to come.

She's fifteen now. A complicated age. There's a gulf between us. It's been growing for years, a distance subtly accrued. I tell myself it's natural. She's not my little girl anymore, and it's selfish of me to want that. Still, sometimes the thought flies through my head: *You're losing her, man.*

There's some debate with the guard about us wearing haz-mat suits. After a call with his superiors, we're told they're not necessary.

"Just stay away from *that* area." The guard points to the southern side of the school. The old furnace room.

My daughter and I head in the opposite direction, into the heart of my old high school.

My daughter may be my only means of understanding this story—finding it through the eyes of someone it resonates with deeply. I'm a middle-aged man. Both of those facts, that I'm old and male, stand against my aligning with the truth of this.

In the end, it's a story of two friends, isn't it? Two teenage girls who were in the process of drifting apart as they moved into new phases of life.

But what *is* that narrative? Is it a thwarted love story, a revenge story, or a story of madness? In our teenage years, is there really such a clear division?

Over the months, a surprising polarity has developed.

Team Margaret versus Team Charity.

At first both sides drew equal support, and why not? Margaret Carpenter was the scarred survivor. The friend who—as the facts now bear out—was subjected to the equivalent of a daylong scavenger hunt organized by her childhood friend Charity Atwater, who pushed, cajoled, and threatened Margaret via an iPhone to ensure her compliance.

And Charity? She was a warped Cinderella: the poor girl who, denied her prince and gala ball, simply *took* them for herself. Another corollary would be Victor Frankenstein's creation: misunderstood, unloved, never asking for the life it'd been given—and fueled by rage. Justified rage, as Charity's army of admirers see it.

As the facts continued to trickle out, a groundswell of anger built against Margaret. You can see the war playing out on her Wikipedia page to this day. It gets updated hourly, sometimes by the *minute*, by pro- or anti-Carpenter factions.

Margaret June Carpenter

From Wikipedia, the free encyclopedia

MARGARET CARPENTER (born 2000) is the sole survivor of the St. Catharines Golf and Hunt Club Tragedy (see Rudyard Crate, Charity Atwater, Harry Cook, Project Athena, Subject Six).

Repeat after me: MARGARET 👏 CARPENTER 👏 IS 👏 A 👏 BAD 👏 BITCH 👏

An update had been made when I refreshed the page ten minutes later.

MARGARET CARPENTER (born 2000) is the sole survivor of the St. Catharines Golf and Hunt Club Tragedy (see Rudyard Crate, Charity Atwater, Harry Cook, Project Athena, Subject Six).

Repeat, kids: MARGARET 👏 CARPENTER 👏 IS 👏 A 👏 **DEVIOUS** 👏 BITCH 👏

Why such division? Much has to do with what came out in the wake of the golf club event. Students at Northfield—a shell-shocked, hollow-eyed bunch—eschewed traditional TV interviews, preferring TikTok and YouTube and other social media platforms. Their narratives colored Charity as the slighted party. The overlooked constant companion. Margaret, whose family had recently come into wealth, was reframed as the snob. The girl distancing herself from her old trailer park pal.

The tide had been turning even before what devout Project Athena drama-watchers refer to as "The Video."

It was filmed at what has become the world's most well-known high-school party, Burning Van. The minute-and-a-half clip shows Charity Atwater crawling out of the van that the party took its name from.

And—as millions of memes and clip dissections show, slowing the footage down to a frame-by-frame crawl—in the seventy-first second, we see Margaret Carpenter amid the throng of onlookers, staring at her friend in stark horror.

That did it. Margaret Carpenter went from survivor of an unimaginable ordeal to supervillain.

She was a *Bad Friend*. In the teenage constellation, is there any more poisonous a star?

My daughter is solidly Team Atwater. It would only provoke an argument to tell her I'm Team Carpenter. I think a lot of adults secretly are. We know how awful it would be to be judged by your actions at what is likely the most impulsive, inconstant, and selfish time of your life.

Of all the ephemera to come out in the wake of Project Athena, the reams of TV and newspaper and online footage, the podcasts and deep dives, one needle in the haystack of that information overload had a profound effect on me.

On the afternoon Margaret Carpenter and Harry Cook were unraveling Subject Six's history, Margaret's father, Verne Carpenter, left four voicemail messages on her personal phone. Before those cell phone records could be seized and sealed, some enterprising soul sold them to TMZ.

Call One: *"Hey, Magoo, it's your old man. I woke up this morning to find you'd left. The first time in weeks. Don't get lightheaded on all that fresh air, hah. Seriously, you okay? You left without telling us. Give us a call, would you? Love you."*

Call Two: *"What's up? Send a text if you're not into the whole speaking-to-another-carbon-based-life-form thing. Don't be a goon."*

Call Three: *"Honey, is everything okay? Your mom and I are worried. Give us a buzz. Send a carrier pigeon, ha-ha!"*

Final Call: *"Uhhh, so I guess you're ignoring your old man now. Mamma told me there'd be days like this. Anyway, you got me thinking of this night a long time ago. You woke up and called out my name.* Daddy, I'm scared. *All I had to do was walk the length of the trailer and lie in bed with you. Presto, problem solved. I remember how happy it made me, and at the same time sad. Happy because you were still small enough that my presence alone did the trick. But sad because I knew that your problems were gonna get bigger and bigger, and one day I wouldn't be able to help fix them—I may not even understand them. Anyway, I don't know why I'm telling you all this. I cried watching an oatmeal commercial the other day. You okay out there, Magoo? Call us, okay? We'd like to hear from you."*

The lost tone in Verne Carpenter's voice stirs something in every parent who's felt their kid pulling away. That helpless disbelief, not at the fact it's happening—most of us are clear-sighted about that—but how *fast*. The world has developed fresh angles, *hungrier* ones, and you're neither strong nor wise enough to stop it from carving into them.

Daddy, I'm scared.

Yeah, kiddo. Me too.

As we round a corner on Northfield's second floor, I settle my arm over my daughter's shoulders. She gives me a look— quizzical, brows pinched in—but doesn't shrug it off.

We approach Mark Foster's class. The overhead lights are gridded with the phantom power common to schools after the students have gone home: they shine for ten yards, go dark for twenty, shine again. Foster's old classroom sits in one of those unlit trenches. The door appears to be open, barely a crack. Tension floods up my daughter's body, her calf muscles bunching.

Something the mind registers as a smell but isn't, old and

stale but still there, wafts from that crack in the door. It sets some primitive area of my hindbrain aquiver.

"This way."

I steer us down an intersecting hallway, away from the classroom. My daughter doesn't argue with this.

———

Margaret Carpenter's whereabouts are presently unknown. The house in the prefab community of Executive Acres where she lived with her parents stands empty. The windows got smashed months ago; they're now boarded up. Online scuttlebutt holds that the family may have entered witness protection, although none of them committed any crime.

The court of public opinion holds otherwise. *Bad Friend.* Tried and convicted.

Charity Atwater's whereabouts *are* known, however, and with a firm degree of surety. Yet while her physical body exists somewhere under the St. Catharines Golf and Hunt Club, her spirit—what she's come to represent for millions—is unshackled, atomized into the atmosphere.

She's no longer a person. Genetically, there's an argument she never was. She has now ascended to the realm of an ideal. And ideals function best without the baggage of personhood. People are always letting you down. People are made of fleshy, failing stuff. Ideals are impregnable.

A few weeks after Project Athena entered the public consciousness, Greta Thunberg addressed the Intergovernmental Panel on Climate Change wearing a plain white tee with FREE CHARITY ATWATER written in black Sharpie.

Days later, the actress Florence Pugh walked a red carpet at a film premiere with another plain white tee slashed in Sharpie.

GONNA EAT SOME SKINNY BITCHES

The slogan was silk-screened onto a shirt that sold 4.5 million units in the forty-eight hours following Pugh's appearance.

Abruptly, Charity-slash-Serena was everywhere. She spread worldwide. She became deathless, the way saints come to be— and in a real way, her life *was* that of a saint. This wasn't fat Elvis croaking on the toilet with a fried-PB-and-banana sandwich poking out of his mouth. Charity went out young and went out burning: the perfect combination of star-crossed fate and violent potential.

Most of all, she died in the pursuit of something noble: revenging herself against her wealthy makers, and by proxy against the suffocating, evil, entitled world of adults and all their unearned power.

She lives forever, encased in an endless teenage-hood. She'll exist—an ant aflame in amber—while the rest of us fall prey to age and become wrinkled, frail, doddery. She'll persist, a matchbox saint just itching to ignite, there for those who need her while passing through the complicated age in which she exists eternally: as fists to curl in rage, as a mouth to scream, as a fount to express the wild, ungovernable power of their adolescent hearts.

I miss you so much already

That was the first text.

so dark

down here

The phone that arrived on Margaret Carpenter's doorstep was recovered two days later inside the van she'd used to escape. There were a series of unread texts sent by her friend. They were never meant for public scrutiny.

> scared

> real scared

> tell them

> my story make

> them notice

> just once

> love

> i

> love you

> LOVE YOU SO SO

Fourteen texts. Twenty-eight words, representing what appear to be the final thoughts of Charity Atwater to Margaret Carpenter. A galloping catalogue of fear, duty, want—oh, such desperate want—desire . . . but mostly, love.

> LOVE YOU SO SO

As I grow older, the recollections of my own youth grow vaguer. Some details remain in pointillistic detail, though sadly they are often ones I'd rather forget. Looking back, I can see that my teenage years were a period when my cohort was inching ever closer to a cliff. Every day our toes drew closer to its edge. We could see what was at the bottom, hazily so—in the defeated stoops of our fathers' backs and in the way our mothers watched the birds take flight from the backyard feeder with something like lust and in the veins spidering across the backs of our grandparents' hands. It was there, but we were only just starting to feel the chill of its breath on our necks.

That fall was gonna be scary as hell. The best we could hope for was to find someone with whom to share the plummet.

Margaret and Charity had that in each other. Those texts tell me so. I want to believe they shared a closeness so profound that when they slept, their consciousnesses skipped the blood-brain barrier to enter each other's dreams. The part of Charity that wasn't of our species—a foreign piece she'd come to accept the way a tree will grow around and incorporate a metal fence—had no impact on what they felt for one another.

They loved each other. With all my heart, I do believe that. I think I *need* to. The love they shared was particular to that time in our own brief existences, the years bridging childhood to adulthood that we call adolescence; that love is feral, it's intoxicating, it's wildly contradictory, it's unstable, and it exists at levels that we can't comprehend or even properly remember once we've gotten older. If anything, as the baying of young wolves in our blood. It's too much for us, that love: It floods our brains like voltage from an overloaded power station, a crackling blue pulsation that our bodily grids are only strong enough to withstand when we're young. A love that peels us open and decays us, all at once.

LOVE YOU SO SO

My daughter and I arrive back at the building's front doors. The tour has ended. As we exit into the bright sunshine, she shifts imperceptibly and my arm, still around her shoulder until then, slips off. I stuff my hand in my pocket, no big deal.

As we walk to the car in the shadow of my old high school, I stumble off the curb. My daughter's there, gripping my elbow to keep me upright. Neither of us remarks on it, but there is to me the turning of a gear. This is how it goes. The parent does their best to hold up the child until they can hold themselves up. For some time, they walk as equals. Then the shoe inevitably winds up on the other foot.

Casting a final glance back, I perceive movement in an upper window of the school. Something past the dark glass, floating and drifting. But it's nothing. Nobody will ever walk those halls again. Nothing is there, unless you believe in ghosts.

But things still move beneath the St. Catharines Golf and Hunt Club. Oh yes, yes they do.

Are you down there, Charity?

We're up here still.

We strange, we fragile, we human.

Call us, okay? We'd like to hear from you.

UNIVERSITY OF IOWA MFA PROGRAM
STUDENT APPLICATION PACKAGE // FALL 2023 TERM
CREATIVE NONFICTION WRITING SAMPLE
APPLICANT #433

You know me. At one point, years ago now, you probably held an opinion about me. If you saw the old photos that showed up online, it would click.

In the most well-known of those photos, I'm standing on a patch of twilit grass. To the left, you can make out the bodywork of a white panel van. My nose is broken. I'm laughing. I look insane.

Nowadays, my face holds a haunted edge. You would hardly recognize me. Walk down the street, nobody knows who I am.

I live somewhere else. Far from my childhood home.

Except part of me is still there. A part of us never leaves home, does it? But with me, it's more specific. There's a kitchen. Stainless steel, white tile, an astringent note of bleach. I live there. Even if I manage to push it away, when I fall asleep my dreams carry me back.

When you're a teenager, grown-ups say you've been infected—you go rabid for a few years, thirteen to nineteen, contracting a madness in your blood. You've got to work that craziness out of your system before becoming one of them.

See you when you're twenty and sane again, they'd say.

I'm twenty-three now. But I'm not sure I'll ever be sane.

My best friend was a monster.

But see, even if she'd been told—even if I'd been let in on the secret—neither of us would have believed that.

A monster. How could she be? She was a nice, regular girl.

We grew up together. In my memories, she's always there. I remember my father carrying us both home, cradled against either shoulder, sun-drugged and sleepy after the Canada Day fireworks, the night sprinklers ticking away like tinfoil crickets.

Sometimes I'd watch my friend from the corner of my eye, catching her at an unselfconscious angle. She wasn't pretty in any traditional fashion. Her eyes were antifreeze green, the color of a potion in a wizard's cabinet. Her tummy stuck out, a smooth round bump above her hip bones. When she sneezed, she'd emit this mousy squeak.

There was no hint of monstrous in her. But it wasn't anything she could guard against. The monster was in her, you see, no different than a stone in a peach. A peach can't grow without its stone.

I wonder now if I'd sensed that monster gathering inside her. Had it given off a smell or a pulse as it spread through her veins and down the long white lines of her bones?

There was a game we used to play, Tell Me.

Tell me who you love so crazy it's a drug in your bloodstream.

Tell me what makes you so scared you can't sleep.

Tell me if there's a place in this world where we can be happy together.

These aren't the games of a monster, are they? It was more she'd been given a framed portrait of herself and told: This is you. She'd accepted that, as any of us would. Then one day a razor blade had shown up in the mail with a note. *Cut around your portrait and lift it from the frame.* When she did, peeling back the picture, another face was lurking underneath.

Two portraits in one frame. The minute she set eyes on that second self, the unstoppable process of becoming began.

So why hadn't I seen that other face? What did it say about me that I could be the best friend of a monster? But what my friend was and what she became were unalike. One of them I loved, up until I abandoned her. The other I never knew at all.

It's that reckoning that's the hardest. That I hurt her. That I was selfish, and thoughtless, and cruel at the time she needed me most. I'll never have a chance to fix that.

Sometimes I think my punishment is to never leave that kitchen. I wake screaming from nightmares where I'm back in it. In these dreams, the certainty dawns that I've never left, that I never will, and there is even the sense that I was born in that kitchen.

I let my best friend walk five miles home wearing my bloody underwear. Do I really need a dream to tell me I'm the real monster?

I've only once returned to the place where the monster and I grew up. I went to the peach groves on the eastern edge of the property and walked to the tree I'd come to find, the one with a milky scar on its trunk.

One summer night, the monster and I were too hot to sleep. We hopped on our bikes in our pajamas and rode through the sweet relief of this peach orchard.

The trees got watered overnight and the mist lingered, cool on the skin of monster and human alike. The Motorola Droid phone strapped to the monster's handlebars was blasting music, and from a distant trailer unit came a cry: "Shut up, we're trying to sleep!"

The monster hollered back: "You shut up, you old thing!"—because at that point in our lives, everyone did feel old, didn't they, old and sinister.

The monster's tire skidded, and she plowed into this very tree. The monster spilled off, howling, sprawled on the ground in a coffin-pose.

"Ohh, I've died!" the monster cried. "Gimme my funeral!"

Then that old tune by Ke$ha got cued up and the monster leapt to its feet on the song's throbbing backbeats, the two of us dancing in the moonlight, proclaiming our love for each other at the tops of our lungs.

And you see, we did love each other, the monster and I. A love we couldn't express to our parents because by then our relationships were crippled by expectations and disappointments . . . a love we couldn't whisper to a boy because he might not whisper it back . . . but a love that needed to be said, because it was a pent-up sickness that had to be shared in order to dissipate.

It's not like I ever needed to be told that the biggest part of my best friend was human, and always had been. But if I ever lose sight of that fact, all I have to do is think of that night in the peaches. All that want, that desire, those wishes, that fear, all that hurt.

All human. Every atom of her . . . well, pretty much.

When the song ended, the monster and I found ourselves tangled on the ground. She swung on top of me. Her fingers made soft manacles on my wrists. She pinned me down, hips pressed on mine, and there came a springy bob of fear in my chest.

. . . let's play spider . . .

She bent down until her bangs brushed my forehead. And she kissed me. Our lips touched for a fraction of a second, though it felt like longer.

"Soulmates can kiss, don't you think?" the monster whispered. "It's not even sexual. It's more like kissing ourselves."

"I really do love you, Cherry."

"I really love you too, Plum."

And I'll never love anyone else quite the same way ever again.

EPILOGUE

THE LETTER

Postmarked August 6, 2023

Dear Margaret Carpenter,

I don't know if this will ever reach you. You have worked hard to make your whereabouts unknown. I promise you will never hear from me past this.

My name is Edward Yates. I am a sergeant in the Marine Commando regiment of the Royal Canadian Navy. You could say I am a Canadian version of a United States Marine.

My wife, Ellen, and I have two daughters. Their names are Eadie and Charlotte. I have turned the idea of writing to you over in my head for many years. I am sorry if it was wrong to seek you. But I think of my daughters. I think of you, even though we have never met and never will. I think of your friend Charity, who also I never met. Not as she really must have been.

I was one of the men who went down there. Into the nest. I was selected due to my experience with undersea rescues.

I also assisted at the Kidd zinc mine in Timmins. There was a cave-in on the No. 4 shaft. Seventeen men and two women buried a mile-and-a-half underground. We could not save all of them, but we did rescue some.

My superiors felt I would be a good candidate to go into the nest. The Midnight Layer, as it was called internally. Myself and two other men, Sergeants Carl Eisen and Kellen Kesey.

We went down wearing Exosuits. Specialized suits for deep-water dives. Nobody expected there to be water under the ballroom, no matter how deep the tunnels stretched. But the air down there was considered unfit for human breathing, thus the suits.

A hole was cut through the nest with a motorized drilling rig, big enough to permit entry into the ballroom. The five cameras had to be turned off if our mission was to remain a secret. Once they were, we mounted the hill of rubble and went down.

I have never been more scared in my life, Ms. Carpenter. I imagine you know more than a little of how I felt—much worse, probably, seeing as you were all alone, and for so long.

Our helmet flashlights lit the blackness under the ballroom floor. Tunnels went down and out from a winding central stem. We had to sit on the shelves of earth and lower ourselves to each new level, like children on a bizarre play structure. For hundreds of feet, we went down. There was little to observe. But I could tell something meaningful had occurred here.

In a way, it echoed human settlements. The cities we live in now are built on top of the bones of old towns, which sit on top of villages, which rest on top of ancient encampments. It was similar, except what happened in the nest was a sped-up version.

At a depth of three hundred and fifty feet, we came upon

a massive bowl hollowed out of the earth. In it were heaped hundreds of bodies. Not human, but not foundationally inhuman, either. All broken open.

The next generation of the nest's occupants had been born here. That's what we were given to believe. And the ones who'd crawled out of those shells had kept going down.

At seven hundred feet, we found another generation. Those shells were smaller and even less clearly humanlike.

The tunnels grew more cramped and complex. Our lights could find no end to them. They twisted out and around in patterns that I felt might be beautiful, but at that time and at that depth only left me terrified. Of course, I have never been to an alien world, but I felt I was on one right then. The human world I had been born into had been swept away.

Just past a thousand feet, we reached a platform carved into the rock. It was just me and Kellen by then; poor Eisen had begun to shake at nine hundred feet, refusing to go any farther. When I asked Command for instructions on how to proceed, all I received back was static. Our comms system wasn't receiving at that depth.

Kellen and I made the difficult choice to leave Eisen and continue on. I didn't know how much deeper I could have gone. My brain was starting to do odd things.

A single shaft continued downward from that final platform. Kellen lit a flare and dropped it. The red light went down and down, bouncing off the rock walls until it hit a bottom almost too deep to perceive ... then, way down there, something moved over the glow of the flare. I never got a good look. I feel blessed for that. But it was big. The sound of it traveled up the shaft, along with the heavy rush of air pushed by its body.

Kellen and I backed away from the ledge, continuing deeper onto the platform. The rock had been carved in curving gouges *that seemed to hold a kind of logic. Runes. Language. Perhaps it was the story of the things who'd built all this down here.*

Kellen and I encountered more specimens. I am sorry to call them that. But they were not people, were they? What we beheld were roughly the size of summer salmon. They crawled and heaved at our feet. But they did have faces . . . kinds of faces.

We progressed to the end of the platform, which is where we found her.

I say "her" because I know she was once a girl. I saw photos of her. A regular-looking young lady, no different than anyone. No different than my own girls.

She lay on a carved altar. A place of worship.

It became quiet and still, as only it can be that deep underground. Even the sound of my breath in my helmet went away.

The only sound was her sound. The only voice was her voice. She still had one, Ms. Carpenter, and I want you to know that it was very small and very human.

My daughter Eadie was three years old at that time.

It was her voice I heard. The voice of a little girl.

I am real.

That is what she kept saying. Over and over.

Forgive me, Margaret. Forgive me for telling you this.

I am real I am real I am real.

I am still a real girl.

ACKNOWLEDGMENTS

First, the usual and vital thanks. To my agent, Kirby Kim, for picking me off the scrap heap lo those many years ago and flinging me back into the fray. To Ed Schlesinger, my editor, who brings something out of these Cutter books that isn't there in the first draft, or the second, or sometimes even the third, but be damned if he doesn't wring the best out of these pages. For that I'm eternally grateful.

To copyeditor Stacey Sakal, proofreader Susan Bishansky, and cold reader Dan Seidel, who whipped this tome into shape.

To Cassidy Sattler, Kell Wilson, and Sarah Schlick at Gallery Books/ Simon & Schuster for all your work. It means the world.

To my mom and dad. To my brother and Kathleen. You will find some of my brother Graham's work in these pages: the advert for the Queen's Tour was created by none other (he also put together the book's very own website, which you are invited to check out at www.queenstour.ca).

To my wife, Colleen-o, my Queen-o, the most beautiful woman I have ever seen-o.

To Nicholas and Charlotte. Love you both so much.

With those formalities duly dispensed, onward we march.

Most novels have at least a few creative mothers and fathers, and certainly the Cutter books have no scarcity of forebearers.

In *The Queen* you may see a shimmer of *Picnic at Hanging Rock*, a flash of *The Perks of Being a Wallflower*, a glint of *Saturday Night Fever*, a flicker of Joe Hill's story "Pop Art," some *Promising Young Woman*, H.R. Giger and Cronenberg and Barker and Carpenter and Bradbury (where *does* thunder go when it dies?), and Linda Pastan's poem "To a Daughter Leaving Home."

Readers may add the *Alien* film series to that list, which is fair, but to my mind both Dan O'Bannon and Ronald Shusett—the screenwriters of *Alien*—and I took our cues from the insect kingdom, where host incubation is *de rigueur* for the voodoo and jewel wasp, among others.

You may find other influences, who knows. I tried to keep a fairly scrupulous accounting as I wrote, but to quote Ed Tom Bell in *No Country for Old Men*, my mind wanders.

Beyond those bits of flashing, there were three primary inspirations for this book.

Years ago, I sat down with Jay Asher's *Thirteen Reasons Why*. I was struck by its hook of audio tapes forming a series of mysteries to unlock. I decided to frame this novel on Asher's narrative engine. A cell phone rather than audio tapes, which provided different inroads—texts, phone calls, etc.—but the bedrock would be Charity's confessional .wavs, delivered in much the same way as Hannah Baker voiced hers to Clay Jensen. So, many thanks to Jay for that.

My first Cutter book, *The Troop*, was heavily indebted to William Golding and Stephen King, among others. Stylistically I patterned it after King, and on the narrative end it used the frame familiar to anyone who has read *Carrie*. Now, when I sat down to write *The Queen*, I can honestly say that *Carrie* wasn't at the forefront of my mind, but as the story developed, I realized that I'd clearly backed into the territory of that fine novel.

A social-outcast-slash-misfit in Charity Atwater, whose powers are "born," so to speak, via a dynamic bodily change. A concluding bloodbath at a public event.

So, yes, the influence is there once again. But if you've got to stand on someone's shoulders, they may as well belong to Stephen King.

Finally, those pesky ants.

As kids, my brother and I watched *MacGyver*. Lushly mulleted Richard Dean Anderson making bombs out of gum wrappers, superballs, and India ink. One episode found our hero facing a horde of murderous ants. I forget how he prevailed—jury-rigged a flamethrower and incinerated them?—but my brother and I would *never* forget watching one of the hapless secondary characters fall into a broiling pit of ants to get eaten alive.

That night, both of us couldn't sleep. The ants, I tell you! They were in our beds. They were on the floor and ceiling. They were every-*goddamn*-where!

Many years after watching that episode I read a story, "Leiningen Versus the Ants" by Carl Stephenson. It was published in *Esquire* back in 1938, and evidently was taught in schools for some time.

In it, the titular character, Leiningen, runs a plantation that gets overrun by—you guessed it, ants. The story's got a highly colonial outlook, which is surely one reason it's not taught anymore. Leiningen is pigheaded, disinterested in the warnings of the local officials ("You don't know these ants, Leiningen!"), and yet the plantation workers remain in thrall of their wise, forthright, and very Caucasian master, who nobly sacrifices himself to save them.

Setting that aside—some things just don't age well; hell, some of my own early work doesn't, and I'm still alive—the scenes of the ants overmastering Leiningen's attempts to kill them with fire or water or other inventive methods remain thrilling to me to this day.

It was obviously the inspiration for that *MacGyver* episode. But more reading showed me that "ant fiction" was a thing even before "Leiningen." Specifically, "The Empire of the Ants," the H. G. Wells story published in 1905, also about ravenous ants and the human settlements they merrily digest their way through.

So, there you have it. The decades-long march of obsession (my own, with ants) that brought Rudyard Crate's nemesis to the preceding pages.

All due debt to the writers who got there before me, and acknowledgment of the devices—lard, gasoline, etc.—I borrowed.

I also did a deep dive on pheromones, particularly QMP. Two articles I used as research were:

"Queen and young larval pheromones impact nursing and reproductive physiology of honey bee *(Apis mellifera)* workers" by Kirsten S. Traynor et al.

Chapter 5 of the book *Neurobiology of Chemical Communication*, entitled: "Chemical Communication in the Honey Bee Society."

Beyond that, I must thank Wikipedia, and Jimmy Wales's army of wiki-soldiers.

I set the novel more or less in modern day—2018, to avoid the pandemic—out of the sense that the underlying science would be more believable. In truth, it's no less supportable now than it would have been thirty years ago, or likely thirty years in the future. But the goal of most authors is to make it *feel* believable, and for that I figured I'd better set it close to the present.

Problem with that decision is that, yeah, I'll be a forty-nine-year-old man when this comes out. I was in my mid- to late forties writing this book. If you're finished, you know I made the choice to write in the first-person perspective of a teenage girl.

I did consider other ways to kick the story along—make Margaret into Mike, maybe?—but the novel resisted those attempts. So I buckled down and tried to get as much right as I could, realizing that for some readers, maybe quite a few of them, I might never make that character click.

But I did my due diligence. I called it my "Kids These Days!" research kick. Thank you to:

The Red Scare podcast.

Teen Girl Talk podcast.

And big shout-out to r/teenagers for the ganked memes.

This book takes place in my hometown of St. Catharines, Ontario. I set most of the books published under my own name in and around the area, but this marks the first Cutter book to stroll those streets. Northfield is basically my old high school, Westpark. There is no Golf and Hunt Club, but there *is* a Golf and Country Club, and they reside at the same geographical locus.

For all those real-life equivalencies, it's crucial that the people who know me, or who I used to go to school with almost three decades ago and who may possibly read this book, understand the following: The St. Catharines of this book is *not* the real place. The characters herein have no basis on the real people I grew up with. None of the events captured in these pages should be seen to mimic or re-interpret incidents that may have happened back then.

It's a tricky thing, navigating your own past when it comes to fiction. In some ways, that closeness helps. Remembering my high school—in a physical sense, its halls and classrooms—helped draw me closer to the story. But the danger is in getting *too* close, yes? Or in not clarifying, and making sure this is true in your own heart, that what you're writing isn't benefiting from some parasitical attachment to the people you grew up with.

Fact is, I can't remember a lot of what went on back then with any clarity. I certainly know I wasn't the best person all the time, and I wouldn't want to be judged by the manner in which I behaved. And I would want to extend the same fairness to anyone else.

So, to the good students and teachers and staff of Westpark circa the early nineties (Christ, was it that long ago?): If you ever read this, know that everything herein is the product of my imagination. No character should be construed as someone I ever knew, had a beef with, or nursed a crush on. You do exist, absolutely, but not within these pages.

Finally-finally, a note on the history of my city as it occurs toward the end of this book.

In those early nineties, when I was in high school, the serial killer Paul Bernardo murdered two girls. Their names were Kristen French and Leslie Mahaffy.

My parents—and this is true—live within spitting distance of

Bernardo's old house. Walk out their front door, down the drive, and look south. There it is, five hundred yards off. It looks much different now. Total gut job. Sometimes you'll see the owner out pruning the bushes or mowing the lawn. Looks to be a decent fellow.

The deaths of those two girls marked the most profound tragedy our town ever saw. But what I remember (or *thought* so) was the differing reaction to their passings.

Everyone had a story about Kristen French. After she died, everybody seemed to have known her. You'd be listening to the tenth person tell you some story about the time they'd done this or that with Kristen, and it dawned: *You never knew her at all. You're just recycling a story someone else told you about her.*

Kristen was attractive. Smart, popular. She was all ambition and potential.

Leslie Mahaffy was all those things, too. They were young women. They were *YOUNG*. Everyone is all potential at that stage in their lives, right?

Except people didn't have the same stories about Leslie. It wasn't that there wasn't sorrow—there was, deep and abiding—but as the kids today might say, it hit different.

I'd always wondered how that could be. I used to think it was because (and this is the viewpoint I set out to write *The Queen* under) Leslie had been poor. But it doesn't seem to be the case, looking at history now. From all I can see, she came from a middle-class family. Kristen may've been slightly better-off, but the difference strikes me as negligible.

That impression—that the difference was based on wealth disparity—was what formed the ticking heart of this novel. But I never realized it was a *mistaken* impression until after I'd finished writing it. I'd mulishly persisted under the belief that Leslie was memorialized differently because she wasn't as well-off.

Funny, and perhaps awful, how memory works. How it can fuel entire books, even when those recollections are wildly off base. And it all happened so long ago, y'know?

My mind wanders.